THE GOOD DOCTOR

"If you decide to go ahead with the procedure, there are some rules we must follow," said Dr. Lipsky. "The first: you must never speak of this work to anyone. Not a word, not to anyone, no matter how close they are. This, of course, is for your baby's sake. But it's primarily for our own safety. Now you must have some questions of your own."

"What other conditions have you treated?" Rackley asked.

"You don't need to know that," Lipsky said flatly.

Rackley felt a surge of anger. "You're asking us to use a completely unproven technique on our child. I do need to know."

Lipsky gazed at him calmly. "I'm not asking you to do anything. You came to me."

Kaye interjected quietly, "How will it work?"

"It's really quite simple. We'll take the healthiest embryo we have and implant it in Mrs. Rackley's uterus. After that, you're on your own. Normal pregnancy, normal delivery, you forget that you ever saw me."

"What are the risks?" Rackley asked.

He paused for a long second. "The primary risk, by far, is that someone unfriendly finds out we're doing this."

"Michael Rogers has combined his talents as a respected journalist and a gifted novelist to create a uniquely engrossing tale about the promise and portent of bioengineering. **FORBIDDEN SEQUENCE** is one of a kind—a thrilling page-turner of a novel that also informs and enlightens, spotlighting some of the deepest scientific and ethical issues yet confronted by our species."

—Timothy Ferris

FORBIDDEN SEQUENCE

MICHAEL ROGERS

BANTAM BOOKS
TORONTO • NEW YORK • LONDON • SYDNEY • AUCKLAND

Author's Note

This is a novel. The names, characters, places and incidents depicted in FORBIDDEN SEQUENCE are entirely fictional or are used fictitiously. Any resemblance to real events, places, or people, living or dead, is entirely coincidental.

FORBIDDEN SEQUENCE
A Bantam Book / January 1988

ISBN 0-553-27080-X

Published simultaneously in the United States and Canada

PRINTED IN THE UNITED STATES OF AMERICA

O   0 9 8 7 6 5 4 3 2 1

For Jan

"Take care to be born well."

—George Bernard Shaw

PROLOGUE

The slim street urchin, no older than eight, was dressed in tattered jeans and an old T-shirt reading "I Ran the San Francisco Bay to Breakers Race." He sat in one corner of the Mexico City police station, surrounded by the noise and bustle of constabulary business. He had been sitting quietly for several hours after being brought in by a foot officer. The teenagers who ran the juvenile sidewalk life on the *avenida* paid the police a few thousand pesos each day to make sure that strange young beggars such as this one didn't encroach on their territory.

Now, untended, the boy watched with large brown eyes as an Indian woman selling meat pastries from an old straw basket limped through the dimly lit station house. A rich scent of roast pork filled the air, but it seemed to have little effect on the child. Had anyone bothered to watch carefully, they might well have noticed an unusual, almost unnatural calm about the boy, as if he were taking in all of the scene about him at once, absorbing it like some kind of human sponge.

Just after the old woman wandered back out into the dusty street, officer Ramon Portillo finally began to question the boy. The interrogation was hardly sinister; the point was simply to find the urchin's home street and thereupon send him packing in that direction. The khaki-clad policeman stood, towering over the thin, slight young man.

"Cómo te llamas?" Portillo demanded.

"Me llamo Alfonso," the boy said softly. *"Número uno."*

The cop tugged on his ammunition belt, pulling his trousers higher, and leaned back. "You're number one, are you? In what neighborhood?"

Alfonso looked down, shook his head, said nothing.

"What neighborhood?"

Alfonso stared down at the rough cobblestones of the station floor, unmoving.

Impatient, Portillo reached down and hooked his forefinger under the boy's chin, snapping his head upright in a quick, harsh motion.

"Where are you from?" Portillo repeated. *"Dígame ahora!"*

The skinny young boy looked directly at Portillo now, his intelligent brown eyes showing a faint curiosity, a trace of resistance, an odd, cold distance, and . . . something else.

There was something sufficiently odd about the gaze to stay Portillo's hand, poised to deliver a stinging slap to the side of the boy's head. The boy simply stared at Portillo, and the officer, transfixed, stared back. This was a strange young one.

After a few moments, Portillo shook his head.

"I said, where are you from? Tell me now!" But the boy, unmoving, continued to stare, and after a few more moments had passed, Portillo noticed something unsettling. The young man was sitting so still that it was . . . as if he were a statue. A perfect statue, hardly alive, not breathing.

Portillo looked more closely at the child. His lips were blue. The child *wasn't* breathing.

As the police officer watched, the boy's brown eyes misted with tears, and under the faded T-shirt his skinny chest gave one sudden shudder. Abruptly, with no warning, the child fell over sideways, striking his head on the rough wooden bench, then falling to the stone floor, as limp as laundry, so quickly that Portillo had no time to react.

Portillo shouted; two more officers ran over. By the time they had picked up the frail boy, his heart had stopped. Efforts at resuscitation proved futile. For the second time in less than a month, a stray Mexico City street urchin had died in police custody. This, by itself, was disturbing. But in both cases the boys had killed themselves, simply by willing their lungs to stop.

Now there had been two little boys in Mexico City who could hold their breath until they died.

C H A P T E R   O N E

The winter had been long, the weather strange and unpredictable, and the last Monday in March yielded another odd morning. The great Pacific fog bank remained far out at sea, but the sky itself was like damp gray plush, vaguely organic, hanging close over San Francisco. As Rackley sat waiting on a bench near the edge of the Berkeley waterfront, the towers and spires of the city, just across the Bay, seemed devoid of color, yet as sharp against the horizon as if etched on glass.

Rackley could also see that there was little traffic on the Bay Bridge, and he glanced at his watch. Kaye was ten minutes late. That in itself was not unusual. Punctuality was not prime among Kaye Caswell Rackley's virtues, and usually her husband found this more endearing than maddening. Today, however, Rackley was tense. As a rule, he disliked medical procedures and their associated sharp instruments. And today there was something more: This appointment marked a final step forward in the wholesale reconstruction of his life.

Rackley's full name was Thomas Benton Rackley, but for years no one had called him anything but Rackley. Even Kaye used the name, and the reason was simple. He somehow looked, entirely and beyond question, like a Rackley: of slightly less than medium height, but powerfully built, with unfashionably long brown hair that appeared perpetually tousled. His face was angular and still bore faint scars of adolescent acne, but in all he had aged well, with only the slightest hint of a belly now pushing his beltline. Depending on his attire, he might pass as a prosperous building contractor, a tough young police detective with a few years of college, maybe even an aging scholarship student working his way through medical school.

But Rackley was none of these. Seven years earlier he had been an out-of-luck journalist, living in a $75-a-week welfare hotel room, overweight, heartsick, wondering where his life had gone and his next dollar might come from. By age thirty he had managed to turn a promising career into consummate failure.

Abruptly, his life had taken a direction he would never have imagined. Now he was married, renovating a house, vice president of a company called United Genetics. He even had stock options, a notion that Rackley of years past would have found altogether unbelievable. Sometimes, hours past midnight, lying in bed, listening to the foghorns across the chill water, he might momentarily wonder whether he had taken the right path. On days like this, however, it almost didn't matter.

He glanced up just in time to see Kaye's small German coupe enter the far end of the big asphalt parking lot, tossing up a slight spray of water remaining from the previous day's rain. She was driving fast, and he stood until the car slowed directly in front of the big Birthtech clinic building, newly constructed just where the Berkeley flatlands reached the Bay. He walked over and opened the door for her.

Kaye emerged from the little yellow car in a cloud of subtle perfume, her fine blond hair slightly disarrayed, her large blue eyes bright and only mildly abashed at her tardiness. She was fully a head shorter than Rackley and quite thin, with a long neck and prominent chin. Bundled in winter clothes, she seemed formed of some fragile material, although Rackley knew well that beneath that delicacy was a core of pure resolve.

"I'm sorry," she said quickly, as she embraced Rackley, then tightened the belt of her khaki raincoat against the chill wind off the water. "I was with a client at the Showplace and she couldn't make up her mind about some stupid cloth wallcovering. I finally just told her that, for God's sake, it wasn't exactly the fate of the free world in the balance."

Rackley looked at her. "Isn't there something about the customer always being right?"

Kaye shrugged. "I'll call and apologize. Are we terribly late?"

Rackley shook his head. "The appointment isn't for another fifteen minutes."

Kaye tilted her chin suspiciously. "I thought you said noon."

"Maybe I did," Rackley said innocently, putting his arm around her as they started toward the clinic doors. "I know your ways."

Kaye stopped for a moment and looked up at the four-story building, its broad glass windows tinted bronze, reflecting the Bay in a massive hazy golden image. "You know," she said, "I don't think I've ever actually been here."

"It's about time," Rackley said with mock reverence. "This is our top profit center."

A decade earlier, in the eighties, Birthtech started as a clinic for in vitro fertilization—the technique that united egg and sperm in a test tube, then transplanted the resulting embryo to the mother's womb. When Birthtech was acquired by United Genetics, it rapidly grew from a single, struggling laboratory to a global chain, expanding as well into the new technique of genetic screening for parents-to-be. Now, from New York to Paris to Tokyo, Birthtech provided prospective parents both high-technology conception and the inside odds on the previously imponderable genetic dice roll.

As the huge glass doors of the clinic automatically slid open, Kaye looked at Rackley with quick curiosity. "Are we paying for this?"

Rackley smiled slightly. Even though Kaye had been raised amid wealth and power as close to nobility as the western United States could manage, she still kept a cautious eye on their finances. "Employee discount," he said. "And we get the full gene scan. Your brother says it predicts everything but sense of humor and diaper rash."

Kaye laughed, but Rackley heard a trace of uneasiness. The exaggeration wasn't far from the mark. Hundreds of diseases and physical conditions could now be predicted by gene scanning, ranging from cystic fibrosis to heart disease and cancer. There was also some information that no one could receive at any price. A new federal law prevented genetic counselors from passing on data about certain nonmedical qualities. One gene sequence in particular, which contributed to high intelligence, was specifically forbidden—counselors could neither confirm nor deny its presence.

Inside the clinic a young nurse immediately ushered them into a small, neatly furnished office. "No waiting room," Kaye whispered, "for a corporate vice president."

Moments later, Louise Allman, senior genetics counselor at Birthtech, entered and sat behind the desk. She was a large, gray-haired woman in her forties, who looked more like a reference librarian than a genetic seer.

"It's a pleasure to meet you, Mr. Rackley," Allman said, then smiled at Kaye. "Hello, Katherine. I've already worked for your brother Edward and his wife. How is baby Erin?"

Kaye smiled. "We just saw her last night. She's a beautiful little girl. And very smart."

Allman nodded sagely. "Doesn't surprise me a bit."

"Edward says you're the best," Rackley said.

"Well"—the woman raised one eyebrow, mildly amused—"let me see if I can live up to that." She glanced down at the file folder in front of her. "Today, it's pretty straightforward. We'll take blood samples and send them to our processing plant." She looked up. "That's actually only a couple of blocks from here."

"I want to know all about it," Kaye said quickly. "If you don't mind."

Allman nodded and began to explain the sophisticated machines that broke down blood cells to extract the long microscopic strands of DNA. These comprised the genetic sum of Rackley and Kaye—the skein of genes which would also shape their child.

"We'll analyze your DNA two different ways," Allman said briskly. "Some gets chemically chopped into fragments. Certain kin. s of fragments can be linked directly to genetic conditions. The rest of the sample, we test with DNA probes."

Kaye frowned. "Where do you get those?"

"We make them," Allman said. "We know that specific genes cause certain diseases. So we mass-produce synthetic versions of those genes, which will bind to similar genes in your own DNA. If there are any. We label our synthetic genes with a tiny bit of radioactivity, so if they do link up to some of your genes, we know they're in there."

"They glow in the dark," Kaye said.

Allman smiled. "Something like that."

Rackley was familiar with the technology; in the early days of United Genetics he had written more than his share of press releases describing gene scans. But he listened patiently; Kaye was intently curious about every detail of the process.

Kaye followed Allman's technical recitation for another minute or so and then finally leaned forward. "But how accurate are these things? I mean, really."

Allman gazed at her evenly. "Extremely accurate," she said with quiet confidence. "We're discovering, more than anyone guessed twenty years ago, that genes are destiny. And also, genes don't lie."

Kaye's expression did not change. "What do you mean?"

"Families," Allman continued, "sometimes lie. Not on purpose, necessarily. But family histories tend to be . . . sanitized. That's what used to make genetic counseling so hard. Somebody would tell you about their charming, dotty great-great-aunt. Back then, if we had gene scans, we could have known the woman must have been a raving schizophrenic and there was some chance one of her descendants might be also. Now we don't have to rely on those histories. The truth is in the genes."

Kaye nodded again, glancing sideways at Rackley. Allman caught the silent exchange and cleared her throat. "Is there," she asked after a moment, "something in particular you're concerned about?"

She looked down at their histories, which were standard forms that inquired only about the most serious hereditary disorders. "I don't see anything here that looks like a red flag."

"I don't imagine so," Kaye said quickly, a bit of cool affront in her voice. "We just want to be certain."

"Of course." Allman smiled for a moment. "Certainty is exactly what we deliver." She leaned forward and touched a button on her desk. "Let me call the nurse in."

While they waited, the talk turned more informal. Allman asked how Rackley and Kaye had met, and soon they were talking about themselves.

Their romance started six years earlier, at the Caswell summer house in the Sierra foothills, an elaborate retreat financed by three generations of timber and mining. Rackley was spending the weekend as the guest of Kaye's older brother, Edward. Early one morning Kaye and Rackley found themselves together, and the attraction grew quickly. Kaye had a smart, quick laugh and it was humor, in fact, that first brought them together: It was as if they secretly, with no prior negotiation, shared the same perspective on life. Eight months after their meeting at the summer house they were married.

"I think I saw a picture in the paper," Louise Allman said.

Rackley nodded. The local newspapers doted on what remained of the Western land aristocracy. "I was the one that looked like the penguin."

Allman glanced up as her office door swung open. A male nurse entered, carrying a stainless steel tray neatly set with medical paraphernalia.

Kaye turned. "I forgot to ask. How long will this take?"

"Day after tomorrow," Allman said. "Make an appointment on your way out."

* * *

When Trina Robbins drove into the Birthtech parking lot, she was surprised to see Rackley's old MG. She was manager of press relations for United Genetics, and her visit to Birthtech today was a minor bit of business that in no way required Rackley's attention. She would be glad, nonetheless, to see him; they hadn't really talked for nearly a week. Trina reached up and smoothed her dark hair back from her face. Perhaps, she thought, she could distract him for coffee in the clinic cafeteria.

Then she saw the car next to his: Kaye's yellow Mercedes. Trina felt a rush of adrenaline and a certain sharp stab. She knew instantly there was only one reason the two would visit Birthtech, and the thought gave her a quick, irrational surge of jealousy.

She shook her head at the senseless response. Rackley had been married for six years now; whatever claim Trina once had on him was even more distant than that. She parked the car, switched off the engine, and leaned forward, resting her smooth chin on the cool steering wheel, thinking for a moment. Of course Kaye and Rackley would have children. She knew that perfectly well. And it had absolutely nothing to do with her.

She gathered up her briefcase, left the car, and started to walk into the clinic. Just before she reached the big glass entrance of the building, the automatic doors slid open and Kaye and Rackley emerged. Kaye had her arm hooked through Rackley's, her head turned toward him, and the two appeared deep in conversation.

Trina stood quietly for a moment. When she had first met Rackley years ago in the hospital, she had weighed less than one hundred pounds. Back then she had a kind of breathtaking, unhealthy beauty, like some nocturnal creature accidentally caught in the daylight, but as she gained health, she gained weight as well and was now in a constant state of declared war with her figure. Today her coat was loose at the neck, revealing a pale lavender blouse, cool against her tan skin. Her dark, curly hair was pulled back, accentuating her cheekbones and brown eyes.

Kaye saw her first. "Trina," she said, clearly surprised. "Hello."

Trina smiled. "Hello, Kaye."

Rackley regarded Trina with some concern. "Is there a problem?" he asked. "No more pickets, I hope."

Trina shook her head. "It's the tenth anniversary of Birthtech next month. I was thinking we might do a press release about it."

Rackley nodded. "We can use all the good publicity we can get."

There was a silence as the three stood for a moment, and then Rackley glanced at his watch. "I should run. I have a meeting with Edward in half an hour."

He looked at Kaye. She kissed his cheek. "Go. I'll talk to Trina for a second."

"See you later," Trina said.

Rackley nodded and walked briskly toward his aging sports car. Both Trina and Kaye watched him for a moment, and then Trina turned back, curious.

Kaye spoke first. "Do you have a minute?"

Trina paused, puzzled; she could not recall the last time she had talked privately with Kaye. She and Kaye were hardly close friends; indeed, she always felt a certain tension between them.

"I just wanted to ask you something," Kaye brushed a wisp of her thin blond hair away from her face as the wind came up more strongly from the Bay.

"Sure." Trina, still puzzled, gestured to one side, and they sat on a textured concrete bench just outside the smoked glass doors of the Birthtech clinic.

Kaye bunched her hands together, looking down in her lap. "Sometimes," she said finally, "I think you know more about Rackley than I do."

Trina shook her head quickly. "Don't be silly," she said. "That's not true. We used to have the same problems. That's all."

"Well," Kaye said. "More than that."

Trina said nothing for a moment. "He really loves you," she said at last. "I don't think I've ever seen anything quite like it."

Kaye nodded.

"You're lucky. He's a good man."

"I know that," Kaye said softly, clearly a bit uncomfortable. She looked out at the rough stone-gray water of the Bay and sighed. "I think he's a worried man, too."

Trina nodded calmly. "He has a lot to worry about. The public offering, and this thing with the escaped rice plant—your brother and Markham act like it's not important, but—"

"That's not what I mean." Kaye hesitated, then spoke quickly. "At the meetings you and Rackley go to, do people ever talk about their children?"

"Sometimes," Trina said tentatively.

"Do their children," Kaye asked, "usually end up the same way?"

"You can say the word. It's not an insult. Yes, some of their kids are alcoholics. Or addicts. Or both."

"Even if their parents are sober?"

"Doesn't seem to make much difference. It's certainly genetic, if that's what you mean."

Kaye nodded. "I know that's what the scientists say." She paused for a moment. "I think Rackley is worried. That he'll think it's his fault if we have a child and—"

"But you don't know for sure, do you?"

"That's why we're here," Kaye said. "To find out. But if . . . anything happened . . . Rackley would blame himself."

Trina shook her head. "That doesn't make sense. He didn't personally invent the disease, you know. I mean, whatever genes he has, he got them from somebody else."

Kaye laughed quietly. "I guess that's true." She looked over at Trina. "He and I really haven't talked about this very much. I don't know why."

Trina nodded. Rackley seemed to shield her from that part of his life, that element of his past. Kaye had never even visited an AA meeting. "Well, maybe you're getting ahead of yourself. Wait for the gene scans. Rackley may be . . . some kind of exception."

Kaye nodded. "I guess I'm just nervous."

Trina put her hand on Kaye's and squeezed for a moment. "I'd be nervous too," she said. "But don't worry. Take it one day at a time."

Kaye hesitated. "I don't really know who else I can talk to about this."

"Well." Trina said. "You can always talk to me."

Kaye nodded again. "I'm glad you feel that way."

They talked for another minute or so, and then Trina stood and walked into the Birthtech clinic. For a moment she stopped, standing in the carpeted lobby. She had entirely forgotten her mission.

Her mind was wandering, she told herself. She was thinking about Kaye being pregnant, trying to imagine Rackley as a bumbling, nervous father-to-be. . . .

Then she remembered; she was putting together a file on Birthtech. And at that moment a thought came into her mind, quite unbidden, altogether treacherous. She realized with a shock that she was wondering whether she and Rackley would sleep together while Kaye was pregnant. Trina shook her head; that kind of thinking belonged in her past.

"Ms. Robbins," a nurse finally said from behind the reception desk, "can I help you?"

"Yes," Trina said quickly, and smiled. "I think you'd better."

CHAPTER TWO

Rackley drove through the Birthtech parking lot, then past United Genetics' main research facility, a scatter of tilt-ups rising on ground previously occupied by a tribe of vagrant hippies, final relics of the sixties, who had lived in school buses festooned with psychedelia.

Times change. A dozen genetic engineering firms were now settled in Berkeley; biologists seemed to prefer its relaxed atmosphere over the kinetic pace of Silicon Valley. Rackley sometimes mused that computers operated at nearly the speed of light, but living organisms, no matter how their genes were tweaked, retained a more measured metabolism. Genetic engineering thus had a different tone than the computer business—although United Genetics intended to eliminate the difference as much as possible.

Before Rackley turned the corner toward the freeway, he paused for a moment and gazed into his rearview mirror. Trina and Kaye were still in front of the clinic, small figures against the imposing structure of golden glass. The day was so clear that if he looked carefully, past the two women, beyond the big new building, far up into the green hills, he could make out the tiny yellow dot of the private hospital where he had first met—and briefly fell in love with—Trina Robbins.

God, he thought. It seemed almost another life altogether, back when he was a magazine writer, earning a reputation for investigative pieces, from African famine to the Alaskan pipeline. For nearly ten years he had traveled the world, and he was always happiest at the beginning of a story. Living out of a suitcase struck him as a nearly ideal existence.

Drinking and drugs were an integral part of that life, and for a time Rackley's chemical proclivities even seemed to help his writing. At a nuclear power plant protest in California, Rackley, slightly drunk, found himself in the middle of a police charge. He was arrested with some Greenpeace activists and wrote his story in a jail cell. His editors thought it a brilliant stroke of participatory journalism.

Gradually, however, his professional day became a matter of achieving the right chemical state in order to produce a few pages of copy. Then the productive periods became shorter and shorter. And one day Rackley awakened in a Santa Monica motel and found that he could no longer write at all—not with drink, not without. He should have been at the peak of his powers; instead, Rackley's career collapsed. His last magazine contract was canceled after he drew $10,000 yet never submitted a word.

By then Rackley could no longer avoid the truth. One sodden night in a decrepit San Francisco residence hotel he found himself staring at a bottle of vodka. With acute clarity, Rackley abruptly confronted something long denied: he had precisely the same disease he had so hated in his parents. The next morning he decided to stop drinking entirely.

On his second dry day, in the midst of miserable withdrawal, Rackley arose shakily from his sweat-soaked sheets and sat in the darkened room, head pounding, limbs trembling. At that moment, sick and shaking and disgusted with himself, Rackley suddenly felt, out of nowhere, the urge to drink renew itself. It was a primal, bone-deep desire, mysterious, impossible to ignore: an urge beyond words that seemed to come not from the mind, but directly from the brain tissue, the blood, the genes.

Rackley sat, hands clenched, resisting with all his strength, but even then knowing the inevitable. In a matter of minutes, as if in a dream, he would find himself gathering together a few dollars in change and going down the street for a pint of drugstore vodka.

But then, just before he stood, Rackley had been engulfed by a massive seizure: a muscular spasm so intense and powerful that it pulled him up out of his chair, flung him backwards, helpless and catatonic, against the dingy wall of the hotel room, limbs flailing as if electrified, where he slid slowly to the floor, unconscious, barely breathing, twitching slightly, a tiny bit of blood running from his mouth.

*   *   *

Now, seven years later, the seizure seemed distant, hazy, mysterious. It was almost as if there had been another Thomas Rackley, so entirely had his life been altered.

Twenty minutes after leaving Birthtech, Rackley parked in the basement garage of a tall marble building in the San Francisco financial district. Twenty-five floors upstairs, the express elevator opened into the lobby of United Genetics. The quiet suite of offices was decorated in salmon and gray, furnished with Italian furniture in clean, international lines. The look was simple and clearly expensive, designed to make both East Coast investment bankers and molecular geneticists from Stanford feel equally at ease.

The receptionist looked up as Rackley entered. Over her desk was a huge oil painting with dramatic, spare lines of bright color. Visitors conversant with contemporary art often identified it as a commissioned piece by a prominent French artist; those who spent more time in the laboratory saw an impressionistic rendering of the human insulin gene. Very few visitors ever recognized both aspects at once.

"Your assistant has your messages," the receptionist said. "Also, Mr. Caswell was just asking if you'd come in."

Rackley quickly walked down one long hall, stopping briefly in his office to pick up a document, then crossing the corridor. Caswell's secretary waved him in. "He's expecting you."

Caswell was on the telephone, but held up one finger to indicate his call was nearly complete. Rackley nodded and sat on one of the low leather chairs across from Caswell's massive rosewood desk.

Rackley first met Caswell in a freshman dorm at Stanford. Even then, Rackley was an adept writer and occasionally helped Caswell with term papers. Rackley liked the young heir's quick wit, and during spring breaks, the two would go trout fishing on Caswell land in the Sierra, at the summer home where he later met Kaye.

Now, Caswell was Chief Executive Officer of United Genetics. "When Edward walks into a room," Rackley sometimes said, "he *looks* like he's somebody." He was a large, imposing man with dark, wavy hair and a heavy beard, always flawlessly trimmed. His smile began slowly, and then as his large white teeth appeared, shifted to something approaching a feral challenge. His dominance was accentuated by broad shoulders and thick forearms from weight training, and his suits were closely tailored to fit his hard-earned torso.

Rackley, however, had known Caswell long enough to learn that his image was as carefully cultivated as his triceps. Caswell had in fact been a quiet, shy child, always in the shadow of a dominating father given to fits of temper and irrational behavior. Two generations of Caswells had managed, through batty business deals, to reduce the family fortune significantly. But young Caswell seemed a throwback to his great-grandfather; Wall Street pundits speculated that if anyone could restore the family ascendancy, it would be Edward.

Rackley leaned back in the chair and listened to the conversation.

"I'll be in New York on Friday," Caswell was saying. "We'll talk then."

Caswell listened briefly, staring out the window, eyes blinking impatiently. "I don't care what the analysts are saying and neither should you. If they're so bright, why are they sitting on Wall Street writing reports instead of out making money like God intended?" He listened again. "Breakfast on Friday. Seven-thirty, the Carlyle. Don't worry about a thing."

Caswell hung up and gazed over at Rackley. "Donahue at Chemical Bank."

"What's he worried about?"

"Oh," Caswell said, waving one large hand. "Something about this Rice Five business. Whether it will delay the public offering."

Rackley leaned forward. "Edward, the only thing I can see delaying the public offering is goddamn Paul Markham. We've got to get some kind of schedule in place and stick to it."

Caswell settled back in his chair and regarded Rackley for a moment, his gaze amused but affectionate. "Rackley," he said gently, shaking his head, "sometimes I look at you and I wonder, where did my spaced-out writer go?"

Rackley relaxed slightly and smiled. "He was driven insane by Paul Markham."

"Well," Caswell said mildly, "if your first idea at age eighteen made you four hundred million dollars, you'd be a little difficult also."

Rackley shook his head firmly. "No. I'd have spent it all long ago."

Caswell laughed. "Probably so." He was silent for a moment, looking across the desk. "It was good to see you two last night. We should do that more often."

Rackley agreed. Sunday night, he and Kaye had visited the

Caswells' apartment, a big old penthouse in a Nob Hill building. They ate pizza and spent the evening playing dumb video games on a projection television screen. It was mindless, relaxing, pure play, something they all did too infrequently.

"I was watching Kaye with Erin last night," Caswell said. "She's very good with children."

Rackley shifted in his chair. "She likes them. They like her."

"What you need is one of your own."

Rackley sighed deeply, trying to stare down his brother-in-law. "What I need is a serious discussion about the public offering."

"Kaye's twenty-nine," Caswell said conspiratorily. "Come on. You can tell me."

Rackley gazed at him for a moment. He owed much to Edward Caswell, but there were times that the man was simply overbearing. Caswell had an almost limitless need to control everything around him. That had long since included the life of his younger sister, and with marriage Rackley had fallen into the same purview. "Edward," he said firmly, "what we're talking about today is the public offering."

Caswell nodded with good nature and raised both hands in surrender. "Fine," he said. "Fine." He looked at Rackley for a moment. "But you and Kaye will let me know your plans, won't you?"

"Edward," Rackley lied, "you'll be the first to know." He reached down and pulled out a thin folder. "This is a tentative timetable on taking United Genetics public. We could have an offering within nine months. And I think it's going to set records."

Caswell nodded quickly. "That," he said, "I don't doubt."

It had been only a handful of years since Paul Markham, the reclusive young man who made his first fortune with PM Computers, had walked into the Caswell family offices with a business plan for a company called United Genetics. At the time no one—except Markham himself—could have foreseen the explosive times that followed.

Markham's plan was simple. Instead of only one application— drugs or agricultural products or medical diagnosis kits—United Genetics would do everything from creating new plant species to performing gene scans for parents-to-be. Markham proposed computerized assembly lines with standardized tools, manipulating genes in all species from bacteria to humans. And there was a fundamental logic to his vision: DNA is DNA, whether it comes from a sea urchin, a cornstalk, or a human baby. "We'll be the

IBM of genetic engineering," he told Caswell that first day. "Only bigger."

Caswell agreed on the spot. He and Markham put up half the money, and dozens of other venture capitalists competed to provide the rest. If PM Computers was any example, the early investors would earn back their investments fifty times over. After months of secret planning, Markham and Caswell purchased seven genetic engineering companies and molded them into a single, massive corporation. Markham had already devised the corporate motto: "The Future Is in Our Genes."

United Genetics had been the fastest-growing technology company in history, and now the time was approaching to sell stock to the public, thus providing the payoff for their investors. Rackley handed Caswell his projected timetable. Caswell picked up the report, fingered the cover, then set it back down on his desk without opening it.

"Fine. I'm glad you've done this. But we don't have to rush."

Rackley stared at him. "Our valuation has never been higher," he said. "The stock market will go crazy trying to buy a piece of Paul Markham's next great idea."

"You and Paul are going to talk to the underwriters next week. What more do you want?"

"Something definite to tell the investors."

"Tell them they're all going to be very rich."

Rackley sighed. "They're on my back every day. Some of those boys are getting very eager to cash out."

"All I'm saying," Caswell said, "is that if the conditions aren't right, we can delay the offering. As long as we haven't made too many commitments in front." He tapped Rackley's schedule heavily with one finger.

"Right now is the ideal market. If we wait much longer somebody is going to sue us."

Caswell rubbed his high forehead with both hands. "Talk to Markham."

"I did. He said to talk to you."

"Well," Caswell said, spreading his hands wide. "Then you've done your job."

In the corridor outside, Rackley paused for a moment. He felt both patronized and dismissed, and what was worse, he was quite sure he was right. He knew that he should go back in and confront Caswell. But then—as was usually the case—Rackley hesitated. His relationship with Edward Caswell was not a simple one.

After his seizure, when Rackley had awakened in a strange hospital room, the first face he had seen was Caswell's.

"Huh?" Rackley had said, staring up at the tall, bearded figure, even as he discovered that during the throes of his seizure he had chewed his tongue into a swollen mass. "Where am I?"

"Mt. Zion," Caswell told him. "Private room. You still had my business card in your pocket. Frankly that was the only thing that kept them from throwing you into county detox. I told them you were on our health plan."

"What . . . ?" Rackley asked, still uncomprehending. "How . . . ?" Then vague, disconnected memories came back: a week earlier, a lunch with Caswell, some talk about a job that sounded suspiciously like public relations for a new company. Pitching rotten story ideas to bad-mannered newspaper reporters: Rackley had taken the lunch, but never considered the idea seriously.

A young doctor approached the bed and gazed at the chart. His diagnosis was simple: acute alcoholic withdrawal. "You've got a real problem, Mr. Rackley," the doctor said solemnly, returning the chart to its hook at the foot of the bed. "I would strongly advise treatment. Next binge, you're probably going to see some brain damage."

"The job offer still stands," Caswell said that night in the hospital. "In a way, you're on the payroll now."

Rackley, groggy, just stared.

"You'd be in from the beginning. Healthy stock options, if you care about that sort of thing."

Rackley struggled to sit up. "Well," he said. "If . . ."

Caswell, taking this for affirmation, held up one hand. "There's only one condition: before you come to work, we'll send you to a little place in Berkeley. They have a twenty-eight-day program that will do you a world of good."

The seizure had literally flung him out of his old existence and into a new one. But even now, seven years later, he sometimes felt as if he was still learning his way. After another moment standing outside Caswell's door, Rackley shook his head and walked away.

Later that night Rackley and Kaye left their old Pacific Heights Victorian and walked up Baker Street to a country French restaurant. They sat in one corner of the small, warm room and ate onion soup and steaks and pommes frites.

With some frustration Rackley described the conversation about the public offering with her reticent brother.

Kaye leaned her head to one side, only mildly interested. "Maybe he's right," she said casually. "He's been in venture capital for a long time."

Rackley looked up quickly. "You're on his side."

"No, no, no," Kaye said, shaking her head. "My God, don't listen to me. My idea of high finance is our balance at Saks."

Rackley was silent for a moment. Edward's undue influence was an old source of tension between them. Unlike many children of the privileged, Kaye had neither completely rejected nor entirely embraced her genteel roots. She ran away from a Swiss boarding school when she was twelve; her parents brought her back to a girls' school in the hills above Silicon Valley. She did well there, and went on to Vassar. About then her father died, and Edward took charge of the family.

Kaye had debuted at Cotillion, but when she returned to San Francisco after college, she tended to take her friends from an artier, south-of-Market set. Her one serious love affair had been with a writer, a year her junior, who went off to Los Angeles to work in the movies.

Rackley still recalled their first long conversation, up at the Caswell house in the Sierra foothills. Early one morning he left the big old Victorian house, just at dawn, fly rod in hand. Rackley was so intent on leaving quietly that he was startled to see the thin young woman, in jeans and a light wool sweater, sitting on the porch railing.

"Hey," he said, catching his breath. "You're up early."

"Mind if I tag along?"

"Of course not," Rackley said, flattered by the attention.

Kaye was a surefooted companion, who walked along and said little, as Rackley made desultory casts into the wide, cold river. The fishing that morning was terrible: a couple strikes and one five-inch rainbow punctuating an hour of uneventful casts. But Kaye was pleasant company; they chatted idly about the woods, restaurants in San Francisco, the birds around them. Kaye worked as an interior designer and had a small office in the warehouse district and a part-time secretary. When they returned to the big house for breakfast, they made a date for lunch back in the city.

Once they became close, Kaye admitted that it had been Edward's suggestion that she accompany Rackley on his postdawn excursion. At the time Rackley was grateful for his old friend's manipulation. But in recent years he had found Edward's attempts to control Kaye increasingly annoying. Now it sounded as if she were taking her brother's side on the public offering. "I wonder,"

Rackley said that night at dinner, "if you'll always take Edward's word over mine."

Kaye glanced up sharply. "I don't do that now."

Rackley simply nodded.

"I do not," Kaye said. "Look at me."

Rackley looked up from his steak.

"Listen. Edward is always going to be a busybody. That's how he is. He thinks he knows everything, and he has a million opinions, and the way I've learned to deal with it is just to nod and ignore him." She reached across the table and touched Rackley's hand. "I don't do that with you," she said. "You're the most important person in my life and I care completely about everything you say and think. Okay?"

Rackley nodded. "Okay." Then he shook his head. "I'm just tired."

"Let's talk about something else." For a moment Kaye sipped a glass of red wine. "I had a talk with Trina today. She was very nice. Very reassuring."

Rackley took a deep breath. The gene scan seemed to hover in front of him, an inevitable moment of judgment. Right now his genetic sum was churning in an automated machine, binding tightly to telltale markers, glowing faintly in some cool laboratory darkness.

Kaye didn't notice his silence. She began to talk about their plans to remodel the upstairs of the old Victorian. They would replace the forbidding library that now filled the back of the house with a nanny room plus a nursery. Typically for San Francisco, the renovation project had turned into a major production: the entire building had to be brought up to a stringent earthquake code, even though the Victorian had already been twenty years old when it survived the last quake.

"I talked to the architect today," Kaye said. "The permits are going to take months."

"Well," Rackley said, still tense. "We have months."

"I already found wonderful wallpaper though," Kaye went on, ignoring his mood. "It's from Spain, and it's just like what used to be in my room at the summer house."

Rackley smiled slightly, sinking into the conversation as if it were a warm bath. "Spain," he said. "Bullfight scenes?"

Kaye made a face. "Tiny flowers." She took another sip of wine. "Burgundy and pink and a kind of soft yellow. It's just perfect. . . ."

So went the conversation, over dinner and coffee, and by the time they walked home through the low cool fog, Rackley felt powerfully content. The talk of nurseries and nanny rooms was another thing the old Rackley would never have imagined. At heart, Rackley thought, he and Kaye shared the same desire for normalcy. Kaye sought release from the powerful influence of her family; Rackley, to close the door on the hazy, dangerous days of his addiction. Although neither ever quite said so, their baby would represent a new beginning: a creation entirely their own, growing into the future, rather than reaching out from the past.

It was nearly eleven when they went to bed. Kaye was slightly tipsy from two glasses of wine at dinner, and feeling romantic, they made love.

"You know," she whispered as she slipped into bed, "I could punch a few holes in my diaphragm and we'd never have to go back to old Mrs. What's-her-name."

Rackley tensed involuntarily.

"I'm joking," Kaye said quickly. "Please don't think about it now." She breathed into his ear. "I love your back," she whispered, running her hand down his spine, caressing his buttocks. He thought for a moment of the first time they had made love, in a little inn in the Napa Valley, surrounded by goosedown quilts.

Kaye had refused to sleep with him until they had been dating for two months, and Rackley came to wonder whether there might be something odd about his new love. But when they finally went to bed together at the inn in St. Helena, it carried their relationship to a deeper level. Kaye was a shy but passionate lover, and from that first night on their bond was set.

"Why did you want to wait so long?" Rackley had asked her that first night.

She whispered that something might not have gone right, and she wanted their romance to last as long as possible. He had reached over and pulled her close to tell her just how right it was.

It was still right. Kaye's body was lithe, muscular: the thought of her small firm breasts, her long neck, the scent of her smooth skin, sometimes came to him, out of nowhere, in midday. She was an eager, imaginative lover who trembled when he stroked the slope of her waist or her smooth thighs. Kaye had infused his life with energy he had thought lost long ago in the gradual dulling cynicism of his previous existence.

With his last conscious effort, Rackley set the alarm clock for six A.M., and they fell asleep in each other's arms.

The telephone rang ten minutes later. Rackley groped to reach the receiver and then heard Trina's low voice.

"Rackley, I'm sorry to call so late, but I just got tomorrow's *New York Times*. Rice Five is on the front page."

"Damn," Rackley said, instantly awake.

"This," Trina said, "is going to be trouble."

In the morning Rackley's secretary had arranged copies of the *New York Times,* the *Los Angeles Times,* and the *Washington Post* across the polished surface of his desk. Rackley's corner office afforded a view from the dry peak of Mt. Diablo in the east to the green undulations of Marin in the north. Normally, Rackley would take a moment to appreciate the vista. But not today. He glanced at the first headline: GENE-ALTERED RICE NEW WEED ON COAST.

"There have been about fifty calls today," his secretary said, standing at the door. "Everybody wants to talk to Markham. The guy from *Time* is calling every five minutes. Trina's handling them."

"Where's Markham?"

"He's here. But he says he'd rather not get involved."

"We'll see about that," Rackley said sharply, rubbing his face.

Rackley returned to the papers. All three had run the escaped-rice story on the front page; in addition, the Los Angeles paper had taken a poll. Sixty-three percent of the respondents now felt that genetic engineering work was "dangerous"; eighty-eight percent agreed that the current ban on human genetic engineering should be continued indefinitely.

"Holy Christ," Rackley said softly to himself as he read the poll results. It was the highest negative response yet. He picked up another paper and scanned the story for a moment.

The account was basically correct. The agricultural division of

United Genetics, up in the California farm country near Sacramento, had spent several years developing a strain of rice that
would be much easier to plant than current varieties. It had been
one of Paul Markham's favorite schemes. The young entrepreneur
had always felt that the Japanese had stolen America's computer
industry. "This time around," Markham told investors, "the
Japanese are going to buy their rice from us. And it won't be
cheap."

Apparently, the Agricultural Division planted Rice Five
outdoors, before greenhouse safety tests were finished. The
modified plant, a cross between a popular rice hybrid and a rare
Asian water lily, had developed the ability to spread on both land
and water with remarkable speed. Before the tendency was
recognized, however, birds consumed seeds from the outdoor
plantings. The seeds passed through the birds undigested and had
taken root in one of the shallow waterways of the labyrinthine
California Delta, seventy miles east of San Francisco.

Rackley set the paper down and closed his eyes for a moment.
He had hoped the outbreak would be eradicated before it received
public attention. The reason was simple: in only a month Congress
would debate the extension of the federal ban on human genetic
engineering—a ban that United Genetics had lobbied hard to
change. The timing of the accident could not possibly have been
worse.

He stood and quickly walked down the hall to Trina's office.
She was on the telephone when Rackley walked in. "No," she
was saying, "we do not know acreage. It may not have spread at
all . . . No . . . We do not know that . . . Yes."

Rackley sat and watched Trina for a moment. She was wearing
a cream-colored silk blouse, buttoned at the neck. A delicate
woven gold chain circled down toward her breasts, and her thick
brown hair caught quick highlights as she moved her head. Trina
was a sensual woman, and Rackley still sometimes recalled
the months they had spent together. It had broken his heart the
afternoon he had walked out, but there had been no choice:
the risk was too great. Behind her demure demeanor, Trina's story
was even more extreme than his.

At twenty, Trina had been an honors student at the University
of California when she met a major northern California cocaine
smuggler, who lived in the secluded hills of west Marin County.
Within three months, Trina lost interest in her studies and drifted
into a world that seemed a blend of perpetual tourism and
sophisticated risk. When she moved into Rand's house, her friends

were baffled: they couldn't understand the attraction of the sullen, hostile young man. Trina, a conventional child from a small Midwestern town, couldn't explain it very well herself. What she didn't tell her friends was that she found herself consuming a great deal of his flaked and powdered product.

The relationship lasted nearly two years, until Trina, in a careless moment, was arrested on drug and firearms charges. After she had spent a night in the Marin County detox and a half-day in jail, Rand posted her bail, then kicked her out. She was too crazy, he said; he couldn't stand to keep her around anymore. For Trina the rejection was an epiphany: a sociopath was saying that she wasn't good enough for him.

Her lawyer advised her to complete a drug and alcohol treatment program before sentencing; she chose the detox facility in the hills of Berkeley, arriving just four days after Rackley. They met on dishwashing duty in the rehab's kitchen. The two had been lovers, first, and then friends ever since.

This morning, Rackley could tell that the reporter on the other end of the line was being persistent. Trina finally raised her voice. "When there is a press conference, you will be the first to know. Now I really have to go." She made a note on a piece of paper, set the telephone down, and looked up at Rackley. Then she held up a hand for another moment, picked up a large bran muffin, and took a bite. A tiny shower of crumbs dotted the newspapers on her desk.

"This is absolutely ruining my diet," she mumbled. "I've been on the phone since six this morning." She finished swallowing. "I assume you saw the protesters."

Rackley nodded. He couldn't miss them: about thirty well-dressed pickets from Natural Progress had been on the sidewalk directly in front of United Genetics' corporate headquarters, marching in a tight circle, carrying hand-lettered signs: "Stop the Mutants!" "Hands Off Mother Nature!" "No Designer Genes!"

"This is exactly the kind of thing Steven Hechinger loves," Rackley said. "Now there's no way the Senate can ignore this, whether they think it's important or not."

Trina smiled slightly. "The guy does know how to make trouble."

"He's a pain in the ass." Rackley said, leaning back. "Period."

Steven Hechinger was the founder of Natural Progress, a national group dedicated to the control of genetic engineering. Over the years, the energetic young activist had amassed a powerful assortment of allies and in Rackley's view, was the single greatest threat facing United Genetics.

Trina cleared her throat. "I've been saying we should do something preemptive on this rice thing. We knew there were reporters around. Markham just refused to talk to them."

"Well," Rackley said, "he's going to talk to them now."

Trina shook her head. "I already asked him this morning."

"And what did he say?"

Trina looked at an open notepad on her desk. "Quote: 'Worse things have happened to the environment.'"

Rackley closed his eyes for a moment. "The man has a natural gift for public relations."

"He's got an ego the size of the Goodyear blimp."

Rackley realized that he had been holding his breath. He exhaled deeply and finally nodded once, twice, staring intently at the maroon carpeting.

Trina watched Rackley for a moment. "I could use a meeting tonight," she said softly. "How about you?"

Rackley looked up slowly. "I'll try."

Trina smiled. "I'll count on it."

Before visiting Markham, Rackley tried to enlist Caswell's support. But he found his brother-in-law far less cheerful than the previous day.

"Hechinger is behind this," Caswell said immediately, "isn't he?"

"I think so," Rackley said.

Caswell tapped one large fist softly on the surface of his desk. "These Natural Progress people are ignorant and dangerous. If you'd told me seven years ago that we were going to run into a movement made of Bible pounders, nature freaks, and liberals, I'd have said . . ."

Caswell's measured voice trailed off as he shook his head, clearly unable to imagine so preposterous a proposition.

"You'd have said, 'nuke 'em,'" Rackley suggested.

"At least," Caswell agreed.

Rackley leaned back in his leather chair and watched Caswell for a moment. Caswell's annoyance with Natural Progress had a special edge: for four generations his family had shaped the western United States—built a railroad, funded a major private university. Questioning a Caswell venture, regardless of the merits, was just plain ungrateful.

Rackley was very conscious of the unspoken class distinctions that clouded his brother-in-law's vision. It was something Rackley could never share. Caswell and his peers all seemed to have attended the same prep schools and summered in adjacent compounds on Martha's Vineyard. They always knew exactly when an Oxford cloth shirt with a frayed collar looked right; Rackley was the sort who invariably appeared to have run out of decent shirts. But Rackley was also the one at United Genetics most in touch with the people out on the street, and as the voices of the demonstrators momentarily drifted up from the sidewalk, he cleared his throat.

"Listen," he told Caswell. "The more we ignore these people, the more public sympathy they're going to get. Did you see that poll in the *Times* this morning?"

Caswell snorted quietly. "And two out of three Americans believe that launching satellites has changed the weather. We're in a new Dark Ages, Rackley."

"In this country," Rackley said quietly, "ignorance doesn't disqualify you from having an opinion. Or voting on it."

"Please don't lecture me." Caswell stood at the window and looked down at the band of protesters.

Rackley walked over to gaze out the window next to Caswell. He didn't share Caswell's inbred sense of divine mission, but he did retain faith in the ability of science to save the species. The hour was late, the planet too crowded, to reject any technologic fix. "As far as I'm concerned," Rackley said after a moment, "stonewalling is not an option here. If we act now, this can be a minor matter. Otherwise . . ."

Caswell said nothing, thrusting his hands deeper into the pockets of his gray wool trousers.

Rackley turned to leave.

"Do what you have to," Caswell said finally.

Markham's secretary saw Rackley coming and smiled. "He's waiting for you."

"I bet," Rackley said softly and he opened the door with a brisk gesture, then stopped abruptly.

A young woman in white was kneeling beside Markham's desk. She had a hypodermic needle and was drawing blood from the young entrepreneur's arm, which was stretched out flat on the blond surface of his desk. Rackley paused for a moment before entering the room.

Rackley used to call Markham and his cohorts "the baby

moguls"—Silicon Valley teenagers who became millionaires in the early eighties by starting computer companies or writing best-selling software. Once they had made their fortunes, the lucky ones hired money managers and retired to quiet hacking in their mansions. The unlucky ones lost their fortunes starting new businesses, trying to re-create those early moments when any computer was golden. Only a few baby moguls—Steven Jobs, William Gates—proved to have staying power. And Paul Markham was the most remarkable of them all.

When PM Computers went public in 1983, Markham found himself worth $400 million, a symbol of Silicon Valley, featured on newsmagazine covers, feted at White House dinners. But Markham knew that the computer gold rush would soon end. Quietly, Markham moved his money out of computers and into Sunbelt real estate and municipal bonds—and waited patiently for the next great technologic opportunity. Caswell claimed that Markham was the only entrepreneur of his generation with the drive and vision of a great railway or steel baron, transferred to the esoteric realms of high technology.

At last Markham noticed Rackley, raised his other hand, and gestured him in. "This is almost done, I think."

"One more tube, Mr. Markham," the nurse said, withdrawing the needle, squirting the dark red blood into a small glass ampule, one of five in a wooden rack. She reinserted the needle into the soft flesh of Markham's inner arm. Markham, showing no sign of physical discomfort, looked up at Rackley.

Markham lacked Caswell's inherent aura of significance. He was of average height, slim and dark-haired, with an aquiline nose, and would have looked rather ordinary were it not for his gaze. His dark brown eyes perpetually watched the world with cool, detached concentration. Whatever entered his realm was scrutinized by an exceedingly sharp critical intelligence, constantly judging, evaluating, discarding.

The nurse and the blood samples reminded Rackley of his own gene scan, and for a moment his attention wandered. He knew that was dangerous around Markham, whose attention never wavered, so he cleared his throat. "This is for the Markham Project?"

Markham nodded. "They're drawing blood every other day now."

"Ah, Mr. Markham," the nurse said quietly. "Could you hold your arm more still, please?"

"Is this healthy?" Rackley wondered.

"They only remove the DNA from the white blood cells,"

Markham said, "so we talked about giving me the rest of the blood back. But apparently that's more trouble than it's worth." He shrugged and looked back at the needle in his arm, the glass syringe filling with crimson fluid. "Anything for science."

"All done." The nurse briskly swabbed the pale crook of Markham's elbow with alcohol, then placed a small bandage neatly across the puncture.

"Thank you," Markham said formally, as the nurse stood and picked up her steel tray of blood samples.

"Thank you, Mr. Markham," she said, and departed quickly.

Markham looked up casually, folding his long, thin hands in front of him. "Rackley. It's good to see you."

"You may not say that when I'm finished."

Markham smiled, very slightly, but said nothing, just listening.

Rackley sat. Markham's tastes were at once expensive and spare; his office was furnished only with a desk of oiled birch, a hanging light of spun aluminum, two chairs upholstered in natural wool, and a flat computer screen recessed into the desktop. Markham eschewed decoration in conversation as well, so Rackley knew there was no point in prologue. "I want to do the full dog and pony show as soon as we can, up in the Delta, right where they found Rice Five. Radio, TV, print. I want you to talk about our role in this, the eradication plans, possible damages, all that. And it's got to be you, standing there next to the goddamned slough." Rackley exhaled deeply, leaned back.

Markham did not move for a moment, nor did his expression change. Then, almost imperceptibly, he relaxed. "Fine. Whatever you say."

Rackley was taken off guard. "Trina said you weren't—"

Markham waved one hand. "I wanted to hear what you thought. And if you think I should stand up on this, I will."

Rackley stood. "Great. I'll start working on the arrangements now." He turned and began to leave the room, then thought better. As long as Markham seemed amenable, he decided to bring up the Congressional hearing. Thus far, Markham had been determined to stonewall any investigator sent out from Washington.

"You know," Rackley said, "I think a similar tactic will work with the Congressional people. The hearings on the gene therapy ban are coming up. The only way we can have a clear shot is to be straight with these guys. If we're not careful, they'll extend the ban to lower mammals too."

Markham's mood changed abruptly. "Absolutely not. This is a

business with proprietary secrets, not some university laboratory that gives free tours."

Rackley looked out the window, then back at Markham. "At least let them look at the public facilities. Jesus, you'd do the same for a newspaper reporter."

Markham nodded quickly, without emotion. "Sure. But I won't set a precedent of giving away trade secrets in return for permission to do business."

"Don't worry. I don't know half the trade secrets you've got."

Markham nodded with satisfaction. "That's fine."

Rackley began again to leave Markham's office.

"Rackley," Markham said softly.

He stopped, turning to face the thin young man.

"We don't do anything wrong here," Markham said. "And at the press conference I won't say that we did. I want to make it dignified." He paused for a moment. "Understood?"

"If we do this correctly, United Genetics can come out looking better than before. We had an accident, but we can take responsibility and we can move forward."

Markham nodded. "I like that," he said. "I like that very much."

As Rackley left, he realized that Markham's quiet approval had pleased him inordinately. "Damn," Rackley said under his breath. He had hoped that by now he was immune to Markham's peculiar spell.

Rackley had seen Markham reduce a world-class molecular geneticist to tears; yet that same geneticist was one of Markham's most loyal supporters. It was as if Markham was some final yardstick of human potential, and his approval—or scorn—could make even the most difficult scientists work like people possessed.

"When you work with Markham," a researcher once told Rackley, "it's like you join a cult. Only you're the center of the cult. He makes you feel like you're the most important person in the world. But then, when he has what he wants—you no longer exist."

CHAPTER FOUR

Rackley walked into the church basement just as the meeting was starting. Outside, the scent of the Pacific was fresh on the wind from the shore twenty blocks distant. Inside, the room was warm and smelled of fresh coffee. Long folding tables had been arranged in a U-shape; Rackley took a seat on the nonsmoking side, nodding briefly to the people around him.

He loosened his tie, slowing his breathing, slowing his thinking. Tomorrow he and Kaye were scheduled to meet Louise Allman. But tonight he would pay attention to the only thing that made his current life possible. He glanced around the room and saw most of the regulars, who ranged from a seventeen-year-old poet with orange hair to a chunky police lieutenant in his mid-thirties.

He was disappointed when he didn't see Trina. Just then, however, she slipped in through the back door and sat at the table across from him. She had changed to blue jeans and an old fisherman's sweater. Trina smiled at him and winked.

Rackley watched her as she shrugged the denim jacket off her shoulders, and she mouthed the words "ice cream" across the table at him.

He nodded, the meeting started, and then briefly his mind wandered. He hadn't seen Trina in blue jeans for months, and somehow it brought back memories of those first days at the rehab.

She had been tough: she used to call her arrest "the roadside misunderstanding." The route to her boyfriend's Marin house had twisted through the coastal hills for twenty miles, a narrow highway hazardous in the best of conditions. The last night Trina drove that road, she'd been drinking champagne since breakfast, taking cocaine to stay up, and was in the kind of hazy yet oddly alert state that only a dedicated substance abuser can achieve. She was driving Rand's Porsche, a modified 911 with a turbocharged engine and racing suspension, and she was hitting speeds, as she put it, in the lower three digits.

The first Highway Patrol car picked her up as she roared through San Rafael, but began to lose her as she climbed at full throttle into the coastal range. Within fifteen miles, three more police cars joined the pursuit, but on the twisting mountain road none was able to come anywhere near the little black sports car. Trina was blissfully unaware of her pursuers, concentrating on her driving, occasionally taking a delicate swig from a can of beer propped in the console.

She might have made it all the way to Rand's house had it not been for a moment of vanity. Near the summit of the winding road she pulled off, parking on the gravel shoulder, to touch up her lipstick. She was sitting peacefully, gazing into the mirror of her compact, when abruptly all four Highway Patrol cars screeched up, surrounding her, pinning her in the glare of their spotlights.

With great dignity she closed the compact and stared haughtily into the spotlights. "What's the matter?" Trina had asked the first patrolman to approach her car. "Can't a girl put on a little makeup?"

Besides various illegal substances, Trina also had a small, unregistered pistol in her purse. A week later, she checked into the rehab, and the day after that, she had been in Rackley's arms.

Rackley shook his head quickly and returned his attention to the meeting. The evening's speaker was a clean-cut young man just turned twenty-one. He looked like a bank teller in training, but he told a nightmarish story of rapid descent into total addiction: starting to drink at age twelve, he was locked up in his first detox two days before his fifteenth birthday. Not, however, before he had robbed his parents' own house five times. Midway in his tale he added that his father had been in AA for ten years, but that had made no difference. "I had to hit bottom by myself," the young man said. "That's the only way you can get better."

Rackley had noticed that the age of AA members was dropping steadily. The World War II generation chugged along until their fifties or sixties, then finally fell apart. Rackley's generation, fueling their addiction with all manner of pharmaceuticals besides alcohol, burned out far more quickly, usually by their late twenties or early thirties. And the younger generation was now showing up in AA even before they hit legal drinking age. It was almost as if the disease itself were getting worse, like some mutating influenza.

After the meeting ended, Rackley tried the theory on Trina. "Like the flu," she said, raising one eyebrow. "That's . . . creative." She returned her attention to the large bowl of chocolate chip ice cream in front of her.

"Figuratively speaking. That's all I mean."

Trina nodded. "Eat your ice cream."

It was their regular binge. Before sobriety, neither had the slightest interest in desserts, but once the alcohol was out of their bloodstreams, a powerful craving for sugar emerged. Rackley glanced around the brightly lit parlor for a moment. Trina looked up again. "Something's on your mind," she said finally.

"About seventeen things are on my mind. You know that."

"Tell me the worst one."

"Listening to kids like that scares the hell out of me."

Trina nodded. "Because you think you're going to have a little alcoholic of your own. Kaye told me."

"Sure," Rackley said. "What do you think?"

"Does seem to run in families, doesn't it?"

"It would be hell to watch your own kid turn into a drunk. These days kids run into cocaine and booze by eighth grade. And if a kid's got the genes, he'll probably get hooked."

Trina raised a spoonful of ice cream. "Seems to me, that it's out of your hands. If some higher power wants your kids to be alcoholic, they will be. And if they're supposed to get better, then they'll get better."

"That's a nice spiritual way to look at it," Rackley said, picking at his dessert. "But it's hard to accept." He looked up. "It's even harder for Kaye."

Trina reached across the table, touching the back of Rackley's hand. "Seems to me she's pretty happy with the alcoholic she married."

"Come on. She never knew me before."

"Things could be worse. What if you married me? God, we'd probably have to send our kid to a preschool detox."

Rackley laughed briefly, without much enthusiasm. Trina watched him for another moment. "I think you just have to go ahead," she said finally. "Some of my best friends are alcoholics."

"Maybe," he said, "my gene scan will come out negative for alcoholism."

Trina looked at him curiously. "Is that possible?"

"We'll know tomorrow." Rackley shrugged. "That would mean I'm just a weak-willed, self-indulgent fool who wasted ten years of his life." He shrugged. "Our kids might turn out to be fools too, but at least they wouldn't have genes that . . ." His voice trailed off. "Cause this uncontrollable craving for chocolate chip ice cream."

Trina hesitated, then spoke again. "You know, sometimes I think you try to be too perfect."

Rackley looked up. "Oh?"

"I mean, you have the perfect wife, the perfect house, the perfect clothes. Now you want the perfect baby. You're always trying so hard. I don't know if you're trying to make up for lost time or what." She smiled. "But you're really just fine the way you are."

"I'm glad you think so."

"I wish you thought so too."

"I'll work on it." Rackley glanced away, then looked back. "You still going out with the biochemist?" Trina had been dating a young scientist who worked in the United Genetics pharmaceutical division.

Trina shrugged. "Yeah. Sort of."

"Seemed like a nice guy."

"Oh, he's real nice. Too nice." She smiled and lowered her voice. "I like 'em a little weird and nasty. Like you, Rackley."

For a moment Rackley thought of those afternoons in the rehab, sneaking into the stairwell, making love on the cracked yellow linoleum, the afternoon sun slanting down through the narrow skylight. "Me?" Rackley said innocently. "I'm a pussy-cat. Captain normalcy."

"Sure you are," Trina said. "Sure you are."

She was silent, then sighed and looked up, her brown eyes large and serious. "Do you ever feel like we used it all up too soon?"

Rackley watched her. "What do you mean?"

"I mean, people like us, we just used up our share of everything before we were supposed to. Drugs, drinks. I mean, we had all our wild times, we ran through the whole thing too quick. And now there's none of it left, for the rest of our lives."

Rackley leaned back. "That's dangerous thinking."

"You know what I mean."

"I know what it's like to feel sorry for myself, yes."

"Oh, forget it," Trina said abruptly. "You know, the hell of it is, men get to be alcoholics, then they get better, and then it's all okay. But women are always . . . tainted. Unclean. We don't get to go off and marry pretty young things and make everything good again." She paused for a moment, shocked by her own vehemence. "I'm sorry."

Rackley shrugged. "I was taking your inventory," he said. "I was out of line."

For a moment, Trina was on the edge of telling Rackley what was really on her mind: she had in fact just broken up with her biochemist boyfriend, her fifth ill-fated romance in two years. The reason was familiar: she had found it very difficult to make love ever since she became sober.

At first Rackley had been an exception, but even sex with Rackley had become more difficult, and that in part led to their separation. Somehow, nothing seemed spontaneous, or graceful, or uncontrolled, or loose and liquid and passion-filled. Straight, there were just too many thoughts in one's head, too many distractions in the dark, elbows and knees, and nothing was mysterious and magical enough. . . .

"What are you thinking about?" Rackley asked after a moment.

"Oh," Trina said. "Nothing. I guess I'm just tired."

"It's been a long week," Rackley said softly. "It's time to go home."

Early the next morning, Rackley and Kaye watched in silence as Louise Allman, the Birthtech genetics counselor, rapidly paged through a dozen sheets of computer printout—the tabulated results of their gene scans. Occasionally she nodded silently, making notes on a pad of yellow paper. After several minutes she looked up apologetically. "I'm sorry. Usually we go over these before the appointment."

"It's my fault," Rackley said, tapping one finger on the frame of his chair. "We're having a press conference later, up in the Delta."

"We just didn't want to postpone," Kaye said.

"It's no problem. Another few minutes." Allman returned her attention to the gene scans.

Rackley sat back in his chair and looked over at Kaye.

Wearing a tailored linen suit, she was perched at the edge of her
seat, staring intently at the gray-haired woman, almost as if the
counselor's attentions were an invasion of privacy, a reading of
some secret diary. For Rackley the process seemed less invasion
than magic: it was both remarkable and frightening that one could
look deeply into the genome itself, and see the future.

"These are also, of course," Allman said as she continued to
read, "extremely detailed gene scans. We don't do these too often.
Some of these things, I didn't even know we could look for."

Rackley nodded. There was an unspoken reason why most
people avoided such extensive gene scans. When insurance
companies paid for the scan, they also demanded a copy of the
results. If the gene scans showed tendencies toward cancer or
heart disease, patients would suddenly see their insurance pre-
miums jump skyward. And they would find it nearly impossible
ever to get new insurance again. Thus most people paid cash for
their gene scans and demanded all copies of the data.

At last Allman was finished. She set the printout to one side
and glanced up. "Very good," she said, "in all. Let me start with
some trivia."

She lifted one page of the pad. "Definite tendency toward
silicosis. You may not want your child to work in coal mining."
She smiled slightly. "Although I doubt that your offspring are
likely to end up in that line of work."

She turned another page. "Also, there's a one in ten chance of
dyslexia, from father's side. Learning disability, easy enough to
overcome with the proper teaching techniques. Often we see
dyslexia tied to brain dominance, by the way. Equal aptitudes for
math and liberal arts, which can be very positive." She glanced up
at Rackley. "Wouldn't be surprised if that's the case with you."

Rackley felt a little shock; he was indeed mildly dyslexic,
although his last remaining symptom was a tendency to confuse
left and right. He shifted uncomfortably in his chair. Someone
once called the human genome the secular equivalent of the soul;
Rackley felt as if someone was looking deep into his essence. And
that, of course, was precisely what Allman was doing.

Looking back down at the chart, she continued to read. "No
male pattern baldness from either side. That's unusual, but nice."

Rackley interrupted. "I didn't know we could scan that trait."

Allman looked up. "Normally we don't tell patients about it.
It's a single gene cosmetic and we're collecting information on its
frequency. Marketing purposes, really. If we ever do more gene
therapy, that's a pretty likely product."

Kaye interrupted. "I'm sorry, but could you get to the serious part?"

"Of course." Allman looked at the pad one more time. "The good news: no schizophrenia, no special cancer sensitivity, no diabetes. All in all, you both have pretty clean genomes."

Allman paused, tapped her fingers on the printout, then sighed. "With one exception. The only real problem I can see here is alpha alcoholism."

Rackley knew it was coming. In a way the news relieved him of responsibility for his mismanaged life. But even so, it felt like some final sentence, some indelible mark of fate now fully revealed, and it hurt, more than he had expected. After a moment he nodded. "I was treated eight years ago," he said quietly. "No relapses."

"I see," Allman said, nodding. "I would have guessed that."

"Please," Kaye said, "what does that mean? What do you tell us now, the odds, or what?"

Allman looked at Kaye. "The fact is," she said softly, "you're both carriers."

Kaye stared at her, utterly shocked. "What?"

Allman extended one hand, smoothing the pages of the computer printout with her palm, as if by touch she might absorb its authority. "It's a very distinctive sequence. And you definitely carry it."

Kaye looked over at Rackley, but he was staring at the wall, lost in thought. Instantly it made perfect sense: the previous two generations of Caswells had not misspent the family fortune on a purely natural high. The afflictions of Kaye's wayward forebears had always been described politely as "a nervous condition" or "melancholia," but the truth was simpler: the Caswells had their own alcoholics rattling in the family closet.

"I can't believe it." Kaye looked at Rackley again, eyes wide. "I don't have any problem with drinking."

"No," Allman said. "You wouldn't." She lifted the printout. "You're only a carrier. It's not what we call 'expressed.'"

Rackley was still trying to absorb this new turn. He felt an instant of irrational relief: their plight was no longer entirely his fault.

"So what does this mean?" he asked Allman. "If we both—"

"Wait a minute," Kaye said, agitated, shifting quickly in her chair as if testing some invisible bonds. "Listen. My brother Edward, you did his gene scan. What happened with him?"

Allman was silent for a moment. "Gene scans are extremely confidential."

"Oh, for God's sake, he'd tell us." Kaye pointed at the telephone. "Call him right now."

Allman hesitated, looked at Rackley, then relented. "All right. Your brother is a carrier also. But if the other parent has functional genes, this form of the disease doesn't occur."

There was a moment of silence as Kaye absorbed this. "And Madeleine has okay genes," she said finally.

Allman glanced at the ceiling. "I am violating some confidences here," she said. "Yes, that's right."

Kaye leaned back as her natural calm reasserted itself. She blinked a few times, very serious, nodding tightly, and Rackley felt a surge of tenderness: she looked solemn, like a college student receiving a terrible grade on her final exam but doing her best to keep up appearances.

"What," Rackley asked again, "does it mean?"

"If your child inherits defective sequences from both of you, the odds on him or her—either sex, this isn't X-linked—having some chemical dependency is extremely high. Perhaps eighty percent." She paused for a moment. "There are several forms of alcoholism, some more environmentally influenced than others. We've known that it was hereditary for decades, from family histories. Now we've found several key genes. In normal people these genes metabolize alcohol harmlessly. But in alcoholics the genes are faulty, and somehow alcohol is turned into a substance as addictive as . . . morphine, or something like that."

"Alpha alcoholism," Rackley said, "is early onset, high probability. The worst."

Allman glanced at him. "I don't usually put it that way, but that's basically correct." The gray-haired woman looked down at her printout. "Even now that the genes are known, there is no physical cure. We just don't understand brain chemistry well enough." She looked at Rackley. "As you're aware, abstinence is the only known treatment."

"So," Kaye said, "what can we *do*?"

"Luckily, you'll know from birth that there is this disease. So there are diversion programs, using behavior modification, that can be started as early as age two. You can try to head the problem off." Allman paused. "That's the good news."

Rackley nodded. It wasn't very good news. He'd followed the prevention efforts ever since the genetic prediction of alcoholism became possible. The results had been disappointing. The child would be embarrassed when his friends learned his diagnosis. And then the diversion programs often didn't work. A teenager, trained since two, might still fall into drinking or drugs at the first opportunity. It was as if the disease couldn't be arrested until it had already started.

"I think," the geneticist said softly, "you should just go ahead. Humans have been doing that for millions of years." She paused for a very long moment, then cleared her throat. "Normally in a case like this, that's what I'd prescribe."

Kaye instantly heard the implication. "Is there something else?"

Allman hesitated for another moment, looking at both Rackley and Kaye. "Would you excuse me for a minute?"

"Certainly," Rackley said.

Allman walked silently out of the small office, leaving them alone.

"I can't believe it," Kaye said, reaching out to hold Rackley's hand.

"It's not really different from what we expected," Rackley said softly. "We knew—"

Kaye shook her head. "It's worse. I mean, it's hopeless." She leaned forward, starting to cry softly. "You know, you think how great it's going to be, you . . ." Rackley moved over and put his arm around his shoulders, brushing her hair.

"I really wish," Kaye said bitterly, "that we didn't know in the first place."

"Knowing is better than not knowing," Rackley said. "We'll make it work, somehow. People with our genes have been having babies for a long time."

Kaye gazed at him. "These days kids get drugs in sixth grade. You can't turn on television without seeing some beer ad. I mean . . ." She held her hands up. "It would be like dropping our child into a world filled with poison."

Allman signaled her return with a brief tap at the door. She walked back in, sat down, and took a deep breath.

"There is," she said quickly, "another option. It is unfortunately not quite legal . . ."

"Tell us," Rackley said.

Allman took a deep breath. "We use IVF, try for multiple embryos, then scan them and implant one that's alcoholism minus."

Kaye, now touching her eyes with a pale yellow handkerchief, shook her head. "Wait a minute. I don't follow any of that."

"Well," said the counselor. "We proceed as if you're having trouble getting pregnant. In fact for legal reasons that's what the paperwork will say. We take some eggs from you, and some sperm from Mr. Rackley, and then we go ahead and fertilize all the eggs. We take the embryos and do a gene scan on each one. We look for one that doesn't have the active alcoholism genes. One that's only a carrier, like Kaye. And then that's the one we implant in your womb."

"And you discard the others," Kaye said.

"Yes." Allman paused for a moment. "Legally this procedure is restricted to life-threatening problems."

"This disease killed my parents," Rackley said flatly. "I consider it life-threatening."

"I understand." Allman cleared her throat. "But at the moment it doesn't officially qualify. We just don't want to get into any situations—"

"Where Natural Progress can take you to court," Rackley said.

"These days," the counselor said, "you have to be so careful. There are people who would like any excuse to shut us down."

"God," Kaye said, "all I want to do is have a baby. I don't want to break laws."

The genetic counselor nodded. "I understand. This kind of disorder—it's the toughest to deal with. It makes my job very hard, being able to predict a problem but not being able to fix it. Someday . . ." She shrugged. "But it's really out of our hands."

"Tell me all about it," Kaye said.

"Well, there are risks. You'll have to take several powerful drugs, the egg harvest is done under local anesthesia, the gene scans can damage the embryos. It's not a stroll through the park. And there are absolutely no guarantees."

Kaye looked over at Rackley. Rackley said nothing.

"Ethically," Louise Allman said, "I simply can't advise you about this." She closed the file folder firmly, not looking at either of them. "Go home," she said finally. "Listen to your hearts."

C H A P T E R F I V E

The narrow Delta levee ran straight as taut string for more than a mile. Ten feet down on one side was a broad green field of new barley; five feet down on the other were the turgid brown waters of Kline Slough.

At the shoulder of the dirt road atop the levee, an old man slowly stepped down from the cab of an aging Ford pickup. It was an hour past dawn, but the muggy Delta air still retained a distinct chill from the night. The man, in overalls and a faded blue T-shirt, carefully made his way down the bank toward the brown, brackish water, one of the myriad interconnected waterways that comprise the Sacramento River Delta.

The previous day the old man had left four wire mesh crayfish traps a few feet below the sluggish waters of Kline Slough. Each contained a can of catfood punched full of holes and a handful of rotting sardines; just enough to entice the little crustaceans into the cone-shaped ends of the trap.

The old man had been harvesting crayfish for nearly thirty years. In the old days the harvest had been sufficiently plentiful that the catch was frozen and shipped in bulk to Norway and Sweden. These days, instead of Scandinavia, the harvest went to the elegant restaurants of San Francisco and Los Angeles; the old man had been told that such places sold four crayfish and a bit of greenery as a ten-dollar appetizer. That he found difficult to believe; but the prices they paid were good, and so this morning he was happy to pull his fourth trap from Kline Slough and see at least twenty of the little creatures inside.

He took a quick walk up the riverbank to survey a new spot for his traps. This stretch of Delta was as familiar to him as his own truck garden; in the forty years since he'd moved out from Kansas, a great deal had changed about California, but the backwaters of the Delta remained much as they had always been. As he admired the graceful low willows that lined the banks, the occasional heron or egret in flight along the surface, he felt somehow as if time really hadn't passed at all.

He found a likely spot to sink his traps and was about to turn back when something caught his eye, perhaps a hundred feet farther up the riverbank. He walked closer, and what he saw then made no sense at all.

Growing luxuriantly in the marshy sides of the slough were hundreds—thousands—of green grasslike plants, waving softly in the early morning breeze. They hadn't been there three weeks earlier, he knew. And more than that, he knew that they shouldn't be there at all.

The old man recognized immediately that this was some kind of rice, growing weedlike in the brown Delta water. Rice was an occasional crop in these parts—he had worked it himself in the past—but it required special tending; there was no way rice could be growing so profusely in the weedy shallows of Kline Slough. The very idea was utterly impossible.

The old man walked another fifty paces up the riverbank and finally halted. For at least one hundred yards the strange rice was growing lushly in the byways of the Sacramento, already crowding out the natural horsetails and slough grass.

Crayfish forgotten, the old man, suddenly uneasy, turned and walked quickly back to his pickup truck. But just as he reached the old Ford, he heard vehicles driving up the narrow levee road from the south.

This was a parade of cars, led by a delivery truck, two pickups, then two government agency sedans, then several vans with satellite dishes on top and television station call letters on the side. The vehicles, all in a line, drove slowly along the dusty old levee road looking like some kind of funeral cortege.

Leaving his traps behind, the old man climbed into his pickup, fired up the engine, and headed down the road just as the first of the strange vehicles passed by.

Two hours later, when Rackley arrived, the levee had been transformed with a small portable dais, a public address system, and seventy-five folding chairs for the press. As Rackley walked over, Trina was wearily considering the bulging sheaf of notes on her clipboard.

She turned to him. "Rackley. How did it go?"

He looked at her for a moment. "We're both carriers."

Trina held the clipboard against her chest. "What?"

"It looks like the Caswells had some drunks in the family before I came along."

Trina shook her head in some wonder. "So what does that mean?"

Rackley sighed. "It's not good news. We just have to think about it."

"If there's anything I can do . . ."

"For now," Rackley said, "I guess we should have a press conference." He stood for a moment, staring around the countryside, the sun now burnishing the surrounding fields to a greenish-golden tone that appeared almost artificial. "Looks good," he said finally.

Trina shook her head. "I still think we should have done this in some nice hotel meeting room."

Rackley gazed at the glimmering water of the narrow levee. "No, this is perfect. When the president of the company himself comes out to the site, pays attention, it looks good. It's reassuring."

"I'd still prefer coffee and Danish."

"So do reporters," Rackley said, and for the first time he smiled slightly. "They like hotels, so they ask nasty questions. But outdoors, the print guys get rocks in their shoes, the on-camera guys have to worry about their hair blowing around."

Trina laughed, shaking her head. "You have such high regard for your former colleagues."

"Sometimes I'm right. That's the sad part."

It was, Rackley thought, a victory for corporate culture. And it made his job much easier. Most of the ambitious kids in journalism school now took their degrees in public relations or television. Television rarely covered anything in depth; it was an intensely powerful spotlight roving the nation. When caught in its glare, you just stood still and it passed, looking for fresh action. Nor was there much to fear from the slick magazines for whom Rackley had once written. Now they devoted their pages to celebrities, fashion, and investment tips. Toss in traditional New York provincialism and even nuclear war between California and Mexico might play as a wacky West Coast life-style story.

A few years earlier a bioaccident like Rice Five would have

drawn intense scrutiny; now, Rackley suspected, he could move it
to the back pages by the end of the week.

Just then Paul Markham's gray Mercedes roared down the
levee, throwing clouds of dust, pulling up in front of Rackley.
Along with his wealth, Markham had acquired excellent but
esoteric taste; monastic opulence, Rackley called it. Markham, for
example, refused ever to ride in a limousine. "Limos are for rock
stars and prom night," he once told Rackley. "These days the
powerful people ride in plain sedans."

Markham stepped out of the backseat; Rackley was glad to see
that he was wearing a conservative business suit. Markham
preferred corduroy pants and faded work shirts, but Rackley
advised that the informality that charmed the public in the
seventies would, these days, alienate them. The rich should at
least have to dress up.

"Isn't this like criminals returning to the scene of the crime?"
Markham said, looking around the green countryside, staring
briefly at the slow waters of the slough.

"Not at all," Rackley said. "This is taking responsibility.
Plus, the camera crews can shoot the Rice Five. It makes a nice
innocuous visual."

"Actually," Markham said quietly, still glancing around the
bucolic scene, "I've never even been up here before."

Rackley nodded. The Delta was little known, even though it
comprised the massive confluence of two great rivers flowing
down out of the Sierra range. Initially it had been an immense
swamp hundreds of miles square. Then, during the 1800s,
Chinese laborers built elaborate levees that held back the waters
and revealed powerfully rich farmland, millennia of swamp
vegetation laid down as black peat soil; the levee network earned
the area the nickname the American Netherlands.

"I wish to hell it hadn't happened here," Rackley said.
"These farmers have spent the last twenty years keeping Los
Angeles from stealing their fresh water, so they know how to dig
in and fight."

Markham turned his head, idly observing an early-morning
water skier speeding down the flat, smooth expanse of the
Sacramento River. "There's nothing to fight about," Markham
said. "This will all work out just fine."

Rackley wiped a thin sheen of sweat from his forehead. Even
this early in the day the Delta heat and humidity were building; it
was the season of luxuriant growth in these parts, and the place
already felt like a greenhouse. He glanced at his watch. "We're

scheduled to start in about an hour. People should start showing up fairly soon now."

Markham glanced around languidly once more, the bright Delta sun reflecting harshly off his dark sunglasses. "I'll wait in the car."

An hour later the narrow levee road was packed with newspeople and a dozen television cameras. On the dais at a folding table were an expert from United Genetics' agricultural division, a fellow from the Environmental Protection Agency, a county supervisor, and Ralph Kline, who owned the surrounding land. Markham took the podium, picked up a wireless microphone, and read a statement quickly, but with nice inflection.

"The plant variety discovered in Kline Slough appears to be a form of rice developed at the agricultural division of United Genetics in Davis, California. Apparently a small portion of an experimental crop accidentally went to seed, was consumed by birds, and was transported to this location. United Genetics is cooperating fully with the Environmental Protection Agency and the California State Agriculture Department to eradicate the plant before further propagation can take place."

When he finished he paused for a moment and then broke into a lopsided grin. Rackley briefly marveled at the boyish, winsome manner Markham, now nearly forty, could still carry off, summoning up all manner of memories of his earlier triumphs in Silicon Valley.

"Damn," Markham said softly into the microphone, pushing his hair back and looking out at the reporters. "After all the terrific things United Genetics has done in the last four years, I hate like hell to have to stand here and talk like this."

Rackley picked up his microphone. "We are open for questions."

A San Francisco reporter was up first. "Is there any information on how far this rice has spread? And what are the plans for removal?"

The EPA bureaucrat, a balding man who looked uncomfortable in the sun, cleared his throat. "As far as we know, it's only in this immediate area. California Conservation Corps crews are removing it and the work is proceeding on schedule. At present we are satisfied that United Genetics is dealing with the problem responsibly."

"Why is this rice a problem?"

Rackley nodded toward the young scientist from the Ag

Division, who hesitated, then picked up his microphone. "Well. It's not really a problem, in so many words. Our intention was to make this crop easier to plant, and this particular strain has the ability to spread by runners. It can also live in a wider variety of conditions. That seems to be why it has temporarily rooted here in the Delta."

A younger woman near the back of the crowd raised her hand. "Mr. Markham. Will this effect the Congressional debate on genetic engineering next month?"

"Absolutely not. Every industry has its growing pains. Compared to the accidents you might see with the nuclear industry, or even the chemical industry, this is really a pretty benign situation."

A local reporter instantly spoke up. "Are you saying you view this as a minor problem?"

Rackley glanced over at Trina, standing nearby at the edge of the road. She averted her eyes; both knew that Markham had a bad tendency to speak without thinking when under pressure.

"Absolutely not," Markham said. "But I think if you'll look around this levee, you'll see a lot of introduced species. For starters, the striped bass those fellows down the road are casting for." He glanced to one side. "Mr. Kline? Do you have a comment?"

The old farmer looked vaguely surprised, as if caught dozing. He took the microphone and coughed softly. Rackley watched with interest; immediately after the Rice Five had been found, Markham's lawyers offered Kline a generous, open-ended compensation agreement that included shares in United Genetics. A Delta barley farmer read enough of the business pages to know that, in the past, founders' shares in a Markham company had made many millionaires.

"We are worried, of course we are," Kline said, "but I've been damn impressed with the work these boys are doing to get rid of the rice. The one thing a farmer has to keep in mind is that these fellows are doing this research for us."

The questions went on, most rather innocuous. Markham appeared in public so rarely that the questions began to range away from Rice Five. Had Markham found genetic engineering as fulfilling as computers?

"Vastly more so," Markham said. "Starving people can't eat a computer. A computer can't cure cancer. And we've only just started."

The press conference was working perfectly, and Rackley's

mind already was wandering. And then, even as he was watching a big white egret rapidly taking off over the slough, he heard a strange voice.

"I have a statement from Natural Progress that I would like to—"

Rackley was at the microphone almost instantly. He found the young woman, standing in the midst of the reporters. "I'm afraid," he said loudly, "that this is a United Genetics press conference. If you'd like to—"

Markham raised one hand. "Let her read her statement," he said softly, looking calmly into the crowd. "You have thirty seconds," he said politely.

The young woman, tall and thin with steel-framed eyeglasses, looked surprised, but resumed her reading. "United Genetics is in the forefront of companies who are attempting to reap profits by permanently changing the genetic nature of our planet."

Rackley returned to his seat. "Damn," he said softly to Trina. This kind of scene invariably made terrific television. Indeed, all the minicam operators who moments earlier had been filming horsetails and dragonflies were suddenly training their lenses on the young woman.

"Rice Five is the tip of an iceberg. It is nothing less than an effort to own the genetic heritage that rightfully belongs to all people. Chemical toxins, even nuclear radiation, can be contained. But when life itself has been twisted beyond its natural boundaries, all for the sake of profit, the changes can never be undone.

"Already the history of ecology is filled with disastrous introductions of exotic species from other continents: the starling, Dutch elm disease, the walking catfish of Florida. Rice Five confirms that genetically engineered creatures can and will destroy the natural balance.

"For further information on this issue please contact Natural Progress." She gave a Washington, D.C., telephone number, then said, "Thank you," and turned and walked out of the press conference, down the road to a dust-covered old Volkswagen. One or two reporters followed her.

Just enough material, Rackley thought, worded tightly to fit into a couple of television sound bites. Steven Hechinger probably wrote it himself. There was a distinct possibility that the carefully orchestrated press conference would turn on them now. Thinking quickly, he looked at Markham. But Markham was already picking up his microphone.

"I'm glad we heard that today," Markham said. "I mean, it's not like we at United Genetics set out to do something wrong. We set out to do something right. Many right things. And I wonder how many of us, even now, would like to close the door on the promise of genetic engineering. The millions of additional mouths being fed, this moment, by genetically engineered crops. The cancer victims who, a decade ago, would have died terribly, today healthy thanks to genetically engineered drugs. Or the babies with fatal genetic diseases, cured by gene therapy, now leading happy, normal lives."

Markham hesitated for a second, looked down, looked up again. "Today we're here because we made a mistake. But it's a mistake we're willing to take responsibility for. And with the support of an understanding public and legislators, we will continue to do our work. Because we think it's the most important work left to do. Our lives, the lives of our children, the life of our planet, all depend on it. And you can depend on us."

Markham paused briefly, his timing excellent. "Thank you, ladies and gentlemen." He turned and walked down the narrow steps of the dais. Moments later he stepped into the backseat of his car.

As Rackley stood to dismiss the press conference, the unobtrusive sedan accelerated down the levee road, rapidly disappearing into the heat waves shimmering on the green horizon.

When Rackley arrived home from the press conference, Kaye was reading in the living room, a light sweater over her shoulders. A year earlier she had redone the dark old Victorian and the interior now had a bright and spacious feel that often raised Rackley's spirits at day's end. But tonight, even before he left the entryway, Kaye stood and spoke to him across the living room.

"Your brother is here," Kaye said, clutching her book in both hands. "He's drunk out of his mind."

Rackley stared, not comprehending at first. "But he's in the hospital."

"He checked himself out. He says it's the worst treatment program he's ever seen."

Rackley sighed as if to expel the sudden wave of sadness that mixed with anger in his chest. "Well, he's seen enough of them."

Kaye's voice was soft. "He's really a mess."

Rackley nodded. "He's been a mess for a long, long time."

"He's upstairs. What will we do with him?"

Rackley dropped his briefcase on the polished wood floor of the entryway hall. "God."

Vincent, two years younger than Rackley, had been in and out of treatment centers from coast to coast, usually at his brother's expense. When things got very bad, he would end up on Rackley's doorstep. Vincent had nowhere else to go. Their parents had died in a spectacular automobile wreck in Los Angeles when Rackley was twenty; at the time both had blood alcohol levels double the legal limit.

Kaye turned away. Gazing out onto the dark street, she bit at one fingernail. "I really don't like having him in the house," she said. "I don't feel safe."

Rackley nodded, sighing again. He took off his tan suit coat, threw it across one of the big overstuffed white couches, then sat heavily. Behind Kaye's words, he knew, was another concern. Besides the potential hazards of having an uncontrolled alcoholic crashing about the upstairs rooms, Vincent reflected a side of Rackley that Kaye had never seen, an unpredictable specter still lurking within.

When Rackley said nothing, Kaye's expression softened. She turned, her thin arms wrapped around herself, and walked over. She sat on the couch next to him and touched his knee. "Listen," she said after a moment, "it'll be okay for a few days."

"No. As long as he has someplace to go, clean sheets, warm food, he's not going to get well. It's too easy for him to walk away from the hospital."

"He's too drunk to put out tonight. He'd get hit by a bus in front of the house."

Rackley considered this. "Drunks are pretty resilient."

Kaye frowned, sympathy engaged. "But he's really—"

At that moment there was a loud crash from upstairs, powerful enough to shake the downstairs windows in their frames.

Rackley rose to his feet. "Oh shit," he said softly. He turned to go upstairs, but before he moved more than a few feet they could hear Vincent in the upstairs hallway.

"Ah-oops!" came his voice, echoing down the stairwell. "Goddamn bookshelf tipped right over!"

Rackley looked back at Kaye, and then Vincent came stumbling down the stairs. He was a tall and sallow version of Rackley, his thin hair prematurely gray, his clothes rumpled; one tail of his yellow shirt was untucked from his creaseless brown pants. As soon as he was halfway down the stairs and saw Rackley, Vincent stopped abruptly and looked contrite.

"Sorry about . . . the bookcase. I just leaned on it and it tipped over."

"What the hell are you doing out of the rehab?" Rackley said.

Vincent shrugged innocently, looking away. "They . . . threw me out."

Kaye spoke from behind Rackley. "The hospital called here. He checked himself out, AMA."

"Against medical advice," Vincent said. "Damn straight. Those people don't know what they're doing." He resumed his careful descent of the staircase.

Rackley did not move. "I want you out of here tomorrow morning," he said quietly. "I don't care where you go, but if you're not going to cooperate with the hospital, then you can just go to hell." He turned and started to walk through the living room, away from Vincent.

Vincent's mood suddenly switched to rage. "Of *course*. You're probably too *busy* to talk to me," he said loudly. "You're the goddamn model. Look at Rackley. Look at how he cleaned up his life, what a great thing he's made of himself." The tall, thin young man slammed one fist on the stairwell balustrade, shook his head, then slammed his fist again.

He looked up angrily at Rackley. "It never fucking occurs to anyone—I mean, not to a single loving soul—that maybe I don't want to stop drinking. I'm an artist—not some businessman like you. I stop drinking, I can't play music anymore. I sit there, nothing happens. Take away drinking, you take away my life."

Rackley knew better than to argue with a drunk. But he couldn't let the observation pass. "It's just the opposite," he said softly. "That's the disease talking. It's a creature living inside you, and it'll lie, tell you anything, make up any kind of story, in order to survive."

Vincent stood still for another moment, not moving. Then suddenly he shouted, "*Fuck* your meetings! *Fuck* your goddamn goody-goody act! You're always the ideal perfect successful example, and I'm *sick* of it." Suddenly he turned to face Kaye. "You should have seen your wonderful husband when he was a drunk. He was the sloppiest guy in the bar. He'd fuck anything that moved. He'd steal, he'd lie, he'd—"

"You," Kaye interrupted, her voice hard yet quiet, "are garbage. And nothing will ever change that." Without another word she turned and stalked out.

Rackley felt the muscles of his broad shoulders tense. "In the morning," he repeated, "I want you gone. And I never want to see you again. Until you decide to do something about your life."

Rackley followed Kaye into the kitchen. Behind him Vincent stood on the stairs, anger spent, now almost gasping for air like some ornamental carp out of water.

Rackley caught up with Kaye, touched her arm, and turned her around. "He's got it bad," he said. "There's almost nothing in him that was Vincent. There's nothing left but the disease."

Kaye shuddered. "I hate it. I hate it so much when he comes around."

In the middle of the night Rackley heard the sound first, barely perceived in the depths of his slumber: low choking noises, halfway between a call for help and pure sounds of pain. Rackley rolled over and turned on the nightstand lamp. The illumination awakened Kaye, who quickly sat upright, listening.

"It's Vincent," Rackley said after a moment.

"God," Kaye said, rubbing her face. "He sounds awful."

The voice grew louder, with a sound that was almost inhuman—quite terrifying in a curiously disconnected way.

"I better go check." Rackley slipped out of bed and pushed a button on the bedside console that activated the hall and upstairs lights. In a moment he was in his brown bathrobe, out the door, and up the stairs to the little guest bedroom on the third floor of the old house.

He stood outside the door for a moment. Now there was no sound and for a moment Rackley thought that perhaps Vincent had simply called out in the midst of some alcohol-fogged nightmare. But then the low moaning began again. "Hey old buddy," Rackley said softly, leaning against the white-enameled door. "You doing okay in there?"

There was silence, followed by another groan. Rackley didn't hesitate; he opened the door, walked in, and switched on the small lamp on the dresser. His brother was in bed, the blankets pulled up over his head, and he was shivering uncontrollably.

"Hey," Rackley repeated tentatively. "You . . ."

With a deliberate motion Vincent pulled the covers off his face, which was so utterly pale as to seem lost in the bed linen. His eyes were open wide, terrified, and he struggled to pull himself upright, one hand tightly clenched over his chest, borrowed pajama top twisted and disarrayed.

Rackley's first thought was that Vincent was having a heart attack, and he stepped forward, but even as he moved another terrible groan came from his brother. Vincent opened his mouth as if to speak, then opened it even wider when no words emerged. Suddenly he coughed, and a thin spray of bright red blood spattered across the sheets. He coughed again—this time nearer a choking sound—and a more concentrated stream emerged from his gaping mouth, a few drops striking Rackley's robe. Then, with no warning save one huge, shuddering groan, a full torrent of blood rushed out of Vincent's mouth, down his chin, dripping onto his chest, a gush of red fluid so copious that, incongruously, Rackley thought momentarily of some kind of stage trick.

But this was no trick. Vincent gasped once, choking on the blood, then wriggled and writhed for a moment among the sheets, as if seized by some giant hand, then fell over sideways, breath rattling twice, then silent, with only an awful gurgling noise—not breath, but simply the passage of blood—coming from deep in his throat as the bright red fluid ran from his mouth, soaking into the Oriental carpet, pooling on the dark hardwood floor.

Rackley's momentary paralysis passed and he rushed forward, hearing behind him Kaye's footsteps on the stairs. "Rackley," he could hear her calling softly, "is everything okay?" He reached the bed and pressed his hand against Vincent's bloody neck. His brother had no pulse. He rolled him over, pulling him back up onto the bed, and Vincent's gory head lazily slumped back against the pillow, disgorging another thin red trickle from the corner of his blue lips.

Kaye came into the bedroom, and when Rackley moved to one side, she took in the scene at a glance. "Oh God!" she cried in a strangled voice halfway between scream and shout. "What . . . ?"

Rackley stood, leaning over the bed, cradling his brother's head, trying to rub away blood with the twisted end of a pillow-case. "Call an ambulance," Rackley said softly. "Right now." He leaned Vincent's head back, propping it with one hand behind the neck, and bent over to blow into the bloody mouth. "You better stay downstairs until they come."

"Massively ruptured esophagus," said the doctor at the hospital. "When all of the tissue goes at once, there's almost nothing you can do. But you don't usually see it in alcoholics this young."

Rackley nodded numbly. "Well. He . . ."

"I assume your brother had a drinking problem."

Rackley nodded again. He was looking past the young doctor

to where Kaye was sitting, quite pale, almost unmoving, on a couch in the emergency room lobby. She had said no more than a dozen words in the two hours since the ambulance had arrived and the two paramedics had double-timed up the staircase, rushing into the guest bedroom, gently pushing Rackley away from where he was still trying to restart his brother's breath.

The first paramedic had checked for a pulse and breath. "Okay," he called to his partner, "we've got a Code."

Rackley's mouth had been filled with the taste of blood, and once the paramedics were in the room, he felt—for the first time— a sudden wave of nausea that sent him spinning into the hall bathroom. On his knees he vomited over and over into the toilet, hugging the bowl in exhaustion just as in his old days of drinking, heaving until there was nothing left to come up.

Now, less than an hour later, all the technology of the Trauma Center had failed to bring Vincent back to life. The young doctor explained that the esophageal rupture had dropped his blood pressure so quickly that the shock alone would have killed him; given the poor state of his health, there was really very little hope.

Rackley looked at the doctor. "He'd just left a rehab unit," he said, as if somehow that might explain matters.

The doctor frowned. "But he was very intoxicated."

Rackley nodded. "It didn't take."

The doctor was clearly ready to move on. "It's a terrible disease. I'm very sorry." He cleared his throat. "There'll be some paperwork. You might want to come back in the morning for that."

"Thanks."

Rackley walked over to where Kaye was sitting, drawn, small against the big upholstered frame of the waiting room sofa. He sat down next to her, putting one hand on her knee, squeezing gently.

"God," she said softly. "I'm really sorry. He was . . ."

"He was doomed," Rackley said, putting his arm around his wife. "He was just plain and simple doomed."

Kaye looked at him. "I don't ever want that to happen to anyone I love."

"Of course not," Rackley said, holding her close, feeling the tears welling warm and fast in his eyes. "Of course not."

CHAPTER SIX

The next morning, in Washington, D.C., Senator Mathew Gordon simply had to interrupt Steven Hechinger. "For God's sake," Gordon finally said. "Just remember: I'm on your side."

Hechinger, a tall loose-limbed blond man in his late thirties, was so wound up from his telling of the Rice Five accident that it took him a moment to catch his breath. There was a brief silence in the senator's large office. "Steven," the senator chided him, "I do believe you've completely forgotten that I'm the one who asked you here."

Hechinger, sufficiently self-aware to be abashed by his own verbal excesses, only nodded.

Gordon smiled easily. He was a powerful legislator in his sixties, a big man with a perpetually red face and a striking shock of white hair. Publicly, he was probably best known for his marriage a year earlier to a twenty-one-year-old stewardess he met on the Washington–New York shuttle. When their first child had been born, the May–December parents produced the kind of front-page photos beloved by newspaper editors. But Gordon was also a pivotal figure in the regulation of genetic engineering and much courted by the biotechnology industry, which had now developed one of the wealthiest political action committees in the country.

For a moment Senator Gordon tallied the delicate political implications of what he was about to offer the hyperactive Hechinger. The man, he knew, was an old left-winger with whom

he shared little in common. But the issue of genetic engineering
had produced some unusual political bedfellows.

"You know I'm sympathetic to your concerns," the senator
said quietly. "I mean, why else would I have named you special
investigator for the subcommittee on genetic engineering?"

Hechinger stared. The thin light of the Washington spring sun
slanted, nearly horizontal, across the senator's desk. There was
another stretch of silence as Hechinger grasped the implications of
Gordon's words.

"You're kidding."

The senator shook his head. "Special investigator. You write
the full report. That is, if you want to do it."

Hechinger could scarcely remain in his chair. "Well, of course
I do. I mean, this is . . ." What he was about to say was that
reporting directly to a Senate subcommittee, at last whispering his
words so close to the ears of power, was something he never
would have dreamed a few decades earlier, when he was being
teargassed for protesting the bombing of Cambodia. He quickly
checked that observation. ". . . a very great honor. I will do my
best to live up to it."

The senator paused, choosing his words carefully. "Steve, I
understand your position on genetic engineering." The senator
also understood the gathering political clout of Hechinger's
constituency. "But the one thing we have to keep in mind is that
Paul Markham is the most successful industrialist of his generation. The fellow is a symbol of high technology. I don't think you
can paint him as some bogeyman without public backlash."

Hechinger nodded. "Personally I don't buy his wunderkind
act. But Markham isn't the issue. The control of genetic
engineering is the issue, and United Genetics just happens to be
the biggest player."

"Of course," said Gordon. "But this isn't a witch-hunt."

"Do I have subpoena power?"

"If you need it, of course."

Hechinger settled back into his seat. "I'm going to bring you a
report that will put this nation on notice."

"I'll count on it."

"Now," said Hechinger, "I just want to finish briefing you on
this rice bioaccident. . . ." ,

The senator's attention drifted as Hechinger began to ramble
on about metabolic pathways and ecological niches and God
knows what else. Science actually bored the senator, and
Hechinger was something of a lapsed biologist.

Raised in rural Michigan, surrounded by woods and creeks, Hechinger had become fascinated with living creatures—from the perch in the ponds to the ironwood trees in the forest. But in college he rapidly grew disillusioned with biology. The emphasis was on what happened inside cells, chemically and electrically, with little mind paid to the great, sweeping intricacy and perfection of nature that had first drawn a child's attention.

Even as Hechinger drifted away from his boyhood dreams, the protests against the war in Vietnam peaked. Hechinger took to activism with all the enthusiasm he had carried for biology—organizing, writing newsletters, learning grassroots politics. The excitement made up for his disillusionment with science, and he developed a national reputation as a superb issues man.

When the war ended, Hechinger began to read about genetic engineering. The moment he understood recombinant DNA technology—the ability to swap genes between species—he knew that those biologists back at the university who wanted to replace spiritual essence with nucleotide sequences and soulless mechanism were now in league with big business. Capitalism run riot had already transformed the face of the planet. Now pure corporate greed would engineer the very creatures who lived upon it. Hechinger sensed that this was a cause that would last the rest of his life.

"Steve," the senator finally interrupted that bright spring morning, "getting back to Paul Markham. I've met the young man, and he may be a little arrogant, but he's no fool. I can't imagine he'd risk a major investment in order to push some research forward." He shook his head. "No. If there's funny stuff going on, if people are breaking the rules, it's happening in the universities. Those people have never given a good goddamn about what the rest of the world thought."

Hechinger, shocked, stared for a moment. At first Gordon had seemed to be among his allies. The senator had been instrumental two years ago when Congress passed a federal law against human gene therapy, imposing stiff penalties. But now Hechinger feared even this powerful man was slipping away. Soon there would be no one to stop the genetic engineering of the planet. He tried once more. "Senator, this new weed in California did not come from a university laboratory."

Gordon's eyes glazed and he began idly to shuffle papers on his desk. "United Genetics," he said impatiently, "is going to get nailed for that one. I hear they might postpone their stock offering."

"They'll survive. But as sure as I sit here, Markham is doing more than designing new weeds."

Gordon nodded solemnly. "If you can prove that, I'll personally attach Mr. Markham's hide to the wall."

Hechinger watched Gordon for a moment, then gathered up his notes and stood. "I'll be out there by the end of the week, and I'm not leaving until I've found what I need to know."

Gordon's expression did not change. "The hearing is in five weeks," he said with heavy irony. "It would be convenient to have you back by then."

"I'll be in touch," Hechinger said, and he left quickly.

Gordon gazed up at the ceiling as the door closed behind the activist and calm silence ensued. Hechinger, he thought, was the perfect choice to be committee investigator. He was radical enough to satisfy even the harshest opponents of genetic engineering, but at the same time sufficiently disorganized that he was unlikely to uncover anything but more of his own overblown rhetoric.

With Hechinger's report in hand both sides would be served, and the senator could still do just as he pleased. Genetic engineering, he suspected, was an issue so powerful that it would either one day propel him into the orbit of possible president or else cost him his career.

He shook his head briefly to clear it. The senator found it enervating to be in the room with so much contained energy. Then he reached over and picked up his telephone. After a moment his secretary came on the line. Gordon glanced at his watch. "Could you get me Paul Markham in California? Try his home number first, then call his car."

That same afternoon, Trina was sitting in her office, going over the text of a speech Markham had dropped on her desk early that day. Rackley was taking several days off to arrange for Vincent's funeral in Los Angeles. He had been in the office only briefly that morning.

"Funny," he'd told Trina as he left. "I just figured it out, that I always thought he was going to get better, and we were going to be two old guys, falling asleep in the back row at meetings. I guess I feel like I lost that, too. And I wonder if there was something else I should have done."

"If there was some magic word, there'd be a lot fewer drunks on the loose."

Then they had held each other, for a long time, before Rackley left.

Now, Trina was having difficulty concentrating on the speech. They had both been so crazy when they had met at the rehab. Crazy and utterly attracted to each other. Maybe they were trying to prove to themselves that they were still worth something even though they were locked up. Or perhaps they were trying to distract themselves from the simple reality that they were addicts, that they had established lives around something false, and now they had to rebuild.

Probably it was a blend of reasons with a bit of real love somewhere down at the bottom. But whatever the mix, the day after they had met they broke into a locked stairwell where they made love on that yellow floor every night, with a kind of desperation and abandon that neither of them had ever known before.

Soon after they had left the little hospital, they heard the classic admonishment: Don't get involved with someone else in recovery for the first year. If your lover goes wrong, you could go wrong also. They ignored the advice. Trina returned to school, Rackley began his job, and they rented a tiny apartment together. But then, three months later, Trina had one particularly dismal day. She earned a C on a paper that deserved better, and then her probation officer ran a surprise drug test on her. Angry, frustrated, filled with some emotions she couldn't even name, she came home, opened a bottle of wine, and smoked a joint. Ten minutes later Rackley came home from United Genetics.

She could still recall his eyes as he smelled the air, saw the slightly glazed look on her face, the bottle on the table. "Give me a call when you want to talk about it," he said, then turned and walked back out.

That night before Trina passed out she called her sponsor. The next morning she was at a meeting, and that proved her last slip. "A convincer," her sponsor told her. "You were just a quart low."

But that was the end of the relationship with Rackley. He told her that staying clean and sober came first. They would remain friends but curb the romance. If after a year the romance was still there, then they could make a life together.

That was the plan and Trina stuck to it. She concentrated on her classes in journalism and public relations, did well, stayed straight. Soon Rackley was named vice president of corporate communications at United Genetics, and he hired Trina as an assistant, in charge of press relations. But about then Rackley went off on a weekend visit to Edward Caswell's fishing lodge, and when he came back, he was talking about someone named Kaye. Over a dozen after-meeting sessions of coffee and ice cream, Trina watched Rackley drift away. In her own mind she had decided to wait for him. But there had never been any deal that he would do the same.

Trina shook her head and looked down at the draft of Markham's speech. Kaye was as fine a wife as someone could want. And Trina did want the best for Rackley; he deserved the best. But sometimes she couldn't help but think that it might have turned out differently. Acceptance was one quality she still needed to work on.

She concentrated fiercely on the page in front of her. She wasn't even sure why Markham was having her read this again. It appeared to be basic boiler plate: the triumph of the private sector in biotechnology, keeping the United States number one in genetic engineering, the need for fewer restrictions.

But then Trina turned to the last page and noticed a new paragraph.

> We now stand on the brink of the greatest medical breakthrough in history: the ability to heal not just individuals, but the species—not just one child, but generations of children. We can eradicate genetic disease from the soul of the human race just as we eradicated smallpox from the face of the planet. All that remains to be seen is whether we have the courage to proceed.

Oh no, Trina thought, staring at the neatly printed text. Markham was talking about embryo gene therapy, the biggest red flag in the entire genetic engineering controversy. Quickly she turned to the front of the speech; she hadn't even noticed whom he was addressing. The upper left-hand corner of the page read: "For Benefit Evening, Caswell Clinic for the Diseases of Overpopulation, March 30, 8:00 P.M., Marin County, California."

Trina frowned. That was tonight. She wasn't sure just what benefit this referred to, but if the press was going to be there, then this reference to embryo therapy simply had to go.

She stood quickly and walked down the hall, which was carpeted in a subtle plum color, the walls lined with bright drawings of gene sequences patented by United Genetics. To untrained eyes each drawing appeared like a nearly identical variant on an elaborate spiral staircase. Yet one of the framed

DNA sequences, when inserted into yeast cells, produced the most powerful anticancer agent yet known. The sequence hanging next to it, spliced into animal cells, generated a substance that prevented a common variety of heart attack.

Just as Trina passed the last sequence and reached the lobby outside Markham's office, his heavy door opened and a man in a light gray suit walked out. The man was tall and well-built, about forty, with dark good looks that blended cultures in a manner that defied categorization; a truly international visage. His black hair was smoothed back, oddly anachronistic, at once fierce yet sophisticated. Trina's breath caught in her throat; she stood, stunned. The tall man's eyes briefly swept the lobby, met her gaze for a moment, then moved on without a hint of recognition.

But Trina recognized Edward Kelley-Delgado. Her memory was instantly taken back eight years to a drug-sotted week in a huge, rented house on the Nevada side of Lake Tahoe. It was the end of a major deal; her boyfriend had moved a camper truck filled with hashish and cocaine into the U.S. through some complicated transshipping arrangement that made it appear that the truck had come from Alaska, rather than more suspicious climes. The connection in South America had been Kelley-Delgado, and for weeks during the deal Rand had told her stories about the ferocious young Mexican-American.

When Kelley-Delgado finally came to San Francisco, they drove to Tahoe for a week of celebration, none of which Trina remembered very clearly—except for one night when she ended up in bed with both men, and Delgado told horrible stories about punishments wrought on disobedient lieutenants in South America. Trina had never been able to forget that bizarre night of sex mixed with tales of homespun torture.

But as nearly as she could tell, Delgado didn't remember her. The tall man, moving with easy grace, nodded to Markham's secretary. "Until next time, Betty," he said and then turned to leave.

Trina, momentarily dazed by this vision from the past, stood briefly, gathering her wits, then stepped forward. "Betty, is Paul busy right now?"

"Go on in."

Trina opened the door. Markham was sitting at his desk, looking at papers, and when the door opened he quickly closed the folder and set it aside. He looked up at Trina, eyebrows raised.

"Who was that man?" she asked as casually as she could manage.

Markham smiled slightly. "You interested?"

Trina tried for an offended tone. "No. But I should recognize people who are on first-name basis with your secretary."

Markham gave her a sidelong glance. "That's Edward Kelley-Delgado. I was sure you'd met him. He's the head of operations in Mexico City."

Trina kept watching Markham, trying to make sense of this, to fit the Edward Kelley-Delgado she knew into United Genetics. It simply didn't match up. On the other hand, of course, she never would have imagined the Trina Robbins of a decade ago now clad in a light wool business suit, toting a Mädler notebook, collecting stock options.

Markham noticed her distraction. "He's up here arranging supplies, enzymes, sequencers, all the stuff he can't get in Mexico. Also, we're planning the official opening for next month. It's going to be quite an event."

Trina nodded. "I know. Rackley told me. Has Delgado worked—"

Markham seemed impatient. "Was there something you wanted?"

"Oh. This . . ."

Markham saw the speech in her hand. "Embryo engineering. Somebody in this country has to have the guts to bring it up."

"You don't have to answer the phone calls the next day."

"This is a private group tonight," Markham said. "Like-minded people. Keep the press out if that'll make you happier."

Trina, although still off-balance, felt annoyed. "It's not me I'm trying to keep happy."

"Of course," Markham said soothingly. "I don't mean to be difficult."

Trina gazed at him. "That will be the day."

Markham looked at her for a moment. "As a matter of fact, Delgado is going to be at that benefit tonight. At my house. Why don't you come too? You should really get to know each other."

Trina frowned. "I'm not sure I can make it."

Markham raised an eyebrow. "Try."

C
H
A
P
T
E
R

S
E
V
E
N

The only sensible thing, Trina knew, was to avoid Markham's benefit entirely. Edward Kelley-Delgado hadn't recognized her, and since Rackley was in charge of the Mexico City clinic opening, she might not encounter him again.

On the other hand, she was now twenty pounds heavier; her hair was six inches shorter. Eight years ago Trina Robbins wore tight jeans and knee-high leather boots. Finally, after pacing the floor of her loft for nearly twenty minutes, she began to dress for the evening. She had figured out so many reasons not to see Delgado, and also so many reasons why he wouldn't recognize her, that in the end it became a matter of simple compulsion. She wanted to do it; and what could it hurt?

Driving up to Marin, Trina tried to remember what she had known about Delgado. He had been born in southern California, his father an illegal Mexican national, his mother a strawberry blonde from Oklahoma who worked in the orange groves. At twenty-two, an army enlisted man, Delgado was arrested in Germany for stealing weapons from the base armory, allegedly to sell to terrorist groups. He spent eighteen months in Leavenworth. When he emerged in 1975, middle America had just discovered cocaine, and Delgado rapidly figured out that it was the business for him. To smooth his dealings he began using a matronymic, creating the construct Kelley-Delgado. He had achieved major success as a low-profile smuggler when Trina met him in their first incarnations.

During that weekend in Tahoe, she and Rand and Delgado had

done some gambling, then visited a nearby firing range. It had been an odd afternoon amid the pines and cool mountain air, the two men competing in pistol prowess as Trina watched. At the time she was herself a decent shot, and Delgado, she recalled, was excellent. Not long after that weekend, when the drug trade became more violent and unpredictable, Delgado quietly retired, living in Mexico City off investments he had made in the U.S. and Mexico. Trina had not heard a word of him in years.

Just past five Trina arrived at the long driveway up to Markham's house and left her car with the valet service. Markham's estate, originally built by a silver baron, was a huge white stucco house on fifteen acres of rolling green California hilltop. From the massive flagstone patio one could look south to the pastel pointillistic lights of San Francisco, or west toward the flat gray expanse of the Pacific.

Markham always intended to tear down the drafty old mansion and build something of his own. He dreamed up all manner of solar-powered pleasure domes, but could never find an acceptable architect. In an odd way it was as if Markham finally adapted to the massive, aging edifice. "He has come into the full flower of his moguldom," Rackley once joked; he insisted on calling the estate Mogul Manor.

Trina walked through the brick courtyard of the house and paused at the ornately carved front door. The house was crowded with perhaps seventy-five people, mostly young, wearing a uniform distribution of diamonds, silk blouses, and thousand-dollar suits. Markham, underdressed in gray wool slacks and golf sweater, was near the door and saw Trina arrive. He walked up and kissed her cheek. "I'm glad you could make it." He glanced around. "Delgado is here someplace."

Trina quickly surveyed the room. She noticed a half dozen of the most powerful venture capitalists in northern California, and three or four other ranking heads of Silicon Valley. There were two university deans, a scatter of bankers, a young newspaper publisher, and a U.S. Representative. "Hey," she said after a moment. "This is definitely the A list."

Markham shrugged as if he hadn't noticed. "They all contributed to building the new Caswell Clinic, five thousand dollars or more." He looked at Trina. "The public doesn't realize how generous these people can be."

"I'm sure they don't," Trina said. Markham excused himself and Trina continued to glance around. This was an unusually bright gathering of influential minds and pocketbooks—indeed, a fair assortment of the hands controlling the great engines of American technology. Set off a bomb in this room, Trina thought, and the U.S. would be set back a decade.

As the eighties closed, San Francisco's influence in corporate America had ebbed—money and power flowed south to Los Angeles or remained in New York. But northern California burgeoned as the world's birthplace of new technologies. Perhaps it was the gold rush heritage; perhaps the proximity of large universities and Silicon Valley. Whatever the reason, billions of dollars flowed in from all over the world, and the venture capitalists, allocating funds to the most deserving inventors, became crown princes of the realm.

Trina walked over to a bar arranged by the two-story stone fireplace and asked for soda water and lime. As she did, she heard Markham talking to two young venture capitalists, both investors in United Genetics.

"I'll tell you," Markham said, leaning forward, one foot on the massive granite hearth as if it were some creature he had felled. "I'll tell you what really amazes me about biotech."

"The huge return on investment," one fellow said cheerfully.

"That's trivial. What amazes me is that, so far, everything has been easier than we thought."

"Paul," the first venture capitalist said, "we're already in for two rounds. You don't have to sell this door to door."

The other venture capitalist cleared his throat. "Unless he's angling for more funding."

The first investor sighed extravagantly. "Unfortunately we're strictly into software this year."

Markham waited patiently. "Okay," he said finally, feigning hurt, "are you going to listen to this sincere observation, or are you just going to make fun?"

"Paul," the first investor said formally. "When has anyone not listened to you?"

"Okay," Markham said. "I remember in the early days of recombinant DNA, you'd ask the scientists, when are we going to see the first genetically engineered human insulin? And they'd hem and haw and say, 'Oh, we can't make predictions, that's too far off.' Four years later the stuff is in every drugstore in the country."

Markham paused for a moment. "Same thing with genetically engineered plants. 'Oh,' the researchers said, 'it will be decades before we have genetically engineered seeds.' Three years later they're on the market. 'Oh,' the researchers said, 'we'll never figure out the human genome.' Now you can walk into any Birth-tech branch and get a gene scan that lists five hundred disorders.''

Markham paused, taking a sip of his drink. "And most of the scientists are still hiding behind that bullshit."

"Well," said one venture capitalist, puzzled, "isn't that—"

"The point is," Markham interrupted, "scientists used to promise miracles they couldn't deliver—nuclear-powered cars, that sort of thing. Now they're scared to make promises because they're hiding from people like Natural Progress and the media and Congress, for God's sake." He glanced over the crowd and shook his head. "We don't have any Galileos anymore, willing to stand up and say the truth."

There was an awkward silence. "And what is the truth, Paul?" one venture capitalist asked quietly.

"The truth is that this technology will change everything we believe. About democracy and equality and human potential and . . ."

At that moment Markham caught Trina's eye and, with an effort, calmed himself. "Now, there's my public relations counsel. I suspect that I've said too much."

Trina smiled easily. "You're among friends," she said sweetly. "I think you can rant and rave to your heart's content."

Markham looked at the first venture capitalist. "She understands my needs perfectly." He took Trina's elbow. "I see Delgado outside."

Involuntarily Trina hesitated. When Markham glanced at her quizzically, she followed.

The tall man was talking to a small group of women; as Trina and Markham approached, she saw him excuse himself and turn. Encountering him once again, years after that vaguely recalled Tahoe weekend, gave her an odd sense of déjà vu, upwelling recollections of a life that she thought was locked away.

Markham introduced them briefly; then in typical fashion said, "Talk now," and disappeared.

There was a brief silence. Delgado, whose dark hair was thinning slightly, had an innocent, charming smile. He appeared about to say something, but then paused. He looked at Trina closely.

"You know, you look very familiar to me. Have we met before?"

"Maybe you've seen me around the office," Trina said uneasily.

He gazed at her. "You do look familiar," he said finally.

"But . . ." He shrugged and smiled. "So. You work with Rackley."

"That's right," Trina said, relieved. "I handle press relations." She lifted her glass of soda and sipped for a moment. "We . . ." Her voice trailed off as she saw the sudden change in Delgado's expression.

"Oh my God," he said softly. After a long moment he spoke again. "You are Rand Davis's friend."

Trina hesitated, not sure how to respond, and then their eyes met and in that instant the recognition was complete.

"Lake Tahoe," Delgado said. "We went to a pistol range."

Trina just looked at him.

"Jesus," he said after another moment, his face registering the first trace of real emotion. "Yes."

"I haven't seen Rand for a long time," Trina said. "I've been clean for seven years."

Delgado's expression barely changed; all Trina could see was a slight rise of one eyebrow.

"Congratulations," Delgado said, clearly gathering his thoughts. "That's wonderful. Addiction is a terrible curse."

He took her elbow and they moved a bit farther from the crowd, toward the edge of the big stone patio, where San Francisco was a collection of bright towers across the water, the Transamerica pyramid a sharp exclamation among them.

"The last time we met," Trina said, "you were importing automobiles. One at a time."

"That was a long time ago."

Trina took a deep breath. "Funny thing," she said. "I thought you were a drug smuggler."

Delgado did not even blink. "And I thought you were a hooker."

Trina winced slightly. "That's not nice."

"Look how wrong we can both be," Delgado said easily. "We really have to learn not to judge people."

Trina gazed out at the city for a moment. "How do you know Paul?"

"Mutual friends," Delgado said, "in the film business, in Los Angeles."

"And how did you come to work for United Genetics?"

Delgado, once again cool and quiet, shrugged. "Paul was having trouble organizing services in Mexico City. It's a difficult city to do business in. So I volunteered to help, and one thing turned to another and finally he offered me a bit of stock if I came to work for him full time."

"Does he know about your previous work?"

"Does he know about yours?"

There was a stretch of silence as both Trina and Delgado regarded the city.

"You look very good," Delgado said. "Very healthy."

"Thank you. I take good care of myself now."

"As you should." Delgado cleared his throat. "Can I get you another drink?"

"Thanks. Soda water with lime."

Delgado went off and she turned to gaze out at the bay again. Her pulse had picked up; her breathing was shallow. She didn't believe it was physical attraction; it was more that Delgado's presence brought some of her former life back to her, a certain tightness in the chest, a kind of low-level adrenaline. There had been some very good times, and some very bad times, and some times she had never even been able to talk about in meetings. Like three in a bed; somehow, that had never come out, not even with her sponsor. In the program people sometimes said you were only as sick as your secrets and perhaps that was true. One thing that was clearly not secret: Delgado was interested in her, and that was an influence she did not need in her life.

When Delgado returned with the drinks, she smiled. "Tell me all about the work you do at the clinic."

"Oh, I hope that you can come down for the opening next month. You can write about the new clinic building, all the work with the poor."

Trina didn't look at him. "Rackley is in charge of that."

"I will talk to him about it."

Trina glanced over her shoulder. The guests out on the patio were now drifting back inside to hear Markham speak.

"Are you going in?" Delgado asked Trina.

"I don't think so. I've heard this speech a few times before."

Delgado moved slightly closer. "Then perhaps we could walk around the grounds a bit. You could tell me about the native plants."

Trina laughed softly. "It's a little dark for nature walks, don't you think?"

Delgado shrugged, his expression amused.

"No," Trina said. "I really have to get home. An early day tomorrow."

"Of course. But I do look forward to seeing you again. I think we could make a wonderful story in Mexico City."

Trina went back inside and she could hear that Markham had started his speech. He wasn't using any of the material she had reviewed earlier. Instead he was describing the Caswell Clinic for the Diseases of Overpopulation. The Clinic had been started forty years ago by Edward Caswell's grandfather to serve the poor of Mexico City, and the Caswell Foundation had financed it until recently. Now a sizable portion of its budget came from United Genetics. The tiny clinic in downtown Mexico City was being replaced by a new building in the suburbs—a 400-bed hospital, a nursery, a day-care center, even a small orphanage.

Like many large American companies, United Genetics' drug division had started to use foreign hospitals to test drugs that had not yet passed the regulatory hurdles in the United States. At first Third World countries protested, claiming that it rendered their populations guinea pigs for American pharmaceutical companies. But the protests quieted when it became clear that the arrangements also involved major new expenditures on facilities like the Caswell Clinic, as well as research positions for local scientists.

Trina walked quietly along the back of the big living room, listening as Markham thanked his guests for their support of the Clinic. "I hope," Markham was saying, "that you will continue to find a place for it in your hearts. Our best years are still ahead of us." Trina was nearly to the front door when she encountered Megan Collins, a woman about her age, the wife of Albert Collins, a venture capitalist who was lead investor in United Genetics.

Megan was a green-eyed brunette, wearing a blue silk princess dress that fit her closely; a tall, elegant young woman, she was given to clothes that showed off her narrow waist and willowy figure.

"Trina," Megan said, "how are you? We haven't seen you in so long."

Not, Trina thought, all that surprising. Trina was not generally A-list in financial circles. "You look wonderful. What a dress."

"Thank you," Megan said. "This is probably my last chance to wear it."

"Oh?"

"We're going to have a baby."

"Congratulations," Trina said, even as she felt an involuntary

tug of sadness. Babies everywhere. She chatted briefly with
Megan, whose bright enthusiasm made Trina feel curmudgeonly.
Sometimes the aura of motherhood seemed overpowering; a half
dozen women at the party tonight, for example, either had a new
child or were pregnant. And there was Edward Caswell and his
wife with little Erin. Now, Rackley and Kaye. Once again Trina
found herself wondering about her own course. Was she going to
spend the rest of her existence writing press releases for United
Genetics and sleeping every few weeks with boring biochemists?

After a polite interval she said good-night to Megan and was
just about to go out the door, down to retrieve her car, when she
heard a voice behind her. "Trina."

She turned to see Delgado, standing in the big slate-tiled
entryway. "Please," he said. "If I said anything to offend you
tonight, I do want to apologize. Sometimes when old lives and
new lives meet . . ." He placed both hands palms upward and
shrugged.

"I know how it is," Trina said. "Don't think about it twice."

When she got down to the big circular driveway, the valet took
fifteen minutes to find her car. She nearly took that as a sign to go
back up to the house and look for Delgado, but then thought better
of it. It was an impulse that made no sense. Before she could think
again, her car appeared.

CHAPTER EIGHT

Vincent's death rendered the decision inevitable. Immediately after the sparsely attended memorial service in Los Angeles, Kaye visited Birthtech, where a physician made the intentionally inaccurate notation that she had been infertile for over a year. This would establish Kaye's in vitro fertilization as medically necessary, in case Birthtech's records were ever audited to see if they were genetically screening embryos.

Birthtech had been nearly bankrupt when Paul Markham bought it. Conventional health insurance didn't cover in vitro fertilization, and few patients were able to afford the thousands the procedure could cost. Markham promptly mounted a whirlwind tour of Congress, arguing that fertility was a right, not a privilege. It was typical of Markham: if a venture wasn't successful for social reasons, his immediate response was to change society. Then—since back in the seventies Congress had banned federal funds for research involving human embryos—Markham spent his own money to create an assembly line approach to IVF.

Kaye began taking a genetically engineered drug designed to force her body to produce ripe eggs. Each morning she put a small metal sensor under her tongue. The sensor was connected to an electronic device not much larger than a box of tissues; by measuring chemical changes in her saliva the small microcomputer would predict exactly when ovulation would take place.

On Thursday morning Kaye was startled and delighted when the tiny gray device beeped twice and its liquid crystal display screen announced: Ovulation: -21 hours.

She immediately took another drug, also produced by the
United Genetics pharmaceutical division. This was a sophisticated
version of a fertility drug, which, during the seventies, sometimes
produced quintuplets and sextuplets. The exotic hormone would
force Kaye's ovaries to produce four or five ripe eggs, rather than
just one. The more eggs, Louise Allman had explained, the better
the chances of producing a healthy embryo.

The morning the little machine sounded, Rackley had long
since left the house. His mission was to meet Steven Hechinger,
who was beginning his investigative junket ninety miles away at
the United Genetics agricultural division in Davis.

"I can't believe they appointed him," Trina had said the day
before.

"Well," Rackley shrugged. "At least we know where he
stands."

Driving through the former farmlands that were now San
Francisco's most distant suburbs, Rackley thought about Birthtech. Kaye's eggs would soon be harvested, close on the heels of
Vincent's death. Life out of death . . . Rackley felt as if there
was some profound link he should make, but all he could think
was how relieved he would be when it was over. He was tired to
the bone, and he simply wanted something to go right. Once past
the endless tracts of cheap housing, he saw that the hills had
turned a new intense green from the spring rains, and somehow
his spirits lifted.

An hour later Rackley arrived on the outskirts of Davis, once a
sleepy university town, now headquarters of United Genetics'
agricultural division: five low earth-toned buildings sprawled over
several acres of industrial park. Behind the buildings as far as one
could see stretched experimental fields filled with crops, dotted
with huge greenhouses.

As Rackley parked, he noticed two television vans in front
with crews shooting exteriors. A sure sign, he thought, of Steven
Hechinger's presence. When Rackley stepped from the car,
Hechinger himself approached.

On the telephone Hechinger sounded like some small bearded
gnome who wore ill-fitting sport coats and backed people into the
corner at parties, talking intensely about important topics as all
they could ponder was how to escape. But Hechinger's looks
belied his telephone manner: he was tall, with receding blond hair,
wearing a blue shirt and tie under a Levi's jacket, with gray

corduroy pants. He carried an aging leather briefcase and looked vaguely like a young Eisenhower.

Hechinger approached Rackley's car and held out his hand. "I was sorry to hear about your brother."

Rackley nodded. "Thank you. He'd been ill for a long time."

There was a moment of awkward silence, and then Hechinger glanced at Rackley's old sports car. "I figured you for a Mercedes for sure."

Rackley pulled his briefcase from behind the seat. "So you're not always right?"

"Only on minor issues," Hechinger said easily.

Rackley straightened up and looked around for a moment. "We should start at the lab. It's a short walk from here. Mind?"

"Not at all," Hechinger said, gazing out at the countryside. "God, I love California. If the steering wheel wasn't in Washington, I'd be out here."

Rackley gestured and the two started to walk.

"Did you know I once wrote you a fan letter?" Hechinger said.

Rackley glanced over at him. "Really?"

"Must have been ten years ago. I wrote you a letter about that 'Rape of Alaska' story." He looked out at the rolling hills behind the experimental fields. "That was a fine piece of writing."

"Thanks. Took six months."

"It showed. So did the feeling." He turned back to Rackley. "I've never been able to figure out what you're doing at United Genetics."

"Maybe I sold out," Rackley said mildly.

"Nah. Small-time newspaper guys sell out. I mean, they realize they're just rewriting press releases for their own papers, why not write the press releases themselves and get paid twice as much."

Rackley smiled at the characterization.

"No," Hechinger said. "With you it's something different."

"I had some personal problems. When I started at United Genetics I can't say I knew what I was doing. But now I do. Those stories I did—famine in Africa, strip mining in Alaska, nuclear power—I was pointing fingers at bad guys. I was great at pointing fingers." He looked over at Hechinger. "But all it did was make readers like you feel good. It never really changed anything."

"That's not true. You influenced—"

"Influenced very little," Rackley said. "Lots of light, little heat." He paused for a moment. "No. Most of our problems don't come from bad guys and good guys. They come from the fact that the planet is overcrowded. But it's too late to fix that. So we have to get much smarter much faster, just to feed people. Just to keep people healthy. Biology is our last hope."

"Now you're quoting Markham."

Rackley shook his head. "Markham was quoting me. I wrote that speech for him." He paused for a moment. "Anyway, that's the story. I had to do something. And this is the best thing I can see."

Hechinger let out a long exhalation of air and said nothing for a moment. "People sometimes asked me what happened to you. They'd guess stock options. I'd say, he turned true believer." He nodded. "I was right."

Rackley shrugged. "I have stock options too."

"And your Mercedes is at home in the garage."

Rackley looked over at the thin activist. "That's exactly where it is. My wife drives it." He stopped. "Here we are."

The two walked into the lobby of the Agriculture Research Center, signed in, and Rackley led Hechinger into the first lab, a big space all in white, with wide work benches covered with glassware.

"I wish," Rackley said, "I was showing you the Ag Division under happier circumstances. The people here have done some great work. It's rough when a bioaccident gets all the attention."

"Then you shouldn't have accidents." Hechinger pointed to the large machine in the corner, about the size of a photocopy machine, but covered with switches and digital readouts. "What's that?"

"That's a nucleotide synthesizer," Rackley said, surprised that Hechinger didn't recognize the device. "It's the basis of this work; it automatically puts together DNA sequences. Organic chemicals in one end, synthetic genes out the other. Then of course you still have to plug those genes into some living organism and make them work, but at least this gives us the genes in the first place."

Hechinger looked over at Rackley for a moment. "You know, nobody has ever really let me into one of their laboratories before."

"It's about time. There aren't nearly as many monsters in the corners as you seem to think."

Rackley glanced around for a moment. "Over there," he said, pointing to another machine the size of a restaurant freezer, covered with digital readouts and topped with a few blooms of elaborate glassware. "That's a sequencer. We can extract the DNA from an organism, run it through this machine, and twenty-four hours later it tells us the makeup of the DNA, bit by bit. It has a hell of a lot of computing power. Markham figured out pretty quickly where computers would be useful."

"I always thought Markham was completely overrated," Hechinger said. "I mean, the media needs somebody to be a star, so they don't have to explain what's really going on. Markham became the star of Silicon Valley, but that was just because he was a nice-looking kid who happened to pick up a few hundred million bucks."

Rackley shook his head. "Markham's different."

"I wonder."

Rackley shrugged. Shortly after Markham cashed out of his first company, he had literally disappeared from sight for five years. One national magazine reported that "the reclusive Markham has lost his Midas touch and turned to Eastern religion for comfort." Another persistent rumor had him addicted to pharmaceutical cocaine; a third said he was buying a motion picture studio. In fact Markham was living in his huge Marin County mansion, devouring technical journals and inviting key scientists over for intense briefings on lasers, robotics, space manufacturing, ceramics—all in search of the next great opportunity.

"He used that money to buy himself the best teachers," Rackley said. "He's so spartan, sometimes he seems like some kind of religious nut."

Hechinger was watching him closely. "You like him."

Rackley inclined his head. "I don't know. He's a very strange man. I do respect him. He's made something remarkable out of his life."

He opened another door, into a large room heated to ninety degrees, its walls lined with shelves. Each shelf held hundreds of round glass petri dishes filled with masses of naked plant cells, floating in their nutrient broths as tiny green globules. The warm, moist air blended the scents of organic chemistry and fresh alfalfa.

"This is where we developed the sawdust tomato," Rackley said.

Hechinger smiled slightly. He had coined the name "sawdust tomato" when, several years earlier, United Genetics achieved one of the holy grails of agricultural biotechnology: the ultra-high-solids tomato. The theory was simple: tomato processors haul millions of pounds from field to cannery each year. But much of the weight is just water. United Genetics found a wild strain of tomato in the Bolivian Andes that was tiny, bitter, and ugly—but it was also almost pure solid content. Researchers extracted the genes for high solids and transplanted them into the most popular American tomato. The result was a patented tomato with the approximate consistency of a tennis ball.

The new tomato swept the industry—until Hechinger and Natural Progress filed suit, claiming that in the course of its genetic engineering the new tomato had lost its vitamin C content. The Natural Progress lawyers even resurrected an old Food and Drug Administration law that set nutritional standards for fruit and vegetables. Hechinger's suit was upheld, and United Genetics was forced to withdraw the profitable tomato for another eighteen months of genetic tinkering; the result was a slight loss in solids, but a return to the old level of vitamin C.

"We do nutritional testing on all our products now," Rackley said.

Hechinger was peering into a green-splotched petri dish. "Did you do it on Rice Five, too?"

"Our next stop."

They walked down a long gray corridor to a steel security door. Rackley inserted his ID card into the lock and the door opened onto a small brick courtyard, where an electric cart awaited.

"We're going out to the rice project," Rackley told the young driver. With a quiet purr the cart started out into the flat green expanses.

The sun, midway in the sky, was already hot. As they moved through the crops, Rackley pointed into the distance where two technicians were clipping buds off plants. "That's an EPA regulation," he explained. "Nothing is allowed to go to seed until it's gone through ecological approval."

Five minutes later they arrived at the small trailer that housed the field operations of the rice project. Rackley introduced Hechinger to the head of the team, a chubby balding fellow in a khaki workshirt, his pockets filled with pens, his forehead shiny with sweat.

The rice project manager immediately confessed that the Rice Five bioaccident had him baffled.

Hechinger stared at him closely. "How could that be?"

The balding man shrugged. "We'd given up on developing Rice Five; it was just too strange, too different than conventional rice. It never would have sold. Farmers want better crops, but not totally new ones."

Hechinger pulled out a small notebook. "So . . ."

"All we can think," the plump scientist said, "is that there was a mix-up in the laboratory. We planted some cell lines that should have been destroyed."

The man looked out over the broad fields beyond, now completely bare, showing nothing but the rich brown soil of the Sacramento Valley.

"You have to understand," he told Hechinger. "The EPA has pulled all of our Experimental Use Permits. We're dead in the water. We have to have all of our facilities reinspected, everything started from scratch. This has set us back at least a year."

Hechinger gazed at him evenly, showing little sympathy. He waved one hand, encompassing the acres of test fields. "Might it be that you're trying to do too much? That you're pushing a little too hard? Not quite keeping track of everything?"

"I wish I knew," the manager said as a slight breeze came up, a bit of late morning coolness in the Valley heat. "Knowing what happened would be better than where we are now. No matter who gets blamed."

"Well," Hechinger said cheerfully, opening his notebook with a flourish. "That's exactly why I'm here."

The next morning, when the gray display of the ovulation detector finally switched to Ovulation: -1 hour, Kaye and Rackley were already sitting in the softly lit waiting room of Birthtech. Timing was crucial: eggs had to be harvested at full maturity or fertilization would not occur.

"I'm finally starting to feel funny about this," Kaye said. "I even have a pain in my stomach. I guess from being nervous."

Sitting next to her on a long couch, Rackley held her hand. "It'll be fine," he said softly. "This is probably the best clinic in the world now."

"Oh," Kaye said, smoothing her tan wool skirt, "I know, I know. It's just . . ."

"Just what?"

She sighed. "For most people it happens in bed, and they don't even know if it happened, and it just takes its course."

Rackley leaned back in the couch. "As long as there's real love behind it," he said quietly, "I don't think there's anything more or less wrong about this than any other way to make babies."

Kaye squeezed his hand, nodded, saying nothing, and at that moment a nurse appeared at the door.

"Mrs. Rackley?"

* * *

Twenty minutes after Rackley and Kaye left the Birthtech waiting room, Trina Robbins arrived. She was there to meet Steven Hechinger. Since Rackley was with Kaye, he had asked Trina to tend the activist for the day. Hechinger's interest, however, was not Birthtech. Instead he had asked to see United Genetics' most controversial undertaking: the Markham Project.

Trina had been sitting for only a moment when, right on time, Hechinger walked into the lobby, tall, blond, wearing a worn leather vest. Trina recognized him immediately and stood. They shook hands.

"A pleasure," Hechinger said.

"I hope your research went well."

Hechinger shook his head. "Actually, it's hard to see how that rice escaped. You guys do seem to be pretty careful about environmental release."

"It's the law," Trina said. "We take it seriously."

"But it did happen. And you don't have it all out of the Delta yet." Hechinger paused for a moment, with a slight smile. "Have you looked into the way those Delta fields are irrigated?"

"No," Trina said, off guard. "Should we?"

"You might. If you people have any liability, that's where it's going to hit."

Trina wanted to avoid the topic in Rackley's absence. "Well, Rackley said he was sorry he couldn't be here. But I'll do my best."

Hechinger nodded easily. "Rackley's kind of a gloomy guy. You look like more fun."

Trina ignored this. "The Markham Project is about ten minutes from here."

"Perfect. I've wanted to see it ever since the first rumors."

"Before we leave," Trina said, "can I tell you anything about Birthtech?"

Hechinger glanced toward the large waiting room, where a dozen young people, some women by themselves, some couples, were sitting on corduroy-upholstered couches and seats. Then he looked back at Trina. "Yes, as a matter of fact. Where are you hiding Stuart Lipsky?"

Trina ignored the reference to the disgraced Stanford geneticist. "Not a whole lot to see here, actually. Birthtech does the standard infertility stuff, plus gene screening. We do thousands of gene scans every month, up to five hundred potential conditions. We've got twenty-one clinics now, on four continents."

"How about gene therapy?"

Trina shrugged. "We do as much as the law allows. We've done a few kids with Lesch-Nyhan, a few with immune deficiency. They're happy, healthy kids now. That's saying something." She turned to a young blond secretary behind the main lobby desk. "Do you have those photos of Bruno X?"

She turned back to Hechinger. "As you know, no other diseases have been approved yet."

"Rumor says that you guys are thinking of patenting genes to correct for baldness and color blindness."

"We can't patent a natural gene," Trina said, slightly annoyed, "any more than you can patent an oak tree. You should know that."

The secretary returned with a legal-length manila folder. Trina handed it to Hechinger. "One of our first gene therapy patients. Before and after. I can't look at it."

Hechinger opened the manila folder and suddenly his breath stopped in his throat. The glossy color photos before him were bizarre and terrible: images of a four-year-old boy with a crazed look in his eyes and nothing but ragged, torn flesh where his lips had been. A close-up of one hand showed fingers that seemed to have been gnawed like barbecued chicken legs.

"Oh God," Hechinger said softly, closing the folder quickly.

"Lesch-Nyhan is the worst disease I've ever heard of," Trina said. "Besides eating his own flesh, that little guy was constantly screaming obscenities, breaking everything he touched. Like he was possessed."

She took the file from Hechinger and turned to the last picture. It showed the same child, now five, smiling into the camera, whole and healthy.

"Reconstructive surgery," Trina said. "Obviously. And also a single gene, inserted into his bone marrow, to produce the enzyme whose absence made him into . . . that pitiful thing."

Hechinger didn't meet her eyes. "I'd never seen pictures of Lesch-Nyhan."

"They're not exactly publishable," Trina said. "There are two hundred new cases a year in the U.S. We treat about half of them."

She handed the folder back to the secretary and turned to Hechinger. "To return to the question of patents. We can't patent genes. What we can patent are novel arrangements of DNA plus delivery vehicles."

"Sure," Hechinger said, quickly regaining his composure.

"Tweak a few nucleotides, then you patent it. Like you did with those tomato genes from Bolivia."

"We won that one."

"Damn unfair, too." This controversy had arisen in the United Nations. After the patented ultrasolid tomato was a success, the Bolivian government filed suit to gain a portion of the proceeds, alleging that the genes belonged to Bolivia. The situation was made more tense when Hechinger revealed that United Genetics was actually selling the ultrasolid tomato in Bolivia.

"You stole Bolivia's genes," Hechinger said, "and sold them back."

"But those genes were useless until we plugged them into our own variety. That's why the World Court upheld our rights."

Trina turned and gazed at Hechinger for a moment. "You know, I shouldn't say this, but there's one thing that really bothers me about you people."

Hechinger brightened up. "I was wondering when the nice guy act was going to wear off."

"You're intellectually dishonest. Your disagreement is really with capitalism and the patent system and private property. But you don't come out and say so, because you know it's too late for that. The sixties are over, the masses didn't rise up, the revolution didn't happen. So instead now you attack genetic engineering, but you're still really going after capitalism and big business."

Hechinger laughed and shook his head. "Christ, Caswell really has brainwashed you. Another five years and you're going to be an out-and-out Commie basher."

Trina felt her face redden. "That's not what I'm saying."

"But you are. You've completely ignoring the real issue—which is that genetic engineering means fooling around with a resource, our genes, that *does* belong to everyone. It's not like the silver in the Caswell mines or the oil in Texas. Genes *are* life, millions of years of evolution, and you're going to twist them around to make next quarter's profit. That's not capitalism as usual, it's a whole new game."

Trina stared off into the Birthtech waiting room for a moment, watching the young parents-to-be. Hechinger made her oddly uneasy, and clearly this discussion would accomplish nothing. "You were asking about our work on humans. All I can say is that we're still characterizing genes. Obviously, with the federal ban, there's only so much we can do."

"Without that ban all hell would break loose."

Trina shrugged, saying nothing. At first there had only been voluntary guidelines controlling human genetic engineering. But then, several years earlier, public outrage over an unauthorized experiment by Stanford researcher Stuart Lipsky forced Congress to pass a formal ban with fines and prison sentences for violators. The law even required the sterilization of any resulting babies.

"So," Hechinger said as Trina remained silent, "why did Markham hire Lipsky?"

Trina found Hechinger's tone annoying. "Lipsky is brilliant. He made a mistake, but that shouldn't disqualify him from science. Personally I've always been in favor of giving people second chances."

"I want to talk to him."

Trina stared at him. "After the way Natural Progress beat him up in the media? You did everything but ask that he be burned at the stake."

"What if I insist? As part of the investigation."

Suddenly Trina realized that Markham's stonewalling instincts had been correct. Trying to cooperate halfway with someone like Hechinger was impossible. Lipsky, she knew, from the few times they'd met, was a bitter and unhappy man—not the sort who should be presenting United Genetics' case to critics. "I'm afraid it's unlikely."

"Please set up a meeting," Hechinger said curtly.

Trina held her temper. By now she had learned a modicum of patience from her dealings with reporters, many of whom were petty tyrants. Even so, silence in the face of boorishness still rankled: sometimes Trina felt that since sobriety she had become restrained, tamed, encased in nice-girl outsides that no longer matched her insides at all.

"Look, I'll ask Lipsky. But he won't talk to you."

"Then we'll subpoena him. He can't disappear into private industry and lock the door behind him."

"Suit yourself." Trina glanced at her watch. "We have to get moving."

Twenty minutes later Kaye, wearing a surgical gown, was wheeled into a small operating room. The door read Oocyte Retrieval, and just outside, the attending physician, a woman in her late twenties with short red hair, turned to Rackley. "I'm Dr. Lindfern." She glanced at the paperwork on her clipboard for a moment. "This is not fertility related, I see."

Her tone was a study in professional neutrality, but Rackley felt a twinge nonetheless. "What makes you say that?"

"I'm guessing," Lindfern said, again with little inflection. "Usually with a fertility problem there's some preexisting condition on record."

"Do you disapprove?"

She looked at Rackley for a moment, then shrugged. "It depends, I suppose. I didn't spend eight years learning IVF so that some rich family could have a guaranteed tall boy or blue eyes or whatever. It hasn't come to that yet, but the way the system works, what with the fudged paperwork, I really can't tell what we're prospecting for."

"Avoiding, in this case," Rackley said. "Alpha alcoholism."

She said nothing for a moment. "You didn't have to tell me that," she said finally, her tone warmer. "Stand over there." She gestured toward a large color video monitor. "If you'd like to observe, most of our work happens on television."

The doctor set a silver transducer, the size of a steam iron, on Kaye's stomach. The transducer generated ultrasonic sound waves, which resonated inside her body, and then a sophisticated computer turned the reflected waves into a visual representation of the body cavity. The imagery, neatly drawn in computer-style animation, almost looked like some educational cartoon on the color monitor that dominated the center of the small operating room.

Rackley stood off to one side. Kaye was on the table, legs pulled up, feet in stirrups. Along with a local anesthetic, she had been given a mild tranquilizer, so she looked rather peaceful, almost dreamy. The young redheaded physician stood at the foot of the operating table and looked up at the big color monitor for a moment.

"Excellent image," Lindfern said quietly. "When there's not much body fat, the image is sharp as a textbook." She studied the image for a moment longer as a nurse took up position at a rack of electronic readouts and a small metal table of instruments, four feet from where the doctor stood.

"Everything okay?" Kaye asked drowsily.

"Just relax," Lindfern said. "Fall asleep, if you'd like to."

She moved the ultrasound transducer on Kaye's abdomen slightly, then reached down to controls mounted under the bed and touched a joystick. Instantly the image on the big overhead television screen moved an inch or so to one side. "There," she said after a moment. "The right ovary."

On the screen in deep red was an organ shaped like a slightly puckered kidney bean, the surface studded with three tiny protrusions, like little mushrooms. "Mature follicles," the doctor said. She touched a button and a scale, measured off in centimeters, was superimposed on the TV screen.

"Two centimeters each. Excellent." She turned slightly to talk over her shoulder to the nurse. "Speculum," she said, and a few moments later, "Retrieval set."

The physician carefully inserted a long, Teflon-coated needle up into Kaye, moving it slowly up toward her ovaries as she watched its progress on the monitor. The needle appeared as a bright blue line on the computer-enhanced image. After about forty-five seconds the tip of the needle was near the right ovary.

"Ready for vacuum," the nurse said.

On the television screen the needle approached, then touched the first little toadstool-shaped follicle.

"Vacuum," Lindfern said, and there was a quiet hum, the tiniest whisper of compressed air somewhere in the complex machinery of the operating room. Then the first little follicle collapsed like a deflated balloon. In that instant the egg—the largest cell in the human body, just barely visible with the naked eye—was pulled from the follicle that sheltered it and sucked back through the Teflon needle and tube, out into a tiny glass dish of warm fluid. "Egg number one," the nurse said.

The doctor immediately moved the needle toward the second follicle. In another five seconds it was in place. "Vacuum," she said again.

Moments later the nurse spoke: "Egg number two."

The young doctor moved the needle one more time as once again the nurse changed culture dishes. "Vacuum."

"Egg number three."

On the television monitor all three follicles now looked like exploded balloons. The young doctor's shoulders relaxed briefly, although she did not move her hands, keeping the needle in place.

The nurse busied herself with some optical equipment over the egg retrieval machine. "Okay," the nurse said after about twenty seconds. "We're three for three."

Lindfern nodded and began to pull back on the needle. Kaye, sleepily alert, was listening to the conversation. "We're doing okay?" she asked.

"Doing just fine." The doctor was once again using the joystick on the operating table to move the sonogram image on the screen. "Doing just . . ."

Lindfern's voice trailed off as the left ovary appeared on screen. It was nearly twice the size of the right, a different color, mottled. The two follicles growing on it appeared to be smaller and more puckered than the healthy ones on the right side. Even Rackley could see that something was very different.

"We have a LH reaction here." The young doctor gazed up calmly at the monitor and spoke over her shoulder to the nurse. "Recorder on." The nurse switched on a small video tape recorder to preserve the image of the injured ovary.

Rackley shifted uncomfortably as he heard the doctor speaking softly to Kaye. "Did you notice any pain during the past few days?"

"A little," Kaye said sleepily, gazing up at the operating room ceiling. "I thought that was . . . ovulation."

"I see." Lindfern watched the color monitor for another long moment. "Ready for vacuum," she said over her shoulder. She maneuvered the needle to touch each of the oddly damaged follicles. "Vacuum," she said once, then again.

"Egg number four," the nurse said in turn. "Egg number five."

"Label those last two separately," the doctor said, and then, without another word, she started to withdraw the needle. Rackley glanced at his wristwatch. The total time for the egg harvest was less than ten minutes.

A moment later Lindfern handed the egg retrieval needle to the nurse, then stepped over to Kaye. She held her wrist for pulse.

"How long had you noticed the pain?"

Kaye shook her head slowly. "I don't know. The last couple of days. I just thought . . ."

The young doctor briefly touched her forehead. "You'll be fine now. We've got some very healthy eggs." She glanced over her shoulder. "Now it's up to your old man to come through."

"Oh, he's good," Kaye said, sounding slightly dreamy from the drugs. She moved her head slightly on the paper-covered pillow. "He won't be a problem."

Lindfern patted Kaye's shoulder, then turned to the nurse. Her tone changed abruptly. "Start one hundred cc's of AnaLutel, I.V. Let's have another sonogram of the left ovary in four hours." Then she took Rackley's arm and escorted him out of the room.

"Your wife had a reaction to the luteinizing hormone," she told Rackley out in the corridor. "We don't see it often, but sometimes nature just doesn't cooperate. We'll probably discard the eggs from the left ovary."

"She'll be all right?"

"I think so. But I wish we'd seen it two days ago. Your wife must have a pretty high pain threshold."

"She really wants this to work," Rackley said. "We both do."

Lindfern nodded. "Then it's good we got three healthy eggs. She won't ever be able to do this again."

"**G**uys do this all their lives," a Birthtech nurse had told Rackley the week before. "Then they get in here, and their wife is in the operating room, and there's a little dish full of ripe eggs waiting for them, and they get nervous and . . ."

The young woman had smiled cheerfully. "So we usually tell men to practice at home—a few days before the real thing, then abstinence, of course."

Rackley had ignored the advice. Today the nurse sent him, plastic cup in hand, into a small room with pink walls, a couch, a low bed, and a table with five or six old *Playboy* magazines. He stood in the middle of the room and opened his zipper. Then, feeling slightly ridiculous, he pulled his pants down. Nothing. The mind, he thought . . . such a skittish organ. He had wondered, when the time came, whose image would fill his mind? Miss August? His ninth grade geometry teacher? Trina?

A moment later he thought of Kaye a few months earlier, sitting on the side of Mt. Tamalpais, looking out over the Pacific, surrounded by the earliest wildflowers. The green hillside had been deserted in every direction. They'd been lying together, and he rolled over and kissed her, tasting the cabernet on her breath, growing aroused, and then Kaye reached down and felt him. She started to open his shirt and kiss her way down his chest, reaching for his belt buckle.

Now, standing in the little Birthtech cubicle, Rackley recalled the moment, the cool breeze coming up from the Pacific, lying

back on the soft wool blanket. He imagined her warm lips kissing
his thighs, her gentle tonguing, the feel of her blond hair. . . .

"Very good," the nurse said, when he returned. "You can see
your wife now."

While he went to see Kaye, the pure concentrate of Rackley
was placed in clear warm liquid just at body temperature, then
taken to the fertilization room: a bright space with chrome-plated
incubators arranged around the walls. Kaye's three fertile eggs
already rested in a small plastic dish. Now, a white-clad technician
used a glass pipette to siphon up a few drops of Rackley's sperm
solution. Moments later a droplet splashed directly on each
microscopic egg.

The technician moved the dishes into an incubator. Within a
few hours, in each shallow plastic well, one sperm cell—bulbous
head containing half the genetic material that defined Rackley—
would merge with one egg, bearing half the chromosomes that
characterized Kaye. Each resulting embryo would immediately
begin its own division and growth.

The dice would have rolled and stopped, and the game would
be set.

It was a ten-minute walk through the sprawling industrial park
to the Markham Project. The briefly sunny day was now giving
way to the fog again, pouring through the Golden Gate, crowding
up against the Berkeley hills. As they walked Steven Hechinger
casually asked Trina questions about her upbringing, and she
found herself telling him about growing up in Nebraska on a small
family farm, then moving to California for college. By the time
they reached the huge corrugated aluminum building that held the
Markham Project, Trina had come to think that for a fanatic
Hechinger was at least fairly personable.

"This is it?" Hechinger asked, puzzled, when Trina stopped
walking. The big building bore no external sign.

"We don't advertise the Markham Project. Too many crazies
around." She inserted her identity card into a slot on the metal
door, and placed her hand over a small glass plate. The plate
briefly glowed orange, reading her fingerprints, then beeped as the
lock on the door yielded with a dull metallic sound. Trina opened
the door wide and gestured for Hechinger to step forward.

Hechinger took two steps, then stopped short.

"There you have it," Trina said quietly from behind him.
"The Markham Project."

Hechinger stood for a moment, staring, as his eyes adjusted to the dim interior. The building was one huge room with a forty-foot ceiling. Around the edges were dozens of sophisticated gene sequencing machines, each in an individual cubicle, each tended by a white-coated operator. In one corner was a supercomputer the size of a refrigerator connected to a dozen terminals, screens glowing green in the dim light. The sound in the big warehouse was a mix of quiet conversations, the gentle hum of the supercomputer's cooling system, and an almost inaudible sucking and hissing from the gene sequencers as they went about their painstaking analysis.

Hechinger took all this in at a glance, but what caused him to stare was an immense diagram, eighty feet long, forty feet high, that completely covered the south wall of the laboratory. The size of a billboard, it looked like a cross between a full-color subway map and an elaborate maze conjured up by some manic puzzle-maker.

Barely visible all along the twisting, turning patterns of the huge billboard were carefully printed notations: tens of thousands of words, none readable at a distance. The giant image still had several huge blank spaces, each the size of a small automobile. Two painters were perched atop tall ladders propped against the giant diagram, at work adding new details.

"My God," Hechinger said after a long moment. "It's big."

"It's not easy," Trina said, "describing a whole person."

And that was precisely the point of the Markham Project: the huge diagram taking shape on the wall was the first genetic blueprint of an entire human being.

Mapping the human genome had first been proposed in the early eighties, but at the time would have cost well over $100 million. The reason was pure complexity: the DNA that comprises the forty-six chromosomes of a normal human is an incredibly long necklace made up of just four kinds of beads: adenine, thymine, cytosine, and guanine. A simple code—but to describe the flesh, chemistry, and circuitry of a human being requires three billion of those A's, T's, C's, and G's. Those three billion beads, in turn, form about 100,000 individual gene sequences, ranging from a few letters to several thousand, each coding for anything from eye color to the fibers of the heart.

Early on scientists identified some individual genes. But no one had ever actually identified each and every A, T, C, and G, thereby filling in the vast areas of terra incognita on that sketchy map. The task was daunting: sometimes there were long se-quences of genes that simply repeated, over and over. Other times there were nonsense genes, which did nothing except confuse the picture. The human genome appeared to be an elaborate secret code, which could take centuries to crack. Some even speculated that the human mind—which itself grew from those twisted coils—might never comprehend it in totality.

Paul Markham believed that the keys were supercomputers and artificial intelligence. United Genetics was the first biotechnology company to buy a supercomputer—a $15 million investment that made Wall Street analysts wonder aloud if Markham knew what business he was in. Now, however, it was clear: Markham had been precisely right.

"Obvious question," Hechinger said. "How'd you choose the lucky subject?"

Trina smiled slightly. "Well, we had to choose somebody. Except for identical twins, no two people on earth have exactly the same genetic blueprint. And of course it had to be a man, since only males carry the full complement of chromosomes."

"No one asked me," Hechinger said innocently.

"Since Markham was signing the checks, I guess he thought the choice was fairly obvious. Every few days he donates blood. They remove the DNA from the white cells, then distribute it to all those sequencing machines."

Standing in the huge laboratory, Hechinger stared at the billboard-sized gene map at the other end of the massive hall. "Will you publish?"

"I doubt it. This is worth a lot of money."

Hechinger looked over at her with surprise. "But this is a historic piece of science. It's incredibly important, like a Rosetta stone. You *have* to share it."

Trina shook her head. "If it's so important, then why didn't the federal government fund it? A month of the space weapons budget would have paid for it, and then it would have belonged to the nation. As it is"—Trina shrugged—"we paid for it and I expect we can do just about whatever we want with it."

Hechinger stared at Trina with a combination of amusement and admiration. "You are a tough one."

"Don't patronize me."

"I didn't mean to," Hechinger said quickly.

Trina gazed at the huge diagram taking shape on the opposite end of the cavernous room. "Publishing that thing on paper," she said softly, "would require almost a half million pages. DNA is really an incredible information storage system."

Hechinger was still staring across the warehouse, examining

the intricate genetic blueprint. "So that's the recipe for a Paul Markham," he said, after a long moment and then looked over at Trina. "Have you guys located the genes for greed yet?"

Trina glanced at her watch. "I think the tour is over."

Back in the recovery room Kaye was already sitting up. She was still wearing the light green surgical gown, and an intravenous bottle and tube perched at one side of her bed, steadily dripping AnaLutel into her right arm.

"It's so strange," Kaye told Rackley. "It was like going to the dentist or something. Not much more. I . . ."

She hesitated as Louise Allman entered. Today the stout, grayhaired woman wore a white jacket that rendered her more medical in appearance. She sat down and looked at Kaye. "How do you feel?"

Kaye nodded. "Pretty good. A little sore, I guess, but all right."

"I'm glad it went well." Allman paused. "They did discard the two eggs from the left ovary. Even with a full gene scan we can't tell detect all the possible damage in an egg."

Kaye nodded, a trace of disappointment showing through her sedation.

"But we've got three very healthy, mature eggs, and sometimes that's all we get from both ovaries. So we're doing fine."

"What next?" Rackley asked.

"When all three eggs are fertilized, we'll monitor each embryo as it grows." She gestured, as if describing expanding dough. "Two cells, four cells, eight cells. When they reach sixteen cells, we use microsurgery to remove one cell from each embryo."

"Doesn't that hurt it?" Kaye asked.

The older woman shook her head quickly. "The embryo continues to grow quite normally."

"Then the gene scan," Rackley said.

The older woman nodded. "Except first we'll freeze all three embryos in liquid nitrogen. We don't really like to implant embryos much older than sixteen cells, so by cryopreserving them, we can decide what we want to do without having to hurry."

Rackley frowned slightly; the process grew more complicated at every turn.

"Cryopreservation is nothing new," she said quickly. "We do it all the time. We even ship frozen embryos overseas."

Rackley nodded. The woman shifted in the small hospital

chair and crossed her legs. "So, we do the gene scans. We'll look for any abnormalities, of course, but particularly for the alpha alcoholism defect. We take the winner out of cryo, prepare it for implantation, and then you're on your way."

Kaye leaned back in the bed. "It all seems so . . ."

"So complicated. Of course it does. But I can tell you this: in two to three weeks you'll be pregnant, just as if nature had taken its own course, and this will all quickly fade in your mind."

"Not so much complicated," Kaye said, "as cold. Calculating."

The older woman shrugged. "But you have a very good reason for doing this. And you could say the same thing about the natural process. Fifty million sperm cells, battling their way up to meet one egg, which they'll maybe reach, maybe not. Only it's even less fair: one could win the race and still produce a defective baby."

"What happens to the other two embryos?" Kaye asked.

"Well, if they're defective, we can dispose of them. At the sixteen-cell stage they're barely even embryos. It's another ten days or so before the primitive streak develops, the little line that becomes the brain and spinal column and so forth."

"And if they're not defective?"

"You can store them here, frozen, as long as you'd like. If you get more than one alcoholism-minus embryo, you should probably do that. You won't be able to go through this procedure again."

Kaye sank back onto the pillow and Rackley noticed just how pale and drawn she looked.

"Go home," Allman said, "and in a couple of days I'll call you." She looked at Kaye and then at Rackley. "Get some rest, and cross your fingers."

Three days after Rackley and Kaye completed their laboratory consummation, an early spring heat was just beginning to build in Washington. And so was the pressure on Steven Hechinger.

The annual hearing of the Senate subcommittee on genetic engineering would take place in three weeks. But Hechinger found himself frustrated. Finally given a turn before the highest audience in the land, he had thus far been unable to produce a damning indictment of corporate genetic engineering. Rackley and Trina Robbins had been almost too helpful, in the end providing not much but reassurance.

The only hard evidence was the Rice Five accident, and even that had attracted far less national attention than he had hoped. Two Natural Progress volunteers in the California Delta had tried to organize a class action suit against United Genetics. But United Genetics people had been there first, providing financial assistance and offering emergency loans. In recent years, Hechinger knew, the multinational corporations had grown uncannily media-hip and adept at avoiding the kind of messy public situations that, in the sixties and seventies, provided rich fodder for radical opponents.

The morning after he returned from California he met with Senator Gordon and an aide. Hechinger planned to overcome the deficiencies in his research with strong language, warning against corporate ownership of the gene pool. But he suspected that canny old Gordon—himself a master of obfuscation—would see through the verbiage instantly.

Less than five minutes after Hechinger walked into the senator's office, Gordon interrupted him.

"So you're telling me that this boy Markham isn't really doing anything against the law."

Hechinger looked away from the portly, white-haired senator. There was a large photo of the senator's infant daughter, and for a moment Hechinger gazed at the image, searching for words. Finally he looked back. "I didn't say that. I said, United Genetics is pushing the law just as far as they can. My people here in Washington have studied their patent applications. They have four times more patent applications pending than the nearest competitor."

"Nothing wrong with that," Gordon interjected. "That's their business."

"No," Hechinger said, mildly annoyed, "of course not. Except that what they're patenting are DNA sequences that look suspiciously like human genes."

"Well, are they or aren't they?"

Hechinger sighed. "They don't really say in their applications. All they say is that their combination is novel and has"—he glanced down at his notes —"'has significant development implications in eukaryotic organisms.'"

Now the senator looked annoyed. "What the hell is a carioca organism?"

The aide leaned over to translate. "Eukaryotic. With a nucleus in its cells. Basically, anything but bacteria. Corn, pigs, humans . . ."

"So," the senator asked, turning back to Hechinger. "Why can't your people figure out what the genes do?"

Hechinger sighed again. "They're basically unrecognizable. I mean, DNA is DNA. We can't really even tell if they come from ducks or sunflowers or what. We think they're all coming from the Markham Project. But those results are secret. And nobody in the public sector is doing the work."

Gordon nodded slowly, absorbing all this. "We considered funding a full human gene scan. But you know how the federal science budget goes. We just couldn't find the money."

"Well," Hechinger said. "Markham found the money."

"Let me get this straight. You're afraid that if we ease up on the genetic engineering laws, these people are going to run amok."

"I think Markham is preparing to start a national chain of

genetic engineering clinics. As soon as you open the door, he's going to push the technology farther than you'd ever believe. And when that happens, the Catholic church, the fundamentalists, the liberals, are going to be all over you."

Gordon nodded. This was language he understood.

"There are some big social issues here," Hechinger continued. "Suppose Markham can offer blue eyes? Or bigger muscles? Will this just go to the parents who can afford genetic engineering? I mean, we could be creating a new genetic underclass of people who can't afford the work."

"As I understand it, the science isn't anywhere near that yet."

"I'm not sure." Hechinger said. "I hoped to find evidence that he was doing the work already, but . . ."

"But he might be playing by the rules." Gordon gazed at Hechinger for a moment, clearly amused. "Kind of makes you mad, doesn't it? Somebody making money, playing by the rules."

Inside, Hechinger was indeed furious. But he kept himself calm. "I'd like to make one more research trip. There's another aspect of United Genetics that I wasn't aware of when I was out on the coast. Something the people in the industry call offshore work."

Gordon nodded. "Fine with me. Just make sure you have a draft on time."

The senator's aide closed his notebook and Hechinger knew that his audience was over. He stood, and then the senator raised one hand.

"By the way, just for your information, Senator Cashman—I believe you know Alan Cashman—will be out in California this weekend. He may pay a little visit to Paul Markham, but not in any official capacity."

Hechinger stopped and stared at the senator. Cashman was a powerful, technology-oriented senator from California, and this sounded suspiciously like an end run around Hechinger.

Senator Gordon instantly read Hechinger's concern. "Oh, for God's sake, Steven," he said jovially. "You see conspiracies everywhere. Can't an elected official even visit a constituent?"

"You look great," Rackley said when Kaye came downstairs in a white silk dress with a soft, low neckline, her bare shoulders smooth, a small pearl comb in her hair.

"My beauty secret?" Kaye said. "Forty-eight hours in bed, with a maximum dose of bad glitter novels."

Kaye seemed to be feeling fine. She had returned to Birthtech two days earlier for an additional sonogram, which showed that the drug reaction had caused no permanent damage. During the visit she had also learned that all three eggs had successfully fertilized, were growing normally, and might be at the proper stage for gene scanning as early as the weekend.

By Friday Kaye felt well enough to dress for a dinner party at her brother Edward Caswell's apartment. Paul Markham would be there, along with Senator Alan Cashman. Cashman was a Silicon Valley entrepreneur who made his fortune in artificial intelligence and then graduated to politics, winning a Senate seat handily with a blend of conservative fiscal politics and a liberal social attitude.

Ostensibly all these evenings at her brother's apartment or Markham's estate in Marin were social, but Kaye knew that neither Edward nor his partner ever separated work from life. She found this curious: her parents had always made a distinction between social and business occasions. Among the nouveau riche technocrats of California, however, there seemed no such separation between life and business. While Edward embraced the style with enthusiasm, Kaye wasn't quite sure what she thought. On one hand it went against her upbringing; on the other it seemed wonderful that one might be so caught up in one's work that it blended seamlessly with life.

"I'm still feeling a little tired," Kaye said as she came down the stairs that evening. "I hope we don't have to stay too late."

"Cashman just flew in this afternoon, so it probably won't run too late."

Kaye picked up her evening purse, and Rackley stepped over to arm the security system in the front hallway. Just then the telephone rang.

"We're already late," Kaye said.

Rackley glanced at his watch, then went into the kitchen and picked up the wall phone.

"Mr. Rackley," the voice at the other end said, "this is Louise Allman at Birthtech."

Rackley came instantly alert at the sound of the genetic counselor's voice. "Yes?"

"I'm sorry to call you so late, but the results of your embryo gene scans just came in, and I thought you should know."

Rackley felt a quick adrenaline rush, but the counselor gave him no time to speak.

"It's some good and some bad, I'm afraid," Allman said, clearly accustomed to delivering news quickly and without unnecessary preface. "You have two male, one female embryos, all genetically healthy in the major disease groups. But all of them do scan positive for alpha alcoholism."

Rackley leaned back against the long ceramic tile counter that divided the big kitchen. Alerted by Rackley's silence, Kaye had walked into the kitchen and stood in the doorway, watching him, concern clear in her eyes.

"What? How can that be? I thought this was—" Rackley gestured for a moment, looking for the right word.

"I'm very sorry," the counselor said, her voice warm and reassuring even over the telephone. "You two did everything you could. But there was always a statistical chance that this might happen. And of course we had a limited number of eggs."

"Of course," Rackley said, now feeling slightly numb.

"I'd like you to come in, so we can talk about this. The embryos are in storage, so you don't have to make any decisions immediately. I have a file on early childhood addiction modification that you might want to look at."

"Fine." Rackley rubbed his eyes with one hand.

"Would you like to schedule a time now?"

Rackley looked across the kitchen at Kaye, whose somber expression registered clear understanding of the news. "No," Rackley said slowly, "I don't think so. We'll call you next week."

There was a long silence at the other end, and then Allman sighed. "Mr. Rackley, I just hope you keep in mind that *any* information is good information. This technology may give us tough choices, but at least it does give us choices, which is a lot more than parents had ten years ago."

"I appreciate that, Mrs. Allman. I do. Thanks for letting us know so quickly."

Rackley replaced the telephone slowly as Kaye watched him. She was still holding her little beaded evening purse. "Three for three?"

Rackley looked at her and nodded. "Otherwise, they're all completely healthy."

"Oh God," she said softly, letting the purse slip out of her hand onto the polished tile floor of the kitchen.

In two steps Rackley was across the room, holding her, smelling the faint fragrance of her perfume, feeling the soft skin of her shoulders, the dampness on her cheeks.

"Damn," she said quietly, angrily, into his ear. She was holding him so tight that her fingers pressed hard into his back. "Damn."

Kaye held him for a moment longer, then pulled back. "We needed more eggs. If I hadn't gotten sick . . ."

"It's just statistics," Rackley said. "The luck of the draw. We'll figure it out."

"Figure what out? What are we going to do?"

"Just because a child has the genes, doesn't necessarily mean something bad will happen."

"Tell that to your brother," Kaye said flatly.

"If they can figure out the biochemistry, there may be a cure someday. A drug or something."

Kaye was listening, but she was also already reaching for a handkerchief, patting at her face. Kaye, who seemed soft and vulnerable much of the time, had a remarkable resilience underlying her nature. Rackley had never seen her fall apart emotionally: when problems arose, she went almost immediately from fear and worry to a firm resolve that he found both endearing and reassuring.

"Well," she said. "So we'll go see Mrs. What's-her-name next week?"

"We should. There's nothing we can decide now." Rackley paused for a moment, watching Kaye closely. "Do you want to go to Edward's? We could say you're still feeling rocky."

"No," she said with a tone of resignation. "We said we'd go. It's business anyway, isn't it?"

Rackley nodded. "These days, it's all business."

Kaye turned to leave the kitchen.

"Another hug," Rackley said, and then they held each other for a long moment.

Edward and Madeleine Caswell lived in an apartment that took up the entire top floor of a white neo-classic building on Nob Hill with a panoramic view of the Bay area. With four bedrooms, a library, maid's quarters, and an entrance done in marble, it was reminiscent of the grand apartments on upper Fifth Avenue in Manhattan. On two sides there were narrow terraces, but these were little used due to the constant chill breeze off the Pacific.

Senator Cashman, an athletic man in his late forties who still retained a collegiate look, stood at one of the huge plate glass windows.

"I've always loved this building," the senator told Edward Caswell. Cashman looked out toward the yellow flood lamps of the bridge in the distance, the low dark rise of the Marin headlands. "I thought about buying an apartment here, before the election."

"My family used to own this building," Caswell said.

The senator turned. "Really?"

Caswell nodded. "Father had to sell it, back in the fifties. A nice piece of property. A shame to lose it." He shrugged. "At least we kept one floor."

"Could be worse," the senator said.

"True," Caswell said dryly. "Father never was the best businessman." He shook his head slightly. "He did love a good party though."

"I imagine he'd be proud of what you've done for the family."

Caswell raised his glass. "We do have a very large number of eggs in a single basket right now."

"United Genetics, you mean."

Caswell's maid approached with a tray of small, fresh Pacific oysters, open on glistening shells. Caswell and the senator each took one.

"Very good," the senator said after a moment. "You don't often get Pacific oysters to taste so sweet."

"Not without tweaking a few genes. We're raising them up at an aquaculture station near Bodega Bay. More like Belon, or Chesapeake, wouldn't you say?"

The senator nodded affirmation, mouth full.

"Someday we plan to build a major marine facility. We think there's a great deal we can do with fish."

Cashman glanced over his shoulder, looking for the tray of oysters. "You're off to a good start."

Ten minutes later Markham, Rackley, and Kaye arrived simultaneously in the private elevator. Rackley noticed that Markham greeted the senator with unusual warmth. The warmth was reciprocated; Markham ran a biotechnology political action committee that had contributed lavishly to Cashman's previous campaign.

At seven the group sat down to dinner in the Caswells' big oak-paneled dining room—grilled salmon, fresh asparagus, an elaborate salad of exotic greens, an excellent white wine from Mendocino. The dinner conversation was pleasant, primarily Silicon Valley gossip, although Kaye, usually a witty conversationalist, was quiet and subdued. As Markham had privately asked him, Rackley gradually brought the talk around to the upcoming Senate hearings on genetic engineering.

"Well," said the senator, "as long as I'm here, I might as well ask directly: What do you really want?"

Markham took a deep breath, folded his hands in front of him. "We'd like to begin some very limited testing with humans."

"I was afraid that's what you were going to say," Cashman said slowly. He gazed at Markham, shaking his head. "You have to appreciate the position that puts us in. We're stuck between the religious right, the Catholics, and the anti-technologists on one side, and then you people on the other." He pushed at the leaves of his salad for a moment. "I frankly have to say that, given the enormity of the decision involved in human genetic engineering, a delay of a few years isn't the end of the world."

"That's pure propaganda from Hechinger and his people at Natural Progress," Markham said sharply. "Even if we start now, we won't have practical applications for a long time. And by then—I don't have to tell you—the Japanese will already be there."

"I wish you could say it was the Russians we were worried about," Cashman said. "Congress understands that."

"I could say it, but it wouldn't be true." Thanks to an ideologic detour a few decades earlier—during which Soviet biologists were taught that a proper socialist environment was a more powerful influence than genes—Russian genetic engineering was still moving slowly.

Cashman looked at Markham. "It's really in Senator Gordon's hands. He climbed on this genetic engineering issue early. By now I wonder if maybe he wishes he hadn't. He has a real tiger by the tail."

Markham cleared his throat. "Gordon has always been straight with us. I'm optimistic about his personal thinking. I just hope that the rest of the Senate will go along with his recommendations."

The senator hesitated for a moment. "I was surprised to see that Gordon brought in Hechinger."

"I imagine he's giving our adversaries the full benefit of the doubt," Markham said mildly.

Cashman raised his eyebrows. "Do they need it? This Rice Five accident was bad timing for you."

"Accident." By now Markham was completely ignoring his dinner, focusing the full force of his gaze on Cashman. "That's the key word. We made a mistake, we admitted it, and we're fixing it. The existing laws are more than sufficient. In fact they're too strict."

Rackley could see that Markham's intensity was daunting even for the senator. He leaned forward. "Any predictions on what the Senate as a whole might say to easing the genetic engineering law?"

"Frankly, I think you'll find they feel as I do. No matter what Gordon's subcommittee comes up with. This is a frightening question, and not one to rush into."

"It's a political land mine," Markham said, "and you're all scared of public ignorance. That's what you're saying."

Cashman set his fork down and looked at Markham. "No, Paul," he said flatly. "That's not what I'm saying."

"Senator." Markham gazed at the legislator. His brown eyes seemed nervelessly calm, his smile oddly narrow. He raised one finger. "Hypothetically. Don't tell me there aren't things about you, your family, traits, talents, that you wouldn't change if you could?"

Rackley glanced across the table and saw that Kaye had started to cry very softly. No one else at the table had noticed.

"I have three children," the senator said. "And I love them exactly as they are." He hesitated. "That prospect goes beyond the limits of my imagination."

"And that is exactly the problem," Markham said curtly.

Madeleine Caswell cleared her throat. "I think that's enough politics for one evening," she asked the table at large. "Don't you?"

Kaye was reaching for her napkin, and then, her voice slightly choked, she said, "Please excuse me," and left the table.

There was a moment of awkward silence as the company watched her depart through a doorway into the big living room.

Markham slouched backward in his seat, toying with his food, oblivious.

"I hope Kaye is all right," Cashman said with puzzled concern.

"Excuse me," Rackley said, and followed her into the living room.

Kaye was sitting in the far corner on a straight-backed antique chair, turned away.

When Rackley touched her shoulder, she looked up. Her face was already slightly puffy from the tears. "I'm sorry. That was rude."

"No," Rackley said. "We shouldn't have come."

She sighed, glanced away. "It's just that Markham is so obnoxious, so sure of himself. He just gets anything he wants, and . . ." She shrugged. "I don't know. I thought about babies and I just felt sad."

Rackley kneeled next to Kaye on the thick carpeting. "It's okay. We'll stay here for a second."

The two remained in the living room, not moving, silent. But after less than a minute there was a sound behind them.

"What's going on?" Edward Caswell said. "Are you all right?"

Kaye sighed deeply, not turning around. "Edward, I'm fine. Go back to your guests, you're being rude."

"Kaye," he said more sharply. "What is wrong?"

She shook her head silently and then Caswell turned to Rackley. "For God's sake, Rackley, what's going on? This isn't like her at all."

For a moment Rackley was torn. They had decided to keep their plans private; on the other hand, the concern in Edward's voice was hard to ignore.

Kaye finally broke the silence. "You'll just keep after us until we tell you, so here it is." She glanced toward the dining room, then in a soft voice quickly described their visits to Birthtech, the gene scans, the in vitro fertilization, the unhappy news.

"You *what*?" Caswell said, too loudly. Then, recalling his company, he stood, staring, listening in complete silence.

When Kaye finished, he struggled to keep his voice down. "*Why* didn't you tell me?" he asked, then turned to Rackley. "For God's sake, we were just talking about this, you *promised* to tell me."

"Jesus, Edward," Kaye said, not looking up at him, "we were going to tell you. But you don't need to know every momentary detail about my life."

Caswell exhaled a great breath, jammed his hands in his pockets, and looked away for a moment out over the city, thinking.

"So," he said finally. "The three embryos are in cryo-storage."

"That's right," Rackley said.

"Here's what to do," Caswell said, his voice low and urgent. "You must talk to Stuart Lipsky."

Now Kaye looked puzzled, pushing back a single wisp of blond hair that had fallen from under the pearl comb. "The little plump man?"

Caswell nodded curtly. "I would have told you this much

sooner. If I'd known. He's the best medical geneticist I know. He'll have some advice."

Kaye watched for a moment longer, as if she expected her brother to say more, but he remained silent. From the dining room they could hear Senator Cashman excusing himself, pleading jet lag and a busy weekend of constituent meetings.

"Just go talk to him," Caswell said finally, ignoring the departure of his guest. "You absolutely must."

CHAPTER ELEVEN

On the day of their meeting with Lipsky, moist, warm clouds up from Mexico rendered the air humid, clinging, almost tropical. Rackley and Kaye had a small breakfast on the back patio of the old Victorian, beneath a young eucalyptus, its foliage mixed gray and bright green.

"So this guy," Kaye asked, "shut down all human genetic engineering work by doing his experiment?"

Rackley poured himself coffee. "Someone would have done it sooner or later. Lipsky was just the first to get there."

Kaye nodded. "What's he like?"

Rackley shrugged. "I haven't spent much time with him. Markham keeps him pretty well under wraps." All he really knew, in fact, was the story of Lipsky's disastrous career.

New York born, Stuart Lipsky had roared out of the Bronx High School of Science, sped through Harvard and then MIT, to become, at age thirty, one of the youngest full professors at Stanford. His specialty was designing vectors for genetic engineering—vehicles to carry new genes into cells. Usually these were modified viruses, and early on vectors had been found for bacteria and plants. But a suitable vector for humans had proven far more elusive. Until Lipsky. For seven years he labored in the laboratory, using exotic enzymes to chop up viruses, reassemble them, chop them up again.

At last Lipsky succeeded. SPL10—tagged, as was traditional, with the initials of its designer—infected any human embryo, incorporated new genes, and then disappeared harmlessly. SPL10 was the key to precision human genetic engineering. Only one difficulty remained: there was no legal way to test it.

Some limited human gene therapy was already being done on children with truly terrible diseases such as Lesch-Nyhan Syndrome. In another case, the immune system deficiency that once forced a young Texas child to live his entire life in a sterile plastic bubble was cured by transplanting a single gene into a victim's bone marrow. But these were special cases: the implanted gene remained only in a single organ of the patient's body.

With SPL10, however, Lipsky could transplant genes into developing embryos—so that the new genes could spread throughout the body as the child grew. This meant that a vastly wider range of genetic diseases could be treated, along with other conditions that were not diseases at all. And any genetic alteration in an embryo would be passed on to all succeeding generations. Embryo therapy raised a storm of protests; groups ranging from the Catholic Church to Natural Progress demanded that the work be halted. Lipsky's research was funded by the National Institutes of Health; in two telegrams and three registered letters the NIH ordered Lipsky to stop his work.

But Lipsky wasn't opening his mail. One month later a graduate student with a grudge revealed that Lipsky had performed gene therapy on a human embryo with cystic fibrosis. The violation made international headlines: STANFORD DOC BREAKS GENE RULES. The altered embryo was destroyed. Briefly it looked as if Stanford might lose all federal funding. Polls showed public opinion strongly opposed to the work, and some right-wing evangelists even asked their congregations to pray for Lipsky's death. Within a month Congress passed the Interim Ban on Human Genetic Engineering.

"And so Lipsky was out on the street," Rackley said that morning. "Disgraced. Until Markham hired him."

"What does he do for United Genetics?" Kaye asked.

"Not much, as far as I can tell." Rackley's voice trailed off. "A lot of our researchers won't work with him; they're afraid he'll do something else illegal and then whoever is on his team will get benched too."

"What good is he?"

"Well, first of all, Markham likes him. And if SPL10 is ever legalized, we'll be out in front on human gene therapy." He shrugged. "But for right now he's basically one very high-priced administrator."

"Are you sure that's all he does?" Kaye asked softly. Rackley drew a deep breath. "No, I'm not."

Lipsky had his own private laboratory on the far edge of United Genetics' Berkeley research campus. He met Kaye and Rackley at the door of the small, bungalow-style building and, with virtually no small talk, ushered them into his office.

Lipsky was a short, plump man in his early forties with perpetual five o'clock shadow and a frenetic, birdlike way of moving his pudgy hands. He listened carefully to Rackley's description of their efforts to avoid the alpha alcoholism genes. Every few moments the researcher would nod his head very quickly, reminding Rackley of a toy dipping bird that drinks from a glass of water. But Lipsky was clearly following every word, and at the end he leaned back and nodded again, this time more slowly.

"Well, of course I'd already seen your records. But I wanted to hear this from you." Lipsky looked over at Kaye. "Your brother thinks very highly of you." He turned to Rackley. "And needless to say, both Paul and Edward consider you an indispensable part of United Genetics."

Rackley said nothing, but noted that Lipsky referred to both by first name.

"So you will understand that what I am about to say must remain the deepest secret possible."

Kaye and Rackley were both watching the little scientist in silence.

"You do understand?" he asked after a moment.

"Of course," Rackley said, and Kaye echoed his words.

"Fine." Lipsky squirmed slightly in his chair, looked down, looked up again. "To turn my back on the most important tool of the twentieth century, to see people continue to suffer simply because we have a government that prefers inaction to decision . . ." He shrugged. "You don't need to hear this. All you need to hear is that I can help you."

Rackley glanced over at Kaye, who was still staring at Lipsky with clear fascination.

"Go on," Rackley said.

Lipsky shrugged and opened the file on his desk. "The alpha alcoholism in your embryos involves three defective genes. We know which genes those are; they were characterized five years ago." He looked up over the papers. "That, obviously, is why we can diagnose the condition." He cleared his throat. "As it develops, SPL10 is the ideal carrier for those genes. They fit nicely into the slot in the vector." He closed the folder, looked up again. "So correct copies of the necessary genes can easily be planted in a developing embryo."

Rackley stared at Lipsky. The researcher had spoken in such a matter-of-fact fashion that Rackley wasn't even sure he understood what he had heard. "Wait a minute. You're saying you can cure alcoholism?"

Lipsky gazed back at Rackley, eyes heavy-lidded, clearly not overwhelmed by the fact. "Only in embryos, of course. Along with a number of other personality disorders. Manic-depressive syndrome. At least one form of schizophrenia." He looked up. "Since this is germ-line therapy, you can assume it permanently removes the disease from your family line."

Kaye looked at Rackley. "That's amazing," she said. "It's wonderful."

Lipsky's expression did not change. "If you decide to go ahead, there are some rules we must follow. The first: You must never speak of this work to anyone. That includes your brother"—he looked at Kaye; then at Rackley—"and your associates."

"But why . . . ?"

Lipsky held up one hand. "These are rules set up by someone who knows much more about keeping secrets than all of us put together. So, not a word, not to anyone, no matter how close they are. No matter how much they know themselves. This also, of course, is for your baby's sake; it lowers the chances that anyone will ever know that the child has had the work done. But it's primarily for our own safety."

Lipsky paused for a moment, blinking. "And a second condition. I do all of this myself. I have no laboratory assistants. Therefore, during some of the procedures, I need to have one of you available as a worker."

He looked at Rackley. "Your continued presence in my lab would be hard to explain. So Mrs. Rackley would have to come in, probably just for a day or two. You can explain that you are . . . helping me decorate my office." He smiled, very slightly, for the first time that day.

Kaye and Rackley, still overwhelmed, looked at each other, saying nothing. Lipsky, puzzled, opened the brown folder again and glanced down. "Ah, did I get that straight? You are an interior decorator, Mrs. Rackley?"

"Oh. Of course. Yes."

"All right. Those are the two conditions: silence and assistance. Now you must have some questions of your own."

"How certain are you that this works?" Rackley asked.

"Very certain," Lipsky said. "We have our greatest success with disorders that require the addition of genes. There are other disorders where a gene needs to be disabled or cut, and that's a bit more difficult to control. But adding genes . . . it's one of those things that has turned out to be much simpler than anyone expected."

"What other conditions have you treated?"

"You don't need to know that," Lipsky said flatly.

Rackley felt a surge of anger. "You're asking us to use a completely unproven technique on our child. I do need to know."

Lipsky gazed at him calmly. "I'm not asking you to do anything. You came to me."

Rackley thought for a moment. "Okay. Then how many patients have you treated?"

Lipsky looked up at the white acoustical ceiling for a long moment, considering this, then looked back at Rackley. "I don't normally divulge this," he said. "But because of who you are . . . Nearly one thousand patients. We have developed some statistically significant data."

Rackley was utterly amazed. "Where are all these patients?"

Lipsky merely stared at him, blinking once, twice, then shook his ponderous head slowly.

"Ah," Kaye interjected quietly, "how will it work?"

"It's really quite simple," Lipsky said, clearly happier with this line of questioning. "The three embryos are still cryopreserved, I assume."

"Yes," Rackley said.

"Fine. On Monday you will call Birthtech and tell them that you have decided to delay implantation. They will put your embryos into long-term storage. Later that day I will retrieve them. Then, when the time is appropriate, we will insert the necessary corrective genes into SPL10 vectors, defrost the embryos, and infect them."

"You mean, the embryos actually get the virus in them?" Kaye asked.

"Oh, absolutely," Lipsky said. "But the virus is completely harmless. Think of it as the biological equivalent of a hypodermic needle."

Kaye looked dubious.

"Believe me. I invented it. Where was I? Right: It takes a few hours for the genes to insert and the virus to self-destruct. Then I'll run a gene scan on all the embryos, make sure that the good genes are in and that no other damage has occurred. We'll take the healthiest embryo we have and implant it in Mrs. Rackley's uterus. After that, you're on your own. Normal pregnancy, normal delivery, you forget that you ever saw me."

There was a long silence in the small, cluttered office.

"You don't have to decide now," Lipsky said quietly, showing the first glimpse of any concern for his potential patients.

"What are the risks?" Rackley asked.

"As I said, gene addition has turned out to be much easier than we expected. There is a small chance the SPL10 can damage the embryo, but we catch that with the pre-implantation gene scan. In any pregnancy there's a chance of miscarriage. But because we scan the embryo before we implant, the odds are actually less than with natural pregnancy. In fact"—he paused for a long second— "the primary risk, by far, is that someone unfriendly finds out that we're doing this."

There was another long silence. Lipsky glanced at his watch. "Any other questions?"

"When would we start?" Kaye asked.

Lipsky opened the manila folder again and looked at Kaye's chart for a moment. "You seem to be fairly regular," he said. "Given your menstrual cycle, we should try for implantation in about eight days. So we'd need to start the process five days from today."

Lipsky concluded the interview by rising from behind his desk. After a moment Rackley stood also, and they shook hands.

"Please let me know one way or the other as soon as possible," Lipsky said. "There are other patients on my list."

Kaye stood also and shook hands with Lipsky. "Thank you." She glanced around the cramped office, strewn with papers, furnished with plain metal furniture. "Your office really could use a little design help."

"Ah," Lipsky said with a faint smile. "Unfortunately I like it exactly the way it is."

Rackley reached for the doorknob, but just then a framed newspaper clipping on the inside of the door caught his eye. He stepped closer and saw it was an old editorial from the *New York Times*. Rackley quickly read the first paragraph:

The human genome, in this agnostic century, has become the secular equivalent of the soul. Any tampering with either soul or genome must be a decision made not by a single researcher, but society as a whole. Whether it takes five years or fifty to decide how to proceed, the wait will be justified. If we err now in handling our genetic heritage, then humans will have the remainder of time to regret our haste.

Rackley looked up. The headline read: "Stop Doctor Lipsky!" Puzzled, he turned back to the researcher, who was watching him intently, short arms folded across his chest. "It's important," Lipsky said quietly, "to remember each day that one does have enemies. I trust both of you will do the same."

CHAPTER TWELVE

Kaye drove over to Lipsky's lab for two days as he prepared for the work on the embryos. Her tasks were varied: sometimes she helped Lipsky mix reagents, handing him brown bottles of chemicals as he requested them. Afterwards she would load the used glassware into a chrome autoclave, which sterilized its contents with intense clouds of pressurized steam.

On the second day Lipsky asked her to clean out a small stainless steel freezer that sat in the middle of a bench at the back of his small lab. This freezer, he told her, would hold the three tiny aluminum vials containing her embryos, soon to be delivered from the Birthtech storage facility.

After a few hours in the lab Kaye came to suspect that Lipsky, in his own odd way, was actually rather lonely; that in fact part of the participatory element of the process might be to provide some company for the young researcher. Even so, Lipsky was by no means voluble. He talked occasionally about equipment and supplies; Markham saw that Lipsky received all the newest hardware. As he puttered around his bright-lit, spotless laboratory—its tidiness in direct distinction to the clutter of his office—he reminded Kaye of a cross between a shambling circus bear and a fussy little old lady.

"It's odd," Kaye said at one point. "Doing this work. I mean, this is something so powerful. So . . . godlike."

Lipsky was calibrating a bright orange digital readout on an instrument in the corner. He straightened up. "Godlike," he mused. "That's one I haven't heard for a while." He smiled slightly. "I guess I travel in rather jaded circles."

"Well?" Kaye asked, tilting her head to one side, her chin set firmly, quite curious.

"No more so," Lipsky said, "than antibiotics. Or open heart surgery. Or kidney transplants. It only seems godlike to people who don't understand it." Kaye frowned slightly and he hastened to add, "I don't mean you. I mean the people who want to stop it. They don't understand it, so they're afraid." He smiled a bit. "As far as I can tell, what I'm doing here is removing a cause of some misery in the lives of your families. And there can't be anything wrong with that."

"Of course not."

On the second day Kaye arrived about ten in the morning. Lipsky was on the telephone, speaking Spanish. It sounded odd: somehow the plump young scientist didn't seem the sort to speak any language but the arcane dialect of molecular genetics. He finished the telephone call as she put on a white laboratory coat, and then they went to work.

For the next twenty minutes Lipsky made the culture nutrient for his SPL10 virus: a precise blend of de-ionized water, sugar, salt, various trace elements, and host bacteria, all mixed under sterile conditions. When the pink fluid was complete, Lipsky poured it into a tall glass incubation vessel and set it under the exhaust hood of a semi-enclosed bench top. He went into the back of his laboratory and came out with a very small glass tube.

"Thanks to the good offices of the United States Congress, possessing this harmless little virus is a felony." He held up the tube for Kaye to see. "Funny," he said softly. "The day I knew that SPL10 worked as a vector for human genes, I danced around the lab. My postdocs thought I'd lost my mind. I thought I was going to win the Nobel Prize."

He shook his head and stepped in front of the negative-pressure bench top. He deftly pipetted a bit of the virus out of the tube, injecting it into the incubation vessel. "There we go. Tomorrow morning we'll have a nice crop of virus particles, and then we'll insert the genes."

"Maybe someday you'll still get the Nobel Prize," Kaye said.

Lipsky touched his cheek and looked slightly wistful. "Frankly, the odds are better that they'll hang me first." He shook his head. "Could you put the glassware in the autoclave now?"

Kaye nodded, and for a few minutes she busied herself loading a stainless steel rack with dirty glassware from the sequencing machine. Lipsky sat at his desk at the front of the lab. Finally he looked up.

"Have you heard of what they call the forbidden sequence?" Lipsky asked casually.

Kaye finished putting the last beaker in the rack, then swung the door of the autoclave shut. "I think so. It's linked to intelligence, right?"

"Correct."

Kaye said nothing, waiting for Lipsky to continue.

"The proper name of course," Lipsky said, sounding almost professorial, "is the Brockman sequence."

Kaye pulled over a lab stool and sat and listened as Lipsky talked. The Brockman sequence was named after the researcher who had first done the controversial work linking intelligence with specific genes. Long before Brockman, back in the seventies, researchers had discovered that a large proportion of mentally retarded men had an X chromosome with a tip that tended to break off. Clearly, genes at the point where the "fragile X" broke were somehow involved with intelligence.

Recently Brockman had taken the work a step further by analyzing the same stretch of chromosome in samples from a special sperm bank in upstate New York. This private foundation collected only from Nobel Prize winners and others of high intellectual achievement. After analyzing hundreds of specimens, the researcher came up with five genes that seemed to be directly related to unusual intelligence.

Almost immediately the federal genetic engineering guidelines put the Brockman sequence off limits for fear that parents-to-be would look for it in prenatal gene scans, then abort embryos without the sequence. "We can't start aborting babies because they won't get into Harvard," as Steve Hechinger put it. Thus the Brockman sequence became popularly known as the forbidden sequence.

"The gene scans on your three embryos," Lipsky said, "included a probe for the Brockman sequence."

"I didn't think that was allowed," Kaye said quietly.

Lipsky shrugged. "The guidelines are ambiguous. We usually do it, but we don't tell the patients. It's just part of the research program."

"And?"

Lipsky looked up, owlish. "What?"

Kaye sighed with impatience. "What did the embryo scans show?"

"None of the three contains a full Brockman sequence."

Involuntarily Kaye felt a constriction in her gut, a bit of the adrenaline associated with bad news. But for a moment she said nothing, carefully tightening the knurled bolts that sealed the autoclave instead. "Well," she said finally, "isn't the Brockman sequence still considered pretty theoretical?"

"Not to people who know."

Now Kaye stopped her work and straightened up. Lipsky, uncharacteristically, was watching her closely.

"Then that's too bad," she said softly.

"Not necessarily," Lipsky said in the same quiet tone of voice.

"What are you saying?"

Lipsky cleared his throat, looked away. "Synthesizing the Brockman sequence is fairly trivial."

Kaye had an almost dizzy sense of what was coming next, but once again she waited for Lipsky to continue.

"Look," Lipsky said, and now he sounded impatient. "There's room in the SPL10 vector we're preparing to include the Brockman sequence. It's up to you." He stood up from his desk and walked over to the nucleotide synthesizer.

Kaye rocked back and forth slightly on the metal laboratory stool. "I see what you're saying," she said softly.

She thought for a moment, staring at Lipsky's broad white-coated back. "How sure are you about this?"

Lipsky didn't turn around. "We're very sure."

"How can you be so sure?"

"We have . . . a reasonable amount of practical experience."

"You mean you've been implanting the forbidden sequence in embryos?"

Lipsky finally turned around, crossing his pale arms across his plump stomach. "I'm afraid that you'll have to take what I tell you on faith."

"That's not very helpful," Kaye said with anger, staring at the researcher's doughy face.

"I'll have to know your decision by the end of the day," Lipsky said calmly. "I need to run the sequencer all night to produce enough gene fragments for the SPL10."

Kaye glanced around the laboratory as if clues might some-where be hidden among the bench tops and glassware. "What else can you tell me?"

Lipsky shrugged. "Not very much. If you want to wait twenty

or thirty years for the world to straighten itself out, then maybe we'll have little color brochures. In the meantime you're on your own."

"Great. That's wonderful. Terrific."

Lipsky looked at her for a moment and his features softened a bit. "I can tell you this," he said. "I have the sequence. Markham has the sequence. And according to your gene scan, you have the Brockman sequence yourself. But it's recessive, so . . ."

"Rackley must not have it."

"You know your biology. Takes two, unfortunately."

"I'll need to ask him."

Lipsky looked up. "We can't allow that."

Kaye was shocked. "But it's his child also. I can't make a decision like that without him."

"I'm afraid that's the only option." His expression didn't change. "As I told you last week, I didn't make up these rules. But they're meant to protect everyone, including the child." He looked at Kaye. "It's best for the child not to know about these operations. And when only one parent knows, the secret is better kept."

"It's crazy," Kaye said, almost to herself, and now she was angry. "Damn. I wish we'd never gotten into this."

Lipsky shrugged slightly. "We've done nothing yet. You can still walk away."

For one brief moment Kaye saw the face of Vincent Rackley, chalk-white against blood-spattered sheets, appearing as miserable in death as he had been in life.

"Of course not," Kaye said quickly. "I just mean . . ."

"I understand," Lipsky said, as if he really did. "These are hard decisions for us all." With that the portly researcher again returned his attention to the big digital synthesizer.

"Just let me know," he said over his shoulder, "by the end of the day."

The next morning Kaye arrived at Lipsky's lab at nine. The SPL10 virus had been growing overnight, and the big glass flask in the incubator was now quite cloudy.

"A healthy crop," Lipsky said with genuine pleasure in his voice. "This is a very sturdy little virus."

He looked up in time to see brief concern in Kaye's expression. "Oh," he said, "nothing to be worried about. You know, a virus is virtually nothing but genetic information. It

sneaks its DNA into a nearby cell and gets that cell to make more
virus.''

Kaye watched him. "And what's so good about that?"

"What I've done," Lipsky said, "and I'm not the only one to
have done it, just the best, is to disarm the virus so that it inserts
the genes I want, rather than its own genes. And I can also
program it with an additional bit of DNA that guides it to just the
part of the chromosome I want." He nodded, gazing at the cloudy
flask, then looked up at Kaye. "Shall we splice some genes?"

The next step was the most delicate of the entire operation.
Lipsky treated the virus particles with a special enzyme that cut
them open, leaving "sticky ends" of DNA. Once the millions of
virus particles were prepared, Lipsky added the gene fragments he
had synthesized in the big machine. These fragments of artificial
DNA also had sticky ends, so they automatically inserted
themselves into the cleaved virus particles.

Kaye assisted as much as she could—bringing pieces of
glassware when Lipsky asked for them, tending a digital timer on
the bench top, keeping notes on each step—but this was
exceedingly technical work, and Lipsky did most of the operation
himself, saying very little.

After about twenty minutes of quiet concentration it was done.
Lipsky delicately picked up the cloudy flask of virus and moved it
back into the big white incubator against the wall. He closed the
door, wiped his forehead with the back of his hand, and turned and
nodded at Kaye.

"That's it," he said. "Let's get the embryos ready now."

In two hours the virus had fully taken up the manufactured
genes. In the meantime Lipsky had carefully thawed the three
embryos and now the three little spun aluminum containers stood
in a neat row on the workbench below the big laminar flow hood,
which expelled a constant stream of air to exclude contaminants.

Lipsky carefully injected a small amount of the SPL10
solution into each tiny cylinder. Then, one by one, he set each into
an incubator. He looked up at Kaye. "In about thirty hours the
new genes should be fully integrated into the embryos. I'll do a
gene scan, choose the healthiest embryo, and then we can refreeze
the other two."

At that moment the telephone on the far wall of the laboratory
rang, startling Kaye.

Lipsky picked up the telephone. "Yes," he said tonelessly,
and then was silent, listening.

Kaye started to turn away to hang up her white laboratory coat when over her shoulder she heard Lipsky inhale sharply. "My God."

Kaye turned back quickly.

"When did it happen?" Lipsky asked, and nodded. "When did she go to the hospital?"

Lipsky nodded again, as if the caller could see him. "And the fetal material?"

"Good." Lipsky listened a moment longer.

"No. We've never seen an elevated incidence in our work. But sometimes it happens, for anyone, you know."

"Of course. I'm very sorry."

He nodded again. "Two months. Then there's no reason not to try again."

"Please," Lipsky said, "convey my condolences."

He replaced the receiver and looked at Kaye. She was surprised: Lipsky was pale, almost trembling. The large researcher moved a few steps and sat down heavily on a lab stool, shaking his head. "A miscarriage," he said, sighing deeply. "A very, very sad thing."

"One of your patients?' Kaye asked.

Lipsky nodded, not looking up.

"It's not because—"

"No," Lipsky cut her off, visibly upset. It was the most emotion Kaye had ever seen from the man. "Definitely not. Of course one would think so, but"—he shook his head emphatically—"if this was dangerous I simply would not do it."

Kaye nodded and Lipsky stared down at the floor, saying nothing, for a long moment. Then, almost as if he had just remembered that Kaye was still in the room, Lipsky looked up suddenly.

"Go now," he said. "Please."

Kaye started to leave. "I'm very sorry about your patient."

Lipsky waved one hand. "You needn't come in tomorrow. I'll call you when it's time for implantation."

Rackley was already at home when Kaye returned from Lipsky's lab. She looked tired and drawn as she set her purse down in the hallway.

"How did it go today?" Rackley asked.

She shook her head. "Something bad happened. He got a phone call that one of his patients miscarried."

Rackley turned quickly.

"It wasn't because of his work," she said. "At least that's

what Lipsky said. But it was the first time I'd seen him upset, emotional. He was really shaken up. Like a real human being.''

Kaye walked into the living room and sank into the long white sectional sofa. She leaned her head back, and Rackley walked behind her and rubbed her shoulders. "So why did it happen?"

She shrugged. "Lipsky says it's no more likely because of the embryo work. It's just always a statistical possibility."

"Did he say anything more?" Rackley asked, curious as to who Lipsky's other patients might be.

Kaye shook her head. "Not a thing. He's pretty careful."

Rackley nodded, considering this. "What else does he talk about?"

"He talks about the equipment. And Markham. He really likes Markham."

"Anything else?"

"I asked him if he wanted to have children someday and he said yes. So then I asked if he'd do any embryo therapy on his own children."

"And?"

"He looked up at me as if I'd asked the very dumbest question in the world. He said, 'I've been writing the sequences for years.' ''

Two days later on a cool, damp Sunday morning just past seven o'clock, Rackley and Kaye arrived at the Birthtech auxiliary clinic, built behind Lipsky's bungalow office. This small facility was a short distance from the much larger eight-bay operating theater where embryo transfers were normally done. Even though there was nothing about the genetically altered embryo to distinguish it, Lipsky still preferred to do the implantation himself, when the clinic was deserted.

Lipsky told Rackley to stand in a narrow observation corridor, normally used for training new physicians. The corridor had two one-way windows, one of which looked into the operating room, the other into the next-door incubator room.

In the OR Kaye was wearing a blue surgical gown, pulled up over her waist. She was on her knees on the gurney, head forward, slim hips thrust up high into the air. The awkward position had proven best to assure that the tiny embryo would attach properly to the wall of the uterus. Kaye's cheek was pressed against the paper cover of the gurney, her head turned away from the observation window, so that Rackley could not see her face.

Normally at least one nurse would be on duty for an embryo

implant, but this, Lipsky said, was unwise. When Kaye had looked dubious at this announcement, Lipsky had waved his hand. "Listen, usually you wouldn't even get an MD. The nurse ends up doing the whole thing." He nodded, and then with a visible effort tried to be reassuring. "Frankly," he added, "I've probably done this procedure as many times as some of the staff. And it's not even my job."

This morning the fat little researcher stood next to Kaye for a moment, making certain that she was in the right position, talking quietly. Then he walked into the laboratory next door and opened the hood on the clear plastic incubator. There in a small plastic dish was the embryo Lipsky had chosen from the three possibilities, a few thousandths of an inch in diameter.

The gene scan had shown that the SPL10 virus had gently incorporated the necessary genes. Now when the embryo grew in Kaye's womb, the gene sequences would find their way to all the organs in the baby's body: liver, brain, marrow. In time the genes would also mix into its children and their children as well, and the particular biochemical torment of the families Rackley and Caswell would finally be put permanently to rest.

Lipsky picked up a stainless steel cannula, a tapered tube about eight inches long. Very delicately, his chubby fingers moving with surprising grace, he leaned over the incubator and aspirated the nearly invisible embryo into the long cylindrical instrument. Holding the cannula tip upwards in both hands, Lipsky walked carefully from the incubator room to the operating cubicle.

Kaye, looking small and thin, turned her head and looked out toward the mirrored glass behind which Rackley stood. Rackley felt a bizarre mix of emotions as Lipsky approached Kaye. The portly researcher spoke a few words and Kaye moved her hips higher, once again turning her head away from Rackley.

Very slowly and carefully Lipsky inserted the cannula into Kaye, moving it with great caution. It took nearly thirty seconds before he had the cannula to the depth required, exactly located in the portion of the uterus best for embryo implantation. Finally, moving one hand around behind the other like a magician performing some coin trick, Lipsky triggered the release mechanism that floated the embryo in a tiny droplet of nutrient fluid into Kaye's uterus.

For a moment there was no movement in this oddly sexual tableau of patient and doctor. Then Lipsky began to withdraw the cannula, as slowly as he had introduced it. Thus began the most crucial hours in the procedure: when the embryo would actually attach to the uterine wall. When IVF work had started, it was more art than science. Now most of the process was routine, orchestrated by genetically engineered chemicals and hormones, but this particular aspect—the actual connection between embryo and mother—still required slow and deliberate moves.

When Lipsky had completely withdrawn the cannula, he leaned over Kaye and said something. Kaye began to gradually ease forward with extremely careful movements, lowering her hips to the operating table so that she could lie flat on her stomach for an hour or so before rising.

Lipsky watched for a moment, then satisfied that all was well, he went back into the incubator room to put his instruments away.

In the operating room Kaye continued her gradual, graceful slide to a prone position. Out in the narrow corridor Rackley suddenly realized that he had been holding his breath, and with a deep sigh he exhaled, filled his lungs, and shook his head. The tension dissipated from his shoulders, and only then did he realize, with a shock and some consternation, that he had an erection.

Lipsky appeared in the hall behind him. "It went perfectly," he said softly. "My work is done."

CHAPTER THIRTEEN

A few days after the implantation, Rackley was sitting in a Nob Hill hotel lobby in San Francisco, waiting for Markham's car and driver. Even though Kaye's pregnancy was underway, Rackley was still tense and distracted. As he sat in the quiet lobby, Rackley realized that he was also growing impatient with the volatile head of United Genetics.

For several days now they had been meeting with a steady parade of investment bankers, all of whom hoped to handle the United Genetics stock offering. The crowning ritual of entrepreneurial success was selling stock to the public. But before shares could be sold, the founder had to choose one of the great gray Wall Street firms to handle the myriad legal details, set the initial price per share, then conduct the first day of sale.

Usually young entrepreneurs made the pilgrimage to New York for the process, but this time all of the potential underwriters were willing to fly out to the West Coast. No matter how United Genetics shares were initially priced, they would almost certainly soar in value immediately. The underwriter would collect millions in fees, plus tremendous prestige—since its own clients could stand first in line to buy shares at the initial price. Five major investment firms had pursued the deal. And so for three days now Markham and Rackley had been meeting with financiers—

usually a few gray eminences and one or two younger partners specifically fluent in the arcane language of high technology.

At first Rackley sat through the meetings with fascination. Markham handled the opening pleasantries with his usual distant charm, then promptly homed in on weakness with implacable accuracy: subtle distinctions, threats, promises, potential deal-breakers. Once again Rackley found himself thinking that Markham's worldly success' was not purely an accident of time and place.

But by now—with the end of the fifth set of interviews— Rackley suspected that the process was going terribly awry. Investors were asking why the offering hadn't been scheduled. Their money had been tied up for years and they wanted to reap profits. So did Rackley: his own shares, worth nearly $2 million, would provide for his graceful retirement from the corporate world. "Paul Markham is as eager to take this company public as you are," Rackley would tell investors. "He just wants to make sure that it's handled perfectly." But privately he was starting to wonder whether Markham was reluctant to give up control of his second company for fear that he would never again have such an idea.

That day in San Francisco they had met with representatives from the largest brokerage on Wall Street, in an airy private room in a downtown hotel. After cocktails the group retired to a light lunch of sand dabs and artichokes.

Today's group had struck Rackley as intimidating to the point of excess. The firm had messengered brief biographies ahead; collectively, the four men and one woman around the table sported academic credentials from Harvard, MIT, Stanford, Oxford, the London School of Economics, and the Sorbonne. One had served a stint in the previous White House administration; another was a consultant to the World Bank.

The two youngest—both in their late twenties—were of a new breed Rackley had seen more and more often: competitors who were sharp, perfectly dressed, ideally mannered. There were no rough edges, no suggestions that they had ever spilled spaghetti sauce on their silk ties. Smart, sharklike, they seemed to have evolved as investment bankers.

Maybe, Rackley mused, they started in the crib. Kaye's friends were obsessed with sending junior to the right preschool in the correct clothes with the best portable computer under his chubby little arm. When a kid has a life like that at age five, he thought, no wonder he looks like a prefab investment banker at age twenty-five. Perhaps the struggle for resources was now so tight that molding one's child early was the only survival strategy.

Sitting quietly at the table, Rackley looked at the young financiers, then at Markham, locked in verbal sparring. Once, after Markham consumed more wine than usual, he had told Rackley an interesting secret. Back in PM Computer days, Markham had known that the business would slump, but he couldn't sell all his shares without depressing the price of the stock. So he brought in a high-powered Eastern management team, then intentionally harassed them with bizarre behavior. At last they forced the young entrepreneur out of his own company—giving Markham the perfect excuse to sell all of his stock at nearly its highest value. Shortly thereafter computer stocks plummeted, but Markham's cash was safely in the bank.

Rackley shook his head, returning his attention to the matter at hand. Markham was gazing out the side window of the private dining room for a long moment. He touched his upper lip. "What else can you bring to United Genetics?"

At this point the young woman spoke up. She was a bit older than the two youngest sharks and had not only a Harvard MBA but a doctorate in molecular genetics. Her hobby was Mayan archeology; during lunch she casually mentioned that two of her discoveries were on display at the National Museum in Mexico City. "With all due respect, Mr. Markham," she said in a low, firm voice, "I think you'll need some particular help with the Rice Five liability question."

Markham's head swiveled toward the young woman; it was as close to a gesture of surprise as he ever allowed himself. "We have the Rice Five situation under control."

"As long as it remains in the Delta, you'll have to address it in the prospectus."

For the first time that day Markham looked uncomfortable. "We're aware of that."

"I'm sure you're also aware that when United Genetics becomes a public company, you'll be playing in a whole new arena as far as disclosure goes."

"I've taken a company public before," Markham said curtly.

"Of course you have," the young woman said. "All I'm saying is that once you're publicly held, any shareholder can stand up in your annual meeting and ask anything they want. I imagine that Steven Hechinger will buy his share immediately."

Markham nodded impatiently, and then he changed the subject

to some obscure discussion about managing an orderly market, which rapidly lost Rackley in the ebb and flow of financial arcana.

For a moment Rackley tried to imagine where Markham's confidence about Rice Five came from. Rackley and Trina were now making regular damage control trips- up to the Delta, arranging public meetings and visiting disgruntled farmers. Natural Progress was active in the area also, recruiting an ad hoc Save the Delta group.

Rackley recalled their last trip. First stop had been Kline Slough, where the original outbreak of Rice Five had been located and, presumably, removed. But it was now clear that the eradication effort by the California Conservation Corps had failed miserably. Their mistake had been simple but fatal: the enthusiastic young workers had done a thorough job of removing the weed wherever it appeared, but in the course of tearing it out they set adrift tens of thousands of tiny rootlets, each one of which had the ability to grow into another complete Rice Five plant.

Rackley and Trina met old man Kline out at the levee. He was still dressed in faded denim, but now seemed far less affable than during the on-site press conference a few weeks earlier. Kline and Rackley shook hands; Rackley took off his linen coat and slung it over one shoulder.

"This," said old man Kline, gesturing toward the acreage all around them, "is a goddamn mess."

Rackley and Trina stood almost exactly where Markham had so eloquently courted the press. Now they were looking out over Kline's fields, which at this time of the year were normally heavily irrigated with water from the Delta. The water flowed over the levees by siphon action into hundreds of narrow channels crisscrossing the broad fertile fields. But these channels were so narrow that each inlet was easily clogged by floating vegetation. For a century this had never been a problem, for such aquatic flora didn't grow in the cool Delta waters.

Now, however, Rice Five was spreading quickly, floating down the hundreds of interconnected channels and sloughs, and finding its way into thousands of fields, each of which had hundreds of irrigation ditches.

Hundreds of channels times thousands of fields times hundreds of irrigation ditches . . .

Standing in the hot Delta sun, Kline on one side, Trina on the other, Rackley gave up trying to do the math. The sun, reflecting off the river behind him, felt unyieldingly intense. Even more distracting than the heat was the high-pitched roar of a dozen diesel-powered water pumps that United Genetics had trucked up to Kline's land. The pumps were pulling water from the Delta and forcing it directly into the fields, bypassing the Rice Five–clogged water inlets. United Genetics had spent hundreds of thousands of dollars on seventy-five-horsepower pumps that now dotted the levees for miles around.

"We pull the damn stuff out," Kline shouted over the sound of the pumps, "every day. But there's always more, drifting in from someplace. The only way we could stop it is to stop irrigating the fields. But you're looking at three hundred thousand dollars worth of barley on my land alone."

"All I can tell you," Rackley said to Kline, speaking loudly, "is that we have two dozen researchers up at Davis working day and night trying to come up with an eradication method."

Kline looked at Rackley, then Trina, then back out at the fields. His face, brown and deeply lined, was past anger, into monumental exhaustion. "I hope the hell you are," he said. "I hope the hell you are."

So did Rackley. What amazed him was that he had managed, thus far, to keep the entire operation out of the media. The national press had dropped the story, and the local reporters rarely traveled into the Delta. Markham had kept influential locals quiet through careful application of United Genetics stock. But Rackley suspected that the story would surface once again as soon as some Delta farmer—assisted by Natural Progress's lawyers—filed a liability suit against United Genetics.

From Kline Slough, Rackley and Trina drove south, following the gentle curve of the broad Sacramento River, to a Prohibition-era hotel that had been recently restored. There they had scheduled a lunch with the young Environmental Protection Agency official in charge of the Delta cleanup.

As they approached the old Victorian hotel, Trina, exhausted by the dense, clinging heat, looked over at Rackley. Her dark hair was slightly stuck to her temple from a fine layer of perspiration, and her face was flushed. She sighed. "Want to hear something funny?"

"I'd love to hear something funny," Rackley said, not taking his eyes off the road.

"I've done one or two illegal things in my time."

"I've already heard your story," Rackley said. "The only part that amazes me is the suspended sentence."

Trina ignored him. "I don't have an overactive conscience. But this Rice Five thing . . ." She searched for a word.

"It's not your fault," Rackley said. "It's not my fault either."

Trina nodded. "I know. But we're the ones running around apologizing for it."

Rackley raised his eyebrows. "That's the job description. Welcome to corporate America."

Trina looked over at him. "You know, I've always been really grateful for the help you've given me, getting me started here, all that."

"I couldn't have done it without you."

She nodded. "But I don't know how much longer I can handle this."

For the first time Rackley looked over at her. "Oh?"

Trina met his eyes. She nodded. "Sometimes I think about being a writer. Like you used to be."

"Well," Rackley said. "I know exactly what you mean." He turned left, off the pavement, into the dirt parking lot of the old hotel and parked the car in the shade of a huge sycamore tree. He looked at Trina before getting out of the car. "Just don't quit before I do."

Trina was silent for a moment. "Have you ever met Edward Kelley-Delgado?"

"The Clinic guy? Once or twice. I've talked to him about the opening next month. He seems nice enough. Very sincere."

"I knew him before treatment," Trina said. "He used to be in a real different line of work."

Rackley looked over quickly, genuinely surprised. "With Rand?"

Trina nodded. "They did a couple of deals together. Delgado was very wired into the Mexican police."

Rackley tapped the steering wheel slowly. "No kidding."

Trina shrugged. "'Maybe he went straight. Stranger things have happened."

"Hmm." Rackley glanced at his watch. "We're late for lunch."

Rackley and Trina walked around to the hotel's patio, an old brick space covered over with a beautifully maintained grape arbor. Unlike the scene at Kline Slough, it was calm and quiet. But even there, sitting in the cool shade eating fried Delta catfish, chatting with the young EPA official, Rackley's sense of impending disaster grew stronger.

The EPA man was in his mid-twenties, tall and thin, and relentlessly earnest. He clearly viewed both Rackley and Trina as dangerous elements to be handled with caution. "The only thing," he said at one point during lunch, "I can think of that's close to this is water hyacinth. You've heard of that?"

Rackley frowned. "Vaguely."

"It's not vague to the people who live near it," the EPA man said sharply. "Somebody brought water hyacinth to this country in the late 1800s to decorate an exposition in New Orleans. It got into the waterways near the city, spread all over the South. The stuff packs a river so solidly that you can't get a boat through. It destroyed the lumber industry in Florida—they couldn't float the logs downriver anymore. They had to apply for federal disaster relief."

"Well," Rackley said. "I . . ."

The EPA man continued, undeterred. "Water hyacinth would close the Panama Canal if they didn't keep it out. The stuff is the most productive plant on the planet. They double every ten days. The only thing that keeps water hyacinth from spreading everywhere is that it needs warm water."

"Question," Trina said, leaning forward. "Warmer than Rice Five?"

"Rice Five," he said solemnly, "seems to be much more tolerant of temperature variation." The EPA official looked at her. "You know, we'd never have granted you permission to sell Rice Five. It's got too many genes from that damn Asian water plant in it."

Rackley nodded. "It was going to be an export product."

"Well, that shouldn't be allowed either, but I don't write the laws." The EPA man shook his head. "I watch this stuff every morning, and I keep thinking that I can see it growing." He picked up his napkin and wiped his lips. "I have a bad feeling," he said, "that the worst is yet to come."

Rackley had returned to San Francisco and given Markham a full report on the Delta situation. But now, just one week later, sitting in the cool hotel dining room, chatting with the New York underwriters, Markham showed absolutely none of the concern that Rackley had tried to instill.

When lunch was over Rackley waited in the lobby for the car while the young entrepreneur went off to use the telephone. Markham's car appeared in front of the hotel just as he returned. The Vietnamese driver opened the rear door of the Mercedes, and Markham, then Rackley, slid in. Once the car was underway,

Markham tilted his head back and asked Rackley what he thought
about their luncheon guests.

"They're the best yet," Rackley said. "And they're the
biggest. That's important. You don't want to get tied up with
anybody who can't handle a deal this size."

"Maybe," Markham said. "Maybe." He stared out the
window at the glass and marble storefronts of Post Street rushing
by. "I didn't like them," he said softly.

"Why not?" Rackley asked, genuinely puzzled.

Markham sighed deeply, shook his head. "They're not smart
enough."

Rackley coughed, hiding disbelief. "Who the hell do you
want, Paul? I mean, Einstein isn't doing new issues just now."

Markham shook his head, visibly irritated. "Oh sure, they're
smart. But I mean . . . like us."

"You got fleas?"

"What?"

"Old joke."

Markham, oblivious, was clearly searching for an explana-
tion. "I mean, they don't think in *levels*. . . . They don't
understand *metaphors*."

"They don't put metaphors in a stock prospectus."

"I know, I know. Maybe it's just that they think so . . . East
Coast."

"Well," Rackley said, loosening his tie, "that's where their
money is."

"I don't know," Markham said. "You know, we see these
people, politicians, bankers, publishers—powerful people—who
think they're well educated, just because they speak French or
they know the difference between Nietzsche and Niebuhr. But not
one of them can tell you the second law of thermodynamics or the
base pairs in DNA. Yet they try to run the country." Markham
sighed. "Sometimes, Rackley, I fear for the world."

Rackley closed his eyes and took a deep breath. "Well, why
not take United Genetics public first, then worry about the
world?"

Markham simply nodded, his clear brown eyes showing no
awareness of Rackley's irony.

Rackley leaned back in the smooth leather seat, puzzled.
Markham had managed thus far to veto five of the best brokerage
houses in the U.S., and Rackley couldn't understand why. Perhaps
Markham was finally taking revenge on the gilt-edged financial
community that, during his early years, often mocked him as a

transient wunderkind. Or—and more likely—it was yet a further phase in Markham's endless search for perfection.

As Markham grew older, his standards for performance only increased. His obsession in everything, from furniture to molecular geneticists to high fidelity equipment, even to women, was to find the best in the world: an endless, unsatisfied quest. It was beginning to make Rackley distinctly uncomfortable, and he looked forward to the day he could gracefully retire from United Genetics.

"Sooner or later," he reminded Markham, "you're going to have to pick one of these firms."

Markham touched his index fingers to the sides of his nose. "When the time is right," he said, "it will happen."

Rackley suddenly felt very tired. The future, he thought, is being divided between the financiers and the technologists: that was the real negotiation today. And damn the public, who might understand neither the technology nor the finances, but whose lives would be shaped by money and science just as surely as the changing of the seasons.

Abruptly Markham turned to Rackley with a reassuring, boyish smile. "Rackley, don't worry. It really will all work out just fine."

CHAPTER FOURTEEN

At nine A.M. on Wednesday, Kaye arrived at Lipsky's lab. The occasion was her final blood test to determine how well the tiny new embryo had implanted in her uterus. Lipsky, Kaye suspected, was just being cautious; he had already told her to begin seeing a regular obstetrician. If for some reason the implant failed, there were still two more embryos, one male, one female, both already genetically modified, sitting in his small stainless steel laboratory freezer.

That morning in fact Lipsky had opened the door and showed her the two aluminum vials, each one no bigger than the smallest segment of her little finger. In another week if all went well, the additional embryos would be surreptitiously returned to the regular Birthtech freezer, where they would wait in perfect cryopreservation until Rackley and Kaye decided to add to their family.

This morning Lipsky seemed more lighthearted than usual. He was planning a trip to Mexico City, a regular monthly visit he made to oversee the Caswell Clinic's research program. After he had drawn the blood sample, he set the little crimson tube aside, and for a moment he and Kaye chatted. During her days in the lab she sensed that Lipsky had come to both trust and like her.

Today they started talking about how Kaye and Rackley had met, their early fishing trips at the Caswell summer house, their mutual love for the outdoors.

"How about you?" Kaye asked the plump young researcher, teasing slightly. She took the cotton wad from the inside of her elbow and rolled down the sleeve of her white blouse. "Why isn't there a Mrs. Lipsky?"

"Oh . . ." Lipsky said, looking away. He shrugged, looked back at her, and smiled. "I'm not exactly a ladies' man type, you know."

"Most good men aren't."

"Well"—Lipsky tilted his head slightly—"actually, there is a woman I see in Mexico City. I mean, that I'm rather fond of."

Kaye smiled. "I suspected as much. Tell all."

"Oh," Lipsky said, touching his small pudgy hands together, "she's a molecular biologist. Undergraduate work at the University of Mexico City, doctorate at Cornell. She works in the research clinic now."

"What's she like?"

Lipsky leaned to one side and pulled out a bulging black leather wallet with a rubber band around it. He opened it and retrieved a small color photograph of a pretty young woman with long dark hair, high cheekbones, and a shy smile. "Maria Aguirre."

"She's beautiful."

"And very smart."

"That's wonderful," Kaye said. "Are you thinking of—"

Her question was interrupted by a sudden rapping sound at the front door of the small laboratory.

Lipsky glanced at the clock on the wall. "Liquid nitrogen delivery. One minute."

Kaye sat back in the low chair for a moment as Lipsky went out to the front door. Not particularly paying attention, she vaguely heard Lipsky open the door, and then suddenly the laboratory dissolved into an abrupt whirl of confusion.

"Dr. Stuart Lipsky," came a man's voice from the front room. "FBI. I have a warrant for your arrest."

Kaye twisted in her seat just in time to see the room fill with men, who spilled through the door behind the agent who was arresting Lipsky. They fanned out through the lab so quickly it seemed as if there were a dozen of them.

Lipsky stood among them, a short, plump, rumpled figure amid suit-coated tigers. The lead agent was a tall, heavyset man in his thirties with broad shoulders and a slight belly and slick black hair. In a single easy move he put one hand on Lipsky's shoulder, rotated the researcher a half turn, and slipped his chubby wrists into handcuffs.

Lipsky finally found his voice. "What the hell are you doing?" he asked, now facing the wall in the front room of the laboratory. "What is this?"

A shorter blond man was now standing in front of Kaye. "There's someone else here," he said over his shoulder.

"Just hold on." The big dark man turned to Lipsky and unfolded a single sheet of paper. "I'm Special Agent Michael Theodakis. I have a warrant authorizing a search of your laboratory and premises."

Lipsky opened and closed his mouth. "I don't know—"

"Hold on," Agent Theodakis said, this time to Lipsky. He called to another of the agents. "You want to read this guy for me?"

The agent came back to where Lipsky was standing and started to recite. "You have the right to remain silent. You have . . ."

Theodakis, moving quickly for such a large man, immediately stepped over to where Kaye was sitting.

"Who are you?"

Kaye's mind was swimming; she felt as if all this were going on behind glass, an unreal diorama, a stage piece.

"Katherine Rackley," she said.

The agent's eyes were already glancing quickly around. He gazed at the small formica table next to her, the tiny tube of bright blood, and the discarded cotton ball.

Theodakis looked back at Kaye. "Are you a patient of Dr. Lipsky's?" he asked in a gentle tone.

Kaye opened her mouth but nothing came out. She had no idea how to answer the question, but even as she hesitated, the agent spoke again.

"Don't answer that," he said. He spoke over his shoulder. "When you're done, please watch Ms. Rackley." He turned to her. "Sit tight."

Theodakis walked back into the front room. "I'll call Larson and see what to do about the patient. Put Lipsky in the car and start packing."

Without another word an agent led Lipsky, hands cuffed behind his back, out the front door. Another agent with a motor-driven Nikon and an electronic flash started shooting pictures, as a third began setting up big cardboard boxes.

As Kaye watched, feeling frozen in one position, two agents wearing white gloves started to pull open lab drawers and desk cabinets, spilling out reams of paperwork, dropping it all into the newly assembled boxes.

Glassware, electronic instruments, even bottles of reagents, went into the cardboard containers. One of the agents unscrewed the big chrome lug nuts on the autoclave and pulled out the racks, still filled with the beakers and test tubes that Kaye had loaded several days before.

"Even this stuff?" the agent asked.

Now Theodakis was back in the room. "Everything. Larson wants it all."

The blond agent was now in the back of the laboratory where the small ultra-low-temperature refrigerator sat. As Kaye watched, he fumbled with the latches on the stainless steel door until it swung open, and a frigid puff of air drifted out.

"There's two little metal things in here," the agent said.

"Everything," the big agent said.

"Wait a minute," Kaye interrupted, her voice rising. "Those are live embryos. You can't take those."

Theodakis looked at her, tilting his head slightly, suddenly interested. "What are they?"

Kaye looked down at the floor, thought for a moment, and looked up. "Those are embryos. From Dr. Lipsky's work. They'll die if you take them out."

The big agent looked at the other man. "Has she had Miranda?"

The other shook his head. Theodakis looked at Kaye closely. "How do you know what those are?"

She looked at him straight on. "Dr. Lipsky told me."

"Why did he tell you that?"

Kaye hesitated. "He's my friend."

"What do I do?" the other man said, one gloved hand still holding the freezer door open.

The big man watched Kaye for a long moment, clearly thinking carefully. "Leave them for now. I better check with Larson again."

The agent went back out the front door. Kaye sat, watching the other two agents pack books, notes, glassware, more bottles of reagents into cardboard boxes. The fourth agent finished taking pictures and left also.

"Who is Larson?" Kaye asked the youngest of the agents.

He looked up from stacking the papers on Lipsky's desk. "Assistant U.S. Attorney."

Kaye nodded, although this meant nothing to her.

A moment later Agent Theodakis returned. "We'll need your name and address," he told Kaye. "Then you can go." He turned to the agent packing boxes behind her. "Larson says everything, including the stuff in the freezer."

Kaye swiveled quickly in her chair. "No!" she said loudly.

Theodakis gazed at her for a moment, his brown eyes bright. "Sorry," he said softly.

"They're *alive*," Kaye said, upset, thinking fast. "They're private property."

Theodakis looked over her head. "In the box," he said to the agent, then turned his back.

In a flash Kaye was up out of the seat, across the laboratory, standing in front of the stainless steel freezer, blocking the way, arms behind her, holding onto the laboratory bench, staring at the agent, eyes wide, jaw set. "If you people touch these, you're in a hell of a lot of trouble."

Theodakis stopped walking. He turned back and looked at Kaye for a long moment. "I think you're a little confused," he said gently. "We have a warrant. If you don't get out of here, you're the one in trouble."

"Call my husband," Kaye said, her voice rising. "Call my brother, Edward Caswell. They can straighten this out."

"You have ten seconds to vacate the premises, and then you're under arrest for obstructing a legal search." Theodakis casually raised his arm and gazed at his wristwatch.

Kaye licked her lips nervously, glanced around the lab, then at the watch on the agent's hairy wrist. "Wait a minute. Whatever you're looking for here, it doesn't make sense to wreck something." She looked at Theodakis. "These are supposed to stay frozen."

"Five," Theodakis said, quite expressionless. He took a step forward.

"Hold it," Kaye said, not moving from in front of the freezer. "Just leave them for an hour. Call your person again. Make sure you're supposed to take them."

Theodakis took another step closer and Kaye tensed her muscles, desperate, not knowing what to do. Somehow, giving up the two tiny embryos seemed utterly wrong. She had seen their gene scans. One girl, one boy.

Kaye reached out, not quite aware, and put one hand against the agent's thick shoulder.

"Hey," Theodakis said easily. "Calm down. Let's just talk about this for a minute."

"Okay." Kaye swallowed heavily, relaxing very slightly. She realized that she had been holding her breath and she sighed deeply, feeling the muscles of her rib cage ease.

At that moment Theodakis moved—so quickly that she didn't even see him coming. In a split second he pinned both her arms to her side and spun her around, bent over so that her face was now almost pushed into the steel top of the little freezer cabinet. She felt his huge hands slide down her arms, gather her hands together, crushing them into a single painful ball.

Incongruously she noticed the scent of his after-shave, and then he pressed against her hard for a moment, pinioning her arms. She heard the metallic click of the handcuffs pinching her wrists. Theodakis put one hand on her shoulder near her neck. He held the chain of the handcuffs with the other and turned her around, away from the freezer.

"Read her," he told the agent in the doorway, "and then put her in the car with Lipsky."

"Stop," Kaye said, recovering, and now uncontrollably starting to tremble and cry. "Stop! You'll kill those little things. Just don't—"

And then she was out the door into the sunshine, pushed toward the corner of the lot where two plain gray government sedans and one big van were parked. She looked back over her shoulder as the laboratory door swung shut. "God damn you people," she said to the agent who was pushing her. "God damn you to hell!"

"You have the right to remain silent," the agent recited, "the right . . ."

Inside the laboratory Theodakis tucked his shirt back into his pants and reached up to straighten his tie. "Larson said to leave the stuff in the freezer."

The blond agent looked puzzled. "But . . ."

"Just shoot some pictures for now."

"I thought—"

Theodakis shrugged. "Larson wanted to see what she'd do." He finished tightening the knot of his bright tie. "Let's get this done."

Rackley was in a meeting room on the twenty-second floor of the United Genetics building in San Francisco. He was talking to Trina and the public relations staff, reviewing plans for how they would handle the "quiet period" required by law during the ninety days before a company sells stock to the public. It was a most delicate time: public relations people had to walk a fine line between providing pure information to reporters and stepping over into the self-promotion that could destroy a billion-dollar stock sale.

Rackley had just finished discussing the SEC regulations and was about to ask for questions when his secretary came into the room.

"Mr. Caswell is on the line. He says it's urgent."

Rackley nodded, secretly hoping that it had nothing to do with Rice Five. He held up one finger, smiled slightly. "Excuse me a minute," he said. "Put it through here," he told his secretary.

He went to a small beige telephone mounted on the wall of the conference room and picked up the receiver.

"Kaye and Lipsky have been arrested," Caswell said without preface. "Lipsky just called from the Federal Building."

"What?" For a moment Rackley could not even absorb the news.

Caswell ignored the question. "I'm going down there now. We're sending a lawyer also. I'm not sure whether you should come or not."

"Wait a minute. Wait a minute."

"Rackley," Caswell said impatiently. "They're going into a magistrate's hearing in twenty minutes."

"Of course I want to come," Rackley said, finally recovering a semblance of composure.

He could hear Caswell take a deep breath at the other end. "Obviously, you're involved in this also."

"I—"

"Okay," Caswell said curtly. "We'll talk about it on the way. There'll be a car at the side entrance when you come down."

Caswell hung up. Rackley stood, phone in hand, stunned, finally sensing that, behind his back, Trina and her assistants were trying not to stare at him.

He turned around.

"Rackley," Trina said tentatively. "Shall we continue?"

"Not now," Rackley said, and without another word, he left.

In the car on the way to the Federal Building, Caswell was grim. "What the hell," he asked Rackley, speaking in clipped tones, "is going on?"

Rackley pushed his fingers back through his brown hair. "I don't really know."

"Well," Caswell said, tapping his fingers angrily on the

armrest in the middle of the seat, "here's what I think. Lipsky was obviously doing some illegal embryo therapy for you. Just tell me: is that what he talked you into?"

Rackley was silent for a long moment, recalling his promise to Lipsky. There didn't seem much point to that secrecy now. Finally he nodded.

"Shit," Caswell said, cutting off the single syllable sharply. He stared out the window for a moment.

"Listen. You told us to go see him."

"I didn't tell you to break the law."

"But we got the feeling . . . I mean, it seemed that this was something he did all the time."

Caswell stared at him for a moment, his eyes very bright, lively. "Did he tell you that?"

"No," Rackley said slowly. "Not in so many words."

Caswell leaned back, closed his eyes. "The man is slightly unbalanced. I assume you noticed that."

"No. He's odd, but . . . ."

The driver turned right and accelerated west toward the Civic Center. "Well," Caswell said. "We'll talk about that later."

Five minutes later the car dropped them off in front of the massive gray Federal Building. They walked up the wide steps, through the metal detector, and stopped in the lobby. Caswell looked at the directory for a moment. "Magistrate's court," he said. "Seventeenth floor."

They came out of the elevator into a big hallway with a marble floor and wooden benches running along both walls. The first person Rackley saw was Alfred Littman, chief counsel for United Genetics. He was a middle-aged man with prematurely gray hair, and at the moment he looked distinctly harried.

The United Genetics attorney walked up to them quickly. "This is a little out of my realm," he told Caswell without preface. "We'll really need someone with criminal law experience here."

"Hold on." Caswell raised one hand, pausing, his voice resonant in the big empty hallway. "Just tell me what's going on."

"Lipsky's going to be charged with one count of violating the federal genetic engineering law." The lawyer looked at Rackley. "Right now your wife's being processed for resisting arrest and interfering with a search. But the U.S. attorney is probably going to ask for another count like Lipsky's."

Two federal marshals walked by, footsteps echoing loudly. "So what's happening now?" Caswell asked.

"They're being processed in the marshal's office on the floor below us. Then they get transferred up here for the magistrate's hearing."

"What's that?"

"It's a formality, to read the charges, determine that they're really the people named."

"Can we see them?" Rackley asked.

"Not right now. I've been down there, just to tell the marshals not to take any statements. And I talked to the U.S. attorney who's handling the case. A young guy named John Larson. We're going to ask for OR, and the magistrate will probably grant that."

"Well," Caswell said, "we can handle bail, if that's necessary."

"I hope not." Littman looked at his watch. "Let's go in now."

The three walked into the magistrate's courtroom, a small wood-paneled room with the judge's bench at the near end. One wall was nearly all windows, with an ironically beautiful view of San Francisco, Nob Hill, and a bit of the Bay. The fog was clearing, and there were patches of bright blue in the sky. One uniformed bailiff stood, rather casually, at a side door. At a table to the left sat two well-dressed men, talking softly.

Littman nodded discreetly in their direction. "This is a big deal for Larson," he said softly. "First time anybody's been prosecuted on this statute. So I imagine he's going to play it very carefully." Littman steered them toward the first row of wooden benches, almost pewlike, and they sat.

At that moment Kaye and Lipsky were brought into the courtroom from a side door, escorted by two heavyset federal marshals in coats and ties. Rackley was relieved to see they were wearing street clothes—he had feared they would be in some strange orange prison jumpsuits—but he was shocked to see that both were handcuffed. "Standard procedure," Littman told him quietly.

As soon as they stepped into the small wooden area set aside for prisoners, the marshals removed the handcuffs. Kaye looked around the little hearing room, saw Rackley, and gazed at him for a moment, her eyes very large, her expression a blend of fear and also relief at seeing familiar faces. Rackley also thought he saw a trace of anger in her look. Lipsky looked over at Caswell, making eye contact, but quite expressionless.

Just then the magistrate entered from a door on the opposite side of the room. "All rise," the bailiff said, and the handful of people in the room did so. The magistrate turned out to be a young red-haired woman, who looked about Rackley's age, wearing black robes and big tortoiseshell glasses.

"Please be seated." She sat behind the bench for a moment, looking over a file of papers, then looked up. "This is the only item on the calendar. Initial appearance of Stuart Paul Lipsky and Katherine Caswell Rackley." The federal marshal ushered both Kaye and Lipsky around from the prisoner's box and they stood in front of the magistrate.

At this the lawyer at the table stood and walked forward, and Littman left his seat beside Rackley and Caswell. "John Larson for the government," said the U.S. attorney.

Littman stood to Larson's right. "Alfred Littman for Dr. Lipsky and Mrs. Rackley."

"Mr. Larson?" she asked. "Mr. Littman? Shall we start?"

Both lawyers said yes.

The magistrate looked up. "You are Stuart Paul Lipsky?"

Lipsky nodded. "Yes."

"And you are Katherine Caswell Rackley?"

Kaye nodded. "I am."

"All right," the magistrate said casually, glancing at Lipsky and Kaye. "The purpose of this initial appearance is solely to determine your identity and inform you of the charges against you." She looked back down at her papers. "Dr. Lipsky—it is Dr. Lipsky?—this complaint charges you with one violation of Federal Code GC one oh three two A, the Federal Genetic Engineering Act, and states that on or about March fifth of this year you inserted a synthetic gene into a human embryo, then implanted that embryo in the uterus of a female patient with the objective of subsequent birth."

She turned one piece of paper. "The government informs me that the maximum possible penalty if you are convicted of this charge is ten years in prison, a fine of two hundred and fifty thousand dollars, and therapeutic sterilization of any offspring resulting from embryo gene therapy." She frowned and glanced up at the U.S. attorney for a moment. "Is that true, Mr. Larson?"

"That is as the act was written, Your Honor."

She looked at Lipsky. "Do you understand this charge?"

"I do."

The magistrate turned to Kaye. "Mrs. Rackley, you are charged with a single count of the same violation of the Federal Genetic Engineering Act, alleging that during April of this year you assisted Dr. Lipsky in the implantation of synthetic genes into a human embryo. Do I need to repeat the penalty details?"

Kaye shook her head.

"In addition the government's complaint charges you with one count of resisting arrest and another of interfering with a legally constituted search. I am advised that if you are found guilty, the maximum penalty for each of these is two years in prison and a ten-thousand-dollar fine. Do you understand these charges?"

Kaye nodded. "Yes, I do."

"Fine," the magistrate said. "I see the government's papers ask bail set at one hundred thousand dollars for each defendant."

Rackley leaned back against the hard bench. "Damn," he said softly to Caswell. "That's ridiculous."

"Your Honor," Littman said, showing none of the uncertainty he had reflected out in the corridor, "we request the defendants be released on their own recognizance. Such a punitive bail turns a case that is merely a technical misunderstanding into something approaching a mass murder."

"Your Honor," Larson said, pushing his dark hair back, "there is nothing technical about this case. These are individuals who have violated a very serious federal statute with international implications."

The magistrate looked at both lawyers wearily. "Gentlemen, this is a preliminary appearance. Please keep your comments confined to bailment."

"Your Honor," Littman said, "Dr. Lipsky is an internationally known scientist with substantial ties to the Bay area. Mrs. Rackley is a prominent citizen of San Francisco and the fourth generation of a pioneer California family. Neither qualifies in any way as a flight risk, so I can only regard the government's bail request as an inflammatory tactic."

The magistrate considered it for a long moment. She turned over the papers in the folder on her desk. "I'm inclined in this case to agree. These are uncharted waters. Does the U.S. attorney's office concur?"

Larson paused for a moment, looking over at Lipsky and Kaye. "We concur, Your Honor."

"Defendants are granted release on their own recognizance, bound over for arraignment at a date to be set."

U.S. Attorney Larson spoke up. "The government requests that arraignment be set for May fifth."

The magistrate gazed at the calendar on the wall. "That is the maximum permissible period."

"We request a more timely arraignment," Littman said, "so we can immediately get to the issues in this case."

The magistrate looked back at Larson.

"Your Honor," he said, "this is a complex case that will require substantial technical evaluation of the evidence seized. Pending outcome of that evaluation, we may file charges against additional individuals."

"Arraignment set for May fifth. Are there additional motions?"

"Not at the present time, Your Honor," Larson said.

"No, Your Honor," Littman said.

"That concludes the calendar. Magistrate's court stands adjourned," the young woman said.

Kaye looked at Rackley; Lipsky glanced up to see Caswell, then looked away. The two federal marshals escorted them out, this time without handcuffs.

Littman immediately walked back to where Caswell and Rackley were sitting.

"They have to sign the paperwork for OR in the marshal's office," he explained. "It should only take ten minutes or so."

As they sat on a bench in the corridor outside the U.S. marshal's office, Littman told them what little else he had gleaned from the affidavit attached to the federal complaints. "They've searched Lipsky's lab, which was where they found Kaye. They cleaned it out pretty well, as I understand it, and they've sealed it as a crime scene."

"How long can they do that for?"

"I can file a motion requesting access, since it's commercial property."

"Do it," Caswell said. "How did they get a search warrant in the first place?"

"The warrant and the complaint are both based on an unnamed informant."

For the first time that day Caswell looked genuinely surprised. He stared. "Who the hell . . . ?"

"There's no grounds for anonymity here. If they won't identify the informant, I'll immediately move for dismissal."

"What happened with Kaye?" Rackley asked.

Littman shrugged. "According to the FBI, she was told to leave the lab and wouldn't. I don't think they expected to arrest her; Lipsky's complaint was drawn up yesterday, hers was just done."

"That doesn't make sense," Rackley said.

Littman turned to Caswell and cleared his throat. "Edward,

you and I have to talk about representation. We have a number of interests here that may produce some conflicts."

Caswell nodded tightly. "We'll discuss that later."

"I don't follow," Rackley said, but at that moment the big oak door of the marshal's office swung open and out walked Lipsky, then Kaye. Rackley stood immediately and took a step and then Kaye was in his arms, holding on as tight as he'd ever felt, pushing her face into the lapel of his suit coat. She was crying now, from relief. "Rackley," she said, "it's really, really awful."

He stroked her soft hair, looking over her shoulder at Lipsky, who made eye contact but appeared almost dazed. "No it's not," Rackley said. "We'll get this straightened out."

She pulled back from him and looked up, cheeks wet. "They were going to kill the other embryos."

Rackley pulled her close again.

Edward stepped forward and put his hand on Kaye's shoulder. "Hello," he said softly, "little sister."

Kaye looked up at her brother. "Edward, this is really bad."

"We have a car downstairs," he said. "Let's get out of here."

The first reporter, a young man in a corduroy sports coat and a loosened tie, reached them just as they left the elevator and stepped out onto the polished stone floor of the Federal Building lobby. Rackley didn't recognize him, but the reporter knew Rackley.

"Mr. Rackley," the reporter said, "have you all been charged with illegal genetic engineering?"

Rackley nearly ignored the young man. "No comment." He took Kaye's arm and kept walking. Just behind them the lawyer, Lipsky, and Caswell left the elevator as its stainless steel doors pulled shut.

The young man glanced around quickly. "This is Dr. Lipsky? Mr. Caswell, were you aware this work was going on?"

Caswell looked at him. "No comment," he said, and pushed past him.

Rackley spoke softly to Kaye. "Someone in the U.S. attorney's office called the newspaper."

They made their way through the lobby of the building and went out onto the street. For a moment they couldn't see the plain gray United Genetics car. "Damn," Caswell said, "where is that idiot?"

Rackley, one arm around Kaye, looked up and down Golden Gate Avenue and finally saw the sedan approaching, pulling up to the curb. But even as he saw the car, just beyond it he saw the first television minicam crew, and behind them, two or three other reporters.

"Jesus," Rackley said. "It's like they put it on the wire services. Larson must be planning to make a career out of this one." He moved Kaye forward. "Let's get out of here."

They crowded into the United Genetics sedan and accelerated down the wide street, back toward the financial district.

There was an odd, protracted silence in the car, until finally they reached the headquarters of United Genetics. The driver pulled around the side of the tall building and into the underground garage. Once the car stopped, Kaye continued to sit in the backseat, arms folded, quite pale, clearly exhausted.

"I think you and Kaye should just go home now," Caswell said softly, as Rackley stepped out of the car. Caswell then turned to Lipsky. "Stuart," he said. "Would you like a car home?"

Lipsky, who had said almost nothing during the brief ride through the financial district, now stood up, his pale skin even whiter than usual in the blue fluorescent light of the underground garage. "No," he said in a surprisingly firm voice. "I think I should go up and talk to Paul now."

A very quick frown crossed Caswell's forehead. "Well, we can see if he's—"

"I mean now," Lipsky said in firm tones that Rackley had never heard him use before.

"Certainly," Caswell said coldly. He turned back to Rackley. "Take Kaye home," he said, his voice softening. "Then give me a call."

Rackley helped Kaye from the back of the sedan and they walked across the garage to where his car was parked. "Hey," she said, "I just remembered. I left my car in the parking lot in Berkeley. I guess it's still there. I—"

The thought of the abandoned car somehow triggered tears. Rackley stopped walking and put his arms around her.

"What's going to happen?" she asked. "How much trouble are we in? Nobody would tell me anything."

Rackley took a deep breath. "I don't think anybody really knows."

"But they know about us, don't they?"

"I'm not sure," Rackley said. "Maybe not." For a moment, he thought of the editorial framed on Lipsky's door. "But Lipsky is sunk. We just have to make sure we don't go down with him."

CHAPTER FIFTEEN

GENETIC ENGINEER
ARRESTED ON COAST

WIFE OF INDUSTRY
FIGURE DETAINED ALSO

SAN FRANCISCO, April 10 — Former Stanford University researcher Stuart Lipsky, 40, was charged here today with allegedly violating the Federal Genetic Engineering Act. Lipsky is now employed by San Francisco–based United Genetics. Also charged was Katherine Caswell Rackley, 29. In addition, Mrs. Rackley was charged with interfering with an FBI search of Dr. Lipsky's laboratory and resisting arrest.

The two arrests are the first under the Federal Genetic Engineering Act. In an affidavit filed here by the U.S. attorney's office, a former patient has accused Dr. Lipsky of performing gene surgery on an embryo, a technique prohibited by the federal law. The procedure was allegedly intended to increase the intelligence of the unborn child. Mrs. Rackley is said to have assisted in a similar procedure at a later date.

Both were released on their own recognizance, and a

preliminary hearing was set for May 5. According to
Assistant U.S. Attorney John Larson, investigation of Dr.
Lipsky's genetic engineering activities continues and addi-
tional arrests may result.

Dr. Lipsky was dismissed from Stanford University
three years ago for attempting an embryo-engineering
experiment, then in violation of National Institutes of
Health guidelines. Federal legislation passed after the
Stanford incident made such therapy illegal. For two years
Dr. Lipsky has supervised a project cataloging human
genes at a United Genetics research facility in Berkeley,
California.

Mrs. Rackley is the wife of a United Genetics vice
president, Thomas Rackley, and the sister of the firm's
chief executive officer, Edward Caswell.

United Genetics, founded seven years ago by computer
millionaire Paul Markham, was expected to make an initial
public stock offering this fall. Wall Street analysts (see
Business, II-3) speculated that the new legal difficulties,
along with an unresolved bioaccident involving California
farmland, may delay the offering.

Rackley—who had been so successful at diverting journalists
from the Rice Five problem—now found himself the center of
media attention. And the *New York Times'* account of the arrest
was the most restrained by far.

That night one television news program opened with film of
Lipsky, Kaye, Caswell, and Rackley walking down the steps of
the Federal Building to their car. Rackley was hurrying them
along, trying to avoid the first minicam crew that was approaching
at a half-run. Lipsky had his head bowed and was waddling
clumsily down the gray concrete steps. Kaye looked small and
vulnerable, her beige wool coat pulled around her narrow
shoulders. Caswell towered above the rest, posture perfect, but his
dark beard somehow sinister in the rushed footage.

On screen, Rackley was shown herding them into the United
Genetics sedan, and as the camera zoomed in, the voice-over
asked:

*"Are these the first people to break the law by custom-building
babies in the laboratory? Tonight the FBI says yes, and this
disgraced genius and his socialite assistant may do their next
experiments behind bars."*

"Oh God." Kaye closed her eyes and leaned back on the big
white couch in the study. "Please turn it off."

Rackley reached out with the remote control and switched the set off. He knew that Trina would be taping all of the network news shows in her office at United Genetics; he could assess the damage in the morning.

Kaye immediately straightened up, pushing her blond hair back. Even though the house was warm, she had started shivering earlier and was now wearing one of Rackley's old wool sweaters. "What," she asked, for the third time that hour, "are we going to *do*?"

Rackley slid over on the couch and put his arm around Kaye, who rested her head on his shoulder. He stroked her hair with one hand, saying softly, "It's going to be all right."

Even as he spoke, he could hear the telephone answering machine on the desk switch on yet again. Months ago Rackley had given his home telephone number to a handful of journalists in case they needed late-night updates on stories. Today the calls had been ceaseless. Rackley had turned the telephone ringer off but left the answering machine on, and he could tell from the clicking sounds of the little machine that calls were coming in almost constantly.

He held Kaye for a moment longer, then stood and walked over to the machine. The green fluorescent digits had counted fifty-eight calls in less than three hours.

He rewound the tape a bit, turned up the volume, and played a call. "Rackley, this is Bill Cunningham at *Time*. I'd really appreciate—" He started to wind forward randomly.

"—the *Los Angeles Times*—"

"—call me before five New York time, or at my house anytime, two one two, three five oh, nine—"

"—producer for *Nightline*. We talked before, about Rice Five, and now I'd like—"

"—keep it strictly background if you'd like—"

"—plenty of space to tell your side—"

"—at the studio in San Francisco for a live interview with Jane—"

"God," Kaye said, listening to the messages from the couch. "They really are like . . . mosquitoes, or something."

Rackley sighed and shut the machine off. For once in his short public relations career, he really didn't need to think about the press. This time his worries were far more personal.

Later Kaye went upstairs to take a nap, and Rackley adjusted the answering machine volume so he could screen calls. He was sitting at the desk in the downstairs study, responding to some vestigial journalistic impulse by making careful notes on the day's events, when Edward Caswell called.

"Rackley," Caswell said over the answering machine, "it's Edward. Pick up if you're there."

Rackley reached for the telephone. "Hello, Edward."

"How is Kaye?"

"She's okay. She's sleeping now."

"Good. Any reporters camped out there yet?"

"None that I've seen yet," Rackley said. "But based on the telephone calls, it's only a matter of time."

"Well . . . " There was a moment of silence. "I want you to know that we're completely behind you in this. That we don't completely understand what you did, but we know you had a good reason to do it."

For a moment Rackley felt almost dizzy. "Wait a minute. What do you mean, you don't understand what we did? You told us to go see Lipsky."

"Of course I did. He's the best medical geneticist I know."

"But—"

"But I didn't tell you to break the law. What's done is done, though."

Rackley held the telephone receiver away from his ear for a moment, shaking his head. Something here was very wrong.

Caswell cleared his throat. "There's one thing I should tell you tonight," he said. "I had a brief discussion with Littman today. He's suggesting that it would be best for him not to represent Kaye, or you, should it come to that. Just in case the company gets dragged into this, we should try to separate our interests. Purely a strategic move."

"So we should get our own lawyer."

"Correct. If you need any recommendations, we can talk about it in the morning."

"Sure."

"Give me a call, I mean," Caswell continued quickly. "At least for the next few days, I think it would be better if you stayed clear of the offices."

Rackley frowned. "Isn't that admitting guilt? You know my preference: business as usual."

"I'm afraid your preference doesn't count right now, Rackley. There's nothing usual about this," Caswell said flatly. "Give Kaye my love."

"Sure," Rackley said quietly.

Caswell hung up. Rackley returned to the living room as Kaye came downstairs, now wearing a white dressing gown.

"That was Edward."

Kaye looked up hopefully. "Does he have any good ideas?"

"Not really," Rackley said, and then he heard the evening paper hit the front porch. "Might as well see what the local guys did." Perhaps, he hoped, it was not as big a story as he suspected.

The evening San Francisco paper made it the front-page headline:

GENE DOC, HEIRESS ARRESTED
ILLEGAL BABY LAB BUSTED

There was a big picture of Rackley and Kaye getting into the sedan in front of the Federal Building. The rest of the story repeated the few public facts, buttressed with a great deal of speculation. A sidebar gave the history of United Genetics. There was a picture, taken from the society pages, of their wedding: Rackley looking slightly pompous in a tuxedo, Kaye cool and elegant in a beaded gown. And at the bottom of the page a box said, "See editorial, page A-14."

Rackley turned to the editorial and started to read: "There are moments when society must say no to science, and human genetic engineering is one such . . ."

He dropped the paper on the floor.

Kaye turned the television back on, just in time to see an odd face on screen. It was a small man sitting behind a desk, law books behind him. The man was clearly somehow deformed; he sat hunched over, his back twisted and bent.

"—and so there is no real basis for this law, as far as I can see," the man was saying. "This sort of work should be controlled, but it must be pursued, for the sake of all humans. Otherwise we're inviting a new Dark Ages."

The screen changed back to the newsreader, who turned a page. "Professor Tortola's view is not shared by Steven Hechinger, the head of the watchdog group Natural Progress. In Washington this morning Hechinger demanded a full federal investigation of the San Francisco case."

Kaye looked over at Rackley. "Who was that first man?"

Rackley was still staring at the screen. "I think," he said slowly, "that's our lawyer."

* * *

Rackley and Kaye slept fitfully that night and were awakened early the next morning by the doorbell. Rackley went downstairs; he opened the small trapdoor at eye level and looked out. On the steps was a reporter from one of the newsweeklies.

"Jeez, Rackley," the reporter said, smiling. "Don't you ever answer your telephone anymore?"

"I'm off for a few days. Call Trina Robbins."

"But—"

Rackley closed the little door and went back upstairs. Kaye was already up and dressing. They had an eight-thirty appointment downtown to meet Jackson Tortola, the only lawyer Rackley could think of who might be able to handle their case. He had called Tortola late that previous night, and the man had simply said: "First thing tomorrow."

Tortola was a national expert in bioethics. He had been involved in several landmark biotechnology decisions—patenting mammals, copyrighting novel genes, the rights of frozen embryos. Now he took very few cases, mostly writing and lecturing at the University of California's law school.

Right on time Rackley and Kaye arrived at Tortola's small campus office. "Come in," the odd-looking lawyer said to Rackley. "It's good to see you again." He turned to Kaye. "And you must be Katherine."

"Kaye," she said, trying not to stare at Tortola. He was a man in his middle years who appeared far older; a rare hereditary illness had given him severely hunched shoulders and a bowed back. His head was always tilted slightly to one side, as if perpetually curious, but his delivery and manner were so sharp and forceful as to make one quickly forget his disability. Rackley had spoken with him a number of times, and for a few months, a year or so earlier, Tortola had been a consultant for United Genetics, until a run-in with Markham drove him off.

"Please." Tortola gestured toward two chairs after introductions were complete. He moved himself around his desk sideways, crablike, and then sat.

"I've already been on the telephone," he said, looking down at a yellow legal pad filled with notes. "Assistant U.S. Attorney Larson has been a busy bee this morning. He's requested a court order to do gene scans on the two embryos in Lipsky's lab. He also wants to subpoena your records from Birthtech."

The short, gnarled lawyer looked up for a moment. "I assume you had gene scans done there?"

Rackley nodded.

Tortola wrinkled his nose and sighed. "I thought so. Larson is very bright, seems to have thought this through."

Kaye spoke up, shifting slightly in her chair. "You think he's going to match the embryos with our gene scans."

Tortola raised his thick eyebrows. "Obviously."

"What can you do?"

"It's always possible to raise civil rights issues about embryos. How old are these?"

"Sixteen cells," Rackley said.

Tortola clucked softly. "That's awfully early. Chances are he'll get his gene scans." He tapped his short fingers on his desk for a moment, gazing off to one side, his head at an odd angle. "I don't think I can block the subpoena of your records. He's got probable cause with Kaye in Lipsky's laboratory." He looked back at Kaye. "The FBI agent's deposition says you took a swing at him."

"No! That's not true."

Tortola shrugged. "That might help." Then he shook his head, looking up at Rackley. "I assume you know that you're going to be charged along with Kaye and Lipsky, sooner or later."

Rackley nodded. "How soon?"

"As soon as Larson can prove the embryos are yours, and that they've been exposed to SPL10. I'd predict he'll bring charges against you by the end of the week."

Rackley thought about this for a moment. "But there's still no proof that we were actually involved. Lipsky could have stolen those embryos from Birthtech without our knowledge."

"How likely is that?" Tortola said gently. "Given your wife's behavior in Dr. Lipsky's lab?"

"Well. There's an element of doubt."

Tortola nodded. "That's probably why Larson has also asked for a blood sample from Kaye."

"What?" Kaye asked.

"That was the third court order he requested this morning. I assume it's to see if you show antibodies to SPL10. That would prove exposure to Lipsky's engineering virus, via the implanted embryo." Tortola shook his head. "I'm not sure that will work. But my guess would be that if it doesn't, Larson is setting a precedent for testing your child when it's born." He paused for a moment and looked at Kaye. "In this case the evidence is really in your womb."

"Can we do anything about the blood test?" Rackley asked.

"We can try. I don't really know. What we can do is raise

enough doubt so we can use the physical testing as an issue to appeal on.''

"Appeal." Kaye looked at him. "You're already assuming we're going to lose.''

"No, not at all. But we have to plan for any contingency. There's some political pressure from Washington to tie this case up. I think they'd like a successful prosecution just to set an example.''

Kaye continued to gaze at him. "Can they really sterilize our baby?''

Tortola shook his head emphatically. "The sterilization penalty can't stick. That was just right-wing nut cases playing with the law for the sake of hearing themselves legislate.''

"Are you sure?" Kaye asked.

Tortola nodded. "I'm sure.''

Kaye shook her head very slightly, very quickly. "I wish I believed you," she said softly.

Rackley began to get angry. "What about arguing that we had a right to do this? Is it a crime to save your child from the disease that killed the rest of your family?''

"Of course it isn't," Tortola said calmly. "But it is a crime to do it when society says you can't.''

"But these are medical techniques that can help people.''

Tortola sighed. "In fact there aren't that many cases like yours. There's already a way to control the genetics of an unborn child: nobody talks about it, but I hear about more and more cases where parents have a gene scan done on their fetus. Then, if they see something they don't like, they abort.''

"But what we're doing is better," Rackley said. "We're not aborting. We're trying to heal.''

"Well, society has been fighting about abortion for a long time. At least it's a fight we're familiar with. But embryo engineering is something else.''

"Why?''

"The point is that the difference between correcting diseases and performing eugenics is very fine. You believe that alcoholism is a disease—and I agree with you. But some people may think it's simply a character trait. And if you begin to tamper with character traits, where do you stop? Blue eyes, blond hair, tall boys, shapely girls . . .''

Tortola leaned back in his chair, gazing out the window for a moment. "With abortion we talked about the rights of the unborn.

Now we're extending it. Are we robbing the unborn of the right to be themselves? And their children, and their children after them?"

Kaye broke in. "I thought you were on our side," she said sharply.

Tortola looked at her. "I'm trying to show you that this is a very complex issue," he said quickly. "I am on your side. Both because I'm defending you and because I think you're right." He ran one hand almost absentmindedly over the oddly hunched mass of his shoulder. "With a gene scan I would have been diagnosed in the womb. And as matters stand now, I would never have been born." He shook his head. "There's something wrong with stopping medicine at a point where it can diagnose but not treat."

Rackley had been saving one last question. "What if we could show that more people than us have done it?"

Tortola stopped moving for a moment as he considered the implications of the question. "Do you know that for a fact?"

"I can't prove it," Rackley said. "But Lipsky could."

Tortola frowned. "If we could argue that this was a treatment already widely in use, that you and Kaye are being singled out . . ." His voice trailed off and then he looked up. "I genuinely do not know. But frankly, at this point almost anything is an improvement."

"I'll talk to Lipsky," Rackley said.

Tortola looked at him. "Do it discreetly. And then have him talk to me. If we're talking about incriminating other people, we have to go very slowly." Again he gazed out the window for a moment. "I don't think anyone else can expect the same immunity Larson gave the Collins woman."

Rackley looked up sharply. "Who?"

Tortola looked down at his notes. "Megan Collins," he said. "The government's witness."

"What?"

"Because of her miscarriage there's no physical evidence, but she's already given extensive testimony. I assumed you knew."

After the meeting with Tortola concluded, Kaye said she felt a bit ill, so Rackley dropped her off at the house, then drove forty miles south of San Francisco down to the exclusive green enclaves high above Silicon Valley. Megan Collins was the wife of Albert Collins, the lead investor in United Genetics and the ranking venture capitalist in Silicon Valley. According to Tortola, she had been so guilt-plagued over her miscarriage—following forbidden sequence treatment by Lipsky—that she finally turned the young doctor in. It had been pure coincidence that Kaye was in his laboratory when the FBI arrived. But the fact that Megan Collins had also seen Lipsky was not a coincidence, and Rackley wanted to know why.

On the way down the peninsula he put in several calls to Lipsky's home number, which was constantly busy. He had almost given up after twenty minutes or so, figuring that Lipsky had left the receiver off, when suddenly the line rang and Lipsky answered.

"Yes?"

"Stuart," Rackley said, driving with one hand, holding the telephone receiver with the other. "This is Rackley."

"Yes?" The strange researcher sounded distant, guarded.

"I figured you left the phone off the hook."

"Oh," Lipsky said vaguely, "it's been a bad day. A problem at the clinic in Mexico."

"Listen, Stuart. Kaye and I spent the morning with Jackson Tortola. You know him?"

"The bioethics lawyer."

"He's going to defend Kaye. I want to talk to you about cooperating in the defense."

There was a long silence at the other end of the line.

"I'm really not sure I can do that, Rackley."

Rackley paused for a moment, changing lanes, accelerating down the broad, smooth highway. "At least let's talk about it. Unless you do something, this guy Larson is going to throw the book at you."

"Maybe. Maybe not."

"Let's talk."

"Where?"

"Let me come by your house," Rackley said. "Tomorrow morning at nine."

There was another long silence, then a sigh. "Make it day after tomorrow. But I don't really know that I can help you."

Lipsky hung up. Rackley set the telephone receiver back on the console and tried to remember the off ramp for the Collins house. Here in the smooth green hills of Portola Valley and Woodside, the barons of high technology lived in manorial splendor. By now most blue-collar manufacturing had long since departed Silicon Valley; remaining behind were the brains and the money. The hills above Stanford University contained the most rarified of the breed: a community that for all intents and purposes was living five years in the future.

Even a simple three-bedroom house here could cost half a million dollars; Collins had a large house in a two-acre compound at the end of a private road. Rackley had visited the Collins home a few times in the past for parties, and as he recalled, the property was gated. But today the gate was open, so Rackley drove right up to the front entrance of the sprawling low ranch-style house, built in a vast L shape around a black-bottomed swimming pool.

He rang the bell beside the two tall, carved entrance doors. He could hear the chimes ring inside the house. Moments later a young au pair wearing blue jeans and a sweat shirt opened the door, revealing a vast tiled entrance hallway. "May I help you?" she asked in a strong French accent.

"Is Mrs. Collins here please?"

The young woman looked very serious. "Mrs. Collins has gone away now. Who is calling?"

"I'm a friend. I need to talk to her."

At that moment a man's voice came from deeper inside the massive house. "Monique, who is that?"

The woman looked over her shoulder.

"Thomas Rackley," Rackley said loudly. "Let me speak to Mr. Collins."

"Tell him to go away."

Rackley put one hand against the big carved door and pushed. The young woman, confused, stepped back as Rackley proceeded into the entryway as if she were not there. "Collins," Rackley called. "I need to talk to you."

Collins, a lean man in late middle age with a confident demeanor reinforced by money and intelligence, immediately appeared at an interior doorway. He was wearing khaki pants, a blue cardigan. "Rackley," he said sharply. "Leave this alone. I'm very sorry Kaye got taken up in this, but Megan can't help you."

"Where is she?"

"Megan is ill. She's in a private hospital. She's had a nervous breakdown."

"Who approached you about gene therapy?"

"I can't tell you. I think you know that."

"New rules." Rackley took another step forward, then felt slightly ridiculous. What was he going to do: beat the man about the head and shoulders?

Collins blew a stream of air through pursed lips, shaking his head. "Please leave now. I've already called the security people."

Rackley heard tires on the long driveway behind him. A sedan with a private guard service shield on one side pulled into the space behind his car. A guard with a side arm got out of the car and started toward the front door.

"Just tell me this. Who sent you to Lipsky?"

Collins leaned against the doorway, touched one graying temple, and said nothing.

The guard, a huge man in his twenties, was behind Rackley now, taking his arm. "Sir, you've been asked to leave."

Rackley pulled his arm away. "I'm leaving." Then he turned back to Collins. "This isn't over."

The man stood in the doorway of his home and gazed at him steadily. "Rackley," he said softly, with the most genteel measure of threat in his voice. "Leave it alone."

Rackley drove back to San Francisco. On the way he called home, but heard only the answering machine. At first concerned, he quickly reassured himself that Kaye simply wasn't picking up the telephone.

But as soon as Rackley opened the front door that afternoon, he knew something was wrong. The house was too quiet—not in any audible way, but in some more subliminal sense.

"Kaye?" he called quietly, walking quickly into the big living room. "Are you here?"

There was silence. Rackley set his briefcase down by the shuttered bay window and began to search the house.

Five minutes later he found the note—pinned to the pale peach bedspread in the master bedroom. The message was simple, written in black ink on a sheet of Kaye's stationery.

Love:

> *I don't see what else I can do. I have to be away from all this or I'll lose the baby the way Megan did. So I'm going away for a while, not because I want to leave you, but because I want to save this baby. The lawyer said it: The evidence is in me. I know you and Edward will figure out something, and then I can come back. Don't worry*

*about me. I'll be taken care of, and as soon as it's safe, I'll
tell you where I am.*

I love you and I know this will all be fine.

Kaye

Rackley loosened his tie, took a couple of steps backwards,
and fell into one of the wicker chairs in the corner of the bedroom.
He stared at the paper, holding it, gazing at the words until they
ceased to make any sense.

But the act itself did make sense—a certain kind of desperate
sense—and he knew instantly that this was indeed something
Kaye might do. Beneath her smooth manners and easy charm
Kaye had a core of pure survival instinct. Once, not long after he
met her, Kaye had walked into her apartment in the midst of a
robbery. Confronted by two lean, nasty teenagers, one with a
knife, she reached into her purse to hand over her credit cards,
then coolly sprayed both youths with Mace. "Three eyes out of
four," she told Rackley later. "The cop said that's the best he's
seen."

In Kaye that instinct combined with the ineluctable sense that
came from being a Caswell—a family that was simply not
accustomed to hearing that anything was impossible. Even
running away from the federal government. As Rackley recalled,
the founding Caswell was himself fleeing some sort of East Coast
financial scandal when he arrived in California to launch the
family fortune.

Rackley roused himself from the chair and went to Kaye's
closet. Not much was missing. He wished he had paid more
attention to her wardrobe—he couldn't even tell what kind of
clothes she had taken. He went downstairs, and two suitcases
were gone from the storage closet.

He immediately called Caswell. His wife, Madeleine, answered.

"Rackley, I'm so sorry—"

For a moment Rackley thought she was talking about Kaye's
disappearance, then realized she was simply referring to the
arrest. "It's a bad law," he said. "We'll win. Is Edward there?"

After a moment Edward's deep tones filled the earpiece.
"Rackley, how are you? How's Kaye?"

"Kaye's gone. Listen." He pulled the note out of his jacket
pocket and read it quickly.

When he was done, there was silence, then a long sigh at the end of the telephone. "Damn," Caswell said. "I wish to hell she hadn't done that."

Rackley frowned. "She never talked to you about it?"

"Not a word. If she had, I'd have told her to stay." Caswell was silent for another moment. "On the other hand, maybe it will turn out for the best."

"I can't see that. I want to find her."

"Why?" Caswell asked sharply. "What good will that do?"

Rackley was puzzled by the question. "But—"

"You have to think what's best for everyone. There are times, when the law is insane, that it's best just not to obey the law."

"What does that have to do with finding Kaye?"

"She may be safer without you poking around."

Rackley had a sudden, odd feeling that Caswell knew more than he was saying; the same feeling Rackley used to get as a journalist when a source suddenly turned too glib, too quick. There was nothing one could exactly identify; it had less to do with the words spoken than the way they flowed.

"Rackley?" Caswell asked, his voice concerned, after the silence stretched on unbroken.

"I'm here," Rackley said in guarded tones, still thinking fast, staring at the wooden paneling that led up the stairwell.

"Rackley, Paul and I want to talk to you tomorrow. We need to plan some sort of strategy for the rest of this problem."

"I'll be there first thing."

"No," Caswell said quickly. "That's not a good idea. There were pickets and reporters in front of the building all day today. For everyone's sake we need to get United Genetics out of this picture."

Rackley considered this for a moment. "All right. Where?"

"How about," Caswell said, "a nice public park?"

It was a long night for Rackley. He called Trina immediately, but she was out, and he left a brief message on her answering machine: "Call whenever you get in." Then Rackley sat and stared at the telephone and tried to think what to do next.

The certainty grew in him that Edward Caswell knew more about Kaye's disappearance than he had admitted. A bit after ten o'clock he dialed the Caswells' number again. Madeleine answered.

"Hi," Rackley said. "Let me talk to Edward."

There was a long silence. "He's . . . not available."

"Not available," Rackley said impatiently. "What does that mean?"

Madeleine was clearly unsure what to say. "He can't come to the phone, I mean. Can he call you back?"

"Sure. When?"

"I don't know."

Rackley took a deep breath. "Madeleine, this is Rackley. Where the hell is Edward and why can't he talk to me?"

"Okay," Madeleine said, her high voice tight with tension. "He's out. On business. He won't be back . . . until very late."

"Tell him to call anytime. I'll be up most of the night."

Rackley stayed up, but the only other call, about two in the morning, was from London. A young woman from the BBC was most apologetic. She had, she said, completely forgotten the time difference. But as long as he was on the line, could Rackley answer a couple of quick questions?

Rackley quietly hung up, and only near dawn did he find a few, fitful hours of sleep.

Caswell had insisted that they meet at noon in Washington Square in the heart of North Beach, a patch of green below the tall white spires of St. Peter and Paul's. Rackley, restless, walked the two miles from Pacific Heights.

North Beach was in transition, its longtime Italian population ebbing as a new wave of Asian immigrants settled in. Italian bakeries were being replaced by banks bearing clocks that told the time in Hong Kong. Washington Square reflected the shift. As Rackley walked into the park, he saw the same old Italian men as always, stooped and gray, overdressed in heavy wool suits, sitting on benches. But among them were small knots of children, Chinese, Vietnamese, Laotian, playing in the sun, dashing across the bright green lawns under the high white spires of the old church.

A moment after Rackley entered the park, he sighted Caswell and Markham, sitting on a bench midway along Vallejo Avenue. As he approached, he saw they were eating lunch: on the bench between them was a big square of white paper with sandwiches from a local delicatessen. Although clad in business suits, the two didn't look out of place in the sunny green space. San Francisco was a sufficiently indulgent town that even ranking executives occasionally lunched in the parks simply to enjoy the weather and the view.

Rackley walked up to the bench quickly, his arms close to his sides. "Where the hell is Kaye?"

"Sit," Caswell said, gesturing to the end of the bench. "Please."

"I want to know where Kaye is."

"Please, sit."

"No."

"Rackley," Markham said, looking up, smiling slightly. "Be reasonable. We're not the enemy."

Reluctantly Rackley sat at one end of the bench. "Where is she?"

Caswell shook his large, leonine head, hands spread wide. "Rackley, I do not know. Do—not—know. She did call me, she did say that she knew she had to get out. But she didn't tell me where."

Caswell offered a sandwich. Rackley ignored him. "I want to know what's going on."

"She wouldn't tell me. And that's how I want it. The fewer people who know something, the safer life is."

"That's exactly what Lipsky told me once."

"Think about it," Markham interrupted, leaning forward, characteristically intense. "It's your baby she's protecting. We live in crazy times. But it's not always going to be like this. The laws will change. But not before your baby is born."

"You'll see her again," Caswell said. "I promise that. But for now . . ."

"For now," Rackley said, his stomach suddenly tensing, "what?"

Caswell cleared his throat. "Paul and I have a proposition. In return for a substantial block of United Genetics stock, we'd like you to plead guilty to the federal genetic engineering charge."

Rackley looked up, stunned. "I haven't even been charged yet."

"It's only a matter of time," Caswell said. "Littman thinks the prosecutor will go to the grand jury by the end of the week."

Markham raised one thin hand, his voice as soft and soothing and conciliatory as Rackley had ever heard it. "*Think* about it, Rackley. If this thing gets dragged through the courts it could take months. Years. If you plead innocent, there will be that much more pressure to find Kaye. If her blood test shows antibodies to SPL10, that's the lock on the case. On the other hand, if you plead guilty . . ."

Markham fell silent as a young Asian couple, hand in hand,

strolled by the bench. As soon as they had passed, Caswell took it up. "If this drags on, it will tear United Genetics apart. We'll spend all of our time in court. Forget the public offering. We'll be bankrupt by Christmas."

"But we've got a case. We can fight this. We're *right.*"

"Rackley, Rackley, Rackley," Markham said. "You're still a goddamn idealist." A breeze came up, carrying the sound of quiet Italian being spoken somewhere nearby. "Sometimes being right isn't enough. This country is a lynch mob about genetic engineering and embryos. The nut cases are coming out of the woodwork. Now throw in an admitted alcoholic. That's not the most sympathetic disease we could have come up with."

Rackley said nothing, staring off at a small knot of kids kicking an orange plastic ball across the lawn. He felt utterly lost, adrift, hopeless.

"I've talked to our lawyer," Caswell said. "If you plead, you'll get a few months down at Lompoc. You'll serve half of it, and the place is a country club. Some perfectly respectable people have been in Lompoc. And when you get out, you'll be worth about twenty million dollars."

"People in the past have gone to jail for scientific causes they believed in," Markham said.

Rackley ignored him. "What about Kaye?"

Caswell raised his hands. "When she doesn't show up for the arraignment, the feds will put a warrant out. I don't expect they'll deal on Kaye. But there won't be any blood tests. No evidence. So your child is safe for sure."

"And the laws will change," Markham said quietly. "The world will change. I promise you that. Kaye will never be prosecuted."

Rackley leaned forward for a moment. A cool breeze off the Bay came up suddenly. For the first time in years he thought about a drink. About just how nice it would be to crack open a cold can of beer and sip and think all this over from a great distance. What was that old AA saying?

"When things go bad," Rackley said aloud, "don't go with them."

"What?" Markham said, puzzled.

"Folk wisdom." Rackley looked up at Caswell and Markham. "Listen, I need to think about this. I'll call you tomorrow."

Rackley stood and so did Caswell; he was the kind to use his height and bulk as a rhetorical device. "Rackley, I know you're upset and confused. But I'm Kaye's brother. I want what's best for her and the baby. And this is it. The sooner you see it, the sooner we can put a cap on all this."

Rackley looked at Caswell, then Markham. "I need to talk to Kaye."

Markham gazed up at him with his placid, imperturbable expression. "I don't see how you're going to manage that," he said softly.

Without another word Rackley turned and walked out of the park. He walked quickly for two blocks, and then in the heart of North Beach he stepped to a pay phone and called Trina.

"Trina, we have to talk. Something's going on."

There was a very long silence at the other end of the line. "Trina?" he asked finally.

"Rackley, we should talk later."

"Okay. Sure."

"Rackley," she said after another long pause. "I'm supposed to be writing a press release right now. About you."

Even standing in the sun Rackley felt a quick chill. "What does it say?"

"I think I'm going to quit."

"What does it *say*?"

"I've got a bunch of notes from Caswell here."

For a moment Rackley could hear paper rustling, then Trina was back on the line. "It says that you're relieved of your duties and that United Genetics has severed all connection with you. That we had no knowledge of your illegal relationship with Lipsky, that it was against all company policy, and we strongly condemn any violation of the law." She paused. "It also says we're considering taking civil action against you and Lipsky."

Rackley stared at his reflection in the chrome face of the pay telephone and then began to laugh at the purely ludicrous nature of the idea. "They're going to *sue* me?"

"I'm sitting here and I'm staring at this stupid piece of paper, and I'm thinking that I'll quit, right now."

"No," Rackley said quickly. "Don't do that. Not right now."

"But Jesus, Rackley, they're railroading you. They're throwing you to the wolves."

"That's what they're doing. But I want you to stay there, stay inside. You're my only contact. If you leave, I'm really out in the cold."

"So you want me to—"

"Throw me to the wolves. It's already happened. This just makes it official."

There was another long pause. "Rackley," she said finally. "You know, you've always liked hanging around rich people. And I never knew why. But one thing I do know, no matter how nice rich people treat you, sooner or later, one day they turn to you and say, 'Here, hold this sack of shit, I've got to run.'"

"Just write the press release."

"All right," Trina said slowly, with great hesitation. "If that's what you want."

Suddenly Rackley realized that they were talking on United Genetics lines. He would tell Trina about Kaye's disappearance later. "Do it right. I'll talk to you tonight."

Rackley didn't feel like going home yet, and so he spent the next two hours on what had been his favorite walk with Kaye: out along the stretch of rock-strewn cliff where San Francisco met the Pacific, the rugged, beautiful bit of coastline called Land's End.

Rackley had walked Land's End in many states of mind. Once, during his worst moments while he was still drinking and his life and career were collapsing around him, he had come out here one late afternoon. He had stood on the craggy rocks, the scrub brush around his feet dusty red and soft green, and gazed down at the breakers a few hundred feet below, crashing violently against the rocks as they finally dissipated the energy of their long run across the Pacific. He had stared down and considered a single step into space, a moment of freefall, then a close, sudden and final, to his daily torment.

Something—perhaps the approach of some bicyclists—caused him to hesitate. He'd returned home that day and a few weeks later had his lunch with Caswell and been propelled into a new life, a new world.

Today he couldn't even imagine the kind of black despair that must have held him then. Now, as he strolled along the rocky path, gazing out at the rusting red bridge, the verdant hills of Marin across the choppy inlet, he thought instead of his walks along this same path with Kaye. On a Saturday they'd bring a blanket and picnic and just sit among the joggers, the lithe young men walking down to the nude beach, the other corduroy-clad hikers. They'd sit and stare at the Pacific, stretching far out of sight.

He had to find Kaye. He could not imagine that it was her own idea simply to disappear without so much as a hint of her where-abouts. He pulled out the crumpled piece of notepaper again.

Her brother seemed too sure, too certain of her health and ultimate return. If Caswell didn't know, then he was showing far too little concern considering his normal role as utterly over-protective older brother. Obviously his hand was in it. Rackley sat for another moment, watching a huge tanker slowly come into view on its way into the Bay.

Maybe he could make a deal with Caswell: agree to consider the guilty plea in return for learning where Kaye was hidden.

No—he had no intention of pleading guilty. With Lipsky they would fight this. Tortola the lawyer had said there were prece-dents- -denial of proper medical treatment. And clearly Kaye and Rackley weren't Lipsky's only patients. Who else? Rackley stood quickly and brushed the dry grass off the seat of his trousers. Too much about the genetic engineering industry had been bottled up too long: it was time to bring it all into the open.

In an odd way, Rackley realized, he was returning to his original occupation: investigative journalist. Only this time, *he* was at the center of the story.

That night the unseasonably warm spring weather broke. Once again the hot, dry air of the Central Valley drew great gouts of fog through the Golden Gate, blanketing Pacific Heights in a damp gray chill. As Rackley walked quickly uphill toward his house, the fog was broken only by streetlights and the yellow glow of living room lights, horizontal bars of gold between the slats of shutters on the Victorians along Baker Street.

Rackley felt for the moment quite distanced from the rush of events that had overtaken him in the previous two days. Somehow walking up the quiet, cool sidewalk toward his house filled him with a real sense of loss, an odd homesickness almost. He loved the neighborhood: the old squash courts at the gym up the street; the tiny boutiques that flourished, then vanished, on Sacramento Street; the markets for fish, meat, and cheese attending the community's obsession with fresh comestibles.

Baker Street had actually been his first home, he thought, after all the wandering of his earlier years. And he was, as he reached the wooden steps slightly damp with the moisture of new fog, glad to be home. He slowly walked to the front door, put the key in the lock, and turned. Nothing happened.

He tried the bottom lock. Again the key would not turn.

He held the key up to make certain it was the house key; it was, and he tried again, and still nothing.

With a certain tension now rising in his chest he went down the stairs and tried the street-level door that led to the side yard. It was locked as well, and once again his key would not work.

Something very odd was going on, he thought, and after a moment he crossed the street. Directly across lived Lucy Spinel, a widow who had been in the neighborhood for decades and had been friendly with Rackley and Kaye. He rang her doorbell, and after a long wait the diminutive white-haired woman opened the door.

"I saw you coming," she said. "I've been really sorry to read about your troubles."

Rackley nodded, not sure what to say. "Well—"

"Whatever Kaye did, I'm sure she had to do it."

"Thank you. It's a bad law and we're going to fight it."

"Come in."

Rackley stepped in, then stopped on the Oriental carpet in the hallway. "I'm having trouble getting in the house. I—"

"There was a locksmith truck there this afternoon," Mrs. Spinel said. "They were there for about an hour. They didn't fix the problem?"

Rackley was baffled. "No, I guess they didn't." He thought briefly. "Can I borrow your telephone for a minute?"

"Of course." Mrs. Spinel gestured toward the old telephone on the hall table, then discreetly withdrew.

Rackley quickly dialed Caswell's home number, and after two rings Caswell answered.

"Edward, I'm trying to get into my house. What's going on?"

There was a long silence at the other end. "Well," Caswell said finally, "there's a great deal going on, as I'm sure you're aware."

"I mean, about the house. The locks have been changed."

"Ah," Caswell said. "Your house."

"Did you do this?"

"Actually, we did. Let me explain why. As you know, the house is technically owned by the Caswell Trust. And given your current legal status, the family investment, Kaye's disappearance . . . I just think it's going to look better for us . . . that is, I think we can help you more, if you stay at arm's length. We're in a very delicate position here, and I'd expect you to be the first to recognize it."

"I need to get in the house."

"Our people packed some of your clothes. They're in a room under your name at the Stanford Court. Please, Rackley. Cooperate with this. Do you need money?"

"You're cutting me loose, aren't you? Just washing your hands of the whole business?"

"Of course not," Caswell said. "We've already discussed the solution to this problem. I said, do you need money?"

"I need to know where Kaye is. And I need to know about Lipsky's other patients."

"If you do need money, I can advance you some personally. Aside from that, I'm afraid United Genetics counsel has suggested we separate ourselves from your situation as much as possible."

Rackley pushed one hand back through his thick hair. "But you set this up. You told us to go to Lipsky."

"Wait a minute. You had questions about genetics. So I sent you to the best geneticist I know. And that's the beginning and end of it."

"But—"

"This is rotten, Rackley. You're family. But now it's up to you to do what the family needs." There was a long silence as Caswell took a deep breath. "Rackley, don't be selfish."

The line went dead. Rackley stood there for a moment, staring at the telephone. A great rush of blood went to his head, pure anger, absolute rage at being pushed aside so casually, as such a bug, a speck, a . . .

He picked up the telephone and dialed Caswell's number again, only to hear a busy signal.

Rackley took a cab to the hotel, on the crest of Nob Hill. There was indeed a room in his name and as he signed the registration card he saw that it was to be billed to United Genetics.

Rackley went up to the room, a large suite with a view east over the Bay. Standing at the window he could even see the laboratory complex of United Genetics; a cluster of light by the dark Bay. He had intended simply to pick up the two suitcases that were packed and set by the big bed, but as he approached them, he felt so exhausted that he stretched out on the bed fully clothed, just for a moment, just to rest.

When Rackley next opened his eyes, the lead-colored light of a San Francisco morning filled the big hotel room. It was nearly eight A.M. Rackley rubbed his face, moved stiffly up from the bed. He hadn't fallen asleep with his clothes on since he'd recovered; an odd feeling now, almost as if he were slightly hung over. Then the full recollection of the previous two days struck him again, and his malaise was quickly dissipated by a rush of adrenaline. He glanced at his watch; his meeting with Lipsky was for nine that morning. He had over an hour; Lipsky lived less than twenty minutes away.

He called room service and ordered a big breakfast. As long as United Genetics was paying, he was eating. But even as he did so, he decided that he would not stay at the hotel another night. Caswell and Markham were now his adversaries. And it would not do for them to know where Rackley was at any given moment of the day. Suddenly Rackley felt that his world was growing small and constricted.

Breakfast arrived; he wrote an extravagant tip on the room service bill, then turned on a morning news program as he ate his eggs. The local news reader was an attractive blonde, recently imported from Chicago; Rackley vaguely remembered meeting her at a party at Caswell's house a few months ago. Now she was reading a story about him.

The visual behind her head was the garish red outline of a baby, encoiled in the familiar double helix of DNA. "The case against Katherine Rackley and Stuart Lipsky," said the newscaster, "the San Francisco residents who two days ago were accused of illegal genetic engineering, may soon widen. Sources inside the federal prosecutor's office say that charges against Thomas Rackley, husband of Katherine, will be filed by week's end. Yesterday Rackley was fired by his employer, United Genetics. The giant genetics conglomerate may also sue their former PR man for theft of trade secrets.

"In a related story, this morning in Washington, D.C., the Reverend Gene Dixman, leader of Christians for Natural Progress, asked that Senator Mathew Gordon investigate the Lipsky-Rackley case during his upcoming hearings on genetic engineering."

The newswoman turned the page of her script, looking at the camera. "Reverend Dixman said yesterday, 'These are crimes against both God and humanity. Time is running out, and we must attack with a swift sword. There must be no secrets.'

"In other news . . ."

Rackley reached over and tapped the switch on the bedstand; the television fell silent. Everyone was getting into the act, he mused. He recalled a few years earlier when a major detergent conglomerate proposed genetic engineering to "downsize" cats to fit smaller living situations and require less food. Steven Hechinger had landed a single mention on the Reverend Gene Dixman's satellite-distributed Sunday morning Inspiration Hour.

"The hand of the devil itself," the old preacher had thundered, "is reaching out to touch the soul of Fido and Fluffy!" The company was deluged with thousands of complaint letters along with the threat of a national boycott. The next week the firm moved its bioengineers back into laundry enzyme chemistry.

Rackley sat and stared at the blank television screen. Dixman didn't even believe in evolution; Rackley idly wondered how the powerful old preacher explained genetic engineering to his followers. In the end the details didn't make much difference; all it meant was additional pressure to make an example of Kaye and Rackley.

If Larson, the federal attorney, brought charges against him, it could mean an immediate trip to jail. If the prosecutor even suspected that Kaye had disappeared, Rackley would become a flight risk also, and his bail would likely be astronomical. Clearly, Caswell wouldn't provide bail. And Rackley's own fortune was almost entirely on paper. United Genetics paper.

He had to disappear. He had to find Kaye. And for the first time in his life he found himself agreeing with Reverend Gene Dixman. There must be no secrets.

CHAPTER SEVENTEEN

Twenty minutes later Rackley took a cab from the hotel across town to Lipsky's house. After twice getting lost on the narrow, winding streets, the driver dropped Rackley off near the top of Twin Peaks. Old-time San Franciscans had fought a valiant but ultimately hopeless fight against the development of the last open land on the city's hilltops. Bit by bit houses and condominiums had appeared, crawling up through dusty vacant lots toward the peaks. The last houses built, on the land most contested, had the most remarkable views.

Lipsky's house was stunning: perched back on a very narrow lot, built three stories high, four counting the garage under the house. It was little wider than a single room, but even the front porch had a view not unlike the vista from a low-flying airplane: the city below, the hills of Marin and the East Bay out beyond.

The sliver of land alone must have cost half a million, Rackley thought; the passive solar house, all gray redwood and glass, probably twice as much. Markham had always suggested that he had rescued Lipsky from scientific oblivion by hiring him at United Genetics. Looking at the house, Rackley suspected that the rescue must have involved a spectacular salary as well.

Rackley rang the bell, hearing it chime electronically deep within the tall narrow house. He idly noticed that Lipsky's house had an excellent security system, including a tiny, low-light video camera on the porch. He recognized it only because he'd admired the same Japanese device at Markham's house; the monitor was in the kitchen, along with a little printer that automatically produced a picture of everyone who rang the doorbell. He'd suggested buying one for Kaye, but she demurred: too many gadgets in the house already, she'd said.

After a moment, when there was no answer and no sound from within the big house, Rackley pushed the doorbell again. He glanced at his watch; he was actually five minutes late for their meeting. Odd, he thought; Lipsky struck him as the compulsive sort who would never miss an appointment. Past that, he had sounded willing to talk about the case. Rackley shifted his weight from one foot to the other, turned, and admired the expansive view.

Standing on the porch, he recalled his first conversation with Lipsky three years earlier. It had been a cold winter day, out on Markham's huge stone terrace. Lipsky, shoulders hunched, sipping a Coke, was looking mournfully out at the Bay. Out of the blue he suddenly blurted, "I was at Asilomar, you know."

Rackley had looked at Lipsky with surprise. "You must have been a kid then."

Lipsky shrugged. "I was the youngest invited."

Rackley was impressed. The Asilomar conference, back in 1975, had shortly followed the discovery of recombinant DNA technology. Those were heady times. For biologists the ability to manipulate genetic material was the equivalent of nuclear fission. And perhaps as dangerous. For the first time in history scientists voluntarily declared a research moratorium.

In a secluded California meeting place two hundred of the brightest molecular geneticists on the planet wrestled with the consequences. Never before had scientists acted with such collective social conscience—and never would they do so again. The press seized on the story, quoting small-town mayors who inveighed against "Frankenstein monsters" in their communities. The damage was done: the public didn't trust the genetic engineers, and the genetic engineers no longer trusted the public.

"That must have been quite a meeting," Rackley had said that chill afternoon on Markham's veranda.

"I think of it often," Lipsky said softly. "I think how naive we were to believe that two hundred of us could control that technology. I don't think at Asilomar we ever believed that it would lead so quickly to . . ."

"To human genetic engineering."

Lipsky had merely nodded. "We live and learn," he said lightly, and raised his glass.

Now, standing on Lipsky's porch, Rackley finally reached out and tried the front doorknob, which turned. He hesitated for a moment. If the alarm system was on, a huge din would break loose when he pushed it open. He hesitated again, then pushed.

The door swung open and no great clanging ensued. Rackley stepped into the foyer, a small alcove of white walls and a bleached oak floor. Directly ahead was the living room, long and narrow, ending in tall French doors that looked out on a tiny, deep green garden.

"Stuart," Rackley called out. "Dr. Lipsky? Are you here? Anyone home?"

The house had the sound of vacancy. Rackley began to walk around the first floor, which had only a guest bathroom, living room, a small dining room, and kitchen. The house was filled with very modern, tasteful furniture and a few well-tended plants. There was a slight, odd odor in the air that Rackley could not place, but there was not a speck of dust anywhere, not a single dead ficus leaf. A regular housekeeper, Rackley guessed.

He passed through the living room, turning into the dining room with a long glass table for eight, dried flowers in the center. A handful of mail was scattered on the table; Rackley glanced at it and saw mostly junk advertisements, along with an American Express bill. Rackley picked up the bill. Lipsky owed $2,398; all new charges, converted from pesos, primarily from a ticket on Mexicana Airlines and a week in a Mexico City hotel.

Rackley put the bill back on the table and walked into the kitchen. It was blinding white, ultra high tech, with a Sub-Zero refrigerator and a restaurant-sized stove. Rackley wondered if Lipsky had ever even used his status appliances. Over by the sink he saw the porch monitor, a tiny five-inch flat-screen TV. He glanced around for the printer and saw it attached to the cabinet. From the bottom of the small dull silver box a strip of thermal printer paper uncurled. Rackley reached out and ripped it off. There was, as he expected, a picture of himself. And then one other photo: an ethnic-looking man with long hair. The time/date stamp in the corner said that it had been taken at 9:17 the night before. Rackley folded the two photos and put them in his jacket pocket.

It was about then that Rackley finally focused on the odd odor he had noticed when he first opened the door. The smell was stronger in the kitchen, and when he saw the stairs in the corner, descending to the garage level, he suddenly recognized what it was.

"Oh shit," Rackley said.

He opened the door and was met by dense fumes. He went back to the sink, found a cotton dish towel in a cabinet, soaked it in cold water, and wrapped it across his mouth and nose.

He started down the steps into the dim garage until he found a light switch and clicked it on. From his vantage point above he could look down on the concrete-floored parking space, where a new burgundy BMW was neatly parked. He descended the stairs two at a time, and as he came down, he could see a crumpled figure in the backseat of the car. The BMW's windows were open. On the right side of the dashboard the red ignition light glowed dimly: the car's engine had run until it exhausted the oxygen in the closed-off garage, then stalled.

Rackley opened the back door of the sedan. Lipsky, in a checked sports coat, was lying with arms folded across his chest, head turned so that one cheek pressed against the black leather of the seat, eyes half-open. His face was pale white, his lips and fingernails as blue as periwinkle blooms. When Rackley lowered the cold, wet rag from his face, the sharp scent of urine pierced the dense smell of stale exhaust. He didn't even need to touch Lipsky to know that the luckless geneticist had been dead for hours.

That same day Caswell and Markham asked Trina to lunch in the small private dining room on the top floor of the United Genetics building, set off to the side of Markham's office. If one looked carefully from the wide windows, it was possible to make out in the distance the United Genetics research facility sprawling along the Berkeley shoreline. The room was elegantly furnished, lacking the eccentricity of Markham's own office, and the china and silver were first quality. The menu, however, reflected Markham's spartan appetites: salad, broiled fish, steamed vegetables.

As they ate, Trina briefed the two executives on the plans for the Caswell Clinic opening in Mexico City. "It's good timing. By scheduling the symposium on the diseases of overpopulation for the same week, we'll get a lot of legitimate reporters from the U.S. who wouldn't come down just for a press junket."

"It's very important, especially now," Markham said, "that

we make it clear that United Genetics is doing socially important work. Between Lipsky and Rice Five we have all the bad publicity we need."

"Oh, I think that's going to be obvious. Have you looked at the papers for the symposium? There's some good science and some good medicine." She smiled slightly. "And the clinic opening itself sounds like quite an event."

Caswell nodded. "Delgado's got a bunch of Mexican honchos showing up. And we might even get one or two senators down also."

The talk about the clinic opening lasted for the rest of lunch, until the uniformed waitress had removed the dishes and left a carafe of coffee. Only then did the topic turn to Trina herself.

"We want you to take Rackley's position," Markham said without preface. "We'd like to name you as a vice president immediately. Announce it today, if possible."

Trina simply stared for a moment, absorbing the news, feeling at once wonderful and torn. Eight years ago she had been up on three misdemeanors, one felony, and was washing dishes in a rehab unit. Now she was being offered a vice presidency at a major corporation. There was a saying in the program—if you keep coming back, the promises come true—and this was something that would once have seemed an utter impossibility. But her own feelings about United Genetics were now changing quickly. More to the point, she was earning this over Rackley's fallen body.

"You've been doing a fine job," Markham said, clearing his throat as the silence stretched on, "and we don't see any reason to go outside the company."

"Well," Trina said, "I mean, I'm honored. This is . . . ."

"It's important," Markham continued, "that we keep a sense of continuity with the press. I don't want any uncertainty now that Rackley's left us."

"I hope," Caswell said, less warmly than Markham, "that your association with Rackley won't make it more difficult for you to handle this. There's bound to be some unpleasant publicity about him."

Trina gazed at both of them for a long time. "Before we go any further, I have to know one thing. Rackley says that Lipsky had done this work before." She pursed her lips, looked down at her coffee, then decided that there was no diplomatic way to phrase the question. "Just tell me: Are we covering anything up here?"

There was a long silence in the little dining room. Caswell looked at Markham, his eyes very brown in the bright light from the window overlooking the Bay. After a moment Markham cleared his throat. "If we are covering up anything, it's that Stuart Lipsky is . . . a little crazy."

"For God's sake," Caswell exploded. "Make that very crazy. The man was falling to pieces as we watched."

Trina looked puzzled. "So why did you send Kaye and Rackley to see him?"

Caswell appeared pained. "Kaye was upset. I hoped that Lipsky could say something about the biochemistry of the problem, that there might be a cure at some point." He shook his head. "I didn't think it would do any harm. And I certainly didn't think Lipsky would see it as an opportunity to recruit some guinea pigs."

He looked at Markham, then Trina. "I'll admit it: I was stupid. I should never have sent them to Lipsky."

"No. We should have let Lipsky go months ago," Markham said. "He was useless. Worse than useless. Just moping around that lab, planning experiments that we could never allow him to do."

"But what about Megan Collins? How did she get involved?"

"Did you ever spend time with her socially?" Markham asked.

Trina frowned. "Just nodding acquaintance, really."

"Megan is as crazy as Lipsky," Caswell said. "Strictly off the record—although it might help reporters understand this story—Megan Collins is in a very expensive psychiatric ward right now, and her husband doesn't expect her home anytime soon. God knows what she and Lipsky came up with together. Frankly, between them the whole thing could be fantasy."

Trina shook her head quickly. "This is really confused."

"Exactly," Caswell said. "And what we have to do is separate United Genetics from all this as quickly as possible."

"Do we have a new vice president?" Markham asked softly.

Trina nodded. "You do."

"I'm very happy," Markham said. "You're going to do a wonderful job. And I don't think there is anything but good news to come."

At that moment a secretary knocked quietly at the door of the small dining room. "I'm sorry to interrupt, Mr. Markham. But there's a call from the U.S. attorney's office. Dr. Lipsky has killed himself."

* * *

Rackley's call to 911 set off three long hours of controlled chaos.

After giving his name and Lipsky's address, Rackley sat in the living room for only a few minutes before an ambulance plus a police car pulled into the driveway. There was a loud knock at the front door, and when Rackley opened it, he directed the two paramedics to the stairway in the kitchen.

"He's in the backseat of the car," Rackley said as they disappeared into the house. Rackley turned back and was startled to see that one of the two officers on the porch was a regular from his AA meeting.

Michael G. was in his early thirties, with red hair and a fleshy face and a slight paunch. Rackley had heard his story a few times and knew vaguely that he was some kind of police officer. Rackley had only seen him in blue jeans and vinyl windbreakers; today, Michael G. was in full uniform. While his eyes clearly showed that he recognized Rackley, he gave no outward indication past a quick, almost imperceptible nod.

"I'm Officer Gillespie, this is Officer Jankins. You are Thomas Rackley?"

Rackley nodded.

"Of United Genetics?" Gillespie asked. "You worked with Lipsky?"

Rackley nodded again.

"Okay," Gillespie said. "You take a statement," he told his partner. "I'm going to make a call."

Rackley and the other officer stood in the foyer of the expensive house for a moment. While the cop took notes, Rackley related simply the events of the morning: he had a meeting with Lipsky, there was no answer to the bell, the door was unlocked, he followed the smell of exhaust.

"What was the nature of your visit?"

"Just business."

Moments later Gillespie came back into the foyer. "That's enough," he told his partner. He looked at Rackley. "You'll need to come down to the station." For the first time his voice softened slightly. "Just for a statement. The feds are going to take it from there." He paused for a moment. "You could call your lawyer from here."

"I think," Rackley said, "that's a good idea."

By the time they reached the Mission District substation, an investigator from the federal prosecutor's office was already on the

scene. The lawyer Tortola arrived shortly after, taking a cab down
from the university, and instructed Rackley to say nothing beyond
the statement he had made earlier.

After two hours Rackley was told he could go. "But don't
leave town," the desk sergeant told him. "We may need to take a
longer statement after the autopsy."

"I second that advice," the prosecutor's assistant said. "We
will definitely be in touch."

Thirty minutes later Trina picked him up in an alley around the
side entrance of the station.

"Rackley," she said as soon as he climbed into her small car,
"could you have made this any more difficult?"

Rackley raised his hands. "I went to see Lipsky. He was dead.
What was I supposed to do? Sneak out?"

"You could have called me first."

"God. That sounds like something I'd say."

Trina sighed deeply, shaking her head, both hands on the
steering wheel but not yet starting the car. "Okay. I have to go
back to the office and finish a press release about Lipsky. People
want bios, background, all of that."

"What does Markham say?"

"He's incredibly pissed off. I've actually never seen him so
angry. I'm not sure why."

"I think he liked Lipsky."

Trina shrugged. "Beats me. But at least we're not stonewalling it. That was my fear. Having to pick up the telephone and say
'Lipsky who?'"

She sighed again. "Shall I take you home?"

"I can't go home. Caswell locked me out."

"How can he do that?"

"That's not all." Rackley turned to face Trina, and a chill puff
of air blew through the side window of the car. Bracing, the air
made him feel keenly, almost supernaturally alert. It was, he
knew, an adrenaline high: after years of abstaining, his body was
extremely sensitive to its own stimulants. He forced himself to
think carefully. "This has to be a dead secret. Promise?"

"Of course."

"Kaye's gone."

"What?"

Rackley took out the note he had been carrying and handed it
to Trina.

She read it quickly. "Oh boy," she said. "Oh boy." She looked at him. "You don't know where she is?"

"I have no idea."

Trina looked back at the note for a long moment. "You can stay at my place for now."

"No one should know."

Trina nodded. "That goes for me too."

For years Trina had lived in the same big, white-painted loft south of Market Street, with polished wood floors, filled with plants, light and airy. The neighborhood, once decrepit, had grown fashionable; the artist who originally inhabited the loft had been driven out when rents rose. Trina had taken the loft as soon as she saw it; somehow it seemed less bourgeois than a condominium on Nob Hill or a restored Victorian flat in Noe Valley. It was big and modern and industrial, and Trina liked it.

Rackley spent the rest of the afternoon at the loft, while Trina returned to United Genetics to finish covering Lipsky's death. Rackley was still exhausted, and after sitting for a few minutes, making notes on the events of the day, he stretched out on the big couch in the middle of the room and fell asleep.

Sometime during the afternoon he found himself dreaming of faces of people he knew—Trina, Kaye, Caswell, Markham. In the dream, however, they were all curiously elastic, constantly transforming themselves, blending into one another as if the flesh itself were some kind of mutable rubber. Then, from a great distance, he seemed to be looking down on his friends, reclining, relaxing, their bodies at ease amidst a green meadow of grass. Again, however, their flesh itself began to intermix in an almost liquid fashion, entwining, blending, in an altogether asexual yet terribly disturbing fashion, bodies flowing together, transmuting, all in some phantasmagoric biological stew. And then suddenly, out of nowhere, a great wind came up across the grassy field and picked up all of the intermixed, transmuted bodies, none now recognizable as a single individual, picked them up as if they were nearly weightless and blew them away like the driest and lightest of autumn leaves, leaving behind nothing but the green meadow, now empty, lonely, silent.

It was dark when he was awakened by the sound of a shower, coming over the high walls of the bathroom in the far corner of the loft. He shook his head to dispel the last images of his dream and sat up to see Trina's leather briefcase on the chair. He leaned back

on the sofa, and after another minute or so the shower stopped and
Trina came out of the bathroom.

Her dark brown hair was tangled and wet and she was wearing
a white terry cloth bathrobe.

"How'd it go?" Rackley asked.

Trina pushed her damp hair back. "Oh, we were on the
telephone all afternoon, answering questions about you and
Lipsky. I'm beat. I took a shower to wake up."

Rackley looked at her. "Has the official line changed?"

Trina sat for a moment on the arm of the couch, pulling the
robe closer around her. "Not really. We're shocked, a full
investigation, et cetera."

Rackley said nothing, leaned his head back against the head of
the couch, and closed his eyes.

Trina reached out and rubbed his shoulder. "Listen," she said
finally, "I have to dry my hair, then let's get something to eat."

"Sure." Rackley literally had not thought about food since
breakfast in the hotel, which now seemed like weeks ago.

Trina turned and went back into the bathroom. He heard a hair
dryer click on with a high electric whine.

Rackley pushed aside a stack of newspapers piled on the couch
next to him. Trina had never been a terribly tidy housekeeper. As
he leaned over to set the papers atop another scatter of junk mail
and magazines, his gaze stopped on one of Trina's oak end tables.
In the center of the table, next to a glass vase with six drooping
daisies, sat a small pistol, the grip made of neatly turned walnut,
the barrel dark shiny blue.

Staring at the gun, Rackley felt a sinking depression. What
was Trina doing with a pistol? It was as if all the people he thought
he knew were no longer the same—as if he were living in the
world he had dreamed, filled with false assumptions.

He sat for perhaps another thirty seconds, gazing at the gun,
and then he heard the hair dryer snap off. "Trina," he called over
the walls of the bathroom. "What the hell are you doing with a
gun?"

Trina came back out of the bathroom, fastening a silver
bracelet on her wrist. "Oh," she said, clearly discomfited, "that's
not a real gun."

Rackley reached over and picked it up gingerly. "Looks like a
real gun."

"It's an air gun. I just got it last week. It's used for
competition, in the Olympics, stuff like that. Made in Germany.
Cost three hundred and fifty dollars."

Rackley continued to examine it dubiously, and Trina walked over, taking it out of his hand. "It can't really hurt anybody. I don't know, maybe you could kill a squirrel with it. And here's the nice part."

She cocked the little air pistol and raised it to firing position, aiming at the other side of her loft, fully seventy feet away, beside a long line of high windows. She aimed carefully. There was a quiet *pfft* of air as she squeezed off a shot, and a dull thud as the pellet buried itself in ballistic putty. Only then did Rackley see the small metal target box at the other end of the loft.

She turned back to Rackley. "See? It's quiet. You can come home and blast away to your heart's content." She walked across the loft and examined the target, then turned back to Rackley, tossing her dark hair to one side. "I used to be a pretty good shot."

Rackley was still gazing at her, relieved, but still slightly bemused.

Trina shrugged, putting the air gun down on the dining room table. "I don't know. I just felt like it."

Rackley shook his head. "Well," he said. "I suppose it's better than collecting Avon bottles."

She stopped in front of the couch. "What are you going to do?"

"I want to find Kaye. And then I want to find out what Caswell and Markham know about this."

Rackley could smell a trace of perfume as Trina approached the couch. She stood in front of him for a moment. "You know, I still can't believe you did it."

Rackley frowned. "What's not to believe?"

"I don't know." She turned away, walking toward the other side of the loft, idly turning the bracelet on her wrist. "Markham says that Lipsky was a fraud."

Rackley nodded. "I don't know why he's saying that."

"So you really think it will work. That your child won't be a drunk, won't be an addict."

"I think so," Rackley said. "It's just surgery, that's all. Very delicate surgery."

Trina was silent for a long moment, then sighed. "It feels funny to me. It's like you hate something inside yourself. It's like rejecting a part of yourself."

"It's a part I hate. Something that causes a lot of pain."

Trina stood at one of the big windows on the west wall of the loft and looked out at the city. "Sure. Funny thing, though, some of the best people I know used to be drunks or addicts. What do the Irish call it? 'The good man's weakness.'"

"Take away the weakness and you'll still have the good man."

"Sure," Trina said, and then turned quickly. "I think it's that in a way you're rejecting me, and all the other people in the program. I guess that's what it feels like."

Rackley felt his anger rise. "It's a *disease*. That's all I'm rejecting."

"Fifty years ago nobody knew it was a disease. What if people decide that"—she gestured vaguely around the room, trying to come up with an example—"being heavy is a disease, and they want to fix my kids. God, if we ever got really good at gene therapy, they'd eliminate half the traits I have. What if . . ." She shook her head. "I don't know. We all want blond hair, or blue eyes, or . . . Do we end up with a world full of Kaye Caswells?"

"Look," Rackley said, deadly serious. "I have no idea what the answer is and nobody else does. All I know is that Kaye and I didn't want to raise a child and love it and teach it and suddenly see him come home one night with that look in his eye and know that the cute little kid was on his way to hell."

Rackley stood up. "Damn. Of all people, I would think you'd understand. You know what the life is like. You know how Vincent died. You're recovering, I'm recovering, but nine out of ten alcoholics die drunk. Maybe you need to think that being an addict and an alcoholic is some soul-strengthening experience, some wonderful learning experience. Maybe you need that. But not for my child. And deep inside you know better. It's hell, it's degrading, and if you don't die, you wish you did. I've been there, you've been there, and now you're saying it's something we're supposed to keep."

Trina said nothing, standing stock-still.

"Jesus." Rackley raised one hand, dropped it. "Of all people . . ."

Suddenly he felt utterly isolated. Trina was his last real contact—and now she seemed to have turned against him also. "Jesus," he repeated angrily. "Just forget it. I don't need to hear this." He turned to leave. "I don't need your help."

Trina rubbed her forehead for a moment. She took a deep breath. "I'm sorry," she said softly. "I didn't mean . . ." She pursed her lips, trying to think what she did mean. "I guess that this thing—AA, NA, all that—I guess it's the one thing we still have in common. And I feel threatened when it looks like you're just going to turn your back on it. That somehow you can just buy your way out."

Rackley felt his anger begin to ebb. "Well. I'm not turning my back on anything. I can't. It's in me, and you and I will be going to meetings until they carry us out. But that doesn't mean I have to pass it on."

"Okay." Trina said. "Sure," and she took a few steps forward. "I'm sorry." She put her arms out. "Hug?"

Rackley, shaking slightly, took Trina in his arms. She held him tightly, and her warmth was the most reassurance he had felt all day. "It's going to be fine," she said softly, "just fine." They held each other, and he stroked her hair and gradually became aware of her perfume, and then involuntarily he became aroused. Trina held him and turned her head slightly and suddenly she was gently kissing his neck, and he felt a strong surge of desire, like an electrical charge in his limbs, tingling, his legs momentarily weak.

Her lips moved across his chin and in a moment they were kissing. Her tongue began to probe his mouth, and abruptly he pulled back, still holding her, not looking at her face.

"I'm sorry," Trina said quietly after a moment. "I don't seem to be doing anything right today."

"Trina—"

"I've really, really missed you, Rackley."

Rackley took a deep breath. "I have to find Kaye. Will you help me?"

Trina's grip on him loosened slightly, changing in emphasis almost imperceptibly. "Of course I will," she said. "You know I will."

On the morning the old crayfish hunter finally returned to Kline Slough, the Delta sun was still low, casting long shadows over the green fields. It had been weeks since the appearance of the bizarre water plant and the parade of odd vehicles had chased him from his favorite fishing ground, sending him twenty miles north to a less-traveled corner of the Delta.

Now, however, the word was out: the strange weed was some sort of rice—a hybrid, he supposed—that was causing no end of trouble in the local irrigation systems. As he walked slowly down the bank, the old man noticed that farmer Kline had a set of gas-powered pumps lined up along the levee to pull water from the river into the fields. In the cool of the morning the motors weren't yet operating. But the fisherman had heard the unfamiliar sound of the small pumps all over the Delta recently. Rumor had it that the company that came up with the hybrid was paying off farmers left and right to keep them quiet.

It sounded as if the world was settling down to business as usual, and so the old man was also gradually returning to his habits. Today was the first time he would pull a trap from Kline Slough, and he was already anticipating the haul. This was always

a productive area for the sweet little crustaceans, and he had
missed the harvest in weeks past.

He made his way down to the edge of the calm water. Here
and there the new water plant was still growing in bright green
stands, scattered among the horsetails and blackberries and
willows. To the old man, however, it no longer looked like some
alien intruder. The plant seemed to be settling in as part of nature.
That was how it worked, he thought: people can do whatever they
want, but sooner or later nature has the last word.

A moment later he found the galvanized chain staked to the
muddy bank. He pulled up the stake and then started to reel in the
chain, feeling the trap rise up from the bottom, about eight feet out
from shore. It felt light as he pulled, and when the old wire trap
broke the surface, he saw that there were fewer than a half dozen
little crayfish within.

"Damn," he said half aloud. That was barely enough to pay
for the can of catfood he used as bait. He continued to pull, and as
the trap came closer, he saw that the situation was even worse than
he had thought.

Five dark blue-green crayfish in all—scrawny ones, too,
smaller than usual. And then he looked more closely. Four of the
five were floating free in the water, quite dead.

"Damn," he said again, setting the trap down on the bank. He
hitched up his overalls and squatted down to look more closely.
Even the single live one was waving its tiny pincers in a distinctly
debilitated fashion. It was unlikely to survive, dumped in a bucket
with fifty or sixty more lively brethren. Right unusual, he thought,
opening the top, pouring the miserable catch back into the river.
As he watched, the dead crayfish drifted slowly downstream,
passing the upturned white belly of a small bass floating stationary
in the weeds.

"Damn," he said a third time, standing up, brushing off his
knees, looking up and down the still, bright water for a long
moment. Kline Slough, he thought, just seemed like more trouble
than it was worth.

Trina Robbins sat in her office at once dreading and anticipating the lunch appointment, momentarily dawdling at her desk
even though she knew a company car already awaited her in the
basement garage.

For Trina the last few days had passed in a vague haze of
confusion and stress. She was still embarrassed about the scene
with Rackley in the loft and felt like a fool each time she thought

of it. Rackley had said nothing more, bedding down on the big white couch, far too absorbed in his own turmoil to sense the sexual tension that Trina found hard to ignore. Since that night, however, she had been scrupulously formal and sisterly around Rackley.

In fact, after the lunch with Caswell and Markham, the business of filling Rackley's position ensured that her thoughts rarely strayed from work. Her first priority was to deflect reporters' questions about Lipsky and Katherine Rackley, following Markham's instructions to disassociate United Genetics from the case as quickly as possible. In addition she was now overseeing the preparations for the opening of the new Caswell Clinic and the Conference on the Diseases of Overpopulation.

The Conference had been scheduled for months, and there was no way it could be delayed. In fact Markham insisted that the event go on as planned: the Conference had been intentionally timed to precede the Senate hearings on genetic engineering; it would not hurt, Markham knew, for United Genetics' name to be linked with solid science.

And United Genetics needed all the favorable press it could garner. There was now a steady parade of pickets in front of corporate headquarters, protesting either Rice Five in the Delta or the Lipsky case. It had reached the point, in fact, where Trina couldn't even keep the demonstrators separate. Luckily, after an initial media blitz, they attracted relatively little attention: demonstrators alone were no longer enough to earn air time. But another development promised to be far less tractable: The day after the Lipsky case broke, the Natural Progress leader Steven Hechinger once again flew to San Francisco.

"He's calling this the smoking gun," Markham had warned Trina after summoning her to his office early that morning. Markham's Washington connections were legion, and he always seemed to have excellent information on Congressional activity. This time, he told Trina, Hechinger hoped to use Kaye's arrest and Lipsky's suicide as proof that commercial genetic engineering was out of control.

"He's going to be disappointed, of course," Markham said with easy confidence, leaning back behind his oiled birch desk and stretching his thin arms. "I really don't think there's anything he can learn here, besides the fact that Lipsky was unbalanced and irresponsible." He finished stretching and leaned forward, suddenly focusing on Trina. "But I want you to set up a meeting with him as soon as you can. And make sure he does as little damage as possible."

Trina opened her mouth to tell Markham that in fact Hechinger had already called her, then hesitated. "Of course," she said. "Consider it done."

During Hechinger's previous trip to San Francisco, Trina had found the energetic, balding activist far more appealing than she had expected. On his last afternoon in the Bay area she had taken him on a brief visit to a botanical garden, a little pocket of exotic greenery in the hills above the University of California campus. It was in fact not far from the rehabilitation clinic where she first met Rackley; back then, once they were allowed off the grounds of the facility, the two had taken long walks together on the arboretum's quiet trails.

That day, only a few weeks earlier, Trina and Hechinger had spent an hour or so strolling the same paths, looking at the remarkable range of plants, many of them rare species soon to be extinct in the wild. The oddly unseasonable weather of the previous weeks had temporarily yielded to a crisp, blustery spring afternoon. Already there were tiny shoots everywhere and the garden was filled with a thousand subtle shades of new green. Dozens of the cacti and succulents were in flower, with bright, incandescent blossoms in unlikely shapes and extraordinary sizes.

"God," Hechinger had finally said that afternoon. "When you see this incredible diversity of species, all these wonderful creations, you end up wondering. I mean, why we don't spend our resources saving the species we have? Instead we wipe out whole populations, then try to create new ones in the laboratory."

Trina had sensed no anger in the observation; Hechinger was so enthralled by the beauty of the garden that his voice had lost its inquisitory edge. He seemed to become a little boy who simply loved nature, and who couldn't figure out what was happening to his world.

"Maybe we need to do both," Trina suggested. "United Genetics does a lot of work in the rain forests, trying to locate species before they're extinct. We've donated quite a few specimens to this garden, in fact." She caught herself. "But that's not why I brought you here. I just thought you'd like it."

"But you don't search out these plants to save them in nature," Hechinger said with a trace of sadness. He stopped for a moment, kneeling to touch the variegated leaves, green and orange, of a rare African succulent. "You do it because you think you might need the genes someday to plug into some organism. You don't want the plants; you want their genes." He looked up at her. "It's unnatural."

"I wonder," Trina said. "Why do you call it unnatural just because humans do something? Is an engineered plant any less natural than a termite mound?"

"Yes," Hechinger said quickly. "If it's something like Rice Five. We have intelligence, and we can make choices, and when we choose to damage the planet, we're acting unnaturally."

He stood again and shook his head. "No, I'm afraid your Rice Five is only the beginning." He looked over at Trina. "What was the first major nonmedical trait genetically characterized?"

Trina frowned. "Eye color?" she guessed.

"Read the journals. It was the forbidden sequence. First thing we did was clone the sequence for intelligence. Not compassion, not charity, not love. Pure cold intelligence." He reached out and brushed a frond of a spidery green fern beside the pebbled path. "We're already too smart for our own good, but we still want more."

That afternoon Trina had glanced at her watch. "We better get back."

"I'm sorry. I didn't mean to lecture."

"I didn't mind," Trina said, and she felt, for the first time, a certain warmth toward the tall intense man. For a moment she nearly invited him to dinner, but she hesitated, uncharacteristically shy. Later that day Trina dropped him off at his hotel; he had flown out the next morning.

Now, less than a month later, they were meeting again under far different circumstances. Hechinger had specified a small Italian restaurant in North Beach; he insisted on paying for all his meals and kept a scrupulously tight budget. Ten minutes late, stomach knotted with apprehension, Trina walked into the dim-lit old restaurant and saw him sitting in a Leatherette booth at the back. Hechinger was wearing a corduroy sports coat and a knit tie, loose at the neck. For a moment she found herself hoping, against rational expectation, that there might still be the beginning of a relationship between them.

She walked up to the booth and he stood and they shook hands. But then Hechinger's first words made it clear that he was very angry.

"I want to talk to Thomas Rackley."

Trina flinched at the tone of his voice and busied herself for a moment unfolding her napkin. "I can't help you with that," she said finally.

"Are you lying to me?"

"Wait a minute," Trina said, already reeling from his quick anger.

"The way Rackley lied to me?" Hechinger leaned across the table. "Lied to the goddamn world. You took me around, gave me the whole dog and pony show, and all the while you were doing embryo engineering in the back room."

"You don't understand. He was . . ." Trina stopped for a moment, blinking, trying to sort out whose side she was on.

"I really don't care what the official line is right now," Hechinger said coldly. "I want to hear the story from him."

Trina paused, trying to steady her emotions. There was not a shred of the warmth she recalled in Hechinger. "You'll have to find him yourself," she said, retreating into her corporate role. "We really don't have any contact with him now."

"I'll subpoena him," Hechinger said. "I hope you know that."

"It's really none of my business."

"But what I'd really like to do," Hechinger said, "is to help him."

This sudden turn took Trina by surprise. "What?"

"Jesus." Hechinger rubbed his face with both hands. "I'm sorry. I'm not mad at you. I'm mad at Markham, I'm mad at United Genetics. Not you."

"Hard to tell," Trina said cautiously.

"I'm sorry. I truly am. I haven't slept for two days, since all this started. I mean, it's all in front of me, and I can't seem to put it together." He raised his head, stroked his chin, pausing for a moment. "What I'm wondering," he said, "is whether . . ."

He raised one hand. "Let me back up. United Genetics threw Rackley and his wife to the wolves. And I think they put Lipsky in a position where he had to kill himself." He looked at Trina for a moment. "Did you know he called me the night he died?"

"What?" Trina said, baffled. "Lipsky called you?"

Hechinger leaned back, clearly satisfied by Trina's reaction. "He said we needed to talk. That there was something I had to know."

"What was it?"

"That's all he said. We were going to meet this morning."

Trina sat back in the red booth. "I'm sorry," she said, "about him."

"I'm sorry that he ever got hooked up with Paul Markham." He shook his head. "It's too late for him. But I was thinking about our talk in the arboretum that day. And I'm wondering whether you might not have some mixed feelings about your employer right now."

"What do you mean?"

"Is there any kind of background you can give me, strictly off the record?"

"What you're wondering," Trina said, "is whether I'll be an inside source for you."

Hechinger looked away, looked back. "I think you're the kind of person who would like to know the truth. And I don't think you're being told the truth. I'd like to help you."

Trina watched him, weighing this in her mind. She had to give him credit for excellent instincts. He had immediately sensed just who might turn into a source for him and had courted her sufficiently that under different circumstances she might well have been inclined to help. But her first loyalty was to Rackley.

"Sorry," she said. "You read me wrong. What you see here is the truth, and if it disappoints you, then go make something up. But I'm not going to help you hang my friends."

Hechinger's face hardened, and after a moment his initial anger returned. "God," he said in low, almost guttural tones, "I can't understand people like you. I mean, a whole generation has completely lost its sense of outrage, of responsibility. It's the most critical moment in history—when evolution turns on itself, when we control the destiny of all humans to come. And it's being run by people like you—goddamn cookie-cutter MBA's and PR hounds and accountants and junior bankers who can't see further than making your first million."

"Wait a minute," Trina said, involuntarily reaching one hand across the smooth tabletop. "That's totally unfair."

"No." Hechinger took the napkin from his lap and threw it on the table. "You just listen for a minute, instead of spouting the party line. It's tragic. We finally have the power to control nature and the controls are in the hands of the most amoral, greed-driven generation in history, destroying the environment with idiotic new species, selling human qualities to the highest bidders."

Hechinger abruptly stood up. "Maybe it's what we deserve. Maybe this is how the species ends, drowning in greed and avarice and the stupidity of a generation that never learned anything but how to make money."

He gazed down at Trina for a moment. "Funny thing," he said. "When I first met you, I thought there was something different about you. That maybe the corporate intelligence might have some kind of heart. But I was wrong."

Hechinger turned, began to walk away, then turned back. "I'll see you in Washington," he said. "Under oath."

"Steve—" Trina started to say, rising from her chair, but the tall activist was already halfway through the restaurant, striding fast, not once looking back.

She sat back down, sighed deeply, and toyed for a moment with her fork, suddenly realizing that her hand was shaking. She felt terrible. Her stomach was churning and she wished devoutly that it didn't have to be this way.

After a minute the waiter came by. "Is everything all right? Can I get you anything?"

For the first time in a very long time Trina thought for the briefest moment that a tall vodka-grapefruit would taste very good just now. She shook her head briefly, as if to clear it.

"I'm sorry." Trina carefully set her fork down, gazing for a moment at the chair where Hechinger had been sitting. "I'm afraid our lunch has been canceled."

The Environmental Protection Agency man remembered Trina from their meeting at the old hotel in the Delta, and so he called her first. It was just past two in the afternoon, and she had returned from her disastrous lunch to find another assignment from Markham sitting on her desk. The previous day he had requested a complete position paper on human genetic engineering in case he was called to testify at the upcoming Senate hearing. She had delivered a rough draft to him that morning.

It had been a difficult job: she was to distance United Genetics from Rackley and Lipsky as much as possible, yet still press to loosen the restrictions on research. In her first draft she had suggested that if the restrictions were eased, there might be less pressure for individuals to take matters into their own hands. The draft had come back from Markham with a red X through that paragraph. *"Keep us out of Rackley's problems,"* Markham had written in the margin. *"We're not making any excuses for him."*

She was just pondering this delicate point when her telephone sounded and her secretary announced the EPA agent.

"Hi," Trina said, grateful for any distraction. "How's it going?"

"Ms. Robbins, it's not going well at all."

Trina reflexively ripped a page from her yellow pad and started taking notes. "Not well," she repeated.

"We started getting complaints from fishermen two days ago," he said. "So we asked DFG to do a fish mortality survey in the Delta."

"DFG?"

"Department of Fish and Game."

"Right, sorry."

"These are preliminary results," the agent said, "but we're seeing a definite upward trend in fish mortality, measured on the basis of floating carcasses. Seven percent increase striped bass, twelve percent in catfish, five percent sturgeon. A couple of salmon, but not enough to be statistically significant. The commercial crayfish harvesters report a definite decline in catches."

Trina realized that she was copying all these figures without understanding what was going on. "What does this mean?"

"Fish are dying in the Delta," the agent said. "We're not sure why."

"But you think Rice Five is involved?"

"Maybe not. But DFG is pretty suspicious."

"I don't get it," Trina said. "How could a rice plant kill fish?"

Trina immediately called Caswell and Markham. An hour later both arrived at the Research Center and went straight to a small, sound-proofed conference room. Trina had set up a teleconference between the EPA agent in the Delta, the Rice Five project engineer in Davis, and the room in Berkeley.

Neither Markham nor Caswell had hesitated when Trina called them, and now both appeared deadly serious. Caswell was wearing a dark blue business suit; Markham was in blue jeans and a loosely woven beige sweater, his hair slightly unkempt.

When the conference operator completed the connection and everyone had introduced themselves, Markham went straight to the point. "So," he said at the small box in the center of the table, "have you done pathology on the fish?"

"That's happening now," said the EPA agent, his voice slightly tinny through the loudspeaker.

"Why are you assuming that Rice Five has anything to do with this?" Caswell asked.

"Listen," the agent said. "DFG has spent the last two days

trying to come up with alternative explanations. They've never seen a transspecies die-off like this without some toxic. We've got normal weather, normal runoff—an ordinary Delta springtime."

"Can I ask an obvious question?" said the United Genetics scientist in Davis, his tone metallic through the speaker. "Have you measured dissolved oxygen in the water yet?"

"It's normal range," the agent said. "You've really got to have a lot of floating plant matter before there's enough oxygen deficit to kill fish."

There was a long silence in the little conference room. Caswell and Markham were staring at each other across the table, almost as if Trina were not even in the room. She could not recall seeing either of the entrepreneurs ever look quite so tense.

Finally Markham spoke. "Obviously, we'll do anything we can. But without further information . . ."

Caswell broke in. "I think you'll understand that, simply because of the Rice Five situation, we can't be blamed for every unexplained ecological upset that comes along."

For the first time the EPA agent's voice hardened. "No one is blaming anyone yet. But I can tell you this: If your goddamned Rice Five is killing fish, then the feds, the state of California, everyone and his brother are going to be all over you."

The angry voice hesitated for a moment, and Trina winced at the suppressed fury in the young man's tone. She seemed to be encountering a great deal of hostility today.

"There's no point to talking more until we have more data," he said, clearly forcing himself to be civil. "Do what you can at your end and I'll be back in touch."

As the EPA agent hung up, there was a burst of static and a low buzz on the speaker. Then Markham spoke softly. "Larry, are you still on?"

The project manager at the Davis laboratory answered affirmatively.

Markham leaned back in his chair, stretching for a moment, now almost preternaturally calm. "What's going on?" he asked quietly. Trina momentarily admired his grace in crisis. Under similar circumstances she'd be shouting into the phone.

"Honest to God, Mr. Markham," Larry said, "I have no idea."

Markham nodded, almost to himself. "Do you have a copy of the gene scan on Rice Five handy?"

"It's hanging on my wall," the man said, "right in front of me."

Trina spoke up. "I thought you might need that. I had another copy faxed down here."

She reached into her leather portfolio and produced a sheet of shiny fax paper eight inches wide, perhaps twice as long, and spread it out on the surface of the conference table. Both Caswell and Markham leaned forward to study it.

The image on the paper was a classic gene map, utterly incomprehensible to the uninitiated: a straight line, broken into dozens of shorter sequences like a history book time line, each one numbered with a cryptic alphanumeral—UKD2, ALP+, BGD. At the bottom of the genetic blueprint was the United Genetics logo, a large stamp reading "CONFIDENTIAL," and another line reading "Patent Pending."

Caswell glanced at the sheet briefly, then stared at the opposite wall. Markham smoothed the paper with one thin, pale hand, gazing at the bare genetic bones of Rice Five for a long moment. He smiled very slightly. Trina recognized the pure pleasure of a true technophile regarding an elegant piece of engineering, devoid of any value judgment past admiration.

"Very compact," he murmured after a moment. "Makes me think of some of the really tight computer code we used to write."

There was silence at the other end, and then Markham focused on the issue at hand. "Remind me," he said more crisply. "What do we have going in the root development and structure sequences?"

"Oh, jeez," said the voice on the speakerphone. Trina could imagine the little balding researcher, sweating in the Davis heat, peering at the chart.

"Let me see," the voice said. "It looks pretty much like our standard packet of root genes. We're putting that into most everything these days. It's got fungus resistance, mild saline tolerance, rootworm resistance. Uh, it's got—"

"Hold it," Markham said quietly, frowning slightly. "How do we get the rootworm resistance?"

"Oh, that's an old gene sequence we've used for years now. Makes a very mild, low-level pesticide that coats the roots so it kills any worms that try to take a bite. Then, once it's in the soil, it breaks down as a nontoxic decay product."

Markham looked sharply at Caswell, then Trina, to see if they caught the drift. He looked back at the speaker. "But some of the Rice Five is growing free in the water now. What happens to that pesticide if it goes directly into water, rather than soil?"

This time the silence at the other end was so long that for a moment Trina thought the connection was broken.

Just as she cleared her throat to say something, the Davis scientist spoke up. "Well, that's not supposed to happen, so I don't think we have test data on that. I believe we got an EPA waiver, since . . ." His voice trailed off at the implications of Markham's question.

"Check and see," Markham said. "And get back to us right away."

"I'm on my way," the researcher said and hung up.

Markham looked across the table at Caswell. "I think we might have a situation here," he said quietly.

Caswell looked at him with a serious, level gaze. "Should we announce it ourselves?"

Markham raised his eyebrows slightly. "We may not have to."

Trina glanced back and forth between the two, trying to follow the cryptic exchange. "So what's the plan?" she asked finally.

Markham rubbed his eyes wearily, smoothed his brown hair. Finally he looked over at her. "This time," he said, "the plan might just be out of our hands."

CHAPTER NINETEEN

As Trina received the unsettling news from the Delta, Rackley was sitting quietly in her loft, staring at the yellow notepad and telephone in front of him, trying to decide just what to do next. Over the past two days he had drawn upon the full repertoire of his investigative skills, calling all over northern California, tracking down any hint of where Kaye might be and just how Lipsky had run his embryo engineering operation.

Early on, Rackley managed to find the hospital where Megan Collins was being kept; a small private institution in the hills above Santa Barbara. But after a few more telephone calls he realized that he would waste his time making a visit. She was in a costly celebrity sanatorium that specialized in keeping public figures with problems out of the limelight. The hospital was as effective a silencer as Albert Collins could possibly have found.

By visiting laboratory supply companies he learned that Lipsky's operation had received regular deliveries of liquid nitrogen for months. Rackley assumed that the young scientist had used the supercold fluid for previous embryo experiments, but on the basis of his standing order with the supply firm, he clearly didn't do any great volume of work. If Lipsky had been telling the truth about the extent of embryo engineering, the work had to be done somewhere other than the little lab in Berkeley.

Between telephone calls Rackley found himself thinking of the community of financiers and scientists who lived in the hills above Silicon Valley in those elegant homes and gated estates. Might they have been Lipsky's clients? Yet that didn't make sense either: Lipsky's initial experiments couldn't possibly have been done on the children of the technologic elite.

Even as Rackley pursued his own investigation, the rest of the media world was trying to find him. Reporters had quickly determined that the house on Baker Street was locked and unoccupied, but that was no deterrent. Messages of every kind were left with Trina. Senior editors from both *Newsweek* and *Time* offered Rackley generous space in their magazines in return for an exclusive interview. "Six columns," one of them told Trina. "My God, woman, some people would kill for six columns." *Asahi Shimbun, Paris Match, Stern,* and a dozen other Asian and European newspapers and magazines all ran long pieces, usually accompanied by bizarre artwork. The *National Enquirer* offered $150,000 in cash for Kaye's story. A half dozen movie producers called from Los Angeles with various deals. "Just pass on three words for me," one television agent told Trina over the telephone. " 'Five-part miniseries.' "

Rackley had worked with the media long enough to learn that it was impossible to cooperate halfway. One could play the press fairly well from a position of power—say, within a large corporation like United Genetics—but an individual, thrown into the media maelstrom of late twentieth-century America, is rapidly torn to pieces. In such a situation, Rackley knew, the only solution is to disappear. And Trina's loft turned out to be the perfect sanctuary. "In seclusion" was the way frustrated reporters usually described his whereabouts. " 'In confusion,' " he told Trina, "is closer to the truth."

His only consolation was that no one else was having any more luck. Tortola the lawyer had assigned a private investigator to the case, but he reported stone walls in every direction. This afternoon Rackley had even called Steven Hechinger. Contacting him directly was a calculated risk: Rackley assumed that by now Hechinger saw him as the enemy. On the other hand, Hechinger might be of some help. In the middle of the afternoon Rackley dialed the investigator's hotel and identified himself.

"That was quick," Hechinger said.

"What?" Rackley didn't understand.

"Trina Robbins didn't tell you to call?"

"No. I . . . " Rackley hesitated for a moment.

"You lied to me," Hechinger said quickly. "You lied to the whole damn world."

"Wait a minute."

"The forbidden sequence. You of all people."

"It's not that simple," Rackley said. "I want to explain."

"Okay." Hechinger said briskly. "I'm listening."

Rackley took a deep breath. "I'm an alcoholic. Lipsky gave our embryo the genes for proper alcohol metabolism."

There was a long silence at the other end. "What?" Hechinger asked finally.

"That's all he did for us. And that's the truth."

Hechinger made a brief clicking sound. "You're going to be indicted, you know."

Rackley said nothing.

"What will you do now?"

Rackley knew he couldn't say anything about Kaye's disappearance. "Wait and see what happens, I guess."

"Rackley," Hechinger said urgently. "Let's meet someplace. Maybe we can work something out."

"I'm afraid that's not a good idea." Without a pause he hung up the telephone.

Markham was precisely correct about the newest development in the Rice Five story: the situation was out of their hands. Less than one hour after the Environmental Protection Agency first contacted United Genetics, a Natural Progress worker in the Delta heard the rumors. Two hours later Steven Hechinger was on the telephone to his favorite press contacts, and by that evening the news had broken.

Most of the editors who shape the national news are city people for whom irrigation problems in the Delta were less than a sexy topic. But dead fish were another matter altogether.

The first headline that night read "MUTANT RICE A KILLER?" and from there on the story was completely out of Trina's control. She found herself longing for Rackley's help. In the past, vestigial professional respect for him had served to blunt direct assaults on the company. But now, his abrupt departure from United Genetics and subsequent silence raised speculation that something was truly rotten at the genetics conglomerate. Reporters were clearly moving in for the kill. Between the federal charges, the Lipsky suicide, and the Rice Five fiasco, Trina had inherited the worst job in public relations: managing the news for a company whose news was nothing but bad.

Rackley's absence was even more damaging in his other specialty: investor relations.

By six A.M. the morning after the fish kill became news, Trina had stopped worrying about reporters. Suddenly she was fielding hysterical calls from the East Coast investment bankers and venture capitalists who had money in United Genetics. The rumor on Wall Street—that United Genetics had canceled the public stock offering—was so clearly true that no one even bothered to ask about it. The darker fear, first hinted at in a *Washington Post* story planted by Steven Hechinger, was that all of the current investors in United Genetics would be held liable in lawsuits.

If Rice Five poisoned fishing waters in California, the lawsuits could prove awesome: bigger than Three Mile Island, bigger than the Bhopal chemical disaster. The *Washington Post* cited "reliable sources close to the Senate genetic engineering subcommittee" as saying that the total bill could run into billions of dollars.

Late that morning Albert Collins, the lead investor, called from his office in Portola Valley.

"Where the hell is Markham?" he asked Trina. "I can't get him on the telephone."

Trina coughed quietly. "He's been in meetings since dawn. He's got a lot to worry about just now."

"I would say so. What does he plan to do? These liability figures I'm hearing—are they in the ballpark?"

"Well. Number one, we don't know that Rice Five is the bad actor in the first place. Number two, those numbers are just guesses, and most of them come from Steven Hechinger and Natural Progress. Obviously they're trying to scare investors out of biotechnology."

"It's working," Collins said curtly. "I've been getting calls all day from firms with money in United Genetics."

"Tell them to stay tuned. At this point we really don't know how it's going to fall out."

"Our lawyers say that we may actually have some exposure here. And if we do, our risk on this could be enormous."

Trina tapped her fingers on her desk for a moment. "I don't know what else I can tell you."

"I want Markham to call me. Soonest."

"I will tell him," Trina said, and then she paused for a

moment. She softened her voice and spoke quietly. "How is Megan, by the way?"

"She's fine," Collins said abruptly.

"She's back home?"

"No. She won't be able to come home for some time. Tell Markham I must talk to him." And with that he hung up.

Trina sat for a moment, gazing at the telephone. Almost against her will she seemed to be spending all of her time protecting United Genetics; virtually nothing she did seemed to have any value for Rackley. She reached over to pick up a rough draft of a press release and uncovered the half-eaten blueberry muffin that had been on her desk since sunrise. For the first time in hours she smiled.

That afternoon the EPA issued the results of preliminary autopsies on more than one thousand fish of seven different species chemically analyzed in the state laboratories in Sacramento. Minute quantities of a natural pesticide had been found in the tissues of ninety-seven percent of the samples. An identical natural pesticide was found on the root surfaces of one hundred percent of 374 samples of Rice Five harvested at random sites in the Delta.

The EPA agent was courteous enough to call Trina and read her the press release just before it went out. A joint statement from the EPA and the California Department of Fish and Game, it announced tersely that "initial research suggests a direct connection between the introduced species Rice Five and the present fish mortality situation in the California Delta."

"We're putting that on the wire services immediately," the EPA man said.

Even though Trina had known, almost certainly, that the news was coming, she still found herself nearly light-headed at hearing the words themselves.

After a moment the agent cleared his throat. "Shall I read that again?"

"No thanks," she said softly. "I got it. We'll probably have a statement later today. I'll let you know." She hung up the phone and stared at it for a moment. Her assistant stuck her head in the doorway, curious about the short call and subsequent silence.

Trina looked up. "We're nailed."

She stood and walked over to Markham's office. The executive floor of United Genetics had taken on the atmosphere of a beleaguered battleship with distinctions of rank falling away. As

Trina approached Markham's imperious secretary, the woman simply waved her on into the young entrepreneur's office.

Trina opened the door to see Markham sitting at his desk. His head was slightly back, his eyes closed as if in meditation. She hesitated for a moment, then saw that he was having blood drawn for the Markham Project. Without altering his posture he opened his eyes, took in Trina's expression at a glance, then gently touched the shoulder of the blond nurse kneeling by his desk.

"We'll finish this later."

"Would you like a Band-Aid, sir?" the nurse asked.

Markham looked up at Trina for an instant and raised one eyebrow. "I think it's going to take more than a Band-Aid this time."

That same night, well before Trina returned from United Genetics, Rackley went to his first AA meeting in several weeks. The meeting was his old favorite, out toward the ocean on Geary Boulevard, but this time, as soon as Rackley walked in the door, he sensed that people were looking at him differently. And then he realized: his picture had been in every newspaper, on every television newscast. So much for anonymity, he thought. Thomas R. was now distinctly recognizable.

He arrived just as the meeting started, the reading of the Twelve Steps already underway, so he had no time to talk to anyone. A well-dressed woman named Beth was speaking that night. She was in her mid-twenties, blond, and something in the way she talked reminded Rackley of Kaye.

Beth had been a buyer for an expensive Union Square department store. She had started drinking in high school, continued in college, and by the time she graduated she was already alcoholic. She had been in and out of AA three times, putting together a few months of sobriety, then slipping. On her last slip she had driven her Fiat through a plate glass window, earning her third DUI conviction; now unemployed and awaiting sentencing, she would almost certainly serve time in county jail.

"But there's nothing I can do about that," she said in even, calm tones. "I just have to accept. I've spent my whole life trying not to accept things, trying to make myself believe that I'm sup- posed to be rich or famous or prettier or something. And all I've done is end up going to crummy bars and waking up feeling sick with guys I don't know. Now I have to work on acceptance. There's nothing wrong with me except that I'm an alcoholic. As long as I accept that and let my higher power work, I can stay well."

Moments later she proposed "acceptance" as the topic for the meeting, and for the next half hour Rackley listened closely to the people around the big U-shaped table.

Acceptance was his problem as well. He had never been satisfied with who he was, what he did, what he had. He had always suspected that deep inside him there was some tragic flaw, some error of character, that would ultimately destroy him. He had compensated by trying even harder to succeed in the world, to keep up appearances, to maintain a perfect veneer. In the end he had nothing.

Now, of course, he knew that he did indeed have a tragic flaw: his addiction. It was, moreover, a flaw so deep in his tissues that he would never be rid of it. After weeks of therapy in the little hospital in Berkeley, when he finally accepted the truth, it had come as a wonderful relief. His much-feared flaw was real—yet in accepting the truth, the fear disappeared. Rather than growing weaker, he gained strength from acceptance.

Tonight Rackley realized that he had lost sight of that fundamental lesson. Perhaps it had been all those hours with Caswell and Markham, men who refused to accept anything and thrived. Perhaps it had been Rackley's own success: as Trina never tired of pointing out, he had garnered the rewards of corporate America in record time. And more to the point, he had desired them.

A few years ago, when Rackley still regularly told his story at meetings, he would credit the principles of recovery. "The promises," he would say, "do come true." By now he hadn't spoken at a meeting for months. And tonight he saw clearly that once again he was trying to control the world around him.

More than that in fact. With the embryo therapy, he was trying to control the world that would come after him.

Trina had said: "If some higher power wants your kids to be alcoholic, they will be. And if they're supposed to get better, then they'll get better." Rackley suddenly understood why she had reacted so strongly to the embryo therapy: he was turning his back on her own belief, investing faith instead in Stuart Lipsky's nucleotide sequencers.

Rackley raised his hand, and after a moment Beth called on him.

"My name is Thomas," he said, "and I'm an alcoholic."

"Hello, Thomas," came the familiar refrain from around the table.

He hesitated for a moment. Suddenly he wasn't even sure what he wanted to say. "I haven't been to a meeting for a while," he said finally. "It's good to be here. I need to be here."

He paused again, looking around the table at the twenty or so faces turned to watch him, expectant, accepting, gently curious.

He took a deep breath. "I don't really know what to say," Rackley said, and then he was aware that against his bidding, against his will, there were tears in his eyes. "I'm in the middle of a . . ." He stopped for another moment. What was he trying to say? "I guess," he said after another long silence, "that I need to listen tonight."

Beth quietly intervened. "Thanks, Thomas," she said softly. "You're in the right place. Keep coming back."

After the meeting he lingered by the door, and a half dozen acquaintances came up to talk, not saying anything specific, although several clearly knew his situation. Instead they offered sympathy and the assurance that things would get better. A minute or two later, however, Michael Gillespie, the police lieutenant who had investigated Lipsky's death, walked up.

"Thomas. Let's talk for a second."

"Sure." Rackley glanced at the others around him. "Excuse us."

He and Gillespie walked to one corner of the church basement.

"Just between us, I want to tell you the disposition of the Lipsky case. We've turned it over to the feds now." He paused for a moment and ran one hand through his curly red hair. "I hope you've got a lawyer. There's a lot of heat on this thing."

"Yes?"

Gillespie lowered his voice. "We even had a call from some senator's office. Senator Gordon. Asking about the status of the case."

Rackley nodded. "Gordon's in charge of the genetic engineering subcommittee."

Gillespie shrugged. "Whatever." He glanced around the room for a moment. "Anyway, Larson, the federal attorney, is really on this one. His investigator was even trying to get you for Lipsky."

"That's crazy," Rackley said quickly. "I'm the one who reported it."

Gillespie raised one hand. "Don't worry. That's not going to happen. It's a clear suicide."

"Oh?"

"Your friend Lipsky had a BAL of point two four when he climbed into that car."

"What?" Rackley said, not comprehending at first. "Blood alcohol?"

Gillespie nodded solemnly. "Drunk out of his mind. We found a quart of Cutty in his trash."

"Damn," Rackley said, shaking his head, looking away. "I didn't know the guy drank."

Gillespie raised his eyebrows. "You don't get a load like that without practice."

"I know." Rackley frowned, thinking back. Had Lipsky been unusually sympathetic to their case? "But usually I can spot it."

"He maybe could have used this program."

Rackley said nothing.

"Anyway, that puts a lock on it for us." Gillespie looked at Rackley for a moment. "Seventy percent of suicides in this city are legally drunk, did you know that? Sometimes I think that's what we should put on the cert, instead of suicide."

Rackley, still absorbing the news, nodded absently.

"Anyway, the feds took custody of the body so fast that we didn't even process the paperwork. They're all over this case." Gillespie was silent for a moment, then sighed. "Listen, I hope this whole thing works out for you and your wife. It's a tough one."

Rackley nodded again. "Thanks for your help."

Gillespie waved one hand, started to turn, turned back. "You know, the church says this genetic stuff is out of bounds. But I'm a drunk, too, and . . ." His voice trailed off and he shrugged his heavy shoulders.

"You said it right the first time," Rackley said. "It's a tough one."

Trina departed the loft very early the next morning for a private meeting at United Genetics. A professor of ecology from the University of California was to present a report on the current and future status of Rice Five. Markham paid lavishly for the research; the professor hired the top names in academia to collect evidence, ranging from satellite photographs to supercomputer simulations.

"This guy is world-class," Markham had told Trina the previous day. "If anyone can predict what's happening, it's him."

The meeting took place in the audio-visual conference room on the fortieth floor, a wood-paneled room with plum carpeting and thirty gray swivel chairs mounted in three curving rows facing a wide screen and a big overhead video projector. Most of the chairs were empty; only Markham, Caswell, and Trina were present. The reason for the secrecy became clear to Trina very quickly.

The middle-aged professor stood stiffly at a lectern; behind him, projected on the wide screen, was a map showing central California in a light green outline. The current spread of Rice Five was overprinted in bright orange, and thus the Delta area appeared almost ablaze; north, toward Sacramento, there were a few scattered dots. There were even two or three bright orange dots near the coast, fully eighty miles from the main Rice Five outbreak.

"How did it get over there?" Markham asked sharply from one of the swivel chairs closest to the screen. "I thought none had gone to seed yet."

The expert looked at the orange dots on the big projection screen. "We're fairly sure that's transmission by water birds. They somehow get a bit of Rice Five vegetation stuck in their feathers or feet. It's bound to happen, but it's not the major worry at this point."

"What do the weed-killer tests show?" Caswell asked from his seat next to Trina.

"So far, not so good," the man said. "Rice Five is highly resistant. I don't need to tell you that herbicide resistance genes are included in the standard United Genetics plant modification package. They seem to be fully expressed in Rice Five."

Markham nodded, saying nothing. It was ironic: in the early years United Genetics' success at creating herbicide-resistant crops had been a major source of income. Farmers who planted their herbicide-resistant tobacco, for example, no longer had to hire workers to hoe fields and remove weeds by hand. Instead they could spray potent herbicides from the air, promptly killing every living green thing in the field—except the tobacco, engineered to resist weed-killers. United Genetics herbicide-resistant crops were best sellers. Now, however, herbicide resistance had come back to haunt them.

"Of course," the expert went on, "there are herbicides that will kill Rice Five. But these are military defoliants, the newer versions of Agent Orange. I don't think we can even think about using them."

Trina spoke up. "And removal by hand . . . ?"

"We've designed a few tools—scoop basket types of gear—

that let us take out plants and capture most of the floating material at the same time." The professor shook his head. "But it's a little late. Damn shame the California Conservation Corps didn't use those to start with. Of course, back then we didn't know what kind of plant we were dealing with."

"So," Markham said after a protracted silence. "What's the bottom line?"

"The bottom line is that, even with maximum manual removal, some amount of Rice Five will go to seed in late August and early September. This almost perfectly coincides with the Pacific Flyway bird migration. That's about fifty million birds, all of which pass directly through the Delta on their way south. They will almost certainly consume and then excrete vast quantities of fertile Rice Five grains."

"Oh my God," Trina said involuntarily.

The man took a deep breath. "We're looking at a dispersal pattern something like this. Next slide please."

The new map showed all of the Western Hemisphere in bright green and was labeled OCTOBER. There was a dribble of orange down California, across the Mexican border, into Mexico and Central America.

"So this is basically following the migration pattern," Markham said.

"So far," the ecologist said. "Next slide."

This one was labeled NOVEMBER-DECEMBER. The amount of color showing Rice Five had doubled. The orange tint had now spread, like blotting ink, across Mexico, as well as spreading out in fingers across South America as far south as Argentina.

The ecologist cleared his throat. "I believe this is self-explanatory." Next to her Trina heard Caswell grunt softly.

The slide changed again, to JANUARY-FEBRUARY, and the orange blush now covered most of Mexico and Central America. The progress in South America had stopped at Chile, but the orange had now spread in a huge stain all across the Amazon Basin in a giant splash of color.

"After February," the expert said, "a lot depends on how quickly Rice Five spreads in the Amazon, and whether the growth rate will accelerate nearer the equator. But, given a conservative growth rate, we can expect to see something like the following, once the bird migration path turns north again."

Now the slides changed in rapid succession—MARCH, APRIL, MAY, JUNE. With each slide the orange blush spread northward again, in two distinct waves. One veered toward the East Coast of the United States, appearing first in Florida, then quickly climbing up the eastern seaboard. Another moved back through Mexico, then into Texas and Oklahoma. The orange color seeped through most of the Midwest, finally spilling over into Canada.

"One year from today," the expert said, "the distribution of Rice Five could be what you see here." He gazed at the final image on the screen for a moment. Most of the map was now tinted orange, from California to New York, from Montreal to Mexico City. "Migratory waterfowl are probably about the most efficient plant distribution system one could devise."

There was a long silence in the conference room. Trina shifted uncomfortably, realizing that she had not moved a muscle since the beginning of the presentation.

"Well," Markham said, "just to cap things off, do you have a projection on environmental impact?"

The expert sighed. "Very hard to say. We simply don't understand enough about ecology to look at a loose cannon like this plant and figure just what it's going to do in various other ecosystems."

Caswell spoke up with an edge of impatience in his voice. "So much for the disclaimer. Given that you're paid to have some opinion about this, what might you guess?"

The expert gazed at him evenly. "Mr. Caswell, depending on this plant's tolerance for temperature and rainfall variation, and the question of—"

"Oh, for God's sake," Caswell said, "get to the fucking point."

"I would say we're easily looking at damages in the several billions of dollars. Uncontrolled, this plant could destroy fish populations throughout the Western Hemisphere."

Another long silence ensued, finally broken by Markham's even tones. "That's astounding," he said softly, as if a remarkable natural phenomenon had suddenly caught his attention, akin to some beautiful butterfly landing on the back of his hand. "Truly astounding."

Markham's voice was so abstracted, so . . . odd . . . that for one moment Trina wondered whether the news had driven the young entrepreneur mad.

"I have one more chart," the expert said. "Next slide."

The final image was a simple list:

Options for Rice Five

1—Improve Manual Removal Techniques
    Cost: $50–150 million
    Probability of Success: Low
2—Investigate Novel Herbicides
    Cost: $1.5–5 million
    Probability of Success: Low-Moderate
3—Develop Genetically Engineered Disease or Parasite
    Cost: $2–4 million
    Probability of Success: Moderate-to-High

"'Options,'" Markham said sarcastically, his tone returning to normal. "I don't see that there are options. You're suggesting we develop another genetically engineered product to get rid of this genetically engineered product."

"More or less. Something you could spray on from airplanes, preferably, that would attack and kill Rice Five. There are some rice diseases that might be modified to work."

"And what if that turns out to be a pest also?"

The expert shook his head, clearly frustrated. "I have no idea. But this might buy you some time."

Caswell interrupted. "What do you mean, you have no idea? What are we paying you for? Processing slides?"

The man shifted his gaze to Caswell, summoning up a full complement of professorial dignity. "We are in uncharted waters, Mr. Caswell, when we begin to throw novel organisms into the environment. We understand very little about natural ecology as it is. When we begin to modify millions of years of evolution—"

Markham cut him off. "We're running late." He turned to Caswell. "Any more questions?"

Caswell shook his head.

"Trina?"

There was dead silence in the small conference room. Markham turned back to the ecologist. "Thanks very much."

The screen went dark, and moments later when the lights came up completely, Caswell and Markham were already standing, ready to leave.

One day after the secret briefing, Trina stood at the edge of a big hotel ballroom, looking out over the audience of reporters, and beyond them the television camera crews, floodlights dimmed. She was nervous: this was her first solo press conference. Mixed with the nervousness was also an odd wistfulness; she knew that her remaining days at United Genetics were few. And considering the announcement to be made this morning, the company itself might not last much longer.

Not that Trina cared much. Without Rackley it seemed a different firm altogether. Trina had intended to go off and try writing on her own for months; now seemed the moment. First, however, she would see United Genetics through this press conference and then the Caswell Clinic opening in Mexico City. And in those remaining days she would do whatever she could to help Rackley.

Trina had slept no more than a few hours the previous night, regularly wandering out of her bedroom to where Rackley was sleeping on the couch.

"Rackley," she had said at one point in the darkness of the loft. "You asleep?"

Rackley sat up, an outline against the big windows. "Not really."

"I want this thing to go well." She hesitated, sitting on the edge of the coffee table. "No. I mean, I don't care what happens to United Genetics. But I want to do my job right. That's what I mean. Just for myself."

"Trina," he said. "Considering what Markham is going to say, you could hold this press conference on an ice floe in the Arctic Ocean and nobody would complain. This is the financial story of the year."

Trina sighed. "I know." She looked at Rackley, pulling her thin robe closer around her shoulders. "There's going to be ten thousand questions. I mean, I'm not that familiar with the financial stuff."

Rackley scratched his head. "When in doubt, just say 'details haven't been finalized.'"

"I still can't believe Markham and Caswell are doing this."

"It surprises me," Rackley said. "But I figure it matches my luck."

"How so?"

"I mean, it'll cost me about two million in stock options." He shrugged. "Funny. A week ago that would have killed me. Now . . ." He shrugged and reached up and squeezed her hand. "You'll do fine. Go to sleep."

Hours later Trina watched with incredulity as reporters continued to troop into the vast hotel ballroom. She had hesitated at first to reserve such a large space, but Markham insisted. And indeed he had the better sense of United Genetics' news value. First Kaye's arrest, then Lipsky's death. Now the Rice Five fish kill had been a major story for two days, making the national papers each morning and the network news each night as the full implications of the situation gradually emerged.

Initially Steve Hechinger and Natural Progress provided much of the material on how Rice Five might spread. But now a dozen other experts were speaking out as well. What amazed Trina was that no one had yet come up with as dire a prediction as United Genetics' own expert. It was directly after that presentation that Caswell and Markham had disappeared into the latter's office for nearly an hour, finally calling Trina in to break the news.

Trina immediately sent out by messenger and wire service a brief announcement: "At 9:00 A.M. PST, Paul Markham, President, and Edward Caswell, CEO, will make a significant announcement regarding the future of United Genetics." The morning papers today speculated that Markham would announce United Genetics' voluntary bankruptcy—an ethically questionable but technically legal technique for avoiding the full impact of massive lawsuits.

For a moment Trina continued to watch the television camera crews jostling rudely for position in the front row. Just then her assistant came up behind her. "Paul and Edward are both here now," the young woman said quietly. "And the satellite link is open." The press conference was being transmitted by satellite to hotel meeting rooms in New York and Chicago as well.

Trina took one more look at the audience and glanced at her watch. Nine A.M.: showtime. She walked up to the front of the room and stood behind the podium. To one side there was a long walnut table with two chairs; ahead the television lights blossomed into full glare.

Trina tapped on the microphone, then cleared her throat. Quickly the audience fell silent. "Ladies and gentlemen. Thank you for attending. I'd like to introduce Paul Markham, President of United Genetics, and Edward Caswell, Chief Executive Officer. Mr. Markham and Mr. Caswell will each read a brief statement, after which we will take questions for ten minutes. Copies of the statements will be available at the door as you leave."

She looked to the right, and Markham and Caswell walked out. Markham was in a gray suit, Caswell in a dark blue one. They sat at the table and then Markham removed a sheet of paper from his coat pocket. His hair was carefully blown-dry, his tie neatly knotted; it was, Trina knew, his best public persona. As she recalled, he hadn't looked half so tidy the last time he dined at the White House.

Markham cleared his throat and leaned into the chrome microphone in front of him.

"Ladies and gentlemen. As you know, an experimental United Genetics product, known as Rice Five, has temporarily established itself in the California Delta. While we are continuing vigorous efforts to remove the plant, Edward Caswell and myself, as majority owners of United Genetics, have decided to take an additional step."

Markham paused for a moment, and the silence in the hotel ballroom was total.

"As of noon today, the Caswell Corporation and I will buy back all shares held by outside investors, on a dollar-for-dollar basis calculated on their initial investment. In so doing we will become sole owners of United Genetics and thus assume all present and future responsibility for the consequences of Rice Five."

A low murmur spread through the audience as full realization

of Markham's words set in. He and Caswell were bailing out all of
the early investors in United Genetics, placing themselves directly
in line of the massive lawsuits that might arise as Rice Five spread
throughout the hemisphere.

"We will still," Markham said, continuing to read from the
single sheet of paper, "use all our resources to eradicate Rice
Five, and we expect those efforts to prove successful." He paused
and for the first time looked up from the piece of paper. "As soon
as this press conference is over, I will personally take charge of
the eradication research team at our Davis, California agricultural
facility."

Markham set the single sheet of paper down and looked over
at Caswell. The tall, bearded man cleared his throat and began to
read his own statement. "This in no way compromises the
activities of any of United Genetics' divisions. Our international
chain of Birthtech clinics will continue to function, as will the
pharmaceutical arm of the company. This week, the new United
Genetics–Caswell Clinic in Mexico City will open on schedule,
hosting our First International Symposium on the Diseases of
Overpopulation. We foresee no structural changes resulting from
the refinancing; only a clearer delineation of fiscal responsibility."
Caswell looked up. "Are there questions?"

There was a moment of silence during which a half dozen
reporters slipped out to commandeer the pay telephones in the
lobby, and then abruptly the room was transformed into a forest of
waving hands and shouted questions. Trina stood at the podium,
calling on reporter after reporter, one after another, until their
faces and questions seemed almost to blur. . . .

"Will this mean the bankruptcy of United Genetics?"

"Will you have to sell your remaining assets?"

"How have your investors reacted?"

"What will this mean for the upcoming hearing in the
Senate?"

As Trina watched, Caswell and Markham handled all the
queries like smooth professionals, never flustered, utterly assured.
Even though she felt the two had betrayed Rackley, she was
impressed with the straightforward confidence they brought to a
situation that was in fact an utter nightmare. United Genetics
would go on, Caswell promised. "The Caswell family has been in
business in this country for a long time, and we plan to stay for a
long time to come."

Markham pledged his full financial resources to fight Rice
Five and set the environment right. "If worse comes to worst, it

may mean I have to start over back in Silicon Valley in a garage,"
he said, and then smiled boyishly. "But I'm sure somebody will
loan me one."

Trina finally called the press conference to an end, twenty
minutes later than planned. It had been a brave performance, but
the truth was inescapable: If Rice Five caused even a tenth of the
damage predicted by the university ecologist, United Genetics
was doomed.

At best the profitable divisions might be sold off. With luck
some employees would even keep their jobs, working for new
bosses. But as the inexorable process of damage suits and costly
litigation wore on, in the end, two victims would find escape
impossible. Odds were good, Trina knew, that both Caswell and
Markham would be bankrupt within a year. And whether either
would ever recover from the worst debacle in the history of high
technology was anyone's guess.

That night, back at Trina's loft, Rackley carried in the first
armload of evening papers and the two sat around the big open
living area, reading aloud.

The previous evening he had helped Trina assemble notes for
her background conversations with reporters; the incidental color
that, properly planted, could slant a story. Modern business
journalism, Rackley knew, rarely offered much moral context,
instead leaning heavily on adjective-dense hyperbole. Myth-
making for capitalists: even the most boring bit of business
competition became corporate titans clashing on blood-soaked
battlefields.

"Give them something that looks like a plot out of primetime
TV," Rackley had told Trina, "and that will be the lead."

This time the elements were perfect. The story played in the
press precisely as Rackley had predicted: heroism and tragedy.
The heroism was the fact that Caswell and Markham were
committing their entire fortunes to United Genetics in an attempt
to shield others. Obviously this was at some cost to the original
investors, who had tied up millions in United Genetics for years.
Now instead of turning a huge profit they were only getting their
original investment back. But at least they were escaping with
their money intact and avoiding years of lawsuits. The joke on
Wall Street was that the flight of top-tier investors from United
Genetics was the first recorded case of "ships deserting a sinking
rat."

The tragedy—depending on one's sympathy for the very

rich—was that two great American fortunes were on the chopping block. One was old money—the Caswell family fortune—which, according to the *Wall Street Journal,* totaled about $2 billion between the various real estate and media holdings of the family members. Markham, through shrewd investments, had doubled his original $400 million stake from the sale of PM Computers stock. Adding in United Genetics, Markham's personal fortune was slightly over $1.5 billion.

When Trina and Rackley finished trading the papers back and forth, they ate pesto pizza from a box and watched the evening news on several channels. Again the story had heroic overtones, although one network did a short piece on the possible long-term effects of Rice Five. All ended optimistically, however, noting that now Markham's legendary technologic prowess was being marshaled to pursue the enemy.

Rackley shook his head. "If they want to get anything done at the Davis labs, they should keep Markham as far away as possible. He'll drive them crazy."

"Quiet for a second," Trina said, pointing to the television. One of the evening news shows was concluding with a brief editorial commentary.

"In short," intoned the silver-haired announcer, "this ranks as one of the most dramatic episodes yet seen in American business. These two young men, Edward Caswell and Paul Markham, are taking full responsibility for the actions of their company—even though that responsibility could ultimately cost them dearly.

"Some may argue that the entrepreneurial capitalism of Silicon Valley is merely an updated version of business as usual. But today's announcement makes clear that this new high-tech generation has not lost its ideals. By putting themselves on the line Markham and Caswell are harking back to an earlier tradition of individual responsibility too easily forgotten in this era of big business.

"For that reminder we all owe them a vote of thanks."

Trina shut off the sound and looked over at Rackley, who was chewing on his pizza, staring at the television with bemusement.

"That's incredible," she said. "United Genetics may end up poisoning half the fish population of the Western Hemisphere, and this guy is thanking them on network television."

Rackley raised his pizza crust in an impromptu toast. "Good work."

"I feel sick," she said. "This is crazy."

Rackley leaned back and put his feet up on the coffee table. "Trina, you need to work on your sense of irony."

"You need to work on your sense of outrage," she snapped.

"Outrage"—Rackley's voice was suddenly very quiet—"has nothing to do with it. I want to find Kaye." He looked back at Trina. "And then I want to get even."

The morning after the press conference Trina was sitting on a vinyl couch in the plainly furnished office of U.S. Attorney Larson.

Once again she had not slept well that night, and to compensate she was wearing a lavender suit that she thought rendered her eyes larger, her waist smaller. Before she had left the loft, she had asked Rackley his opinion.

"That's always been my favorite color on you," he said.

She was about to say something flippant, but then hesitated. "Rackley, when you met me, back when we were in treatment, when I weighed a hundred pounds, did you think I was pretty?"

"I thought you were gorgeous. You're still gorgeous."

Trina looked at him for a long moment. "I hope you always feel like you can say that to me. The other night when—"

"Forget it," Rackley had said, waving one hand. "What's a little nuzzle between friends?"

This morning Trina felt as if she needed every advantage. She was trying the kind of damage control at which Rackley had been so adept. People always trusted Rackley; he had the kind of face that simply looked too open to deceive. But this time it was Trina, sent by Markham to pledge the full cooperation of United Genetics in the Lipsky-Rackley case—to forestall the possibility that the reclusive entrepreneur might actually be called to testify.

"Look," Trina told Larson, crossing her legs, leaning forward slightly. "It's in our best interest to put this behind us. We have enough difficulties as it is. This is an isolated incident, and we want to give you full access, anything we can do to help."

Larson was not showing any signs of cooperation. He looked at her dolefully for a moment, his small eyes quite blue. "Bring Lipsky back to life. That would be a big help."

Trina tightened her lips, turning her head slightly. "That was . . . tragic."

"That's not the half of it," Larson said sourly. "Tortola got a restraining order on the embryos. We can't touch them for gene scans." He flipped through a stack of legal documents on his desk for a moment. "Here it is." He stared at the page. "The argument

is that the embryos would be incriminating themselves, since, as
the law is written, they're at risk of punishment." He looked up.
"Can you believe that? Sixteen cells and they get to take the
fifth." He shook his head. "We have enough on Rackley to go to
the grand jury anyway, but—"

Larson's telephone rang and he picked it up.

"Hold calls, please," Larson said, and then stopped and
listened. "Sure. Put him on."

"What's up?" Larson listened for a moment, his expression
gradually turning even more dour than before.

"What the *hell* do you mean you can't *find* him?" Larson said
suddenly, the words nearly detonating into the telephone. "What
about his wife?"

He was silent for another moment, and his sudden anger
quickly crystallized into an expression of chill resolve. With one
hand he reached up and loosened his tie with a quick jerk.

"Fine," he said finally, cutting the single word ominously
short. "Do that. We'll have that indictment tomorrow night. And
if they're not there, I want flight warrants. And then I want them
in custody. They can't do this to us."

He hung up the telephone and looked across the table at Trina,
taking a moment to focus, as if he had briefly forgotten her
presence. "We can't find Rackley," he said flatly. "And we can't
seem to locate Mrs. Rackley either."

Trina frowned. "What?"

"I knew we should have set bail." He looked at Trina. "But
shit, that wouldn't have done any good. What's a hundred grand to
a Caswell, right?"

"Listen. I'm sure there's just some—"

"When was the last time you saw him?"

"United Genetics hasn't had contact with Rackley since
Lipsky was found."

"After *he* found Lipsky." Larson stared at Trina. "Why aren't
you in touch with him?"

Trina uncrossed her legs and leaned forward. "Frankly, he's
not our problem now."

"If he's really gone, he's going to be your problem. I'm going
to put this case together one way or another. I will take United
Genetics apart, if I have to."

So much, Trina thought, for her attempt at damage control.
"Listen. Rackley isn't going to run away from this. He's probably
just avoiding reporters. I'll put our people on to locating him; he
may have been in touch with someone in my department."

Larson looked at her for a moment. "Okay," he said finally. "But I can't screw around here. I'll give you forty-eight hours, then I'm going after him, both barrels. Got that?"

Trina nodded. "I'm sure there won't be a problem."

"Sure," Larson said, glancing at his watch. "Listen, can we cut this short? Now is not the best time."

Trina left the Federal Building, crossed the street, and immediately went to a telephone booth. She called her home number, waited through the answering machine message, then spoke. "Rackley, it's me."

He didn't pick up the telephone. Finally she spoke again. "Larson's going to get an indictment pretty soon. And he's looking for both you and Kaye."

She paused again, thinking that he would finally reach the telephone, but then continued. "Rackley, you should probably stay inside. I'll be home as soon as I can."

As she hung up the phone, she thought, even in the midst of all this, she liked the sound of "home" and "Rackley" in the same breath.

The telephone answering machine in Trina's loft was speaking to an empty room. Rackley at that moment was two hundred miles away, driving fast in the foothills of the Sierra Nevada. He was leaving a small farm town and heading into the bright green pastureland, low oak forest, and occasional apple orchards that surrounded San Tomas, the Caswell family summer home. San Tomas was a beautiful wedge of land, two hundred acres, on the way to Yosemite Valley. The first arrivals to slice up California had their pick of real estate, and the first Caswell, in Rackley's view, had selected admirably.

In crisis the Caswells always seemed to retreat to San Tomas. Leticia, Edward's and Kaye's mother, had moved there permanently after the death of her husband a decade earlier. Now, as other trails proved fruitless, Rackley began to surmise that it might well be the place that Kaye had thought to run. His suspicions had been heightened when he called and asked for Leticia. The housekeeper who answered said that no one was home. "Everyone," she said, "is in New York." But when Rackley called the Caswells' Manhattan apartment, there was no answer.

The green forests and granite escarpments of the Sierra had for years given Rackley solace, as well as providing what seemed an elevated platform from which he could view the topography of his life. As he drove, he considered the events of the previous three days. The collapse of his careful existence had been inevitable, he thought. After recovery he knew that he had to work hard to make up for lost time. This time around he had chosen to play by the rules, speak the language of corporate America, wear the clothes. He had even, for a time, convinced himself that through United Genetics he was making the world a better place.

But there was still an uneasiness he couldn't quite name. Rice Five had been the first challenge to his complacency. That he managed to keep the severity of the problem away from the public seemed to him less an accomplishment than an antisocial act. The entire situation had simply felt wrong, in ways he couldn't even quite identify. The problem, he realized now as the pine forests of the Sierra passed his windows, was simple: he'd taken the wrong side. Technology might still save the planet, but if it did, it would have to be with new understandings.

After another twenty minutes at the wheel he approached the entrance to San Tomas: a big iron gate, mounted on two granite pillars. Beyond the gate the road wound out of sight through oak trees mixed with scrub pine; the house and stables were nearly a quai: er mile away behind a low rise, snuggled into an almost perfect crook of land at a Y where two wide creeks came together, providing excellent fly-fishing just off the front porch of the huge old house.

As he came within sight of the gate, Rackley slowed his small car. Usually the gate was locked, even when company was expected, and the housekeeper's husband would drive out to open up. This afternoon, however, there were two uniformed guards standing just within the tall iron gates below the elaborately wrought SAN TOMAS that arched over the top. Rackley pulled his car off onto the gravel shoulder, stepped out, and walked quickly up to the gate. As he approached he could see the two guards wore the gray uniforms of the contract security service that Edward Caswell hired for his parties and for special duties around United Genetics.

The younger of the two guards, a heavyset blond, came to the gate. "Can I help you?"

"I'm Thomas Rackley. I'm here to see Leticia Caswell."

The younger guard looked at the other, dark-haired man, who walked over slowly, gazing at Rackley with the jaded suspicion of a career cop. "If you're a reporter, this is private property."

Rackley took a deep breath. "I'm a family member. I'm here to see my mother-in-law, Mrs. Caswell."

The older guard's disdain evaporated, replaced by quiet alertness. He walked back over to one of the granite pillars; leaning against it in the shade was a clipboard. He picked up the clipboard, looked at several sheets of paper, looked up at Rackley, and back at the clipboard.

He was shaking his head even before he returned. "Sorry, Mr. Rackley. You're not on the list."

"But I—"

The older guard continued to shake his head. "Can't help you. Sorry."

Rackley opened his mouth to say something more, then thought better. If he didn't cause a commotion, the guards might not report his visit until the end of their shift. He shrugged. "Orders are orders," he said. "I'll make a few calls and be back."

The guard hesitated, unsure as to how respectful his attitude should be. "You do that, sir."

Rackley drove up the road through the cool pine forest another half mile, then pulled off to one side where the forest gave way to a broader open pasture, bright green from the spring runoff. He glanced around briefly, left the car, and found a break in the fencing that ran on both sides of the road. He carefully slipped between two strands of loose barbed wire, then briskly walked up the pasture to the woods. He ducked under a tree limb, and after a moment he located a well-worn horse trail that circled around to the stables at the back of the compound.

He knew this trail well; almost every visit up to San Tomas with Kaye they had gone riding. As he walked quickly along the dry horse path, he remembered a day when they were out with Trina, on her single visit to San Tomas. They were riding at a fairly quick pace and Trina had fallen behind. Rackley and Kaye waited for her at the top of a rise, but as they watched her come up the grade on the other side of a low ravine, her horse stumbled and fell. Horrified, Rackley stared, uncertain what to do. Kaye immediately pulled her horse around and charged off down through the rocky, brush-filled ravine toward Trina.

Neither Trina nor horse was hurt, although the experience confirmed Trina's worst suspicions about the equine species. "Glue factory" were her parting words to her $35,000 Caswell thoroughbred. But what Rackley recalled most was Kaye's calm

grace as she rode down into the dry, thorny brush, her back
straight, hair shining, as if such rescues were something she did
every day.

Ten minutes later, after walking quickly through another long
stand of scrub oak, Rackley, sweating in the intense mountain sun,
arrived at the edge of the corral behind the San Tomas stable, a big
old redwood building. He paused at the locked wooden gate that
separated the stable area, then quickly climbed over the top. As he
swung over and landed on the other side, Stan Kihn, a young
cowboy who ran the stables and exercised the horses, came
around the corner of the barn.

"Hey," Kihn yelled. "You. Hold it there."

Rackley stood still as Kihn approached and finally recognized
him. "Rackley," Kihn said, brushing his hands off on his well-
worn blue jeans, and eyeing the intruder with an unsettled mix of
suspicion and welcome. "What you doing here?"

Rackley folded his arms. "I'm looking for Kaye."

Kihn stopped about twenty feet away. "You're not supposed to
be here."

"Says who?"

Kihn shrugged, said nothing, looked away, squinting in the
sun, clearly uneasy.

"Has Kaye been up here?"

Kihn looked back at him, head tilted. "You two got arrested, I
hear."

"Has she?"

Kihn shoved his hands into the pockets of his blue jeans.
"We're not supposed to talk to anybody."

"And?"

"And I like my job." He started to turn away.

"Do me a favor," Rackley said quickly.

Kihn stopped and looked back at him. "If I don't tell the rent-
a-cops about you, that's already a favor."

Rackley nodded. "You wouldn't do that."

"Not if you climb back over that gate."

"I need to talk to Mrs. Caswell. I know she'd talk to me."

Kihn watched him for a moment, then inclined his head.
"Wouldn't hurt to ask."

Rackley retired to the shade behind the barn, leaning against a
big old live oak. After ten minutes Leticia Caswell came around
the barn.

Leticia was wearing a soft denim blouse and a long, almost

Victorian skirt. She was about sixty-five now, her stride quick, appearing a decade younger. They touched for a moment as she kissed his cheek. She seemed puzzled to see Rackley.

"I thought you were supposed to stay down in the city."

"No one told me that." Rackley folded his arms. "This place is an armed camp. Did you know the guards at the gates wouldn't let me in?"

"That's a mistake. Edward was just worried that we'd have reporters all over."

"I think he's trying to keep me away. He's afraid I'm going to find Kaye."

"I don't understand . . ."

"I don't understand either," Rackley said. "I just want to know where Kaye is."

The elder Caswell gazed at him for a long moment, squinting in the bright sunlight. Finally she shook her head. "From the way Edward talked, I assumed it was all your idea."

Rackley fished the note from Kaye out of his back pocket and handed it to her.

"That's right," she said after reading it quickly.

"I knew nothing about this. Not a thing."

Leticia was now clearly confused. "Rackley, I don't know what I can tell you. Edward was up here, and he says that he had it fixed. That all we have to do is what he says."

Rackley looked at her with disgust. "So what else is new?"

Leticia smiled slightly. Both outsiders, Rackley and Leticia often shared notes about particularly egregious examples of Caswell hubris.

Leticia only shook her head however. "They didn't tell me," she said flatly. "No one told me anything."

Rackley pursed his lips, considering this, and tilted his head to one side. "And you didn't see anything yourself?"

Leticia blinked her eyes, gazing past Rackley at the wind moving slowly in the ponderosa pines beyond the corral. "You kids are in a lot of trouble, I guess." After another long moment she sighed. "Kaye had a map of Mexico City in her suitcase. I saw it when she was packing."

"How did she leave?"

"Edward drove up, stayed over, they left early. I think they went to the airport in Modesto. Where we used to keep the plane."

Rackley stepped forward, reached out, and kissed her cheeks. "You're great."

"I hope this wasn't a mistake."

"The truth is never a mistake," Rackley said. "In this family it's just a little uncommon."

The San Francisco air was already chill in the early evening when Rackley parked in the alley behind the loft and came up the stairs two at a time.

"I know where she is," Rackley said as soon as he walked in the door.

Trina was sitting on the big white couch, legs stretched out, shoes off, looking exhausted. "Where did you put your car?" She asked in a flat voice.

"I said—" Then the import of her question hit him, and he fell silent. "The indictment?"

Trina nodded. "Real soon." She told him about her visit with Larson; then Rackley told her about Kaye and the map of Mexico City.

"Caswell's not going to admit it. And I can't ask him anyway." Rackley looked up at Trina. "I want to go to Mexico City."

"Well," Trina said. "I'll be there tomorrow. I'm leaving early in the morning." She sighed. "Jesus, I still have to pack, too."

Rackley stood again, took a few steps, and stopped, agitated.

"Wait one day," Trina said finally. "Let me look around. I'll find a safe place for you to stay."

Rackley sat heavily on the other end of the sofa. "Where will you be?"

Trina paused for a moment. "I'm staying at Delgado's house."

Rackley looked up. "What?"

She shrugged. "He has a guest room. I don't like hotels. And maybe I'll learn something."

He suddenly felt overwhelmed. "Is all this a good idea?"

Trina considered it. "You won't have any problem getting out; they'll ask for your passport at the check-in, but that's it." She looked at Rackley. "Coming back in is a different thing. Customs and immigration have pretty good computers these days. If there's a warrant out, they'll pop you right away."

"Well," Rackley said. "One day at a time."

"That's the truth," Trina said, putting her feet up on the table. "And I'm real glad this one's over."

CHAPTER TWENTY ONE

The next morning Trina took a plane to Los Angeles, then transferred to a direct flight. As the airplane approached Mexico City late in the afternoon, she gazed through the scuffed plastic of her window. The sky was leaden gray, a mix of clouds and industrial pollutants, occasionally split by lightning strikes that lent a nearly primeval aspect. Below, the urban landscape stretched on almost endlessly, by now the largest city on the planet, growing so uncontrollably that the last census attempt, in 1980, had never even been completed.

Trina had lived here for five months with Rand, and she knew it to be a city collapsing under the sheer weight of too many bodies. Besides the nightmarish population growth, the city had never managed even the most rudimentary controls on air and water pollution. The result was a population besieged by a spectacular variety of ills. Markham sometimes called Mexico City "our test tube of the apocalypse"—a landscape in which all the forces that threatened the existence of the human species had collided, with a vengeance.

But Trina was not likely to see many symptoms of apocalypse out at Delgado's house. He lived in the Lomas district, near the center of town, just above Chapultepec Park. This was a neighborhood too rich even for Rand's best Mexican connections; Lomas housed the old rich or the relatives of former presidents. She was in fact most curious to see just how Delgado lived.

She recalled one night she and Rand had visited Lomas. The

sister of a ranking government official was building an elaborate
estate for herself. She had imported a million-dollar earth
compactor from the States to build the foundation for her tennis
courts. On the first day the brand-new piece of equipment fell into
a deep pit. The army was called out; a huge helicopter appeared.
But all efforts to raise the machine failed, and ultimately the
contractors decided to bury it. Rand insisted they watch the burial:
"It's important we see the real Mexico," he'd said.

When Trina's cab arrived, she saw that Delgado's house was
not far from the estate with the buried earthmover. He lived in one
of the more modern mansions in the district; from the street one
only saw a high wall of black volcanic rock and a huge polished
wooden door—more gate in fact than door. On the wall in tiny
raised aluminum letters was the name of the architect; atop the
stone wall ran discreet loops of black razor wire, twisted and very
sharp. Once inside the gate, however, the scene changed. There
was a courtyard witn polished tiles, a small fountain, and
luxuriant plantings nearly concealing the real entrance to the
house, which was another tall carved wooden door.

The driver carried her luggage to the front door and she paid
him and then turned and rang the bell. After a moment a young
Indian woman in a blue uniform answered the door. "Señorita
Robbins?"

"Sí." Trina said.

"Habla usted español?"

"Un poco."

"Come in, please," the woman said, and then she spoke over
her shoulder. "Rafael?"

Trina stepped into the entranceway and paused, slightly
startled at the vista. The entranceway opened into a two-story
space that actually fell away, following the contour of the hillside,
so that from the elaborate slate foyer one looked down, over a
wooden railing, to an immense living area in pure white carpeting,
with modern stone fireplaces, also two stories high, at each end.
The interior was all squares and angles, with twenty-foot ceilings
and great expanses of glass.

Just as Trina was taking all this in, a huge, heavyset man in a
poorly fitting sports coat appeared. He had long black hair
covering his ears, but was bald on top. His complexion was poor,
and he was wearing very dark sunglasses. He picked up Trina's
bags and disappeared, so she assumed this was Rafael; he was,
she thought, a most curious houseman.

"Please," the Indian woman said, gesturing down the curving

stairway to the living area. "Señor Delgado will be here in a
moment."

Trina stepped down into the living room. The furnishings were
quiet and tasteful, black lacquer and blond wood, the kind of
smart European imports Trina used to admire in the windows of
the Zona Rosa, wondering who could ever afford to pay the import
duties. Sprinkled amidst the sleek furniture was spotlit Mexican
artifacts of stone and pottery.

Tall glass doors led onto a wide deck. Trina stepped out and
leaned over the railing and looked down. The house hugged the
hillside, and she counted at least four levels below her, dropping
down to the lushly landscaped grounds. There was a big tile
fountain, a small lap pool with a black bottom, even an ornate
greenhouse tucked away at the corner of the property. The
perimeter was encircled by both a high fence and dense plantings
of cacti.

"Ms. Robbins," came the quiet voice from behind her.

She turned quickly to see Delgado standing in the doorway. He
was wearing gray slacks and a wrinkled white linen jacket over
some kind of European polo shirt. "I'm very glad to see you." He
extended his long arm and they shook hands rather formally.

"Quite a house," Trina said as she stepped back into the living
area. "You put some money in this place."

"I think of it as the best of Mexico and the U.S."

"U.S. dollars, I would guess."

Delgado smiled modestly. "The cost of living here is low. I
would have a hard time moving back to the States now."

"Even so," Trina said. "You must be doing well."

"Perhaps. I am . . . adaptable."

The young Indian woman appeared. "Would you like a
drink?" Delgado asked.

"Agua mineral," Trina told her. *"Con gas."*

"Johnny Walker sin hielo para mí," Delgado said, and the
young woman went away.

At that moment a little boy emerged from the far door and ran
across the deep white carpeting of the living area at full tilt,
building up considerable velocity before colliding into Delgado's
legs.

"Ay!" Delgado said, putting his hands on the boy's shoulders,
pretending that the force of the impact almost knocked him over.
"Calm yourself, Pablo!"

Trina smiled. The little boy looked to be six or seven, dressed
in blue jeans and an American T-shirt, cute, bright-eyed, with

shiny dark hair and a dimpled chin. His face was plump, mischievous, eyes perpetually in motion.

"*Hola*," she said.

The little boy promptly wheeled about and presented his hand with a self-confidence almost unnerving in a child so young. "Good evening," he said in only slightly accented English. "You are Señorita Robbins, yes?"

"Yes," Trina said, shaking the small warm hand. "And you are . . . ?"

"Pablo Kelley-Delgado," the little boy said with a neat half bow.

"It is your dinnertime," Delgado said, looking past the boy to where an older gray-haired woman in a blue uniform stood by the big door.

The little boy looked up at him, brown eyes wide. "*Tío*, I am only trying to be polite."

Delgado tousled his hair. "Well. You've done so. Now have your meal."

The boy turned, shook hands with Trina again, and then ran back out of the living room as quickly as he had arrived.

Trina looked at Delgado, curious. "He calls you Uncle."

Delgado nodded. "Please, sit down." Trina settled into one of the leather couches that extended out from both sides of the high lava fireplace. Delgado sat on the couch across from her, crossing his long legs, taking a moment to tug a pant cuff into place, smoothing the fabric.

"He is your nephew?"

"No." Delgado said, settling back. "Pablo is a boy I adopted several years ago. A street child."

"An orphan?"

Delgado shrugged. "Maybe yes, maybe no. He doesn't seem to recall."

"Then . . ."

"It is a sad new twist in Mexico. Something you would think to find in Rio perhaps, but not here, where the family is so important. But when the population pressure grows too great, the young are pushed from the nest. It is a disease of overpopulation," Delgado said, "just as surely as late-stage malnutrition."

He looked away for a moment, then focused again on Trina. "Anyway, Pablo was one of the youngest; he was brought to the clinic. A three-year-old boy with a knife wound. After he healed I brought him home with me."

"His English is excellent."

Delgado nodded. "He is very bright," he said, smiling paternally. "Sometimes he frightens me."

The maid reappeared with two glasses on a small silver tray. She served Trina, then Delgado.

Delgado raised his glass. "To a successful and memorable visit."

They drank, and then Trina watched him for a moment. "Somehow," she said, "I don't recall you as being such a humanitarian."

Delgado took a sip of his Scotch, his expression slightly remote.

"Whatever happened to your friend? What was his name? Rand?"

Trina shrugged. "By now I figure he's either dead or in NA."

"Pardon?"

"A self-help group. Sometimes I fantasize that I'm going to walk into a meeting and there he'll be, sitting across the table."

"Do you think that's possible?"

She shook her head. "It's probably better keeping it a fantasy."

Delgado nodded. "As I recall, he was a strong man. Not a very honest one." He looked at her for a moment. "Are you still interested in talking about the past?"

"Not necessarily."

"Good," he said. "I think . . . that the past is sometimes best forgotten. People like us, we have more to contribute to the future. We should talk about the future."

"Fine." Trina raised her glass. "To the future."

They talked about the old clinic that had stood in Tepito for decades. Tepito was the Harlem of Mexico City, a tough, gritty neighborhood best known for producing infamous criminals and famous boxers. But in fact Tepito was no longer where the truly poor lived: now the worst areas were squatters' camps around the perimeter of the city, where country people, driven out of rural areas, had set up piecemeal communities on unoccupied land.

"More than a million come every year. Absolutely destroys urban planning." Delgado waved one hand vaguely toward downstairs. "Pablo came from one of the squatters' communities, in an area that was to be maintained as parkland to provide oxygen. Now . . . it would take the army to get them out." He looked over at Trina. "Perhaps tomorrow or the next day we can go with Pablo to his village. He's the best guide. Then you'll see what I'm doing here." He smiled slightly. "Besides living well."

"You look around Mexico City," Trina said, "and everybody is childbearing age. I mean, this is just the start, isn't it?"

Delgado shrugged. "Who knows? Mexico has survived a great deal in the past. But this . . ." He shook his head. "We'll see."

Trina nodded. "Have you seen the papers for the conference?"

"I have. We have two hundred attendees registered, thirty reporters, from around the world."

"And the opening?"

"On Tuesday night a reception, and then a huge gala under a giant tent on the clinic grounds. Caswell and Markham will fly down for it, much of Mexico City society, maybe even the President will be there, certainly some ranking ministers. It will be heavily covered in the newspapers, a symbol of what United Genetics is committing to Mexico City."

Trina raised her eyebrows. "Sounds as if there's not much for me to do."

"I think you will find the preparations to be exceptional," Delgado said. "I will, of course, leave the journalists for your care. I assume that you will have balloons and ice cream for the reporters."

"You don't take what I do seriously, do you?"

"On the contrary." Delgado gazed at her steadily, his brown eyes large and placid. "Paul Markham has great respect for you and your predecessor, Mr. Rackley. In the U.S. what you do is very important. Here . . ." He shrugged.

"Why is here different?"

"Oh, in Mexico they admit the connections between us all more easily. If a reporter, for example, writes about a certain ministry, then every month the ministry sends him a little money, just to help out, knowing that reporters are so poorly paid. It is an accepted way here."

"And is that what you do? Send money to reporters?"

Delgado ignored the question. "I remember, once, talking to a reporter who told me about a ministry dinner he attended. There were cocktails and a nice meal, and the minister gave a little speech. Then the minister went to the bathroom. And his press secretary came around the table to each reporter, one after another, and said, 'It's your turn.' And each would go to the bathroom, where the minister would hand him an envelope of cash."

Trina was shocked. "That's totally corrupt."

Delgado shrugged and sipped his scotch. "I would call it totally honest. We all work for someone." He looked at his watch. "Let me show you the rest of the house."

Trina followed Delgado down a circular staircase. The house descended the hillside in four levels, the kitchen and a huge dining room below the living room, then bedrooms, then finally, when the property approached the bottom of the hill, the servants' quarters. Also on the lowest level was a large entertainment room complete with a small wooden dance floor, an elaborate sound system, two big projection video screens, and a wide wet bar made of mahogany. From the discotheque the back of the house opened in high French doors onto a large flat patio area. In front of the doors was another small dining area, the table already set with linen and silver and candles.

"We'll eat down here," Delgado said. "The dining room upstairs is too big for only two. It echoes."

As soon as they were seated, the Indian maid appeared with a cold pumpkin soup, and they began dinner.

"Kaye Rackley is missing," Trina said after a moment.

Delgado, spoon midway to his lips, showed no surprise. "How do you know that?" he asked quietly.

"Her brother told me."

Delgado nodded, sipping his soup, saying nothing.

"Where do you suppose she went?"

Delgado shrugged elaborately. "The very rich have many options."

"Where would you go?"

Delgado thought for a moment. "Tangier perhaps. Although that's more difficult for a woman." He appeared disinterested.

"I might come here."

"Here?"

"Mexico City, I mean."

Delgado shook his head. "Too close to home. Most unwise."

There was another long silence, and then Delgado looked up, his eyes very dark brown in the candlelight. "There was another reason I told you that story about journalists."

"Oh?"

"To make a point. We Americans are very judgmental people, I think. And so, if you see things here that are not done the way you would do them . . ." He held out one hand, rocked it slightly from side to side. "Try to accept."

"I'm pretty good at acceptance."

Delgado smiled, teeth very white, and for a moment Trina thought how really attractive he was. "Very good. I knew you must be."

At that moment Rafael, Delgado's houseman, came in. *"Teléfono. Señor Markham."*

Delgado picked up his napkin, dabbed at his lips, raised one finger. "Trina," he said. "This will take a minute. Why don't you go out and look at the gardens? They are really very nice."

"Fine."

"Please excuse me." Delgado gestured toward the high glass doors that opened out onto the huge tile patio. "Enjoy the grounds."

Trina stepped out onto the patio, and her eyes quickly adjusted to the bright moonlight. The back courtyard of Delgado's estate was characteristic of modern Mexican design: great expanses of tile broken by flying arches of concrete, pools of water plants in carefully maintained fountains. The immediate patio was surrounded by tropical plantings with manicured footpaths of crushed volcanic rock.

She followed one of these paths farther back, past philodendrons and tree ferns and banana plants, and came around a corner to see, a dozen feet distant, a long greenhouse with a solid white metal framework and big glass panes. It was in scale to the rest of the estate: at least sixty feet long and half again as wide.

Trina walked closer, pushed open the old rusting door, and stepped inside. In the moonlight she could barely make out the silhouettes of the plants within, but even in the dim blue light they looked oddly uniform and familiar. With one hand she groped along the rough metal doorframe. At last she felt an old-fashioned toggle switch, threw it, and the greenhouse was suddenly, blazingly illuminated.

Her breath stopped in her throat. The greenhouse was filled with waist-high tables, covered with crudely fashioned wooden containers. The containers, in turn, held hundreds of tall, healthy Rice Five plants.

Trina stepped closer and examined the plants more carefully. No doubt about it: the plants were Rice Five. She recognized it easily from the visits she and Rackley had made to the Delta infestations.

She started walking slowly through the musty old greenhouse, stepping carefully on the uneven wooden floorboards between the rows of Rice Five. At the other end she could see a laboratory bench, its stainless steel top covered with sophisticated instrumentation and elaborate glassware. It looked utterly out of place next to the rough plank flooring and wavy, hand-poured glass panes. As she drew closer, she could see that the bench was a kind of small office with two cane chairs off to one side.

Trina paused, baffled. What could Delgado be doing raising

Rice Five in his greenhouse? Did he have some fantasy of trying to sell it as a crop in Mexico? Regardless of his motivation, Trina sensed that this was something she was not supposed to know. Simultaneously, she felt a quick pulse of fear. With the interior lights switched on, the greenhouse would be a glaring beacon to anyone who glanced out the rear windows of Delgado's house.

Trina looked around once more, then walked quickly back to the door. She reached the exit and had one hand on the light switch when Delgado appeared at the door.

"Edward," she said, the pitch of her voice raised by fear and surprise.

Delgado stared at her, his eyes showing little expression past some mild surprise of his own. He reached around the corner and flipped off the light switch himself, casting them both into sudden darkness.

They stood there a moment in silence as Trina's eyes gradually accommodated to the moonlight.

"You're growing Rice Five," Trina said finally. "I don't—"

"I've always been interested in plants," Delgado said mildly.

"But this is a very dangerous plant."

"Perhaps that's why it interests me."

Trina said nothing. After a few breaths she could see that Delgado was smiling slightly. "It does get chilly out here at night, doesn't it?" he said softly. "People forget that Mexico City is at such a high elevation."

Trina simply nodded. She was in fact shivering, but not from cold.

Delgado didn't move. He leaned forward, putting both his arms on the doorframe behind her so she was momentarily trapped between his outstretched forearms. "You used to like dangerous things. Didn't you?"

Trina cleared her throat, turning her head to one side. "When I was very young. No longer."

Delgado nodded, leaning closer. With one hand he gently touched her hair. He leaned even closer and very softly kissed her ear. She trembled involuntarily at the feel of his warm breath on her neck.

"I'm not going to sleep with you," she said quickly. "I'm . . ."

Delgado drew back. For a moment he was angry, then his expression changed to amusement. "Not that kind of girl?"

"I'm not a girl," Trina said, shifting, her back against the cold metal frame of the greenhouse. "And I think we'll be better off with a . . . professional relationship."

Delgado inclined his head, raised one eyebrow, said nothing. Then he leaned forward abruptly, and suddenly he was kissing Trina, not hard, but with firm pressure. At the same time she felt his arm slide around her back, pulling her forward, and she smelled the faint but pleasing scent of his cologne.

"Really," Trina said, pulling back.

"Really." Delgado held her more firmly and she relaxed, just slightly, appreciating the warmth of his embrace, the enveloping strength of his long arms. Tentatively, not precisely knowing what she thought, she returned the kiss. Then after a moment she felt one of his hands come around her waist, under her blouse, warm on the smooth flesh of her stomach, moving upward.

"Edward," she protested, but mildly, and then his hand was under the elastic of her bra and he was pulling her close. She could feel him hard against her thigh. A heat was building within her now, and she opened her mouth and returned his kiss with full passion, pressing into him, no longer thinking at all.

In the morning Delgado was already gone when she awoke in his bed. The room was huge: one wall was made of volcanic rock with a big fireplace, and the floor was polished dark wood, scattered with fur rugs. The bed was on a raised portion of floor, with an elaborate television and stereo system built into the footboard. Filtered gray light fell from two tall glass sliding doors. Beyond the doors a small deck overlooked the grounds and canyon behind the big house.

Trina moved slightly in the bed, feeling the silk sheets against her bare skin, stretching, still drowsy, then realized that a quiet tapping at the door had awakened her.

"*Sí?*" she said, and the door opened and Delgado's maid, a young Indian woman in her twenties, walked in with a tray, which she set on the table beside the big bed.

"*Buenos días,*" the young woman said shyly.

"*Buenos días. Gracias.*" Trina held the sheet over her breasts and sat up and examined the tray. There was a small silver pot of coffee, some sliced fruit, a basket of Mexican breakfast pastries. There was also a vase with a single orchid and a folded sheet of paper.

She unfolded the note.

I am glad you decided to stay with me. My driver can take you to the clinic. Or perhaps you could take a tour with Pablo. E.

Trina put one of the pastries on a plate and leaned back with a cup of strong coffee.

Jesus, she thought. Now what? She had to admit that she felt good. Just to feel her flesh kneaded, her body caressed, her breath quickened. She hadn't slept with a man for two months, and Delgado was an energetic, exciting lover, who had carried her to peaks she had not felt for years.

He been precisely correct last night: she did like dangerous things and crazy men. In fact, she thought, gazing out at the profuse garden beyond the glass doors, that was her problem. Crazy men, she knew, usually ended up with sane women. That was how they survived: Rackley and Kaye, for example. But what was a crazy woman supposed to do? Sane men wanted sane women too.

She shook her head and reached for a piece of Mexican sweetbread, and then heard another tapping at the door.

"*Sí?*" she said, thinking for a moment that this was a very busy bedroom.

Once again the door opened, and this time the visitor was Pablo. He was wearing new blue jeans, incongruously creased, and a striped shirt. His dark hair was slicked back, and even in child's clothing somehow his bearing was that of a tiny adult.

"Good morning, Señorita Robbins," he said brightly. "Am I disturbing you?"

Trina tugged at her sheet and straightened up. "Well . . ."

"I only wanted to say," Pablo rushed on, "that Tío said you might want to see my village. If you do, I am ready to go."

Trina frowned slightly. "Don't you go to school or something?"

"Tío has tutors come here for me. But not until after lunch."

Trina nodded without much enthusiasm. She had promised Delgado that she would visit one of the squatter camps, and she might as well do it before the conference began. "Well, okay. Maybe before I go to the clinic."

"Very good!" Pablo said, his large eyes catching a reflection of the big glass door at the end of the room. "I will wait for you downstairs."

CHAPTER TWENTY TWO

Ten minutes from landing, Rackley leaned back in the narrow airplane seat and recalled his only other visit to Mexico City. It had been a year ago, just after Markham coined the name Caswell Clinic for the Diseases of Overpopulation. Markham and Rackley had flown down for a single day and had first been driven to the old clinic in a crowded section of Mexico City. Outside in the cobbled streets of Tepito a long line of patients waited, old and young, some in Indian garb, others in tattered clothes, surrounded by decaying buildings, the smell of boiling tripe strong in the air, wafting up from the pots of the sidewalk taco vendors.

Markham and Rackley had been taken quickly through the old clinic, upstairs to a small third-floor dining room, for a lunch with Edward Kelley-Delgado and a young Mexican scientist, Maria Aguirre, who was the head of research.

The lunch was an odd affair. Aguirre's English was hesitant, so Delgado, expansive, ebullient, exceedingly cosmopolitan, did most of the talking.

"You name it," he told Rackley over fresh spiny lobster flown in from the Sea of Cortez. "Any disorder. We see it here."

Rackley looked at him sharply. "You seem almost proud of that."

"Not at all," Delgado said. "It's simply a fact of life on this planet."

Delgado raised his water tumbler. "Fill this from a city tap here," he said, "and you have Love Canal in a glass. No one has even tried to identify the industrial chemicals in the drinking water. We are seeing forms of cancer now that truly boggle the mind." He nodded, ate a chunk of lobster. "And that's among the people lucky enough to have tap water. The squatters from the country, who live in the shantytowns, God knows what they drink."

Maria Aguirre interrupted. "We have a specialist here," she said quietly, "who likes to say: 'If intestinal parasites were fireflies, Mexico City would be as bright as the sun.'"

"Jesus," Rackley said.

"The government does what it can," Markham said. "But if we can help the poor of Mexico City, we can help the world. It's a little laboratory of suffering right in our own backyard."

"Do you need more mayonnaise?" Delgado asked, pronouncing the word with a French emphasis.

Rackley, who was already feeling queasy, simply shook his head.

They had spent the rest of that day in Mexico City, paying a courtesy call to the ministry of health, then attending a dinner Delgado had arranged at an elegant restaurant in the center of Chapultepec Park, the huge park that ran through the middle of the city. The restaurant was a vaulted glass structure that overlooked a brightly lit lake; amid the linen, silver, and European cuisine, the dusty and decaying streets of Tepito had already seemed very far away.

Now, a year later, Rackley found his recollection of the entire visit to be vague, uncertain.

He looked back out the airplane window. The plane was now descending through a low level of clouds on final approach to Mexico City. Below, the city sprawled toward and over the volcanic hills that ringed it: huge, diffuse, ominous. On this visit he could not afford the luxury of vagueness. He had to think clearly, quickly.

At the airport, just before boarding the flight in San Francisco, he called the lawyer Tortola to tell him that he was going to disappear.

"You can't do that," Tortola had said, the concern sharp in his voice. "You'll only make things worse."

Rackley hesitated a moment. "Kaye is already gone. I'm trying to find her."

There was a long silence at the other end of the line. "I had a feeling," Tortola said finally, "that might be the case."

"You said the evidence was in her womb," Rackley said. "She heard that very clearly."

Another long silence. "That is, unfortunately, more true than ever. I was going to call you. Larson is dropping the request for the embryo scan. I'll go over to Berkeley myself to see that they're returned to storage."

"Thank you."

"An ironic turn of the law," Tortola said. "My objections were based on precedents that blocked embryo engineering in the first place. Now they're protecting you. At least for the moment."

"It does get complicated."

Tortola sighed. "On one hand we pry into the very souls of these embryos, and on the other we protect them as if they were full humans. Sometimes I think the law may never catch up."

"Maybe," said Rackley, "this is one time our hearts should lead and the law follow."

"You can't avoid this by running away."

Rackley's flight was being called. He put his hand over the receiver of the telephone, then spoke. "I'd understand if you wanted to drop the case."

"Just when it's getting interesting?" Tortola had asked. "I'm not going anywhere. When they give you your dime, call me."

Rackley tightened his seat belt as the plane lost altitude. As he did, he checked the location of the money belt that rode just below his navel. Even after Rackley had been sober for years, he still recalled what it was like to be down to one's last dollar. Somehow he found himself collecting lines of credit at various banks—far more than he needed, always chiding himself for his insecurity. Now he was glad for his little fetish. Two hours after leaving Trina's loft this morning he had visited five banks and collected fifteen thousand dollars in cash: no sense in leaving a credit card trail.

Rackley leaned back in the seat as the stewardess announced their final descent. He closed his eyes and tried for a moment to relax. But the tension and fear that had settled into his chest remained, a sense of pure uncertainty and hard news still to come. He thought of Kaye, but the image of Mexico City remained in his mind: mile after mile of tile roofs and dots of green parkland and gray concrete and the cluttered sprawl of squatters' towns. It was the kind of city where a person could disappear forever.

That same morning Trina had visited the clinic only briefly, checking in with the administrator, Maria Aguirre. Then, excusing herself with a story about picking up lost luggage, she borrowed a small Ford from the clinic carpool. She promptly headed out of town and now was sitting in front of the modern, stressed concrete international terminal of the Mexico City airport. Rackley's flight had arrived twenty minutes earlier, so she expected to see him emerge from the terminal building soon.

She had slipped the airport cop five hundred pesos the first time he had come around, and now she sat idly in the car's front seat in a line of what seemed to be perpetually double-parked cars. As she watched, she saw a street kid of eight or nine working his way up the line of cars, slopping a soaking wet rag onto each windshield and doing a bit of desultory cleaning, then holding out his hand for a coin.

She sat back and idly watched the kid approach. Curious, she thought. Yesterday she had felt disoriented, a bit off-balance— half from the altitude, she supposed, half from the pure hustle and fever produced by the competition for resources in the largest city in the world. For Trina the intersections symbolized the city best: there, in the midst of stalled traffic, peddlers sold everything from songs to gum to fire-breathing, going from car to car, earning the equivalent of perhaps a dollar a day. But now she was already beginning to feel at home in Mexico City again. Even her Spanish seemed to be still serviceable.

Ten years ago she and Rand had lived here for five months in the Polanco district, atop a fancy new building whose primary distinction was a facade made of imported English stone. It had looked like any other stone to Trina, but their penthouse had an excellent view of downtown, and on the rare occasions that the searing, choking smog lifted, one could even see out to the hills at the edge of the city.

Rand had been arranging new contacts in the Mexican provinces, flying occasionally to Peru and Colombia. Trina's job had been to take care of the apartment, which, with a full-time maid and cook, was not terribly trying. It gave her ample time to wander the city, and she had departed with a curious mix of love and hate for the place. She never adjusted to the stark juxtaposition of wealth and poverty, the sight of Indian women with tiny babies begging pesos in front of chic interior design shops filled with costly merchandise from Paris and Rome.

The kid with the bucket and the wet cloth was getting closer. She shifted in her seat, glancing up to see whether Rackley was approaching. Rand used to say that in the U.S. we tried to be shits to each other without actually breaking the laws. In Mexico they ignored the laws and just acted like human beings, which meant being shits part of the time, surprisingly sweet the rest.

The kid with the rag approached. It would be the third time today someone had washed the windshield unbidden, so in the moments before the kid's hand touched the glass, Trina reached out lazily and flicked on the windshield wipers. As the wipers skittered across the dry glass, the boy drew his hand back suddenly and stared through the windshield, clearly surprised that a gringa knew this trick. She shook her head, very slightly, but then just as the kid started to move on to the next car, she held a fifty peso coin out the open window.

Shitty and sweet, Trina thought. The boy, she thought, reminded her of some of the kids she'd seen earlier that morning with Pablo. She shifted slightly in the seat. The visit to Pablo's home village had been disturbing, and she was still trying to figure out just what she'd heard there.

"Why do you call this a parachute town?" Trina had asked Pablo when they had emerged from the car to stand at the top of a rocky hill looking down on the gigantic squatters' encampment below them. A warm wind swept up the hill, carrying the scent of wood smoke and sewage and frying cornmeal.

"Because," Pablo said seriously, "one day you look and they're not here. The next day they're everywhere. Like they dropped out of the sky."

Trina nodded. She had read about the phenomenon that had in recent years swelled Mexico City's population to the largest on the planet. Poor people came in droves from the countryside, commandeering open land. The loose-knit groups would even rent bulldozers to knock down trees and level the land. Buildings of loose rock and scrap wood with corrugated metal roofs would appear overnight. Wires strung randomly through the sparse trees brought in free electricity from the nearest powerline.

"And this is where you were born?"

"I think so," Pablo said. "I'm not sure. But this is where Tío found me." The little boy gestured down the rocky path, rutted, filled with water, broken by broad patches of mud. "Would you like to walk?"

They started down the roadway. One hundred yards in was a collection of fifty-gallon metal drums for drinking water, the barrels bright blue in the middle of a muddy clearing. Surrounding the barrels were dozens of shacks. Some were built of lava rock, a few of brick, and some were made only of plywood and cardboard. The detritus and debris of industrial scavenging were everywhere, and all manner of hoses ran crazily across the ground. There were goats and chickens in some of the trash-strewn yards; dozens of small children ran and played in the midst of scrap metal and shattered bricks. There was a faint, pervasive odor of fresh sewage everywhere.

"*Momentito.*" Pablo disappeared into the doorway of one of the huts. He returned a minute later with two dusty green prickly pears. The child extracted a pearl-handled pocket knife from his neatly creased jeans and deftly peeled the fruit as they walked. At last he speared the sweet pink fruit on the end of the knife blade and offered it to Trina.

"Thank you."

"Parachute people," Pablo said, looking around. "You don't have this in California."

"No, we don't. And these are the people who come to the clinic?"

Pablo nodded solemnly, concentrating on peeling the second pear. "Yes. Tío sends buses up here twice a week. All the ladies go to the clinic for their babies. They love Tío very much here. He walks through and everyone says hello."

Trina glanced around. "And you used to live here too?"

"Once," Pablo said. "Not for years. Tío came here, and took me and my brother, and two of our friends." He looked up at Trina. "We were very sick. Our parents had come from the country, but they had troubles and finally they went away."

"And left you here."

Pablo nodded solemnly. "But then Tío came along." He tapped the side of his head. "We were sick."

"Sick?" Trina frowned. "I thought you were . . . cut with a knife."

Pablo shrugged. "I don't know about that. But we were . . . turning stupid. From bad food, bad air."

"And he took you to the clinic."

Pablo nodded. "He gave us medicine, good food, a place to sleep."

"That was very kind of him," Trina said. "Where is your brother now?"

Pablo was silent for a long moment. "He's . . . dead."

"Oh. I'm sorry. I thought . . ."

Pablo hesitated and looked up at her. He lowered his high, thin voice. "Can you keep a secret?"

"I think so."

"The police killed him," Pablo said softly, solemnly.

Trina stopped walking and looked down at the precocious little boy. "What?"

"Because he would not tell secrets," Pablo said, nodding seriously. He gazed at her, eyes bright, quick. "Do you want to stop walking now?"

"What secrets?"

Pablo shrugged, looked away, shaking his head in a combination of childish self-importance and uncertainty. "Oh, secrets about Tío. Things that Tío told us never to say."

"What things?"

Pablo gazed at her. "Are you going to live in our house?"

"No," she said, a bit too sharply. "I mean, I have my own house. In California."

He nodded sagely. "You'll have to ask Tío about his secrets."

"Of course," Trina said. "Of course."

"Would you like more fruit now?"

Trina shook her head, but smiled, touching the little boy's hair. "No, thanks. I should go to the clinic now."

"*Bueno.*" Pablo pivoted on one heel in the rutted, muddy pathway and gestured formally back up the hill. "I'll tell the driver."

Trina, roused from her reverie, glanced over her shoulder and saw Rackley approaching, looking harried, walking quickly, trailed by four pirate cabdrivers and two young boys hanging onto his suitcase. She stepped out of the car quickly and walked up.

"*Gracias no,*" she said loudly to Rackley's assorted hangers-on. "Now go."

"Jesus," Rackley said as Trina took his suitcase and kissed him quickly on the cheek. "What a mob scene."

"Big city," Trina said, "and there's not enough of anything to go around." She popped the trunk on the Ford and put Rackley's small valise within. Then she turned and they embraced, leaning into each other, relieved once again to be together.

Ten minutes later Rackley was sitting, utterly pale and quite silent, in the passenger's seat. Once out of the airport sprawl, on the highway into town, Trina had accelerated to eighty miles an hour almost immediately. Then in town she ran two red lights and—from Rackley's perspective—barely avoided a half dozen accidents ranging from minor scrapes to head-on collisions.

He said nothing until Trina missed a turn on a wide boulevard and, without hesitation, made a U-turn in the middle of the *avenida* by cranking the wheel hard, jumping the curb, and clunking over the grass-covered center strip.

"God damn, Trina," Rackley said at last. "You're driving like a crazy person."

Her concentration momentarily broken, Trina looked over at him with surprise. "Hey," she said. "Mexico City was made for drivers like me. If you learn to drive here, you can drive anyplace . . . Cairo . . . Singapore . . ." She shrugged and smiled. "You get stopped, you just pay the guy off and you're on your way."

Rackley stretched out in the seat, staring out at the crowded sidewalks, the grubby gray shop fronts and open stalls, but his attention snapped back when Trina hit the brakes full on as a small VW bus cut in front of them. She rapped on her horn five times, very quickly, in short bursts. The driver's head appeared from the window of the bus, glaring back at her.

"Five toots," Trina explained, "means—ah—'Screw your mother.'"

The bus honked back at her twice, quickly.

"And that means 'No, your mother,'" she said, smiling slightly. "Great system, no?"

Rackley was silent for a long moment. "What do we do?"

"First we'll get you settled at the hotel. It's a nice place, a little out of the way, right next to the toxic waste dump. Then . . ."

She slowed briefly for a crowded intersection, then accelerated straight through, barely clearing a slow-moving bus packed with passengers.

"This is a hell of a big city."

"There aren't all that many places you can stash a rich gringa though."

"At Delgado's house?"

Trina shook her head. "It's a mansion near the park. You should see it—eight bedrooms, disco, kind of *Playboy* goes to Mexico. Also, he's got this little kid living with him."

Trina made another heart-stopping turn off the Paseo de la Reforma, straight through a column of jaywalking pedestrians, who scattered, quite unconcerned.

"God," Rackley breathed.

"One thing. Delgado has a greenhouse filled with Rice Five."

"Well," Rackley said. "At least it's safe in a greenhouse. That's what we should have done with it too."

She glanced over at him. "But why . . . ?"

"Markham used to talk like that stuff was going to make a fortune. Maybe Delgado still thinks it can." He shrugged. "If he wants to play Luther Burbank, that's his business." He tapped his foot on the floorboard of the little Ford, staring out at the traffic. "I want to see the old clinic. Let's start there."

"There's nothing there now. Everything's been moved to the new building in the suburbs."

"Humor me."

"*Bueno*," Trina said. "At your service."

They drove down the crowded *paseo,* finally reaching the Tepito district, the traffic slow and crowded, edging along dusty streets between two- and three-story buildings. At last Trina parked the car in front of a pharmacy; when Rackley peered through the open door, he saw that the counter was behind steel bars.

Trina stepped out and went around in front and opened the hood of the little car. She peered inside for a moment, then reached in delicately and pulled out an ignition cable.

She saw Rackley staring at her. "A little insurance," she said. "Cars can disappear. Once I was down here and parked for five minutes, and when I came out, my headlights were gone. This kid, no more than eight, came up and said he was sorry to see my headlights missing, but he had two just like them he could sell me cheap." She smiled and slammed the hood. "The clinic is this way."

She headed off down a narrow sidewalk, the street alongside torn and potholed. Chickens scratched in the alleyways, and they walked past dozens of little outdoor stalls selling toys, shoes, car parts, bolts of bright fabric. "This is where all the really good boxers come from," she said. "Also, there's a *mercado* near here where you can get all kinds of hot goods, illegal imports, but then as soon as you come out on the street the cops bust you and you have to pay them off too."

In the next block they passed two stands selling beautiful little pastries. "That's one thing I didn't appreciate the last time I lived here," Trina said as she admired a display of tiny white and pink frosted cakes on wooden boxes balanced on the curb. "This country really knows how to handle sugar."

Around the next corner was a crowded *taquería,* open to the street, with a huge pot of boiling organ meat out in front, overpowering, odorous. Rackley felt slightly dizzy; already the air was making his eyes burn, and his senses were overcome by smells and crowds. Across the street a young woman leaned out of a second-story window, hanging wash; below her on the sidewalk a terribly crippled young man moved slowly, pushing a handmade walker in front of him.

At last Trina and Rackley reached the old clinic, a massive, four-story dirty yellow building half the length of the block, erected back in the previous century when the neighborhood had been a posh locale. It had elaborate carved stonework over the entrance and a big sign that read "THE CASWELL CLINIC," and under that in smaller letters, "United Genetics, S.A."

Trina and Rackley strolled by slowly and Rackley studied the building. It did appear deserted; the first floor windows had no curtains, and the front door was chained and padlocked with two armed guards standing on the stairs.

"Are those cops?" Rackley asked quietly.

Trina glanced sideways. "I don't think so," she said. "Private security. Hard to tell though. Around here even the shoeshine boys wear uniforms."

"What are they guarding?"

"Oh, Delgado has some idea about refurbishing it as an orphanage. If somebody doesn't watch the place, folks will strip it down to the studs for building materials."

Rackley nodded again and they turned the corner, past an old Indian woman selling freshly peeled mangoes, bright orange atop a big block of ice. "There's a small parking area behind the building," Trina said, "and a loading dock too." As they passed the alleyway that led to the back of the big old building, she stopped for a moment, staring at a shiny metal-flake bronze automobile parked halfway up the sidewalk.

"Huh," she said. "That's Delgado's car."

Rackley studied the sleek vehicle. It looked odd—like an American car, but somehow different, more streamlined. Abruptly he realized it had no chrome, no manufacturer's insignia, and the grill had been replaced with an all-black frame, vaguely ominous but also quite stylish.

"Let's keep walking," Trina said, slightly nervous now.

"What's he doing here?"

Trina raised both hands, dropped them. "Who knows. He seems to get around everywhere, except I can't ever figure out what he's supposed to be doing. Fits the local style perfectly."

"What kind of car is that?"

"Oh," Trina said, "it's a Chrysler, I think. With the import duties a Porsche costs one hundred and twenty thousand dollars here. So rich guys take Mexican-made cars and customize them.

Delgado's got tuck and roll leather, a hand paint job, new sheet metal. The engine's so supercharged it'll probably blow up in a couple of months."

"He really did go native," Rackley said, glancing back over his shoulder.

"He's very proud of that car. I asked him last night, and he wouldn't let me drive it."

Rackley looked at her closely, surprised by this note of familiarity. "Are you . . ."

"Sleeping with Delgado?" She glanced over at him. "That's none of your business."

"So you are."

Trina stopped walking and looked at him. "Does it bother you?"

"Well," Rackley said, "he's . . ."

"He's an attractive man. I think he trusts me. And that's good for both of us."

She started walking again. "Seen enough? I have to get back to the clinic now."

"I haven't seen anything yet," Rackley said, catching up with her. Although, even as he said it, he knew that wasn't quite true. Something about the big concrete loading dock behind the old clinic looked wrong, but at the moment, his eyes burning, his throat swelling, his chest newly short of breath, he couldn't quite figure just what it was. "But I think I should go lie down for a while."

C H A P T E R T W E N T Y T H R E E

Kaye Rackley stood at the upstairs window of the old colonial-era house and gazed down, through leaded glass, on a cobblestone courtyard. Beyond the courtyard was a flawlessly maintained lawn, a sheet of lush green, and past that, a high brick wall, topped with shards of broken glass. Outside the gray clouds of the morning had now given way to the constant dull haze of Mexico City pollution, warmed by yellow sunlight. It would be nice today, Kaye thought, and returned to her dresser, selecting a white embroidered blouse.

For a moment before she pulled the blouse over her head, she turned and examined her thin torso in the big mahogany-framed mirror on the white plaster wall. There was no visible sign of her pregnancy. Not that she expected any. Were it not for the carefully monitored process, she might not even yet be aware of her condition, although this morning she had arisen feeling slightly queasy, and in recent days she had taken unaccustomed naps in midafternoon.

Kaye watched herself in the mirror for another moment. In the midst of all the problems she at least felt secure about the child she was carrying; she and Rackley had done the right thing. She wondered how it must be for women who have no idea about the nature of the child growing within them. For most women, she thought; for women through all history, until now.

Her naps, Kaye thought, might be the first signs of pregnancy.

But they could just as well be symptomatic of utter boredom. She had been in this house for over a week now, and she missed Rackley more each day. Her brother Edward called regularly, telling her to wait, to stay out of touch, that they were taking care of the situation. He passed on the news that the lawyer Tortola had regained custody of the two other embryos, now safely in cryogenic storage at Birthtech. But he also warned that Rackley was being watched, was in danger of being indicted, and not to write or call him. Not that Kaye could have, even if she wanted: the only telephone in the house was in a locked study downstairs, protected by Señor Gutierrez, the large, balding retainer who ran the household. Gutierrez's favorite English phrase whenever Kaye requested anything was "No problem." She had come to realize that this didn't mean yes; it meant no problem for Gutierrez if he ignored her.

But Kaye knew the stakes were high. She had been shocked to see in the Mexico City English language newspaper that Stuart Lipsky had committed suicide. It seemed to her so sad and pointless that a man who had created so much would end his life simply because society wasn't ready for his work. But Edward, over and over, during their long telephone conversations, reassured her: it would all be straightened out soon, he promised, perhaps after the Congressional hearing. In the meantime, he told her, she should stay calm and think only of herself.

Kaye heard the big front gate scrape on the cobblestones. She went quickly to the leaded glass window and looked down on the yard. Involuntarily she froze for a moment. The visitor was a police car: dark blue and gray with the motto *"Protección y Validad"* emblazoned on both doors. The vehicle pulled slowly into the courtyard and the uniformed officer at the wheel leaned out to talk to the young guard. Kaye watched, then turned away.

The first time she had seen the police was just after she and Edward flew down on the chartered Gulfstream from the little airport in Modesto. She had been so frightened that she ran around the big room, looking for a place to hide, tossing her clothes under the bed. She had been crouched in the closet when Gutierrez, the burly houseman, came up to announce dinner.

Her fright proved quite unnecessary. "Señor Delgado," Gutierrez had told her the day he found her in the closet, "is a very good friend of the police." The big man seemed confused by her concern. "They are looking in only to make sure that no one is bothering you." He smiled, showing widely gapped teeth. "No problem!"

A strange arrangement, she thought, coming from a man who was supposed to be the administrator of a medical clinic. But Delgado had proven to be very thoughtful, visiting several times to make certain that she was comfortable, even sending over his own cook when Kaye complained that the cook who came with the house seemed unable to prepare anything but soggy imitations of French cuisine.

Yesterday when Delgado telephoned to say that her brother and Markham would soon be in town, Kaye had mentioned her boredom. Her Spanish was limited to a domestic vocabulary; she would like, she told Delgado, someone new to talk to. Delgado had thought for a moment and then promised to send over a young English-speaking woman the next day. Perhaps, he suggested, they would go for a walk in the park.

"But," Delgado had said, "no real names. I will tell her that you are here for . . . some cosmetic surgery. She'll call you— ah—Julia. You don't mind?"

Odd as this sounded, Kaye immediately agreed. She longed to get out of the house; she hadn't thus far once used the big map of Mexico City that Edward had given her the night they left the country. She saw now that the map was little more than an attempt to make her think this trip some kind of adventure. Instead she increasingly felt as if she was a virtual prisoner in the gloomy old house.

Just as she finished brushing her hair, she heard the gate open again. This time when she looked out, it was a small Volkswagen she hadn't seen before. The driver was known to the young guard, who gestured the vehicle in with a lazy wave of one arm. The VW pulled up in the cobblestone courtyard and parked. When the driver's door opened, a small Mexican woman, wearing a gray skirt, high boots, and a black shawl, stepped out. The woman shut the car door and then looked up at the house, pushing her long dark hair back. Kaye stared, startled: the young woman was Maria Aguirre, Lipsky's lover, the woman in the photograph he had shown her the morning they had been arrested.

In the big downstairs hallway Gutierrez introduced Maria. When he called Kaye "Julia," Maria showed no indication that she knew who Kaye really was. "I'm the technical administrator at the clinic," Maria said. "Señor Delgado said that you'd like some company."

In the Volkswagen on the way to the park Kaye considered whether she should keep her identity secret. It made little sense, but then Maria didn't seem to know who she was, and Kaye had thus far kept her promise to Lipsky: mention the work to no one, no matter who they were. As it was, Maria was just about Kaye's age, and they exchanged easy small talk about the weather and Maria's shawl and how lovely Mexico City could be but how little of it Kaye was able to see. After driving for twenty minutes through the perpetual rush hour traffic, they arrived at Chapultepec Park. They left the car and walked in through the main gates.

Kaye had noticed one other possible symptom of pregnancy: constant hunger. As soon as they were in the park, she and Maria stopped at a stand selling fruit—papayas and watermelons—carved into bright, fanciful shapes. It was only Friday, but already the park was filled with families, the sidewalks lined with little stalls selling every imaginable kind of food from tiny cheese sandwiches to huge cotton candy cones. The ground was already littered with bits of paper, half-eaten tortas, discarded toys.

"You know," Kaye said, "in the U.S. we go to the park to get away from people. Here I think you go to be with people. People versus nature. In the U.S. we draw murals of whales or empty forests. Here, when you draw a mural, it has hundreds of people."

"Maybe because that's what we've got." Maria swept one arm across the vista of parkland ahead of them, the hundreds of strollers, the drooping trees, the algae-filled ponds, the scrubby grass turned brown by acid rain. "The problem is that too many of us don't even see nature anymore. It is as if the environment doesn't exist. Maybe we love people too much."

"I don't know," Kaye said. "I don't think you can love people too much."

"Perhaps not." There was a long moment of silence, as if some unspoken understanding passed between the two women.

"You are—were—Stuart Lipsky's friend," Kaye said.

Maria looked over, her large brown eyes wide. "How did you know?"

"I was a patient of his. My name is Kaye Rackley."

"Oh no," Maria said, covering her mouth. "You were arrested."

Kaye nodded. "You can't tell anyone you saw me."

Maria shook her head, still stunned. "Of course not," she said, and then she spoke quickly. "May I ask you: Did he talk about me?"

Kaye put her arm around the thin young woman. "Of course he did. He showed me your picture."

For a moment Maria said nothing. She gazed at the ground and her pace slowed.

Finally Maria looked up. "He did not kill himself."

Kaye took a deep breath. "My brother said he was . . ."

"Very drunk. I know."

"People do bad things when they're drunk."

Maria looked at her. "He didn't drink. He didn't like it."

They stopped walking. "Do you want to sit down?" Kaye asked.

The two women sat on a white wrought iron bench, just off the sidewalk. On another bench a dozen feet away a young couple necked with extravagant passion. "He would never," Maria said, "leave all his work behind."

"Then what do you think happened?"

"I think he was killed," Maria said flatly. "Maybe by Edward Kelley-Delgado."

"Why? Because of the arrest?"

Maria shook her head, over and over. "No, no, no. Not because of you. Because of the experiments. I think they were afraid he was going to talk about the experiments." And then for the first time that morning Maria began to cry.

"Hey," Kaye said softly, rubbing the young woman's back, touching her hair, "it's all right. It's all right."

Finally Maria looked up at her. "Do you want me to tell you?"

Kaye sat back on the bench. Her initial thought was no, absolutely not, just let me get up and walk away from this. But it was too late for that. "Tell me," Kaye said, "whatever you'd like to."

"I don't know how it started. Well. Yes, I do. It was three years ago, just after Stuart first came. We were talking one day and I was describing to him one of the saddest things we see down here."

"What is that?"

"Now that food is scarce, in some of the poorest parts of the city there is not enough nutrition for very early brain development. So we see slight mental impairment. In some, more than others. We're not sure why. It is as if in certain children, their developing brains are more sensitive to the lack of nutrients."

"That's terrible."

"It is not as if they become morons," Maria said quickly. "It may be twenty points of IQ, a little slower motor response, some associated symptoms." She took a deep breath, steadying herself.

"We had been trying some early childhood enrichment

programs, that sort of thing, but you know, the damage is done.
But I was describing this to Stuart, and instantly his face grew
bright—he usually looked so sad, you know, it was wonderful to
see—and he said that he wondered if the Brockman sequence
might help."

Maria saw the change in Kaye's expression. "You know about
the Brockman sequence?"

"Certainly. In the U.S. it's called the forbidden sequence."

Maria nodded and pushed her dark hair back. "Anyway, Stuart
suggested this. We had to be very careful. The church is so
powerful here that it could have caused a lot of trouble, you know.
So Stuart cultured some SPL10 in Berkeley and cloned the
Brockman sequence from the Markham Project. We started work
with some of the orphans and street kids—implanting the
sequence in four- and five-year-olds."

"I thought it was for embryo therapy."

"Ideally, of course, yes," Maria said. "We also started some
work with embryos. Pregnant women like to come to the Caswell
Clinic because the national clinics are so crowded. We would
sometimes treat their babies in the womb."

"Let's walk," Kaye said, and the two stood and began to stroll
down the sidewalk past families, lovers, food and toy stands. A
new breeze had come up, bearing a dozen scents, from fresh
flowers to sharp cooking spices.

"Anyway," Maria said, "we began, and then Delgado found
out. He was furious. Very, very angry, and Stuart was afraid that
Delgado would turn him in. He'd had problems before, you
know."

Kaye nodded. "I know."

"God knows what would have happened to him here,
experimenting on the children, on the mothers."

"Do you think it was wrong?"

Maria looked up quickly. "Oh no—we knew it worked, it was
the only way to help."

Kaye nodded. "But Delgado didn't turn you in."

"No. Just the opposite. Stuart spent a lot of time talking to
him, and Delgado became very interested in the science. He came
by the lab all the time, and used to send over new students he had
hired, just so they could have the experience of working with
Stuart. He was always very admiring, very kind to Stuart."

"So why would Delgado do something bad to him?"

"Now," Maria said, with a sigh, "we are beginning to see
problems in the children who received the sequence after birth.

The first ones are growing up—the oldest is eight now—and they are very, very smart." She glanced over at Kaye. "It is almost frightening to see. One little boy lives at Delgado's house and is like an adult. Speaks four languages, perfectly. But there's also something strange about them, as if . . ."

"They're too smart for their own good."

"Exactly. In the last month two of them have been picked up by the police, for acting strangely on the street. And both times, once the boys were in the station house, they died."

"The police . . ."

"No," Maria said. "They killed themselves. Just held their breaths, until they suffocated."

"That's impossible."

"They are very loyal to Delgado. He saved them, of course. And he made them promise to keep the secret."

"But to die that way . . ."

"We picked up the bodies," Maria said flatly. "There was no other cause of death. Nothing organic. It was as if their minds could"— Maria momentarily hesitated, trying to find the correct English—"could overcome the survival instincts of the flesh."

Kaye stopped for a moment, gazing at the big lake crowded with families in small rental boats, laughing, splashing the water with their paddles. "What about the children who received the sequence as embryos?" she asked distantly.

"They are still very young. Most are already several years ahead in development," Maria said. "We'll have to wait and see."

"You've stopped the work?"

"We have now. The first boy died three weeks ago, and then we thought it was perhaps a fluke."

Kaye nodded. "Stuart never mentioned it to me."

"He didn't know about the first boy. I wasn't sure, so I waited until the second autopsy. Then I called and told him right away. It was just before he died."

Kaye looked at her quickly. "Please excuse me for saying this, but you don't think that would be enough to make him very upset or depressed? That he'd done something dangerous to so many patients?"

There was a long silence. Maria's expression suddenly grew agitated and she stared at Kaye. "Did he . . . ?"

"Give it to my baby?" Kaye returned her gaze evenly. "He left it up to me."

Maria covered her mouth, eyes widening very slightly. "We

don't know," she said quickly. "It seems to work perfectly as long
as you implant in embryos."

Kaye shrugged. "I decided not to."

"Thank God," Maria breathed.

Kaye shook her head, smiling slightly. "You know why?
Because Stuart said my husband didn't have the sequence." She
pushed her blond hair back and shrugged. "I don't know. That
made me mad. I remember thinking, what the hell business is that
of yours?"

Maria nodded. "You may be very lucky."

"What did Delgado say about this?"

Maria shrugged. "He was very upset, but mostly he said we
must keep it a great secret. No one must know."

"I can understand that."

"He said to continue to track the children, and then he shut
down our lab the next day. Took out all the equipment and put it in
storage somewhere."

"Where was your lab?"

"On the fourth floor of the old clinic building. We were going
to have a much bigger lab in the new clinic, but, no longer."
Maria shrugged. "Sometimes I think Delgado would even like to
replace me, to get rid of the evidence." She looked at Kaye and
lowered her voice. "He is a very strange man, you know. Not
really like a scientist. Stuart used to say that sometimes he would
come to the lab and some of the SPL10 vector would be missing.
He wondered if Delgado was selling it on the black market. I
thought that was a little crazy."

"But now . . ."

"Now," Maria said, "especially late at night, I think that
Delgado did something to Stuart so he wouldn't testify against
him."

Kaye said nothing. Lipsky had seemed to her like a man who
had already borne more than his share of troubles; hearing about
the deaths from the forbidden sequence work might well have
simply pushed the morose little researcher over some psychic
edge. "So what will you do now?"

"I may do nothing. Stuart is dead. The experiment is over.
What more is there to do?"

"Why do you stay here at all?"

Maria sighed. "I could go back to the United States. I am
really a very good molecular geneticist. I could get a fellowship.
Many of my friends have done that: they leave Mexico and never
come back." She sighed. "But my family is here. And no matter

what happens, the knowledge I have can help the people here."
She looked at Kaye. "You must understand that. The work we did
here with the forbidden sequence was only meant to help."

"Of course." Kaye was silent for a long moment. "Perhaps,"
she said finally, "you should tell Trina Robbins about all this."

"Señorita Robbins?" The young Mexican woman's voice rose
and she appeared shocked at the suggestion. "Oh no. She works
for the company. She seems so close to Delgado." She shook her
head firmly, her long hair shiny in the dull sunlight. "No. That
would be a very bad idea."

"I see," Kaye said. "Then will you do me a favor?"

Maria looked at her.

"This is for Stuart's sake. And yours. I want to write a note
and have you take it to Trina. Only to Trina."

Maria gazed at Kaye for a long time. "All right. I'll do that."

"Fine," Kaye looked around the park. "I'll write it right now.
But first, would you mind if we got something else to eat?"

CHAPTER TWENTY FOUR

The new Caswell Clinic was an imposing four-story structure, fifteen minutes south of downtown Mexico City, a spot of green in the midst of random, unplanned suburban sprawl. On one side of the spacious clinic grounds was a cluster of high-rise condominiums; on the other, cactus fences encircled a settlement of ramshackle hovels where chickens scratched in barren dirty yards. Directly across the highway was an auto wrecking yard where long rows of rusting car bodies hung from chains, like carcasses in a slaughter house. The clinic itself rose above it all: an imposing, starkly modern edifice in the gray concrete typical of modern Mexican architecture, with rows of dark-tinted windows flush with the surface, lending the building an ominous sense of purposeful mass.

This morning Trina was sitting alone in a small, equipment-packed audio control booth midway up the back wall of the new conference center auditorium. Through one wide glass window she could look down over the expansive theater. For the moment she was alone, and she took some time to ponder the conference proceedings below.

The auditorium itself was a beautiful space, the stage made of hand-turned blond wood, the seats upholstered in light gray wool, all surrounded by an advanced sound system. The theater seated about three hundred in rows sloping down sharply to the stage. This morning more than two thirds of the seats were filled.

Not bad attendance, Trina thought. And most were top-drawer

researchers, as well as about thirty reporters, from the United
States, Mexico, and Europe. United Genetics, of course, was
paying the bills for all the attendees, but this was not in itself
underhanded. In a sense the company was making a charitable
contribution; without corporate assistance the scientists' travel
funds would have come out of research budgets.

For the company the investment was excellent: the mention of
United Genetics in conjunction with high-minded research was
subtle but very valuable publicity. And, past that, there were some
good papers being presented, ranging from new therapies for
malnutrition to powerful vaccines against the intestinal ailments
that killed so many infants where sewage systems were inade-
quate.

Trina made sure that the automated sound system was set
correctly. She was impressed with the money that had gone into
the new clinic: the A-list benefactors of Silicon Valley had
financed quite a marvel. She remembered something Delgado had
said the previous night: "These days, when you ask rich Mexicans
where they go for medical care, they say 'Houston.' I want them
to say 'Caswell.'"

"I thought this was supposed to be a charity clinic," Trina had
said.

Delgado had smiled. "Of course it is. But one can dream."

Just past nine A.M. Trina went down the narrow stairs to the
main floor of the auditorium. Maria Aguirre was waiting there,
and they talked briefly. Then Trina walked quickly down a long
hallway that led to the stage and stepped to the podium. She
spread her notes in front of her and tapped the microphone.

"Welcome," Trina said, "to the first Conference on the
Diseases of Overpopulation, cosponsored by United Genetics and
the Caswell Foundation. For forty years the Caswell Foundation
has been involved in the health issues of developing nations.
United Genetics has now joined those efforts. One result is this
building, the new Caswell Clinic, which will be formally
dedicated tonight. All conference attendees are invited to the gala
that will follow directly."

Trina smiled for the first time. "In fact, you probably won't be
able to miss it. Just look for the largest tent you've ever seen, on
the grounds in front of the clinic. We look forward to meeting all
of you there."

She paused and turned a piece of paper. "Paul Markham and
Edward Caswell, the founders of United Genetics, have asked me
to convey their thanks to the researchers who have joined us today,

as well as to the members of the world press who honor us with their presence. And without further preface I'd like to turn the day over to Maria Aguirre, Technical Director of the Caswell Clinic, who will introduce the program."

Trina turned and left the stage to polite applause and briefly touched Maria Aguirre's shoulder as the young woman passed her on the way to the podium. As soon as she was offstage, Trina sank into a folding chair for a moment, trying to decide what to do next.

She didn't plan to stay around for the papers. She had already written press releases based on the abstracts, and any reporters who needed additional information could approach the researchers directly. Instead, today she would see to the last details of tonight's ceremony and gala, then pick up Markham and Caswell when their chartered jet arrived at Mexico City airport later in the afternoon.

Both were flying in only for one night. Caswell was completing the massive investor buy-out agreement, making certain that full responsibility for United Genetics would rest only with the two founders. And Markham, true to his word, had disappeared into the Ag Division laboratories at Davis, throwing his full attention toward the solution of the Rice Five problem.

Sitting in the corridor outside the conference center auditorium, Trina leaned back and her thoughts wandered to Edward Kelley-Delgado. She was shocked at how easily she had adjusted to the man, to the familiar sense of quiet, constant menace and unpredictability. He was an exceedingly attentive lover—she had not been courted so extravagantly since Rackley. After first resisting, she found herself lulled into feeling comfortable with him.

In part it was the presence of Pablo: the child seemed so bright, young, innocent, and was clearly very close to Delgado. She found herself wondering about Delgado's other women: his house showed no evidence of full-time female companionship. Perhaps he was like Markham: content to be without a woman, the kind of man who—unlike, say, Rackley—seemed quite whole as a single person.

Last night in bed after they had made love, more slowly this time, without the rough, hard edges of the previous night, they had stayed awake for a time, and Delgado had said something that remained in her mind.

"You know," he said, as she rested her head on his

outstretched arm, "the most important part is that I finally have something I believe in."

She had turned her head to look at him, his profile sharp against the moonlight through the high glass doors.

"Funny," he said. "You know, when I was a child, in California, I was the kid who beat up the Paul Markhams. I hated them, the smart ones who went to the good classes." He paused, lost in reflection. "The college track. Is that what they called it?"

"Something like that," Trina said.

Delgado nodded. "Now, I work with Markham." He looked over at Trina. "You know, United Genetics is only the beginning."

"What do you mean?"

"This science will change the world forever. The power will change." He nodded very slightly. "Sometimes," he said softly, "I don't think even Markham knows how important it is."

She had slept well that night. But then something disturbing had happened this morning. Once again Delgado—who moved with the ease and silence of a large feline—left very early. If nothing else, he seemed to keep positively grueling hours. It was a beautiful morning, so when the maid appeared, Trina asked if she might take her breakfast out on the patio.

"As you wish," the young Indian woman said.

Fifteen minutes later, wrapped in a white cotton robe, Trina was drinking coffee and eating sliced papaya on a glass-topped table in the middle of the tiled patio. The morning air was still cool, but the sun was already bright. As she sat, she looked around, and for some reason her gaze settled once again on the roof of the greenhouse, its white metal frame just visible through the garden foliage. She took a final sip of coffee, then gathered the robe closer around her and walked through the garden to the greenhouse door.

As Trina stepped inside, the warm moist air struck her like a physical force. In the daytime the rows of carefully tended Rice Five, illuminated by sunlight from every side, seemed almost unnaturally green.

She walked down one long row toward the steel-topped laboratory bench she had seen only for a moment two nights earlier. She stopped perhaps five feet away and gazed at a light green map thumbtacked to the rough wooden wall behind the bench. Even from a distance something about the map was vaguely familiar. She stepped up for a closer look.

It was a U.S. Geologic Survey topographic map, thirty minute series, of the California Delta. Marked in red ink on the map and numbered sequentially were the five sites where Rice Five had initially been found. Tacked below the map there was a sheet of graph paper bearing similar numbers with names after each in neat, laboratory-style lettering:

#1—Hernandez, Oaxaca
#2—Fideles, Michoacoan
#3—Guttierez, Mexico, D.F.

Trina stood for a long moment, enveloped in the warm, moist air of the greenhouse, trying to figure just why Delgado had bothered to track the progress of Rice Five. And then she looked more closely and saw that someone had typed a date in at the bottom of the map.

The date was a full month before the initial Rice Five outbreak.

Suddenly she realized that this wasn't a map of where Rice Five had been found—it was a blueprint for spreading the plant in the first place. Rice Five had come from Mexico, not California, carried in by the migrant farmworkers named on the neat sheet of graph paper.

Trina had returned to the main house and promptly packed her two suitcases. She would change into her evening clothes at the clinic. And then, whatever she did, she would not come back to stay with Delgado.

Trina was jarred from her reverie by the sound of distant applause. She glanced out on the stage and realized that Maria Aguirre had finished her introductions. An older man, an international expert in late-stage malnutrition, was walking slowly to the podium, and Maria Aguirre was coming offstage toward Trina.

Trina looked up as Maria approached. "Well done," she said. "You've done so much to organize this it's made my job much easier."

"Thank you," Maria said, slightly shy. "Anything I can do to help." Suddenly she took a deep breath and looked at Trina directly. "I have something for you."

Maria reached into a thin leather binder and removed a long envelope. "This is for you," she said, glancing around the backstage area as if looking for someone. She smiled tentatively. "From a friend."

Trina glanced down at the envelope. Her name was on the front in feminine handwriting she couldn't quite place. "Thanks," she told Maria. But the young Mexican woman was already walking away.

Trina was about to open the letter when she heard a familiar, low voice.

"Trina Robbins."

She tucked the envelope into her bag and looked up to see Steven Hechinger standing in front of her. He was wearing blue jeans, a white cotton shirt, a leather vest, and he looked very serious.

"Steven," she said, standing quickly. "I didn't see your name on the list."

"I'm not here for the conference."

Trina stared. "Then . . . ?"

"I subpoenaed Lipsky's credit card records. The guy spent half his time down here. Why?"

Trina looked at him for a long moment. "Steven, I know you don't believe me, but I really have no idea."

"We'll see," Hechinger said quietly. "Something is going on down here. And I still think you're covering it up."

"I don't know what you're talking about."

"Rackley was indicted yesterday in San Francisco," Hechinger said. "And now there are flight warrants on both him and his wife."

Trina gazed up at him. She was tempted to take him aside, to describe what she'd found in Delgado's greenhouse. But that was too dangerous: there was no way to tell what he would do with the information.

"I wish I could help you," Trina said.

"Sooner or later," Hechinger said, "you'll wish you had." He glanced at his watch. "Change your mind, I'm staying downtown."

Rackley's first day in Mexico City began with nothing but discouragement, gained at great effort. During his tenure as a journalist, he had learned that one of the best information sources in a new town was real estate agents. They were people who paid close attention to arrivals, departures, changes in neighborhoods, and, unlike legal authorities, would often talk freely. That, at any rate, was his best idea for the moment, and so armed with a list that Trina had assembled and a picture of Kaye, he spent the morning visiting realtors and rental agencies.

The American community of Mexico City was concentrated in several areas; the wealthy Mexicans in another half dozen or so. Trina guessed that Kaye almost certainly had to be staying in one of those neighborhoods. Rackley started with the local rental agents: Kaye was a sufficiently striking young woman that someone might recall seeing her arrive. It was a distant hope, but Rackley had no other idea where to begin. After three or four hours of riding in taxis and trying to communicate in broken Spanish, however, he was ready to try something more direct.

In the middle of the previous night he had finally realized what was odd about the old clinic building in Tepito. Most of the big metal cylinders he had seen on the rear loading dock had been standard pressurized gas containers, the sort used for hospital oxygen supplies. But Rackley had sat straight up in bed when he recalled that there had also been several short, bulky double-walled cylinders. Topped with round metal locking wheels, these were used only for very cold contents, such as liquid nitrogen. But what did a charity clinic need with liquid nitrogen? The last time Rackley had seen so many such canisters had been in the storage area in front of Stuart Lipsky's Berkeley laboratory.

Rackley had found it difficult to sleep the rest of that night. He was dressing for the day in a lightweight khaki suit when Trina knocked at the door of his hotel room. As promised, she was carrying a set of keys to the old clinic.

"You're up early," he said.

"Busy day," she said. "I borrowed these from Delgado."

"He didn't mind?"

Trina shrugged. "He trusts me. I told him that I had to go by and pick up Maria Aguirre and she didn't have her keys."

"He wasn't suspicious?"

She paused. "He had other things on his mind." Trina set the ring of keys on the hotel dresser. She was dressed for the opening session of the conference in a beige linen suit, her hair put up, looking very pretty.

Rackley was standing behind her, knotting his tie, looking over her shoulder into the mirror. "I didn't mean to be a jerk about Delgado yesterday."

"Well," Trina said slowly, "there *is* something very strange going on at his place."

"Oh?"

Trina glanced over to one side and sighed, then told Rackley about the map of the Delta she had seen in the greenhouse early that morning. As she described the scene, he stopped tightening his tie and turned to stare at her.

"That doesn't make any sense," he said finally.

"I think that Delgado planted Rice Five on purpose."

"But why?" Rackley asked. "It's going to destroy millions of fish. And it's going to destroy Markham and Caswell too."

"I know. It's insane." Trina sat on the bed for a moment. "Delgado," she said, "used to play in a different league. I mean, he can be very dangerous." She crossed her legs. "You know, on one level he seems like he's really changed since I knew him. There are times he sounds like some kind of weird idealist."

She leaned back on the bed, shaking her head. "But there's still something very crazy underneath there. I mean, if he was really pissed off at Markham for some reason . . ."

"My God," Rackley breathed. "You think he'd . . . ?"

Trina shrugged. "You said it yourself. It's going to destroy Markham."

Rackley just stood, watching her.

"Take care of yourself," she said, standing up. "Wait until afternoon to go to the old clinic. By then everybody will be at the new building for the opening ceremony."

Rackley nodded. "Listen. You've been great. And . . ." He raised one hand, not sure what he meant to say. Trina stepped forward and then they held each other briefly.

"See you tonight," she said, breaking the embrace. "I'll come by here before the gala."

Before she returned to meet Rackley, however, Trina had to pick up Markham and Caswell, who were scheduled to arrive from San Francisco at two that afternoon. Just before then she was at the airport and standing at the edge of the tarmac, watching as the small silver Gulfstream jet taxied toward her. Even though there had been a downpour just after noon and the runway was still damp, the air had already regained its fragrance of diesel oil. There was a slight chill in the breeze, and Trina pulled her light jacket more closely around her shoulders.

Behind her at the edge of the runway was an old Lincoln limousine. Delgado had rented the car, but the driver was Rafael, the pockmarked longhair from Delgado's house. Rafael reminded her of men who used to work for Rand, the kind who seemed preternaturally calm but who turned violent with little provocation and less warning. She had seen him around the house, on and off, for the previous two days, but he seemed to have few duties of an ordinary houseman.

On the ride out from the clinic, sitting in the backseat, she had tried to make conversation, asking how long Rafael had worked for Delgado and where he had come from in Mexico. The long-haired man had said little, and then continued to stare at her in the rearview mirror until she fell into uncomfortable silence. She brushed her hair back and watched the tattered gray cityscape rush by.

Now, the sleek Gulfstream pulled up twenty yards away. The two jet engines shut down, first one, then the other, and for an instant there seemed an almost palpable rush of silence. A moment later two attendants strolled out from a nearby rusting hangar to open the little jet's door and deploy the exit.

Markham and Caswell descended the aluminum stairs, Markham in blue jeans and sweater, Caswell in a newly pressed gray suit. Markham saw Trina immediately and came forward, smiling. Caswell paused by the stairway and talked briefly with the pilot.

As Markham approached Trina, another private jet taxied past, briefly deafening.

"How was your flight?" Trina asked loudly as the sound diminished.

"Terrific," Markham said with unusual enthusiasm. "We've got some bags." He glanced over his shoulder. "Is this the car? It looks like Delgado's sort of thing."

Rafael stepped out of the old Lincoln. *"Bienvenido, Señor Markham."* He opened the back door, then headed toward the plane.

Markham took Trina's arm. "Is there still a press conference for tomorrow morning?" he asked.

"Sure. The closing session of the conference."

"Perfect. I've got some news. I heard it just before we got on the plane in San Francisco."

"I'm not sure I can handle any more news."

"Listen to this," Markham said. "We've solved the Rice Five problem."

Trina stared at him. "What?"

"Solved it," Markham repeated. "We'll have it eradicated by the first of September."

"But how . . . ?"

Caswell approached as Rafael and one of the hangar attendants put several pieces of luggage in the trunk of the Lincoln.

"Trina," Caswell said cooly. "Good to see you."

Trina nodded formally. "Welcome," she said, then looked back at Markham. "So . . . ?"

Caswell glanced impatiently at his small dress watch. "Shall we move on? I need to talk to Delgado."

All three slid into the backseat, and then as the limo pulled away, off the black tarmac and onto the bumpy airport access road, Trina turned to Markham. "And so?"

"Magnesium," he said with a nearly beatific smile.

"Pardon?"

Caswell looked over wearily. "Try not to draw this out."

Markham ignored him. "We'll need a press release on this, of course. Basically, up at Davis, I said: Let's use the computers. So we created a simulation of Rice Five's metabolism in software—a computer model—and then we started to challenge it with every possible substance we could think of. And after about five days we hit it: magnesium. Pure elemental magnesium. The simulation fell to pieces in about a nanosecond."

Rafael pulled the car off the old access road and accelerated onto the highway. Caswell continued to stare out the window.

"I still don't follow," Trina said.

"For some reason," Markham said, "God knows what, Rice Five is unusually sensitive to the element magnesium. Trace amounts it can handle. But anything more and the plant's tissue system self-destructs. Complete osmotic breakdown."

"So what does that mean?"

"Two days ago we took a hundred test plants of Rice Five in one of the high-containment greenhouses at Davis. We sprayed them with an extremely dilute solution of magnesium. By evening they were wilting. They were dead within thirty-six hours. Just a mass of rotting green vegetation. No survivors." Markham smiled. "We broke out the champagne last night."

"That's great," Trina said tentatively, trying to absorb this turn. "I mean, it's amazing."

"The team leaders at Davis are preparing a proposal for the EPA now." Markham leaned back in the black leather seat. "I just called them from the plane. We'll ask for clearance to air-drop powdered magnesium all over the Delta, particularly upstream. Not enough to cause any other environmental problems. But according to our tests, that should be more than enough to kill Rice Five. Wherever it appears."

"But why . . . ?"

Markham shrugged. "Who knows? Rice Five was an unfinished product. It hadn't been fully field tested, and we probably would have caught that sensitivity if we'd had time."

Caswell turned back and spoke for the first time. "So it's over. Thank God."

"What about the buy-back?" Trina asked. "What about the public offering?"

"The buy-back," Caswell said mildly, gazing out the window at the crowded boulevard, "is a done deal. We bought it, we own it, whether we like it or not."

Markham shrugged. "It'll be a while before we can consider a public offering again."

Trina was about to mention Delgado's greenhouse, but then hesitated.

"Are you all right?" Markham asked.

"Oh." Trina shook her head quickly. "Of course. It's just—"

"It's just that you're not used to good news," Caswell said. "That must be it."

"So what do you think of the new clinic?" Markham asked, leaning back, putting one arm back over the seat top.

Trina regarded him out of the corner of her eye. She hadn't seen the young entrepreneur so cheerful, so sociable, in months. "It's beautiful. I never thought it would be so luxurious."

"And the conference?"

"It's going very well." She opened her leather portfolio and handed Markham a sheet of paper. "This is the final list of presentations. Maria Aguirre really pulled in some big fish. I think the guy from the *New York Times* is going to do a feature about this one." She pointed out a paper on the effect of overcrowding on neural development in very young children.

"Excellent." Markham only glanced at the paper, then looked out at the city. "Excellent."

There was silence in the car, and then Trina cleared her throat. "Steven Hechinger turned up this morning."

Both Caswell and Markham turned their heads quickly to look at her. "What's he doing here?" Caswell asked.

"You were supposed to talk to him," Markham said sharply.

"I did," Trina said. "He found out that Lipsky spent a lot of time down here. Frankly, that was news to me, too."

Markham nodded. "Does Delgado know about this?"

"No, I haven't had time to tell him."

"Tell him," Markham said brusquely, his voice now bereft of its expansive tone. "Right away."

"Okay." Trina paused. "Can I ask why?"

"He's in charge of the clinic," Caswell said. "He needs to know these things. That's all."

Caswell and Markham returned to their silences. But now the atmosphere in the old limousine was subtly altered. She was still confused, but about one thing she was certain: she would not say a word to Delgado about Steven Hechinger. It was only then that she recalled the handwritten letter that Maria Aguirre had given her that morning, and that she had carried in her canvas bag all day. As soon as they reached the clinic, she would read it.

C
H
A
P
T
E
R

T
W
E
N
T
Y

F
I
V
E

By the end of the morning Rackley had visited three of the best neighborhoods in Mexico City. Between calls on property agents he had walked through parks: park after park after park. He had started to fantasize that he would wander into one, cool grass dotted with trees, their trunks painted ghostly white against insects. There, on a wrought iron bench, reading quietly, would be Kaye. She would look up: "Rackley! What are you . . . ?" and even before she finished the sentence they would be holding each other, and he would smell the clean fragrance of her hair, feel the warmth of her body against him.

He could see it, feel it, and each time he entered a new little park, it seemed the perfect setting.

But it never happened. Rackley finally ate a small lunch in a little *taquería*, sitting at a tile counter, sipping fruit juice amidst the smells of frying masa and cilantro and chiles. There was a movie poster pasted on the wall across from him; something about Siamese twins named Doony and Roony, showing two goofy young men in a single giant plaid suit with a headline that read *"La Maravilla Humana!"*

Humans, Rackley thought, are perennially fascinated by the vagaries of the genetic dice roll, even in a city falling apart from the weight of its own population. And here was United Genetics with a technology so advanced that it almost made no sense to the daily cares of the poor. It was as if one small part of the planet functioned a century ahead, while the rest tagged along, unsus-

pecting. Human marvels, he thought. The next twenty years
would be strange ones indeed.

But that was no longer his problem. His problem was finding
Kaye. Even then they would be far from clear. He checked his suit
coat pocket and touched the ring of keys that Trina had brought
him that morning. He finished his *carnitas* and took a cab across
town to Tepito.

The cab dropped him off on a main thoroughfare, and he
walked several blocks down the narrow streets of the tough
district, drawing hard looks from young locals. There was little
reason for a gringo to be in the neighborhood; the big stalls selling
foreign contraband were five or six blocks to the north, and the
prostitutes were as many blocks in the other direction. Rackley
paid no attention to the mildly hostile gazes, striding along
purposefully until he was directly in front of the old yellow brick
facade of the Caswell Clinic.

Just as yesterday there were two uniformed guards in the
entryway of the old structure. This time, however, Delgado's
sleek bronze Chrysler was nowhere in sight, nor was there any
other sign of occupancy.

Rackley passed the guards, who barely glanced at him, then
turned right around the corner and entered the narrow, trash-
littered alley behind the clinic. Moving quickly, he climbed up on
the old concrete loading dock, which was stained with motor oil.
Against the back wall of the building he saw a half dozen empty
gas cylinders, including three of the variety used for liquid
nitrogen. The cylinders were chained together, ready for pickup.
Beside them was an old steel hand truck, clearly used to tote the
tanks in and out of the clinic.

Rackley squatted down and studied the wheels on the hand
truck; their well-worn tread was slightly shiny, soaked with motor
oil from the loading dock. Rackley stood and stepped around the
empty cylinders and used the keys to open the metal-grated back
door of the clinic.

The interior of the clinic was dark and deserted. As Trina had
promised, the remaining staff was at the reception for the clinic
opening. She was certain of the timing; she herself had arranged
for a minibus to transport the workers to the new building.
Rackley stood in the narrow yellow corridor; the plaster near the
ceiling was water-stained, and in some places wallpaper peeled
beneath the old paint. The only light came from the street through
high windows, filtered through layers of dust and grime.

As his eyes adjusted, he looked at the old linoleum floor. It appeared to have had been kept fairly clean, and he bent down to examine it more closely. After a moment he saw the faint but discernible track of motor oil, a slight stripe of iridescence perhaps an inch wide left by the wheels of the handcart as it had transported the big steel gas cylinders.

Rackley straightened up and began to follow the almost invisible trail of oil. As he walked, he glanced around and noticed that the examining rooms themselves were cleaner, more hygenic. In some of the common patient rooms there were still a few old beds and pieces of antiquated medical equipment, apparently not deemed worth moving to the new clinic in the suburbs. There was a scent of mold and despair in the air, decades of human pain met and settled.

He suddenly recalled something that Stuart Lipsky had said to him after Lipsky's first visit to Mexico City. "The doctors in the clinic work so hard," the scientist had said, "but still the people come, more and more, fouling each other's water, breathing each other's air, taking one another's food. And always, always, so very ill. Sometimes after a day at the clinic I would forget what health is." Lipsky had looked at Rackley for a long moment. "I would do anything to help them, if only I knew what."

Rackley realized that he had lost track of the wheel mark. He shook his head and tried to recall the layout of the building from his view of the exterior. All of the upper floors had appeared deserted. The gas canisters, he thought, must have remained on this floor, but he had passed no doorways that seemed to lead to any suitable laboratory. He began to retrace his steps.

And then there it was: the thin sheen of oil had taken a quick right turn ten feet earlier. He straightened up and saw the sign over the door: BIBLIOTECA. That was it; he turned and followed the track into the small medical library.

Once inside the small room Rackley saw that there was an old wooden table and three comfortable chairs for reading. All of the books and journals remained as well, lining the shelves, floor to ceiling. Curious, he thought. Perhaps there was an altogether new library at the suburban clinic. He continued to follow the oily trail of the hand truck until suddenly, against the far wall, it swirled itself into confusion, the result of back and forth movement.

Rackley looked up. The track stopped directly in front of one of the big walnut bookshelves built into the wall. The shelf, the size of a double door, was filled with leather-bound volumes of medical journals in English and Spanish.

Rackley studied the books on the shelf; they were, he noticed, texts on human genetics. Quickly he began to remove the large leather volumes at waist level. He had pulled out no more than a dozen when a bit of reflection caught his eye from the back of the shelf. Rackley leaned down, peered inside, and there was the lock: an incongruously bright chrome plate set into the dark wood, with a circular key slot similar to that used in American security systems.

He looked at the set that Trina had given him; in the middle was a stubby new key that matched the slot.

When Rackley inserted the round key, he almost instantly heard the dull clunk of an electrically actuated solenoid lock, solidly installed somewhere in the wall behind the shelves. He placed one hand on the side of the tall walnut cabinet and pulled toward himself gently; the entire bookshelf swung open easily on well-maintained hinges.

He pulled the shelf far enough open to see ahead of him a narrow stairwell descending into darkness. On one side, just at the level of his head, there was a small gray rack of electrical circuit breakers, bolted to unpainted wallboard. He reached over and flipped several: the stairwell slowly filled with cold blue light as fluorescent tubes flickered on, one after another, in a large room below.

Rackley quickly descended the sturdy wooden stairs and then at the foot stopped abruptly.

The big space ahead of him looked utterly unlike anything on the floor above. It was perhaps seventy feet long and half as wide, and it was packed, ceiling to floor, with modern genetic engineering equipment, absolutely spotless, antiseptically clean.

Walking slowly, glancing around quickly, Rackley saw nucleotide synthesizers, digital gene sequencers, a half dozen workbenches with gleaming glassware and biological protection hoods extending up to the ceiling. In one corner was an American minisupercomputer, the size of a small filing cabinet, worth at least a half million dollars. The computer was connected to two artificial intelligence workstations with monitor screens the size of television sets.

The room was as advanced as anything Rackley had ever seen in the States. In fact the supercomputer was almost certainly in Mexico illegally; the Department of Defense would never approve the export of such sophisticated equipment without a license, and he knew that United Genetics had never applied for any supercomputer export permits.

That single piece of contraband computer hardware was

reason enough for Delgado to be paranoid about visitors. But Rackley continued to look around the laboratory. In moments he saw the object of his search: an elaborate supercold refrigeration unit built into the far end of the room—a full wall of man-high brushed aluminum doors with big chrome handles. While liquid nitrogen made little sense in a neighborhood charity clinic, it was a necessary element of a full cryogenic storage facility.

He quickly crossed the polished linoleum floor and stopped in front of the first big refrigerator door. With both hands he tugged at the chrome handle, and slowly the huge insulated door swung open. A puff of frigid air drifted out, instantly forming a fine mist in the warm air of the lab.

Inside on racks of chrome shelves were dozens of the little spun aluminum containers used at Birthtech for embryo storage. Rackley looked over on the side of the big refrigeration unit; a pair of protective gloves and tongs were hanging from a hook on the wall. Donning the gloves, he reached in with the tongs and pulled out one of the containers. It had a small, neat label, generated by a computer printer. Rackley turned to the light in order to read the fine print:

132Z89—Beauvoir, Alain, Paris.

He carefully returned the tiny aluminum unit and pulled out the one behind it.

234D34—Goldman, Joseph. London.

Then another and another.

389Y23—De la Mancha, Ernesto. Mexico, D.F.

498T99—McDonald, Steven. New York.

He replaced each canister and finally leaned forward to stare into the big refrigerator. The lines of tiny aluminum containers continued as far back as he could see into the cryogenic unit.

Rackley closed the door slowly and returned the gloves and tongs to the workbench. Then, past the big freezers, near the back of the laboratory, he saw a small pile of Styrofoam shipping containers. Walking closer, he could see that each bore a preprinted label:

RUSH—LIVE VACCINE—MUST BE REFRIGERATED

He turned to survey the entire laboratory from this perspective. That was when he noticed, on the wall above the nucleotide synthesizer, a long chart that appeared curiously familiar. It looked, he thought, much like a bit of the massive billboard that he had watched slowly develop in the Berkeley warehouse devoted to the Markham Project.

As indeed it was. When Rackley approached, he saw that it was a tiny segment of the massive genome chart, showing a few thousand base pairs. Like most gene maps it would have been quite unintelligible to the uninitiated, except that it was neatly labeled in what Rackley recognized instantly as Stuart Lipsky's birdlike scrawl:

BROCKMAN SEQUENCE—MARKHAM PROJECT
Do Not Synthesize Without Supervision

And then there on the bench in front of him, Rackley saw the computer printout. It had been run off in a compressed typeface so that each letter was very small, and the long sheet contained hundreds of lines. Rackley picked it up and studied it closely. He was looking at a list of clients, complete with dates and fees in American dollars, ranging from $15,000 to $30,000.

His breath seized in his throat as he saw Albert Collins's name near the bottom of the client list. And then Edward Caswell. He thought briefly of the Caswells' daughter, Erin, so quick and bright and coordinated at only a year of age. And then he started to recognize more names.

He saw two bankers he knew well, and three venture capitalists. One was a man who had helped finance PM Computers, Markham's first company. Several names were San Francisco society figures—one, a childhood friend of Kaye's—most of whom were also major contributors to Markham's fund for the Caswell Clinic.

Other names, one after another, came into focus: several film actors, one professional athlete, two television commentators, a semiconductor tycoon . . .

Suddenly Rackley heard footsteps on the floor directly above him. Someone was walking upstairs. He immediately guessed that the guards stationed in front were patrolling the interior. He glanced back at the stairs that went up to the library and realized with a sudden rush of adrenaline that he had left the fake bookcase open.

He quickly folded the client list into a long narrow strip and stuffed it into the money belt under his shirt. He pushed the money belt down, firmly in place, well out of sight. Then he walked quietly toward the stairs, hoping that he could reach the top and pull the deceptive door shut before the guards walked into the little library.

Rackley reached the foot of the stairs and started up, moving carefully, hearing no sound from above. He stepped onto the top stair and, balancing himself, foot pressed against one riser, reached out to tug on the small chrome doorknob mounted on the back of the false bookshelf.

And then, as if from nowhere, a young guard, tall and thin, no older than twenty, with a wispy black mustache, stepped directly before him, looking down the narrow staircase. He seemed completely startled to see Rackley.

The guard stood at the top of the stairs for a moment, staring, mouth open. In that instant of surprise Rackley reversed direction, pushed off with all his weight, and threw his shoulder into the guard's groin. As Rackley hit him, the man grunted and doubled forward, losing his balance, shouting out. Then, balance completely gone, the guard fell over Rackley, tumbling down the steps into the hidden laboratory.

Rackley stepped up into the little library and saw a second guard appear in the opposite door. Also very young, but shorter and more athletic in appearance, this guard was fumbling at his leather-holstered pistol as he shouted, *"Alto! Alto!"*

Rackley didn't hesitate. He turned and ran the way he had come in, through the back door of the library, running down the old yellow corridor as fast as he could, bouncing off the walls, holding his arms wide to keep his balance. As he reached the back door he heard the second guard shout again, but couldn't understand the words.

Rackley ran out onto the loading dock, past the tall empty gas canisters. As he passed them, he tugged hard on the chain that held them together. Surprisingly light, the metal cylinders tipped over, creating an incredibly loud clatter as they smashed into the concrete of the loading dock and rolled in all directions.

Rackley jumped down the three feet to the alley. He glanced both ways, and then ran in the direction from which he had originally come. Halfway down the alley he could hear the sound of the gas tanks smashing against each other again and some muffled shouts in Spanish as the two guards kicked their way through the overturned canisters.

Out on the street Rackley hesitated again. No cabs cruised this neighborhood, so there was no choice but to run. He knew that about eight blocks to the east was the main thoroughfare, six lanes

wide, filled with cabs and buses. If he could make it that far, he
would probably be safe.

He began to run east, down the rough sidewalk. Children and
adults both moved out of the way, staring but not interfering, and
then from behind him he heard the voice of one of the guards.
"Alto!" he shouted, *"ladrón!"* Rackley didn't look back,
continued to run, and then seconds later he heard what sounded
like a firecracker going off behind him.

It took a moment before he realized that the guard must be
firing his small pistol. That was crazy: there were people all
around. He dodged off the street into the next doorway he
reached. It was a wide entrance to a large public building, with a
sliding overhead steel door that was now fully raised.

Once inside he paused, glancing around, and realized that he
was in some kind of shoe market: the biggest shoe market he had
ever seen, altogether cavernous in its dimensions. For as far as he
could see in every direction, there was nothing but aisles of shoes
up on high racks, acres of shoes, each rack tended by an
individual proprietor.

"Señor," the nearest young man said, holding up a pair of
shiny black leather boots. "Very nice, very nice."

Rackley started off down one of the aisles at a slow trot, then
took a right at the first intersection of racks, then a left, hoping
that he could zigzag his way through the sea of shoes and come
out on the other side of the building. As he jogged along, the shoe
vendors watched with great curiosity and some amusement; then,
moments later, he began to hear loud angry voices behind him and
once again the shouts: "Stop! Thief!"

Now, as he jogged down the endless aisles of shoes—pumps,
high heels, boots, sneakers, slippers, loafers—the sellers began
watching him with distrust. There were shoppers everywhere,
young, old, carrying big parcels or straw baskets. He could almost
feel hands reaching out to catch him, hold him.

Finally Rackley started running full out, turning first right,
then left, time and time again barely missing spectacular collisions
with package-bearing matrons or tiny children watching the crazy
gringo, transfixed. He had ceased to think or plan, trying only to
put as much distance as possible between himself and the angry
voices behind him.

At last, trapped amid the aisles of shoes, stumbling, nearly
tripping, he came to a shuddering halt as he saw three or four
young shoe sellers standing shoulder to shoulder, blocking his
way a few yards ahead. Panting hard, trying to catch his breath, he

realized that he no longer even knew which way the entrance was. He heard hard-soled shoes approaching from behind, and he spun around. The two guards from the old clinic were approaching at a full run.

Rackley turned, bent down, and took off in the opposite direction. But one foot slipped on a piece of wrapping paper left on the market floor, and arms stretched, out of breath, he fell forward across the aisle directly into one huge rack of shoes. The rack tipped over, entwining him in high heels and sneakers and loafers as he tumbled forward, face first, the strong scent of poorly cured leather filling his nostrils.

There was a sharp pain in his ribs as he landed in a tangle of new shoes and metal tubing, and then the next thing he felt was the rough hands of the guards pulling him up out of the rubble of footwear as a dozen voices shouted in excited Spanish all around him. Suddenly out of the corner of his eye he saw one of the guards' hands move quickly. The motion was a barely perceptible blur just at the edge of his awareness, and abruptly a great shock and heat and numbness spread up from the back of his neck, instantly plunging the huge shoe market into darkness.

CHAPTER TWENTY SIX

Early that afternoon the huge white canvas tent for the gala had blossomed like some immense mushroom on the lawn of the clinic. Now, just after sunset, brightly lit from within, it glowed as if phosphorescent. Out at the highway dozens of children stood along the dusty shoulder, staring through the steel bars of the clinic fence at the apparition.

Inside under the canvas the light was filtered and soft. Two hundred guests, mostly Mexican, a handful of Americans, all impeccably dressed, danced to a twelve-piece orchestra that alternated between Europop versions of American standards and up-tempo Latin numbers. Along one side of the tent was a long buffet table with an elaborate fountain in the center, spraying water at the intersection of a dozen colored spotlights.

Trina was standing just outside the door to the tent, leaning slightly against one of the tall aluminum poles that held it aloft, listening to the bright, brassy sounds of the orchestra within. She had changed an hour before in Maria Aguirre's office and was now wearing a black evening dress with one bare shoulder and a small diamond pendant on a white gold chain. Before recovery she had always thought her shoulders were too bony, and she had rarely worn clothes that revealed them. Now, in her view, her shoulders were one of her few features to improve with additional flesh.

Tonight, however, Trina was paying little mind to either shoulders or clothes. She was preoccupied and concerned, glancing occasionally at her watch. She had arranged to meet

Rackley at his hotel two hours earlier on her way to the gala, but he had not appeared. She wanted to show him the letter from Kaye; for his own safety it was extremely important that he understand just how complicated the situation had become. She had pestered the desk clerk mercilessly about the stocky American, but all he could recall was the man had left early in the morning, and his key was still in the cubbyhole in back of the front desk. After ten minutes or so she could wait no longer: she had to be at the gala, since she planned an early departure.

Now, after waiting another ten minutes at the entrance to the big tent, she finally sighed and turned to go in to the party. Obviously there was no way Rackley could show up there. She would simply have to proceed on her own tonight and then find him later.

Trina took two steps into the crowded tent and then stopped, unable to suppress a smile at the elaborate scene before her. Delgado, she thought, had truly gone to great lengths. The orchestra, on a low stage erected at one end of the tent, sounded first-rate; in front of the stage a folding wooden dance floor had been put down on the lawn.

Trina made her way through the well-dressed couples standing and talking and circled the shiny dance floor. She watched for a moment; already a half dozen couples were dancing, some rather stylishly. As dusk fell the damp, warm air had cooled, and the climate within the tent was quite comfortable, almost sensual.

At the other end was the long buffet table. Trina walked by slowly, growing increasingly incredulous at the array of food. God, she thought, she should write this down. Rackley would never believe it. There were quail eggs with caviar, little tacos filled with lobster meat, medallions of lamb, shrimp tempura, escargot and duck breast brochettes, blue corn tostados with crab, several kinds of tiny pizzas, apricots stuffed with goat cheese and pistachio nuts, big pecans dipped in white and dark chocolate, and fresh coconut macaroons.

At the end of the table she nearly ran into Delgado, who was standing, watching her with a trace of amusement. He was wearing a dark blue dinner jacket and a white on white shirt; not her taste, Trina thought, but she had to admit that the combination actually looked very nice on him.

"This is," she told Delgado, "a really"—she cleared her throat, looking for the proper word—"eclectic menu."

"I will take that as a compliment," he said. "Since I was

arranging it, I thought that I might as well have all my favorite foods.''

"You are a man of simple tastes."

Delgado shrugged modestly and looked around for a waiter. "Let me bring you one glass of champagne."

"Just water is fine."

"You really never drink?"

She looked up and smiled at him. "I'm afraid you've seen all my vices."

Delgado nodded. "Most admirable. I'll be right back. Don't move."

As he turned to leave, Markham, also in black tie, walked up, a glass of champagne in his hand.

"Trina," he said quietly, "are we ready for tomorrow morning?"

"I have the statement already written. I messengered it to your hotel. But I have a copy here too."

Markham nodded. "We have to announce this tomorrow morning," he said, raising his voice, slightly annoyed as the orchestra launched into a lively salsa tune. "We have to get EPA approval to do the magnesium spraying. As soon as we file for that, it's going to be public knowledge anyway."

Trina gazed at him for a moment. "Relax," she said. "There are wire service reporters here, the *New York Times*, people from both the newsweeklies. Announcing it here is as good as doing it in Manhattan."

Markham nodded, still dubious.

"Relax," she repeated. "You've finally got some good news to deliver. It's going to be fine."

Markham nodded and glanced away.

"Tell me," she asked Markham casually. "Have you told Delgado about the Rice Five fix?"

Markham frowned. "Not really. I haven't had a chance. Why?"

Trina shrugged. "No reason. I would think he'd be pleased."

Markham looked at her very carefully. "I would think so."

She watched the smooth-skinned young entrepreneur's face, thinking that she would never understand what went on in his mind. Although tonight one thing was obvious: Markham was clearly uncomfortable with this ostentatious gala. His theory was that the truly powerful should remain invisible, and he would never undertake this sort of public spectacle on his own territory. But in this case he was following Delgado's advice, which was that United Genetics should make all the friends it could in Mexico. "Good intentions are not enough," he had told Markham earlier that day. "We must also show hospitality."

When Trina looked up, Delgado was returning, making his way through the crowd, shaking hands and kissing cheeks as he went, until at last he reached Trina. He handed her a glass, then extended his arm. "Would you care to dance?"

"Absolutely."

The orchestra was playing a slow number, and Delgado held her very close. "I'm having a few friends over after this for a smaller celebration. People you probably should meet."

Trina looked up at him. "That sounds fine."

They danced in silence for a minute. "I have," Delgado said finally, "enjoyed having you here."

Trina gazed distantly over his shoulder. "It's been very good for me too."

"I hope that this is only the beginning of your visits."

Trina said nothing.

"There's a great deal for you to see here. Perhaps next time your visit can be for pleasure only."

"Maybe," Trina said. "I tend to take things one day at a time."

Another silence ensued and then Delgado cleared his throat. "There are a number of people here from the government," he said, glancing around the dance floor, "who are good friends to United Genetics. Let me introduce you to some of them."

Even before he was awake Rackley was conscious of the pain behind his right ear, a deep ache low in his neck that throbbed in sympathy with the slow pulse of his heart.

After a moment he became aware that he was sitting up, and that his arms were pulled behind him, the sockets of his shoulders under tension. And then with one abrupt shudder Rackley suddenly came fully awake, recalling instantly just what had happened during his visit to the laboratory in the old clinic.

He opened his eyes. He was in a small room perhaps ten by fifteen, newly constructed, the smell of wallboard and fresh paint still in the air. It was windowless, but the recessed fluorescent lights were bright; on one wall was a stainless steel washstand with shiny chrome hardware, the sort one sees in a physician's examining room. The floor was a pale yellow linoleum. Aside from the washstand the room was unfurnished except for the straight-backed wooden chair in which Rackley was sitting—his hands tied behind his back, his feet tied to the legs.

From far away Rackley could hear, very faintly, the sprightly sound of dance music, accentuated by the occasional blare of trumpets cutting through the distance. He realized that he was in the new clinic building. And somewhere out in front on the grounds must be the huge white tent and the gala that Trina had helped arrange.

Just then the door opened quietly and Markham and Caswell walked in. Both were wearing formal evening clothes. Markham looked momentarily shocked when he saw Rackley tied to the chair. Caswell, just at the periphery of Rackley's vision, at first didn't enter the room, remaining instead near the door. Then, past Caswell, came Delgado, tall and composed in a dark blue dinner jacket; behind him followed another man, who looked like a Mexican national, with long hair, blue jeans. The last man was, incongruously, wearing sunglasses, and he somehow looked familiar—perhaps he was some employee at the clinic—but Rackley didn't bother to try to place him.

The room suddenly seemed quite small with so many occupants. "Oh for God's sake," Markham said to Delgado, his voice high and tight. "Untie him."

The man with sunglasses looked over at Delgado. Delgado nodded curtly. *"Rafael. Por favor."*

"Damn," Markham said to Delgado, shock still tempering his voice, glancing quickly around the bright examining room. "Your treating people like this is"—he searched for words—"the Mafia or something."

Delgado shrugged, unperturbed. "My men acted properly. They assumed Señor Rackley was a thief."

Rafael extracted a switchblade from the back pocket of his jeans, snapping the blade open in the same smooth motion. He quickly cut Rackley loose from the chair. When Rackley brought his arms forward, an intense, painful tingling stretched down from his elbows, and he kneaded his wrists and forearms for a moment. Then he gingerly touched the side of his head below his ear and immediately winced. There was a huge swelling there the size of a small plum.

"Goddamn it, Markham. These guys could have killed me."

Markham took a step forward. "Do you need a doctor?"

"Let me think about it," Rackley said, still trying to restore feelings to his fingers.

"We'll talk by ourselves," Markham told Delgado.

"Bueno." Delgado made a quick gesture at Rafael, and then just before the two left the room, Delgado turned back to Markham.

"We'll stay in the hall," he said. "If you don't mind."

Markham dismissed him with a wave of the hand, then turned to Rackley. The thin young ascetic folded his arms as if addressing a wayward child. "Rackley. Why the hell couldn't you have left this alone?"

Rackley was rocking his shoulders back and forth, loosening his cramped muscles. "Why didn't you just tell me what was going on?"

Markham unfolded his arms, leaning back against the stainless steel washstand. "Would that have made a difference?"

"It might have."

Markham looked at him. "Might have," he said. "That's exactly right." He nodded. "We couldn't take a chance like that."

Now Caswell walked into the center of the room and stood directly in front of Rackley. "We made you a reasonable offer, Rackley. We tried to bring you in on it."

Rackley looked at Markham. "Can I stand up?"

"Of course."

Rackley stood and moved his shoulders back and forward, planting his weight on one foot, then the other, making sure that everything still functioned. He didn't say anything for a long moment, then spoke quietly. "So what are you going to do now?"

Caswell, eyebrows raised, looked over at Markham. Markham was tapping his foot, gazing down at the floor, arms again folded across his chest. "I don't know."

The silence stretched on. Rackley cleared his throat. "What exactly is that, down in that laboratory?"

Markham looked up slowly. "That," he said, "is the most important thing I've ever done."

"Forbidden sequence implants," Rackley said. "The forbidden sequence you isolated from the Markham Project. Your own Brockman sequence."

Markham nodded. "It's much in demand."

"But why all this trouble? Why . . . ?"

"You don't see, do you?" Markham looked away and sighed very quietly. "No one really does. Money wasn't my only reason for starting United Genetics. I had money. I wanted to *do* something. I wanted to make a contribution."

Rackley felt a sudden wave of dizziness, unsuspected, and sat down hard on the wooden chair.

Markham didn't seem to notice. He reached up and loosened his black tie. "Someone had to do it. Someone had to push the science, to make the future happen. Otherwise, the scared people and the stupid people and the religious nuts, together, they'd have stopped it. And I wanted to see it done."

"But I thought we *were* doing it," Rackley said, his light-headedness abating. "If you're talking about improving the world."

Markham shifted slightly, shook his head. "Rackley." He waved his arm vaguely, back in the direction of the soft tinkling music of the clinic gala. "All of this—the clinic, the conference, this diseases of overpopulation business—this is all meaningless."

"It didn't seem meaningless to me."

Markham sighed again, more deeply, pushing his long thin fingers back through his hair. "There is only one true disease of overpopulation, and that is stupidity. The only way this species will save itself is to get smarter."

Rackley nodded. "And that's what you're doing."

"On a small scale." Markham looked over at Caswell. "Edward and I have been wrestling with this for a long time. Ever since Stuart Lipsky came to me and told me what was possible."

"None of this," Caswell said, "was really thought out in advance. You have to understand that. It all just . . . happened."

"At first," Markham said, "I believed that these techniques should be available for all. But then we started to run into the protesters, the legislators, the scared sisters, and I started to think, maybe it's not time to give genetic engineering to society—I mean, society has misused every other technology up until now. Maybe some of the planet needs to die. It could be a natural part of evolution. Our children, smarter than ourselves, will build again. Maybe that's the only solution."

Rackley gazed at him for a moment. "So who does get the forbidden sequence, this time around?"

Markham raised both hands, palms upward. "In a way, nature chooses. The strong, the brave."

"The rich," Rackley said.

Markham inclined his head, unperturbed. "Whatever. These techniques will spread. But only among those who will use them wisely."

Caswell spoke up. "People like you, Rackley. Like-minded people, industrialists, financiers, scientists. We know each other.

We sound each other out. Paul told me. I told you and Kaye. It spreads within families. Gradually you find people willing to take the risks, to use the technology. Almost a thousand so far."

"Where does Delgado fit in?"

Markham and Caswell exchanged glances. Markham shrugged, as if the question was trivial. "He handles the details," Markham said. "Delgado has trained people to insert the Brockman sequence. Our patients have embryos produced at the Birthtech clinics, then Delgado smuggles them into Mexico, frozen. The Brockman sequence is inserted, then they are shipped back to the parents. It fits right into the normal Birthtech IVF procedure."

Rackley shook his head. "For how much?"

"I'm not sure," Markham said impatiently. "Twenty, twenty-five thousand." He shifted his weight against the washstand. "We're not really even making money. Most of our work is simply to keep the technology alive. Until it can be used openly."

"Not making money?" Rackley asked. "You're talking about twenty million dollars so far."

Markham looked at Caswell and cleared his throat. "Most of that stays here to cover costs. What we get is practice in the technology. United Genetics will be far ahead in human gene therapy when it can be done without what happened to you and Kaye." He rubbed his forehead wearily. "That time has been a bit longer coming than I imagined."

Rackley tilted his head to one side. "The problem is that United Genetics will be history by then. Rice Five is going to kill the company." He paused for a long moment, thinking fast, thinking that some kind of deal might still be possible. "But I can tell you who's responsible."

Markham looked over at Caswell quickly. "Can you?"

"Your friend in the hall. Edward Kelley-Delgado." Rackley leaned back, waiting for the reaction.

Markham blinked a few times. "I know that," he said softly. "I paid him to do it."

"What?"

"We staged the Rice Five accident," Markham said. "And tomorrow, we're stopping it."

Rackley looked up sharply. "What are you talking about?"

Markham paused. "Have you ever heard of a suicide gene?"

Rackley shook his head.

"It was an old proposal for controlling genetically engineered organisms released into the environment. The idea was to splice in some genetic Achilles' heel, so that if it got out of hand, you could wipe it out quickly."

He looked at Caswell. "I saw Rice Five in early prototype about a year ago. Just when we officially canceled it because it looked too dangerous. But right then, it stuck in my mind that it might someday be a deal-breaker. I shipped some down here. Just in case."

Rackley nodded. "So there's a suicide gene in Rice Five. You can kill it whenever you want to. Delgado's guys planted it in the Delta. And you scared the venture capitalists to death and got sole control of United Genetics."

"You're very quick," Markham said.

Caswell cleared his throat, clearly uncomfortable. "Listen, Rackley. We didn't have a choice. If we'd taken United Genetics public this year, there's no way we could have kept this work going. We'd have to open the books, let people poke around. There'd be way too much scrutiny." He shook his head. "But if we hadn't taken it public, then the investors would have sued us. They were getting very impatient. So . . . we had no choice."

Rackley gazed at his brother-in-law. "I don't know what to say."

"Nobody lost a penny," Caswell said quickly. "Everybody got their money back."

"Jesus." Rackley leaned back in the chair. "Where's Kaye?"

"Kaye's safe," Caswell said. "She's here in Mexico City. She's a little morning sick, but fine."

"I want to see her."

Caswell nodded. "She wants to see you."

There was a brief silence in the little examining room.

"I don't see," Markham said finally, "why we can't still proceed on the basis we proposed in the park." He shrugged. "Obviously you're facing an additional charge, and we'll have to sort that out. But now that you know what's at stake, maybe you'll see why . . . a few months is really a small price to pay."

Caswell interrupted. "We may have handled this poorly, Rackley, and if so, forgive us. I don't think either one of us is accustomed to this kind of thing."

"Maybe," Markham said, his expression softening, "we should have brought you in from the beginning. But then . . ."

"But then I wouldn't have been nearly as good at keeping the press away from you. Lies work a lot better when you think you're telling the truth."

Markham sighed. "I'm sorry, Rackley. I truly am. But everybody in this business has secrets. You know that."

"I want to see Kaye," Rackley said. "As for the rest of it . . ." He looked away. For now at least he seemed to have little choice. He looked back at Caswell, then Markham. "I'm willing to do it your way."

"We'll take you to see Kaye tomorrow," Markham said.

Caswell smiled for the first time. "Damn," he said. "She's going to be so happy to see you." He nodded. "You're part of the family, Rackley. I've hated this."

He walked over and extended his hand. "We weren't trying to be . . . hoodlums. We were just clumsy."

After the briefest hesitation Rackley reached up, and they shook hands.

"We'll make it as easy as we can," Markham said. "We have friends in Washington. This whole witch-hunt is only temporary."

"Maybe," Caswell said, "you can come back with us on the jet."

At that moment there was a knock on the door, and then Delgado came back in.

"People will notice that you two are missing your own gala," he said. "Very bad manners. You really should get back."

Markham glanced at his watch, then back at Rackley. "So we have a deal?"

Rackley held out his hand and Markham gave him a firm handshake. Markham looked at Delgado. "It's all arranged."

"I'm glad," Delgado said softly.

Rackley stood up again.

"It might be wise," Delgado continued, "if Señor Rackley remained concealed tonight. As long as we have so much company." He cleared his throat. "There are some American embassy people here."

Markham hesitated, looking at Caswell.

Delgado smiled warmly. "Go," he said, shooing them as if they were small children. "Now."

"I'll see you in the morning," Caswell told Rackley. "It's all going to work out."

Markham and Caswell departed. Rackley, trying to sort out the rapid turns of events, sat, unmoving. Delgado walked slowly across the room and leaned where Markham had been standing.

For a moment the tall man studied the tiny gold studs on his shirt cuffs. "So," he said finally, "you came to an agreement?"

Rackley watched him carefully, already feeling the start of cool fear high in his stomach. "I suppose so."

Delgado opened his mouth slightly, his eyes widened, as if innocently surprised. "You suppose so," he repeated in tones almost like those of a child's playground taunt. "Now what does that mean?"

Rackley took a deep breath. "I don't think that's your business," he said. "My deal is with Markham."

Delgado nodded in an exaggerated way, eyes downcast, absorbing this news as if he were some retainer being dismissed. Then suddenly he looked back at Rackley with pure chill rage. "As long as you are supposing, do you suppose that there are parts of this business that Paul Markham is not competent to manage?"

Now Rackley felt his vague fear crystallize into a sharper panic. "What are you talking about?"

"I have heard," Delgado said, "that you like to drink. Would you like a drink now?"

As soon as Rafael walked through the door, carrying two bottles of tequila in his hands and a third under his arm, Rackley recognized him. He was the man in the little security camera picture from Lipsky's house. In the subsequent confusion Rackley had lost the photograph, but now, at last, he recognized its subject.

Rafael set two bottles down on the stainless steel washstand and pulled the cork loudly from the third.

"What the hell are you doing?" Rackley started to rise from the chair, ready to dash for the door. Simultaneously Rafael pulled his knife again and stepped forward so that he was standing directly in front of Rackley.

"Sit still," Delgado ordered calmly. At that moment a fat man with thinning hair, in a tight T-shirt, walked into the room. Delgado nodded, and the fat man stood behind Rackley.

Rackley stared at Delgado, and suddenly he understood. "You're blackmailing Markham," he said. "Aren't you? You took his little laboratory and ran with it, turned it into a big business, and now's he stuck. That's what Markham meant when he said the twenty million stayed here. It went into your pocket."

Delgado shrugged with easy grace. "That's very harsh. I think what has really happened is only good business. Paul and I have simply taken different roles. In return for maintaining security here, Paul lets me run my laboratory and make a little money. It is a fair trade."

"Except that Markham can't really back out. You've got him implicated in all of it."

Delgado scratched his high forehead and nodded easily. "I suppose I do have the final word on certain matters."

He looked over at Rafael and nodded. "How about that drink now?"

Suddenly Rackley felt strong hands grasp the sides of his face. It was the fat man, standing behind him, forcing his rough stubby fingers under Rackley's chin, painfully tugging his hair, pulling his head back, bending his neck hard against the wooden chair, until he was sitting, staring almost straight up at the ceiling. The knot low on his head throbbed in renewed pain, and simultaneously he felt his hands once again pulled around behind the chair as Rafael snapped metal handcuffs onto his wrists.

"Delgado," Rackley gasped. "Listen." Head pulled back, Rackley found himself gazing up at Rafael's pockmarked face, watching Rackley with detached dispassion. Rackley could see his own reflection in the man's dark glasses, and the brand-new white acoustic ceiling beyond.

"Open his mouth," Delgado said, from what seemed to be a great distance.

Rackley felt the pockmarked man's hand across his forehead, thick wrist between his eyes, maintaining a cruel pressure to keep Rackley's head pulled back. Then he pinched Rackley's nose, squeezing the nostrils so hard and painfully that Rackley felt suddenly dizzy, then sick to his stomach, as if he were falling off the hard wooden chair.

As soon as he opened his mouth to breathe, Rafael brought his other hand around the side of Rackley's head, grasping both sides of his jaw. With a grip that felt like forceps, he forced his fingers into Rackley's cheeks and between his rear teeth, almost instantly cutting the inside of Rackley's mouth, jamming fingers hard against the mandibular bone so that his mouth felt as if locked open. Rackley sat, head bent back, staring at the ceiling, and for one wild moment he was certain that his jaw had been dislocated, that he would never be able to close his mouth again.

"*Bueno*," Delgado said. "Give him a drink." Rackley felt the cold glass neck of the bottle brush his lips, bounce briefly against his upper teeth, and then abruptly there was a choking chill liquid, burning, pouring down his throat.

Rackley gagged, his eyes filling with water, but the pockmarked man firmly held his jaws and nose, pressing down on his forehead so hard that even Rackley's shuddering coughs barely caused his head to move at all. The tequila burned and trickled down his throat as tears streamed from his eyes. Rackley choked, once, twice, clearing his throat so that he could breathe again, then took a long, shuddering breath, feeling himself almost losing consciousness.

"All right," Delgado said in soothing tones. "Rackley, relax. Just swallow and there will be no trouble. We want to get you a little relaxed, is all."

Already Rackley could feel the sudden warmth of the alcohol spreading through his stomach—the first time he had felt that hot ethanol rush in eight years. And even as he sat there, head forced back, jaws levered open, nose crushed by the big fingers of the young Mexican, even as all this happened, he felt an unmistakable chemical relaxation, quite involuntary, an utterly inappropriate feeling of well-being spread through his body.

God, Rackley thought, his nervous system was already responding. And then suddenly, cutting through the warmth was a terrible thought, and he realized precisely what was going on.

Between gasps for air Rackley tried to speak, even though each motion of his jaw forced his teeth to tear into the insides of his cheeks where the Mexican held his mouth.

"Delgado," he mumbled painfully. "Listen. I know wha—"

"I am sorry," Delgado said briskly. "But I can't understand a word you're saying. Another drink."

Once again the bottle went between his lips, another long draft of cold tequila filled his mouth. Rackley choked and spouted some of the clear liquid, which ran down his cheeks, over his chin, onto his shirt; but then as he gasped for breath, more of the liquor poured down his throat.

Rackley was choking and coughing, choking and coughing, trying hard to pull in air. "Relax," Delgado said. "We have lots of time."

Rackley caught his breath and managed to speak again. "Lipsky," he gasped. "This is what you did to Lipsky."

"Tequila," Delgado said, "is an interesting drink. It's made from the agave plant, you know. *Otra bebida,*" he said, gesturing with one hand.

Once again the bottle appeared, and another big gout of tequila poured down Rackley's throat; once again, he shuddered through the choking, coughing, burning struggle to breathe. This time even more tequila made it down. Rackley could feel the alcohol now most certainly: a familiar, comfortable sensation, a kind of warm embrace. He struggled to keep his thinking clear by shaking his head, but the Mexican's grip was so tight that when he tried to move it felt as if the muscles of his neck were tearing.

"It's amazing," Delgado was saying, "what the country people can do with the agave. Not just tequila. You know, we Americans are so proud of our high technology, but they—" He paused as Rackley's struggling slowed. "Another."

Once again the bottle, the rush, the coughing, choking; but this time Rackley struggled less. He was exhausted, he could now taste blood in his mouth from where his molars abraded his cheeks, and the tequila stung the wounds going down.

"They make all sorts of amazing things from this cactus," Delgado continued in conversational tones, "not just tequila, but, *por ejemplo*, sewing needles from the spines. They break off the spines, peel back the skin of the cactus, and then twist it into a fiber, so that it is as if there is a little thread, already attached. Remarkable."

Delgado was silent for a moment. "Again."

The bottle appeared and the tequila flowed. Rackley coughed, but also felt a great numbness begin to spread in his body, his brain. Unused to alcohol, his body was extremely sensitive to the drug; already the pain in his mouth, in his neck, seemed to be lessening.

"Another thing they do," Delgado said conversationally, "is to make paper, papyrus maybe you'd call it, by peeling the skin off the cactus. You can write on it. Again."

The tequila once again poured into his mouth, and now it was as if Rackley's throat muscles were becoming affected by the alcohol. He found it difficult, almost impossible, to close his throat and instead just drank, gulping down the burning tequila, feeling his stomach pass through warmth to a sensation as if the drink were searing through its lining.

"Delgado," Rackley said between gasps. "Lipsky. This is—"

"Quiet, quiet, quiet. Hush."

Rackley breathed deep, filled his lungs, then tried to cry out, an inarticulate roar of pure rage at the restraint, his humiliation, the forced feeding of the substance that had once reduced him to a pitiful wreck near death. He roared, but with his nose pinched off, his throat burned by liquor, his mouth contorted by the Mexican's stubby fingers, the sound emerged as less a roar than a cry, like some wounded animal lost in a marsh. . . .

"Quiet," Delgado said. "How much has he had?"

The fat Mexican raised the bottle of tequila; out of the corner of his eye Rackley could see that the bottle was still a bit more than half full.

"Keep going. At least a couple of bottles. Señor Rackley must be sound asleep by the time we finish."

Delgado's words washed away Rackley's anger and replaced it with fear and a certainty that this would be his death. Meaningless phrases about alcohol poisoning flitted through his mind, refusing to settle into thoughts. As the Mexican poured more tequila down Rackley's raw throat, the liquid gurgling in his mouth, some pouring out the side, running down his cheeks and chin, Delgado stepped up close for the first time and looked down at Rackley.

"I don't know why," he said softly, "people cannot leave me alone. Finally I have something in my life that is important. That can make a difference. I've only started what I want to do, and the world comes along and tells me to stop. Again."

Now, to Rackley's dazed mind, the tequila bottle was becoming some great glass nozzle in the sky, attacking him in a steady rhythm, beyond any control or reason. . . .

Delgado's voice rose and his anger became more plain. "What business was it of yours to break in, to go through my laboratory, to root around like some pig looking for apples?" He sighed. "Again."

Rackley choked as he felt the burning liquid on the back of his nasal passages, but even as he did a great relaxation spread over him, and his arms grew limp, and the tequila gurgled down his throat without resistance.

"I'm sick of it, Rackley," Delgado said. "And you were very, very stupid to come to Mexico City. Down here," he said, "this is my territory, not Markham's. Markham doesn't make deals here."

As the liquor poured down his throat, Rackley felt all the muscles of his body relax at once, and a great darkness and sense of peace—peace against all reason—swept over him as his vision went black, focused on a final distorted view of the neck of a shiny glass bottle. . . .

From a distance the last thing he heard was Delgado's voice.

"So much tragedy connected to this science," Delgado was musing. "First, poor Lipsky. Then you come to Mexico City to escape your troubles. But you go back to your old habits. Dependable witnesses see you in the cantinas. Then you disappear, and when they find you . . . Was it an accident? Did you take your own life? I don't suppose we'll ever really know."

* * *

Rackley barely heard the voices as he was pulled out of the rough plywood bed of the small pickup truck. Sensations registered randomly, like fragments of a dream: hands on his arms and legs, the cool dampness of the night air on his face, then wet grass against his back, through his thin jacket, as he was lowered onto the ground. He tried to open his eyes, but they seemed stuck shut. He tried to open his mouth; his face was paralyzed.

Then there was silence, broken by Delgado's voice, speaking in Spanish. "Is he still breathing?"

Rackley's attention drifted away into unconsciousness again, feeling almost frozen, so sleepy that it was as if he were really sleeping, incapable of moving or responding, yet still hearing snatches of words, phrases. . . .

Someone's head pressed briefly against his chest.

"*Sí*."

"*Bueno*. It will look better if he swallows some water."

Rackley tried to think about this, but found himself drifting off again even as hands once again seized his numb wrists and ankles, and he felt himself lifting up off the ground.

"Hurry now. There are cars coming."

"He's heavy."

"Just hurry."

Footsteps, rhythmic movements caused his lolling head to waggle back and forth as he was moved through the night air, eyes closed, too heavy to open, and then he felt himself once again sink into unconsciousness, drunk beyond drunk, drunk to the edge of life itself.

His head, swinging back and forth, back and forth.

"Now."

And then it felt as one feels when passing out, the descent into dizzy oblivion, as if flying—only now he really was flying, and suddenly with a powerful crash of sound he hit cold water.

He inhaled sharply and felt musty frigid water flood his nose, his lungs, as he flailed and inhaled and began to drown, floating facedown, unable to turn himself over. Now his eyes were open, momentarily aware of a bright flash of light as the headlights of the departing pickup truck raked the surface of the water. The light flared and vanished, leaving him struggling in the dark, choking, coughing, so paralyzed from alcohol poisoning that his muscles seemed disconnected from his brain.

He was drunk and drowning, and he let go of his muscles and floated, and then he was dreaming. He was dreaming of Kaye, seeing her walk into a large, perfectly white room, her slender waist now showing the first smooth swelling of pregnancy, smiling at him, her blond hair very bright and clean, swinging free. Kaye moved toward him smiling, and then turned and drifted away, as beautiful as he had ever seen her, clearly happy and at peace, and then she receded into the distance, as if the lights of the room suddenly started to dim, and there was nothing but her face and hair, then just her face, then nothing at all.

Years passed. He floated on his stomach, facedown in the lake, certain to drown except that his respiration was so slow that it was as if he held his breath. And then some survival sense, deep as bone, filtered into his reflexes, and he rolled over slowly onto his back. There was new chill water in his ears, filling his mouth, and something about the water brought him to half-consciousness. With a sudden spurt and sputter Rackley pulled his head up and began to paddle with his arms.

He was in the middle of a big lake in the dark. On the far side of the lake was something that looked like a boathouse, illuminated with strings of white lights that reflected off the water like so many tiny fireflies, surrounded by dozens of tethered rowboats. On the nearer shore was a modern building shaped like the prow of a ship, jutting over the lake, with huge glass windows. Through the windows he could see tables and warm yellow candlelight illuminating well-dressed diners, gazing out at the peaceful lake.

Rackley, seeing double, nearly vomiting as he moved, began to paddle and push his way toward shore. The water was deep right to the edge of the lake, which was circled with half-sections of rubber tires. To protect the boat hulls, he thought. It was the first sensible idea to cross his mind, and as he pulled himself out of the lake, he knew he would be all right.

Soon Rackley was on his hands and knees on a grassy bank, midway between the brightly lit boat docks and the elegant restaurant. He remained there for a long moment, trying to collect his thoughts, feeling once again the sense of being in a spinning room, the final stage of a long drunk gone bad.

He closed his eyes. A smart retort he used early in sobriety suddenly floated through his mind: "Problem drinker? No. I'm a pretty happy drunk, for the first few months." Then the spinning grew worse and finally he vomited, once, twice, an awful mix of bile and lake water and tequila. Oh God, he thought.

At last the shuddering passed, and he began to feel chill as the soft evening breeze blew over his wet clothes. The cold awakened him further, and he gradually struggled to his feet.

He would go to the restaurant. There would be a telephone there, and he could call Trina at her hotel. Except that she wouldn't be at the hotel, he thought. She was at the gala. He shook his head and straightened up, his mind reeling. He would get to the telephone, then figure out how to call her. He began to walk toward the restaurant, perhaps one hundred yards away, up the grassy bank and then across a parking lot, but after the first step he was staggering, seeing double, barely able to control his steps. God, he was drunk.

But he managed to proceed, one eye closed, step by step, up the grass of the slope, onto the parking lot, moving forward, dripping lake water. He would take a few steps, then stop, steadying himself by holding onto the fender of a car. Then a few more steps, then he would steady himself. He gauged the distance to the restaurant and saw he was closer than he had thought. He watched a taxicab pull up, the doorman come forward. From the cab emerged a man, well-dressed in gray pinstripes, then a young woman, wearing too much fur for the mild evening. The doorman bowed slightly in greeting.

Rackley pulled himself forward again and took another dozen steps, still staggering slightly, but now trying not to hang onto the parked automobiles. Soon he was within the bright cone of light thrown out by the two-story entrance to the restaurant. At that moment he realized that the doorman and one of the parking valets were staring at him intently.

Rackley looked down at his clothes for the first time. He was soaking wet, his white shirt plastered to his chest, his khaki suit coat bunched and wrinkled and half off one shoulder, his pants drooping and sagging with water. But worst by far was the fact that he was completely covered with bright lime-green algae, like some bizarre phosphorescent paint on his shirt, his forearms, the sleeves of his jacket.

"Well," Rackley said to himself, mustering drunken confidence, "screw 'em if they can't take a joke," and he set off for the entrance. But by now the doorman and valet were heading toward him, walking quickly as he moved unsteadily ahead.

The doorman, in full-length blue coat, reached him first. "Señor, you cannot come in here."

" 'S okay," Rackley said, barely even looking up. "Only want to use the phone."

He took another step and the doorman hesitated, then fell back, clearly reluctant to ruin his uniform by laying a hand on the sloppy drunk.

"No," he repeated firmly. "You cannot come in here."

Rackley mustered his limited Spanish. *"Teléfono. Solamente para el teléfono."*

"No," the doorman said yet again, and by now the valet had arrived. He was a younger man, built sturdily, in boots and a less splendid uniform, and without hesitation he walked up to Rackley and seized the shoulder of his khaki coat with one hand and the back with the other.

Wordlessly he wheeled Rackley around and in a matter of seconds took three long, hard strides into the darkness, dragging Rackley along, and then on the fourth step heaved him out into the darkness of the parking lot.

"Get out of here," the young man said loudly.

Propelled by the strong push, Rackley tried to keep his balance, but after managing one big step his feet tangled and he fell forward, flat onto his face, skinning the palms of his hands, his cheekbone hitting the asphalt hard.

"Gringo borracho," the young man yelled from behind him. "Get out of here."

Rackley lay on the hard asphalt, facedown, once again overcome by a great gust of dizziness. He could barely concentrate, but he knew that he was going to have to find his telephone somewhere else. This time he was on his feet more quickly, standing, wavering slightly in the soft breeze as he looked around, trying to gain his bearings. All around him was darkness and the black outlines of trees. The restaurant and lake were clearly somewhere in the center of Chapultepec Park. But where would there be a telephone?

From behind him he heard the voice of the parking valet calling something to him again. Without thinking further he decided he would simply start walking and see where it took him. Perhaps, he thought, a taxi would come by.

He reached in his back pocket but there was no wallet. He tried his other pocket, then the inside of his suit coat. Not a peso. Finally he plunged both hands into the front of his pants, and there it was: the little nylon money belt.

The luck forced him into a brief moment approaching stone-sober clarity. Somehow in the confusion no one had thought to search under his clothes. He tightened the money belt, and then, mind slightly clearly, he started off toward the edge of the parking lot.

And then he froze. A car, somehow familiar, was driving down the curving road that led to the restaurant. It was moving very slowly, and as it pulled into the parking lot, Rackley could see it clearly. It was Delgado's big customized Chrysler, smooth curves and metallic bronze paint gleaming in the distance. The car moved along slowly, sharklike, into the parking lot, cruising up and down the aisles of cars, its bright halogen headlights starkly illuminating the lot.

"Holy Christ," Rackley said to himself. Adrenaline rendered his mind even clearer. He glanced around, back at the restaurant, to both sides, ahead, and tried to think what to do. Delgado's car was approaching slowly, cruising down the line of parked cars just ahead of him. In a matter of seconds Delgado would turn at the end of the aisle and head down the row Rackley was standing in. He withdrew between two cars, crouching low, but then from behind him he heard the parking valet.

"*Ay! Señor!* Get out of here or I'll break your legs!"

Crouching, Rackley looked over his shoulder. The stocky parking valet was now striding toward him, fists at his side. And Delgado's car was about to turn around the next line of parked cars and begin down the aisle right in front of him. If Rackley didn't move, the valet would roust him just when Delgado passed by.

He had no time to think. He would have to dash across to the next row of cars as Delgado turned. Then both valet and Delgado would be behind him and he could escape into the darkness of the park.

Rackley took one breath, poised like a runner in three-point position. He raised up just enough to see the progress of Delgado's car, and then when the automobile began a sweeping turn around the end of the parked cars, Rackley bolted across the lane, one step, two steps, three steps—and then just as he was almost to the other side of the dozen feet of blacktop, something caught his foot. His balance still impaired, he fell forward, sprawling onto the ground again. In that same moment the bright lights of the Chrysler completed their sweeping turn and illuminated Rackley in an intense white glare.

Rackley dragged himself forward between the parked cars ahead of him, crawling as fast as he could even as he heard the supercharged Chrysler suddenly accelerate down the parking lane. He moved as quickly as he could, feeling the blacktop cut and tear the knees of his pants, the rocks pressing into his palms, and he tried to pull himself around the end of one car, hoping to stand and run. But just then the big Chrysler pulled up directly in front of him and he was caught.

"Rackley," came a familiar voice from the car. "It's me."

Rackley, tense, shivering, crouched beside a shiny fender trying to hide himself, froze at the sound of Trina's voice.

"It's okay," she said softly. "It's me."

Slowly Rackley stood. Dimly in the reflected light from the restaurant he could see Trina, sitting behind the wheel, one elbow out the window of the sleek automobile. She was looking at him, and then she pushed her dark hair impatiently and spoke again. "Get in," she said, her voice tense and low. "We've got a lot to do."

With a great exhalation, a huge sense of relief, Rackley stumbled forward, both hands out, feeling, involuntarily, tears coming to his eyes. In another two steps he was at the driver's side of the Chrysler, and he collapsed against the side of the car, pressing his forehead against the cold metal of the roof. "Oh God," he said, "I'm so glad to see you."

Trina reached out to steady him, and as she touched and smelled him, she recoiled in shock and surprise. "Jesus. What did they do to you?"

Rackley sat uneasily in the cool front seat of the Chrysler as Trina accelerated away from the bright restaurant, into the darkness of Chapultepec Park. She was wearing a black evening gown, her bare shoulder very white and soft in the dim interior of the car. Rackley was trying to focus his attention on the moment, but the trees and street signs seemed to rush out of the night toward his face. He was still feeling very dizzy.

Rackley shook his head. "What are you doing here?"

"I was leaving the clinic. I saw them put you in the back of that truck." She glanced over. "Jesus, you were so limp I wasn't sure . . ." She shook her head. "I followed you. Just lost them a minute ago, but I knew they had to turn in here somewhere."

Trina concentrated on her driving, taking a wide curve quite fast, heading toward the edge of the park.

Rackley rubbed the back of his neck. "What are you doing with this car?"

"I borrowed Delgado's keys," Trina said. "I told him I needed to get my wrap. He's going to be real upset."

"I found the laboratory," Rackley said slowly. "It's . . . a million bucks worth of equipment. They're doing forbidden sequence work on embryos . . . all over the world. Delgado's running it."

Trina nodded. "So that's how he paid for that house." She

smiled slightly to herself. "Paul Markham finally ran into an entrepreneur who beat him at his own game."

Rackley leaned back in the shiny brown leather seat and sighed deeply. With Trina he was painfully aware of his drunkenness. "Delgado killed Lipsky," he said carefully, trying not to slur his words. "The same way he tried to kill me."

"Delgado," Trina said, shaking her head. "He's so smart. It's the only drug that everyone assumes you took yourself."

"I'm scared. I don't want to drink again."

"Luckily," Trina said mildly, "you're with me, and I have a very good program." She was driving fast, heading out into the countryside, turning onto the big beltway that surrounded Mexico City and accelerating rapidly, passing cars on the left, then the right.

Rackley shivered involuntarily. "Do you remember what you felt like after your slip?"

"I never let myself forget it," Trina said softly.

Rackley nodded, rocking slightly in the seat. "Remember what that old-timer told you?"

"Sure," Trina said with a slight smile. "Pete S. Old coot."

"He said that the only time it would be a slip, would be if somebody held you and poured it down your throat." Rackley shook his head. "I wonder what he'd say about this."

"He'd probably say it was your fault anyway." Trina glanced over her shoulder as she changed lanes to pass a huge tanker truck. "Actually," she said, "you're lucky you're an alcoholic. A couple quarts of tequila would kill anybody with normal metabolism. I wonder if Lipsky was even alive when they put him in his car."

"Poor Lipsky," Rackley said. "Poor, poor Lipsky. He was really a sad, noble kind of—"

"You're drunk," Trina interrupted. "But I want you to listen. We're going to pick up Kaye. That's why I borrowed the car."

"What?" Rackley said, quite confused by now. "How . . . ?"

"She sent me a note this morning. She's scared. It's a big place in the suburbs, a nice neighborhood, about ten miles south of here. There's a gate on the driveway, a guard, and a guy named Gutierrez who's watching her."

Fifteen minutes later Trina pulled off the highway and began to drive down the dimly lit streets of a secluded suburb. Here the houses were mansions, three or four stories tall, set back from the road in guarded compounds. "Damn," she said, looking around. "It's really hard to see . . ."

Then suddenly she straightened up. "That's it," she said softly, "up there."

Rackley's vision focused unsteadily on a large white house of three stories with a red tile roof behind a tall brick wall. Broken glass glittered atop the wall, and the courtyard within was brightly lit by a blue mercury vapor lamp. The cobblestone drive was blocked by a high wrought iron gate crowned with metal spikes.

Trina drove past another hundred yards or so, then pulled over beneath a tall poplar tree some distance from the nearest house. "Get out. Stay under the tree, and I'll be back to pick you up when I have Kaye."

Rackley unsteadily stepped out of the shiny Chrysler. "Sit tight," Trina said, and then she reached over and pulled the door shut. Rackley sat down, hard, on a patch of cool moist grass, hidden by shadows. He took a deep breath as he watched her make a sharp U-turn on the street in front of him and accelerate back in the direction of the house.

Without hesitating Trina pulled into the driveway of the estate and tapped the horn of the big Chrysler. The custom horn made a sound like a quartet of trumpets playing thirds; Trina shook her head slightly as the ornate tones rolled out across the cobblestones. She was very nervous. Her stomach felt light and fluttery, and she was glad she hadn't eaten anything from the gala buffet. She tried to keep her breathing steady and easy. Rand used to say: calm breathing, calm thinking. Seconds later a private guard came out of the shadows on the left; he was in some kind of uniform, Trina noticed, and he had a holstered side arm.

At the sight of Delgado's car the guard suddenly broke into a trot and ran to the center of the gate, fumbling for a moment, then swinging it open. Trina eased the powerful car forward, then stopped when she was alongside the guard, who looked no older than twenty.

"Gracias," she said cooly, trying for the hauteur she had seen in upper-class Mexican women.

The guard looked at her with clear suspicion. *"Dónde está el Señor Delgado?"*

"He is at the party," Trina said in her best Spanish. "I'm here to visit Señora Rackley."

The guard nodded dubiously. "Talk to Gutierrez." He waved her in.

Trina drove into the cobblestone courtyard, then cut the steering wheel and circled halfway around so that the front of the car was aimed at the gate. As she shut off the engine, she watched the young guard swing the gate shut.

She got out of the car slowly, slinging her big canvas bag over her shoulder, quite incongruous with her evening clothes, and walked up to the huge wooden doors of the old house. Even before she reached the door it opened; inside stood an older man, watching her carefully.

"Señor Gutierrez. I am Trina Robbins. Eduardo sent me to see Señora Rackley."

Gutierrez, a fat man, balding, with white shirtsleeves rolled up, stared at her. He was still blocking the door. "He told me nothing of this."

"Tonight is the gala," Trina said. "He's very busy. But he loaned me his automobile."

Gutierrez glanced past her and nodded; as Trina had suspected, possession of Delgado's car functioned as a badge of authority. He opened the door and stepped back. "Please come in." Trina walked into the elaborately tiled entryway, dimly lit by a chandelier with most of its bulbs burned out. Trina could faintly smell cooking oil in the air.

"You may wait in the lounge," Gutierrez said, gesturing to one side. "I will speak to Señora Rackley."

Trina continued to stand in the polished hallway, shifting her weight from foot to foot, concentrating on her breathing. Calm breathing, calm thinking. So far it had gone perfectly. She shifted her heavy bag from her right to her left side and looked up the stairway and at that moment heard Kaye's voice upstairs.

"Trina Robbins? Are you sure?"

Gutierrez's voice was inaudible, and then Kaye came down the stairs, two at a time. She was wearing faded blue jeans and white basketweave sandals and a big muslin overshirt with embroidery. Her blond hair was put up in a small bun. She stopped halfway down the stairs and looked over the metal railing at Trina.

"Trina! I'm so glad—"

"Come on down," Trina said.

Kaye descended the rest of the stairs, reached Trina, and then the two women embraced.

"Oh God," Kaye said softly, close to Trina's ear. "I'm happy to see you. Something really strange is going on."

"That's true." Trina looked over Kaye's shoulder to where Gutierrez was coming down the steps. "Does anyone here speak English?"

"Not really. It's been very frustrating, and I want to know how Rackley—"

"All right," Trina said softly, "I don't want you to say anything, but I'm going to take you to Rackley. We just have to get you out the door first."

"What do you mean?" Kaye frowned. "Why can't we just leave?"

"Act like this is completely ordinary, and I'll explain everything in a minute."

"Okay," Kaye said quickly. "Okay."

As they stood in the big entryway of the old house, Gutierrez approached them. "Please," he said to Trina, gesturing with a clear effort at unaccustomed hospitality. "Go into the lounge. Would you like coffee or a drink?"

This was the moment she had to handle correctly. *"Gracias,"* Trina said, "but it is such a nice night. I think we'll go for a short drive." She turned to Kaye and spoke in English. "A drive, how does that sound?"

"Fine."

Trina turned to open the door and take Kaye out to the car. But Gutierrez stepped forward, blocking the way.

"Momentito," he said. "Señor Delgado can be very hard. You know. Just let me call him and let him know that you are taking Señora Rackley."

Trina hesitated, but then recovered and took one step forward, positioning herself just slightly between Gutierrez and Kaye.

"Of course," she said deferentially. "That's the best thing. He is at the gala, so let me find the telephone number. I have it here somewhere."

Trina started to dig around in her big canvas bag as Gutierrez watched, slightly amused.

"Una bolsa muy grande."

"Sí," Trina said ruefully, and then she nodded, reaching deep into the big purse. *"Aquí,"* she said, and suddenly, in one very smooth motion, she withdrew a small wood-handled revolver and aimed it evenly at Gutierrez's belly.

"Cálmate," Trina said softly, watching the Mexican closely. He froze, glancing at the gun, then up at her eyes, assessing in that instant that she was comfortable with the weapon.

"Go out and get in the car," she told Kaye.

Kaye stood for a moment, staring at the gun, not moving. "Get in the car and wait for me," Trina repeated firmly, and then

Kaye obeyed, walking out the front door and quickly down the stone steps of the house.

"Be calm," Trina repeated to Gutierrez, not moving. She waited until she heard the door of the Chrysler slam, then spoke again. "Turn around and walk down the steps."

He looked at her briefly, then did so. As they came out onto the steps of the house under the bright glare of the mercury vapor yard lights, the young guard at the gate moved forward, watching them curiously.

"I am aiming at your heart," Trina said from behind the fat man. *"Tu corazón.* The neighbors are far away. Tell the guard to throw his gun over the wall and then to open the gate."

Gutierrez yelled the order across the courtyard.

The guard stared at him, cocked his head. *"Qué?"*

Gutierrez repeated the command, his voice slightly higher and harsh, and this time the young guard slowly unsnapped his holster, extracted his pistol, and tossed it over the glass-topped wall.

"Now the gate," Trina said.

The fat man relayed the message. After a moment the guard swung the gate open.

"Now tell him to lie down on the ground with his hands on his head."

She watched as the guard looked over, hesitated, then lowered himself onto the grass at one side of the gate, lying with his face down.

"Walk in front of me to the car."

Gutierrez glanced over his shoulder, then walked slowly, carefully, until he was next to the bronze Chrysler. Trina walked around him cautiously, now raising the pistol so that it was aimed at his broad face. His brown eyes followed her without expression.

"Now," she said. "Turn around."

The fat man just stared at her, clearly measuring her resolve. She raised her other hand and gripped the pistol the way Rand had taught her years ago on the firing range. She aimed precisely between the man's red-rimmed eyes, and subconsciously anticipating the recoil, her lips drew back slightly, showing her teeth.

Gutierrez saw the slight gesture and turned quickly. Now she was aiming the pistol at the thinning hair on the back of his head.

"Ahora," she said. "Run as fast as you can."

He ran heavily into the darkness across the big lawn, away from the front of the house. Trina instantly swung into the driver's seat of the big Chrysler. She had left the keys in the ignition, and

now she had the engine started and slammed into gear in a matter
of seconds. Before the young guard could even rise to his knees,
she accelerated the customized car straight out the gates onto the
darkened street, instantly turning hard right, half-skidding and
then accelerating.

"Trina," Kaye said, recovering from her shock. "What
the—"

"Hold on," Trina said curtly. In seconds the car traveled a few
hundred yards down the dark street; she slammed on the brakes as
they approached the big tree where she had left Rackley.

For a moment she couldn't see him. "Damn." She glanced
over her shoulder, but saw nothing behind her. "Where—"

Just then Rackley appeared slowly from around the back of the
old poplar tree.

"Get in," Trina called, and the back door opened and the
interior light flashed on.

"Oh my God," Kaye said at the sight of Rackley, still damp,
hair arrayed wildly, mottled green from dried algae.

"Kaye." He leaned forward, grasping her for just a moment
over the front seat of the big car, and then Trina saw headlights
emerge fast from the gates of the villa behind her. She hit the gas
and accelerated into the night, throwing Rackley hard into the
backseat. The customized engine of the Chrysler roared, and then
a high whine rose as the turbocharger cut in. In seconds the car
was travelling over sixty miles an hour, streaking down the quiet
suburban street, and the headlights following were already
beginning to recede.

Trina hit the first turn near sixty, but the expensive suspension
of the car held perfectly, and as she accelerated out of the corner,
Rackley groaned loudly, rolling around in the backseat.

"He's *drunk*," Kaye said, utterly baffled, clinging to the shiny
leather bucket seat with both arms, looking first at Rackley, then
Trina, as the Chrysler roared into the night.

"No," Trina said, checking the rearview mirror, a tender
expression briefly crossing her face. "It's more like . . . he's
been poisoned." She glanced around quickly. "Calm breathing,
calm thinking," she said to Kaye.

"What?"

"I'll explain later," she said. "Trust me."

Delgado's automobile easily outdistanced the pursuers, and
twenty minutes later Trina parked in front of the small hotel where
Rackley was staying. It was an aging but neatly kept hotel in an

industrial suburb to the south of Mexico City. The air smelled strongly of sulfuric acid, but the place was clean and the locale was most unlikely for gringos to reside. She and Kaye helped Rackley through the small dark wood lobby and up the stairs as the desk clerk gaped at the green apparition.

"I see you found him," the clerk finally called out to Trina.

"Yes," Trina said over her shoulder. "He has been to a party."

Moments later they were in the room, dimly lit, with peeling pink paint. "Jesus," Rackley said, as he sank into a big chair in the small, overheated room. "I feel really rotten."

"Take a bath," Trina said, stepping back, standing by the front door. "Then get some sleep. We have a lot of thinking to do tomorrow morning."

Kaye went into the old bathroom and ran warm water on a washcloth. She came out and kneeled and started to wipe Rackley's face.

"Where did you get that gun?" she asked Trina, who was still standing.

Trina shrugged. "It's an old hobby."

"She's a great shot," Rackley said.

Kaye glanced at him, as if uncomfortable that he knew such a thing, then looked at Trina. "What will you do now?"

"I've got to get rid of Delgado's car. He'll have the army out looking for it. Then . . ." She shook her head. "Then we have to figure out what to do with you guys."

"What about you?"

"Well," Trina said. "I'm assuming that tonight constitutes my resignation from United Genetics."

"Good guess," Rackley said thickly.

"What will we do?" Kaye asked Rackley.

Rackley leaned forward in the chair, burying his face in his hands.

"We need to get you out of Mexico," Trina said. "This is not a safe country for you right now."

"But they'll arrest us as soon as we land," Kaye said.

"Probably so," Trina said wearily. She sighed, suddenly feeling the exhaustion that rises when adrenaline declines.

There was a moment of silence. Kaye gently pushed Rackley back into the chair and continued to wipe his face. Somehow the touch of the warm cloth on his skin cleared his thinking.

"Hey. I have something you should see." He twisted around on the big chair and pulled up his ruined shirt. There, across his white stomach, stretched the little nylon money belt. He unbuckled it and extracted the thick wad of computer printout. "Take a look at this."

Trina began to unfold the paper, carefully so as not to tear the sheets, slightly damp from the lake water. Finally she sat down on the double bed and spread the paper out on the shiny lacquered top of the nightstand, smoothing the surface flat with the palms of her hands. She leaned over and read the tiny clear printing for a moment.

"Rackley, did you read this whole list?"

"No," he said numbly. "I saw some names . . ."

Trina glanced at her watch, then carefully picked the paper up, folding it once again. "I've got to talk to somebody." She looked at them. "The sooner this stuff is public, the safer you'll be."

It was well past midnight by the time Trina abandoned Delgado's car in Tepito, not far from the old clinic. She took a cab back downtown to Steven Hechinger's hotel.

Hechinger was staying at one of the chain hotels that Americans build everywhere, all vaguely similar whether in Nairobi or Dallas or Mexico City. Trina went straight up in the spotless elevator and knocked on the door to his room. Finally she heard his voice from the other side.

"Who's there?"

"This is Trina Robbins. We have to talk."

There was a long moment and then she heard the chain slide. The door swung open and Hechinger, tall, his hair tousled from sleep, was standing there in a too-short hotel bathrobe.

"What's going on?" he said sleepily, staring at Trina in her black evening dress.

"Listen. How would you like to be a real hero?"

He looked at her, half asleep but fully suspicious. "What are you talking about?"

"I've got some information for you," she said. "But you need to make a promise."

Hechinger swung the door wider and gestured, and she took a few steps into the room.

"I'm listening." He folded his arms, leaning back against the doorframe.

"I want immunity from prosecution for Rackley and his wife, in return for their testimony."

Hechinger turned his head away, looking mildly disgusted. "It's a little late to think of that. They're charged. There's a solid case against them, even if they never say a peep." He shook his head and tried to smile. "Did you have a little champagne at your party?"

"But Rackley and Kaye aren't the interesting case. There's something much, much bigger."

"Oh?"

"Immunity for both of them."

Hechinger looked away for a moment. "I can't promise that. I'd have to call Washington."

"You can't do that."

"Oh?"

"Agree," she said. "Last week you were ready to trust me."

Hechinger gazed at her for a long time, then sighed. "Tentatively, depending on what you have, I'll see what I can do."

"I'd like that in writing, signed and dated." Trina pulled the folded computer printout from her big canvas bag. "Then I've got something for you to read."

As Rackley leaned against the small wooden front desk, it seemed to take forever to pay for his room. His head ached so badly from the combination of alcohol and the blow from the guard's gun that he could barely concentrate on counting out the peso notes. But finally he completed the transaction and walked slowly across the worn carpeting of the lobby to where Kaye was waiting on a cheap black vinyl sofa.

Before he sat, Rackley glanced out the dusty front window of the hotel. The street outside was nearly deserted. "She's late."

"I wonder if she's even coming," Kaye said, not looking at him.

Rackley simply shook his head and sank down onto the sofa beside her.

Trina had called in the middle of the night; Rackley had been sleeping so soundly that Kaye answered the telephone, and Trina had simply said to expect her at eight-thirty in the morning.

"Be ready to leave," she had said. "I think I can get you out."

But this morning Rackley felt anything but optimistic. In fact he felt as hopeless as he ever had. The hangover from the previous night was crushing; he was nauseated, his head aching, his entire body weak and at the edge of a constant quiet trembling. He could not remember feeling so terrible for years; it was as if the alcohol had left every nerve ending raw and sensitive, and the world itself was amplified in color and brightness and sound. But worse than that—worse than anything else he could imagine—was that as soon as he had awakened that morning to the raging pain in every part of his body, he knew exactly what would make him feel whole again.

"What's going to happen?" Kaye asked him as they sat in the lobby of the little hotel, watching the street, waiting for Trina's appearance.

Rackley moistened his dry lips and shook his head.

"Is my brother in trouble?"

Rackley nodded. "I think he is."

"He," Kaye said softly, "wasn't trying to hurt you. Edward just—he just wants to control everything. He's always been like that. He thought Father was a failure, and that it was his job to make sure we were all happy. For him, it's always been the family, first and last. I think he was trying to save us, the only way he could."

"Maybe," Rackley said. "But that's not all he did."

"It's Markham," Kaye said, shaking her head. "I never liked Markham."

Rackley leaned back gingerly on the vinyl couch. "I'm afraid that Delgado is the real problem. Markham finally met somebody he couldn't even begin to intimidate."

"What's going to happen to us?"

Rackley put his arm up on the high back of the couch. "I'll call Tortola today. Maybe he can get us through immigration, if we agree to surrender immediately."

"That sounds terrible."

"Right now," Rackley said, running a hand through his unruly hair, "our main concern is getting out of Mexico in one piece."

"Why can't we just go to the police?"

Rackley shook his head. "Delgado's been making connections for years. If he really started calling in favors, he could probably make things very difficult."

Kaye, recalling the regular police visits to the old mansion, simply nodded. She looked around the little hotel lobby, leaning forward, clasping her small hands together in her lap. "You know," she said finally, "sitting in that big house, I just kept going over it, and . . . I don't really understand how all this happened."

A horn sounded out on the street. Rackley stood halfway and gazed out the big front window. There in a white Chevrolet sedan sat Trina.

Moments later Rackley and Kaye were out on the sidewalk.

"Where'd you get this one?" Rackley asked as he opened the front door.

Trina leaned over. "I borrowed it from the American embassy."

"Do they know?" Kaye asked.

"Get in," Trina said. "We're already late."

Delgado's office on the third floor of the clinic still smelled faintly of new carpeting. It was a corner office with a broad window that looked out on the front grounds. A crew of twenty men was striking the big white tent, now flat, stretching like some giant ruined parachute across the newly planted lawn, with piles of aluminum poles arrayed around the edges. The morning had dawned gray, slightly ominous, and the clouds over the volcanic hills looked heavy and full of rain.

Edward Kelley-Delgado stood silently surveying this scene, hands locked behind his back. As he watched, a few cars entered through the wide gates; early arrivals for the final session of the conference. He noticed with approval that Maria Aguirre was already on hand out in front of the conference center, talking to their guests.

Delgado paid no further attention: he was thinking hard, trying to figure just how to manage the damage of the previous night. At least he had resolved the situation of Thomas Rackley. If necessary, later today he would arrange to have his body found. But now another problem had arisen. At that moment his secretary announced two visitors. As soon as Markham and Caswell walked in, Delgado turned around.

"Kaye Rackley is gone," he said without preface. "Trina Robbins picked her up last night."

Caswell, in a light tan suit, just stared. "What?"

"Robbins had a gun. She threatened to kill one of my men."

"That's impossible," Markham said, sinking uninvited into one of the big leather chairs in front of Delgado's desk. "She's a PR lady. She doesn't know one end of a gun from the other. Your men are just covering up." He shook his head, disgusted, and looked over at Caswell. "That's all anybody does in this country, is lie and cover up."

"She also stole my car," Delgado said quietly.

Markham tapped his fingers together wearily and then smoothed his gray silk tie, still not looking directly at Delgado. "Whatever your personal scene is with Trina, please, leave us out of it. We've got a lot to do this morning."

Caswell cleared his throat. "The press conference is scheduled for nine. And we need to get out to the airport by noon."

"There's something else," Delgado said curtly, leaning back against the windowsill. "Rackley is missing."

Markham turned on Delgado, eyes angry, his thin shoulders tensing. "Jesus. You were supposed to watch him. What the hell happened?"

Delgado shook his head, his expression calm before Markham's subdued fury. He raised one hand. "Last night, after you left, we were sitting and having a perfectly rational conversation. Suddenly he went crazy, yelling, screaming. He threw a chair at me and ran out and somehow got off the grounds."

Delgado paused and looked out the window again, toward the hills. "He seemed very upset. I would imagine he could get in a lot of trouble."

Markham closed his eyes and scowled slightly. "That's perfect. Where's Kaye now?"

"Ask Señorita Robbins," Delgado said.

Markham exploded. "Would you cut the phony Spanish?" he said sharply. "You're as American as I am."

"If I were you," Delgado continued smoothly, not looking over at Markham, "I would postpone that press conference."

Caswell glanced at Markham. "What do you think?"

"We have an auditorium full of reporters. We promised a major announcement. We have to get the Rice Five cleanup moving."

"Rackley would say business as usual," Caswell said.

Markham nodded, then frowned. "But where's Trina now?"

"That's a very intelligent question," Delgado interjected. "My people are looking for her, and I would think—"

Markham was watching him carefully. "Why aren't they looking for Rackley too?" he asked quickly.

Delgado looked at him. "They are. Of course they are."

Caswell cut him off. "I think we can run a press conference without Trina."

"I would delay this if I were you," Delgado said.

Markham turned on him. "You"—he jabbed the air with his forefinger—"have contributed absolutely nothing to this situation except to screw it up. Your idea of security is beating the shit out of our own people and then throwing chairs at them."

Delgado leaned forward for a moment and an expression passed over his face that caused both Markham and Caswell to move back reflexively. It was a look of pure rage, as on a street fighter pushed into a corner, about to lash out at eyes and groin. But then, just as quickly, Delgado's expression shifted into stony calm, and he raised both hands and dropped them, saying nothing. He turned and continued to gaze out the window.

Markham glanced at his watch. "I have the statement Trina wrote. Let's do it." He looked over at Delgado's back. "Call Maria Aguirre. She can do the introductions for us."

"You tell her," Delgado said without turning around.

"You work for me," Markham said. "Do it."

"As you wish," Delgado said, unmoving. Caswell and Markham looked at each other, uncertain. Markham stood, and then both left the office.

As soon as they were gone, Delgado was on the telephone.

"Rafael. I want people at both airports . . . No, Durando too. Is Gutierrez with the police? . . . *Bueno.*" He paused. "That's all for now. Just find them."

Delgado hung up the telephone and once again stared out the window. After a moment he touched the side of his head, as if to take a pulse. His anger at Markham and Caswell felt almost uncontrollable. These two in their suits and superior manners knew very little of how the world really worked, yet they presumed to lecture him.

But worst of all was how Trina Robbins had deceived him. It had been a very long time since anyone had done that to him. If he found the woman before Markham did—Delgado closed his eyes and took a deep breath—he would make her very unhappy.

Half an hour later Maria Aguirre came down the winding staircase from the audio control room. The dark-haired young woman quietly told Caswell and Markham that the sound system was set and ready to go.

"Thank you," Markham said, "for stepping in."

"Please. It is my pleasure."

Maria Aguirre then walked out on the newly finished stage of the conference center, which by now was filled with perhaps slightly over one hundred people, some attendees having chosen to depart Mexico City early.

"Ladies and gentlemen," Maria Aguirre said, "please let me introduce our generous hosts for this conference. Paul Markham and Edward Caswell of United Genetics."

There was extended applause from the group in the small auditorium. A few scientists even rose to their feet, although the journalists, mostly in the front rows, remained seated.

Edward Caswell spoke first. "I'd like to thank everyone who helped make the First International Conference on the Diseases of Overpopulation such a success. There is no doubt in my mind that this is a tradition we will keep and enlarge in the years to come as United Genetics strengthens its ties with the international research

322   M I C H A E L   R O G E R S

community. It is our belief that genetic engineering will increasingly be the key to the survival of our species."

Caswell paused, adding a bit of drama. "That said, we'd like to use this opportunity to make another announcement. For that I'll turn this over to the man who made all this possible. Paul Markham."

Caswell handed the microphone to the thin entrepreneur and then stepped back. Markham moved forward on the small stage and cleared his throat. "Many of you have followed the difficulties we encountered in California with a modified crop plant called Rice Five."

At the mention of Rice Five a low murmur passed through the auditorium, and the reporters, some nearly dozing through what they had assumed was an obligatory thank-you, abruptly straightened in their seats.

"We have," Markham said, "some very good news. Through the use of sophisticated computer modeling techniques, we have determined that Rice Five is highly sensitive to—"

Markham's microphone suddenly went dead. Within seconds Markham heard the problem and stopped talking and tapped the microphone with one fingernail. There was a brief sound of static in the luxurious auditorium, then a harsh, deafening buzz, and then a new voice came over the big public address speakers.

"Good morning, ladies and gentlemen. I am Thomas Rackley, former vice president of United Genetics. It's important for you to know that the management of United Genetics is guilty of at least three significant violations of the law. They are—"

There was an abrupt, rapt silence in the auditorium. Two of the American reporters exchanged glances, confirming with nods and raised eyebrows that the voice they heard was indeed Rackley's. A few others stood, glancing quickly around the big auditorium for the source of the sound as Rackley's voice continued to boom from the big overhead speakers.

Suddenly a young Mexican reporter turned around completely and saw Rackley's face in the small glass observation window of the control room, thirty feet up in the back wall of the auditorium. "There he is!"

"—the intentional release of Rice Five in California in order to gain control of—"

At first Caswell and Markham simply stood on stage, microphones in hand, staring at each other. Then, after the initial shock passed, Markham spoke quickly. "Where the hell is that coming from?"

Caswell was looking around the stage. "He's got to be in the control room."

Caswell looked out at the audience, then tried to overcome Rackley's amplified tones with his own powerful voice. "Ladies and gentlemen," he said loudly, "this is the act of a disturbed . . ."

Caswell's voice trailed off as he saw that even the people in the front row of the big auditorium couldn't hear him. He turned back to Markham, only to see that Markham's gaze, along with that of the audience, was now directed high on the back wall of the auditorium at the small glass window of the control booth.

"Stop him," Markham said to Caswell, pointing toward the booth in the wall and suddenly sounding young and vulnerable, staring up with eyes wide, as if seeing some apparition. "For God's sake, stop him."

"At the same time," Rackley was saying over the public address system, "Edward Kelley-Delgado, with the cooperation of United Genetics, has performed genetic engineering experiments on Mexican children, which have resulted in at least two deaths—"

Caswell left the stage, descending the carpeted steps two at a time. "Where the hell is the control room?" he said to Maria Aguirre as he reached the landing. When she didn't answer instantly, he grabbed both her shoulders and nearly shouted into her face: "Where *is* it?"

"You people killed Stuart Lipsky," she said calmly. "I know you did."

Caswell gazed at her for the briefest moment, baffled. Then he pushed her aside and ran into the corridor that connected the auditorium to the main clinic building.

As soon as Caswell was in the corridor, he saw Delgado running toward him, his sleek gray suit coat flapping behind him. Rafael, long black hair loose, face impassive, was alongside him, a small pistol almost hidden in one hand.

"He has to be upstairs," Delgado called. The three men immediately started up the narrow circular staircase that led to the audio control room on the second level.

Back inside the auditorium, Rackley's modulated voice was still rolling out of the speaker system. "Finally," he was saying, "Delgado, again with the cooperation of United Genetics, has established an—"

Upstairs in the tiny control room Rackley leaned forward over the switches on the audio mixing table, looking out at the upturned faces in the auditorium. Some reporters held their tiny tape recorders up toward the ceiling speakers, others were scribbling quickly in their notebooks. Behind Rackley stood Trina and Kaye, both leaning forward, watching over his shoulder.

Rackley pulled the gooseneck microphone closer. "—established an illegal clinic performing forbidden sequence transplants for clients in the U.S. and abroad. This work has involved a number of public figures." He paused, looked back at Trina and Kaye, then spoke again. "Among them is Senator Mathew Gordon, the chairman of the U.S. Senate Subcommittee on Genetic Engineering."

Looking out over the auditorium, Rackley could see Paul Markham, still standing in the middle of the stage, frozen in place. Only instead of gazing up along with the rest of the crowd, he had his eyes closed tightly, as if in not seeing, none of this could really be happening.

At that moment Delgado and Rafael reached the door of the control room, and there was a loud, vicious rattle as Delgado tried the door, finding it locked from within. Trina and Kaye both flinched at the sound.

"Break it down," Delgado's voice said from the other side of the door. "And kill the power, too."

Rackley cleared his throat and spoke into the microphone again. "Full details have been gathered by the Senate investigator Steven Hechinger—"

There was a stir on the auditorium floor, and for the first time some of the reporters' eyes turned away from Rackley, framed in the high glass window. Rackley paused and leaned forward, craning his neck to see the front doors of the auditorium. Then he leaned back and grasped Kaye's hand. "He's here," he said softly.

Within seconds the auditorium was overrun by men in uniform: Mexican police, along with three observers from the American embassy, and another five or six officers from embassy security. In the midst of them the tall activist Hechinger was striding forward, straight toward the stage, where Markham was still standing.

The arrival of the police finally energized Markham, who opened his eyes. He looked to the left and then to the right and started to dart offstage. But even before he had taken a dozen steps, four big Mexican officers had surrounded him and the thin entrepreneur disappeared from view.

With one quick bound Hechinger took the stage himself and turned and spotted Rackley in the glass window overhead. Hechinger grinned broadly and raised both hands over his head.

At the same moment there were pounding footfalls in the

corridor outside the control room as the Mexican police charged up the circular stairway. Through the door Rackley could hear Delgado addressing Rafael in crisp Spanish. "Drop the gun," he said softly. "Stay calm."

Then, more loudly, he spoke to the arriving police. "No resistance," he said, "no resistance. We are unarmed."

As silence fell, Trina reached out and unlocked the door of the control room and it swung slowly open. On the small landing outside the room the police were quickly handcuffing Rafael, Delgado, and Caswell.

"Edward!" Kaye said, and her brother looked over his shoulder, the fabric of his suit bunched and wrinkled.

He opened his mouth, but Delgado spoke first.

"You are stupid fools," he said to Caswell, biting each word off carefully, precisely, as if they were the last words he would ever speak to him. Then he turned to Trina. "And you," he said, "are still a whore."

A plump Mexican police lieutenant spun Delgado around and began to lead him forward, down the steps. Rafael followed, then Edward Caswell.

Kaye looked back at Rackley, upset by the sight of her brother in chains. Rackley shook his head very slightly. Then after the three men had been escorted down the stairs, Hechinger came up in three quick bounds, positively aglow, hyperventilating from the excitement of the event.

"We've already got extradition in process," the tall man said loudly. "There's no way they can get out of this." Then he looked across the room at Trina, who was standing with her back against one of the audio control panels, her face very white and drawn, clearly exhausted.

"You," he said, "were great."

Within ten minutes Delgado, Caswell, and Markham had been taken to the big police station near the Zócalo in the center of the city. They were accompanied by two observers from the American embassy. At Hechinger's suggestion Rackley, Kaye, and Trina remained in the small control room until the auditorium was empty.

Clearing the reporters was no problem. "It was a mad dash for the telephones," Hechinger told Rackley. "You did just right. It's all on the public record, for sure."

Twenty minutes later additional cars and guards arrived from the embassy and they left the conference center. By then the dark clouds of the morning had arrived overhead, the air thick and moist, rain imminent. As they walked toward the cars, Rackley turned to Kaye. "I need to talk to Trina for a minute."

"All right."

He walked ahead quickly across the big green lawn of the clinic to catch up with Trina, who was walking with Hechinger.

Rackley touched her arm. "Can I talk to you for a second?"

Hechinger glanced at his watch. "I should call Washington. Technically you're under arrest. But it's more like protective custody."

"Thanks," Rackley said.

Hechinger looked at him. "I want the whole story. Every bit of it." He nodded at Trina. "We have a deal."

Hechinger walked off quickly toward a blue embassy sedan parked at the big circular entrance to the clinic.

Trina took Rackley's arm and they strolled slowly across the grass, away from the clinic, toward the hazy hills. "Feel okay?" she asked after a moment.

Rackley nodded shortly, lips tight, saying nothing.

"I suppose," Trina said, "that you'll—"

"I want a drink," Rackley interrupted suddenly. "That's all I've been able to think about since I woke up this morning."

Trina nodded calmly, not changing her pace or looking up. "Well, that's normal. All your old systems have been triggered."

"Trina," he said, tightening his grip on her arm, his voice low. "It's really bad."

"It's the disease talking," she said. "Not you."

"But—"

"I hate Delgado. He's an evil man."

"What," Rackley asked, his voice cracking, "am I going to *do*?"

"I made a call last night. There's an English-speaking AA meeting at noon, downtown."

The sound of it nearly made Rackley crumple. "Jesus. I've lost it all. I'm back to the beginning."

"No," Trina said. "Every day, we're back at the beginning. It's just that some beginnings look bigger than others."

Rackley stared out at the sprawl of buildings beyond the gates, the black hills in the distance, newly revealed as the mist lifted. He shook his head heavily.

"C'mon," Trina said, tugging at his arm. "If I drive, we can be there in ten minutes."

E P I L O G U E

A week after the arrests at the clinic Edward Caswell and Paul Markham were extradited from Mexico to stand trial in the United States. The two were indicted on a half dozen federal charges ranging from illegal genetic engineering to fraud. Caswell and Markham both agreed to plead guilty in exchange for reduced sentences.

Edward Kelley-Delgado, although an American citizen, was bound over to face trial in Mexico on charges including medical malpractice, human experimentation, and corrupting government officials. Delgado's sentence could have totaled several hundred years. But then, while he was being transferred to a prison in Sonora, Delgado's transport was attacked by bandits and he disappeared. After an extensive investigation the Mexican federal police concluded that Delgado had been kidnapped and murdered by former associates in the drug trade.

Shortly after returning to the United States, Rackley appeared before the Senate Hearings on Genetic Engineering for nearly two days. Absent from the hearings was Senator Mathew Gordon, who strenuously denied charges that his young daughter had received forbidden sequence therapy, but who subsequently resigned from the Senate for personal reasons.

The fraudulent buy-back deal engineered by Markham was nullified in district court. A committee of investors formed to reorganize United Genetics' management and asked Rackley to

become acting president. He accepted with one stipulation: that
the company be taken public as quickly as possible, with his
retirement to follow directly.

Seven months later Stuart Vincent Rackley was born with no
complications, nothing even to hint at the baby's extraordinary
genesis. His heritage, however, was a matter of public record—
the supermarket tabloids dubbed him the "gene-spliced baby."
Young Stuart Rackley was, in fact, the only publicly identified
such infant on the planet. Following the arrests in Mexico, ten
anonymous clients from Silicon Valley paid the lawyer Tortola a
large cash retainer to have the list of Delgado's forbidden
sequence patients permanently sealed under court order. Tortola
was successful, arguing that a greater good would be served by
shielding the children involved.

Even though the records were sealed, Trina Robbins, through
delicate negotiation, collected a sample of two hundred of
Delgado's clients in the U.S. and Europe. The parents agreed in
strictest secrecy to allow their children to be monitored in return
for follow-up medical care. These babies, who received the
forbidden sequence as embryos, were all extremely bright, testing
an average thirty IQ points higher than their peers. Some had
started to display slightly odd psychological quirks, but it was not
yet clear whether these were natural aspects of high intelligence or
darker, more ominous changes.

In Mexico City, Trina could locate only a dozen of the hundred
or so subjects who received the forbidden sequence as young
children. Thus far two more had died, both under unusual
circumstances. One had apparently drowned intentionally, the
other was shot during an attempt to steal blank airline tickets.

After Delgado's disappearance Trina arranged to bring Pablo
to the United States and started adoption proceedings, assisted by
Steven Hechinger, who had moved to San Francisco after the
Senate hearings. The brilliant little Mexican boy attended a school
for the gifted and was regularly seen by a child psychiatrist who
specialized in abnormal development.

Nearly one year after the Mexico City arrests, Pablo received a
cryptic postcard in the mail: a bright image of a huge crocodile
lazing on the bank of some lush African river. The brief, unsigned
message read: *Someday we will be together again. We still have
much work to do.*

Trina immediately sent the postcard on to federal agents who
were investigating rumors of an illegal genetic engineering clinic

operating somewhere in central Africa. The inquiry, however, closed after six months. No firm evidence was uncovered, and the investigators reported to Congress that the new technology was now entirely under control.

ABOUT THE AUTHOR

Michael Rogers studied fiction writing and physics at Stanford University. He has published two previous novels, *Mindfogger* and *Silicon Valley*, a collection of short fiction, *Do Not Worry About the Bear*, and the nonfiction *Biohazard*. His books have been published worldwide and optioned for film and television. His fiction and nonfiction have appeared in dozens of magazines and his articles on high technology appear regularly in *Newsweek*. As an associate editor of *Rolling Stone*, he specialized in literature and science, winning the American Association for the Advancement of Science Award for Distinguished Science Writing, for coverage of a total eclipse in the Sahara Desert.

Mr. Rogers has followed genetic engineering since he covered the historic 1975 Asilomar Conference for *Rolling Stone*. In 1984, *Newsweek* published his story revealing plans for the first deliberate release of a genetically engineered organism. The revelation attracted international attention and inspired a flurry of legislation.

Michael Rogers lives near San Francisco, California. He is at work on his next novel.